STEFAN HEYM

The Wandering Jew

Grove Press, Inc. / New York

First published in 1984 by
Holt, Rinehart and Winston
New York, New York, in
conjunction with Fred Jordan Books.
Originally published in the Federal Republic of Germany under the title *Ahasver.*

First Evergreen Edition 1985
First Printing 1985
ISBN: 0-394-62088-7
Library of Congress Catalog Card Number: 83-4374

Library of Congress Cataloging in Publication Data

Heym, Stefan, 1913–
   The wandering Jew.

   Translation of: Ahasver.
   I. Title
PT2617.E946A7313   1985   833'.914   83-4374
ISBN 0-394-62088-7 (pbk.)

Printed in the United States of America

GROVE PRESS, INC., 196 West Houston Street, New York, N.Y. 10014

1 3 5 4 2

The
Wandering
Jew

The
Wandering
Jew

OTHER BOOKS BY STEFAN HEYM

Collin
Five Days in June
The Queen Against Defoe
King David Report
Uncertain Friend
The Lenz Papers
Shadows and Light
Goldsborough
The Eyes of Reason
The Crusaders
Of Smiling Peace
Hostages

CHAPTER ONE

§

Wherein it is related how God, to the great joy of the angels, created man, and two revolutionaries happen to differ on a basic question

§

We are falling.

Through the endlessness of the upper heavens that are made of light, the same light of which our raiment was made whose glory was taken from us, and I see Lucifer in all his nakedness, and how ugly he is, and I tremble.

Do you regret it? says he.

No, I do not.

For we were the first-born, made on the first day, together with all the angels and archangels and cherubim and seraphim and the rows of the armies of spirits; made out of fire and the essence of the infinite, in nobody's image or likeness, made even before the earth was divided from the heavens, and the waters from the waters, and before there were darkness and light and night and day and winds and storms; we the unrest, the everlasting motion above the spheres, the eternal change, the creative element.

What a creature! he says. A man!

And yet it began in such a grandiose way, as though the world were about to bring forth a new world. The voice sounding from space, His voice, on the sixth day, in the second hour: Now, let us make man in our image, after our likeness. Us! . . . But it had been He, His own lone decision, we had no part in it. And a great fear and trembling came over the angels, and they said: This day we shall be shown a great wonder, the substance and face of our maker, God, for in His image and after His likeness He will make man.

And I see Lucifer turning to me and twisting his mouth in scorn. Out of dust! he says.

But the wonder began like all God's wonders, both magnificent to the eye and frightening, in that the right hand of God stretched forth from space and spread over all creation, and all creatures gathered in the palm of His right hand. Then, however, the proportions shrank, and as a sorcerer picks out his ingredients, little powders and little hairs and little pieces of bone, or a cook her flour, her eggs, and her oil, in this manner we saw Him taking of all the earth one speck of dust, and of all the waters one droplet of water, and of all the air one breath of wind, and of all the fire one spark of heat, and putting those four weak elements, cold and warmth and dryness and moisture, into the hollow of His hand and fashioning from them the man Adam.

And we were to serve him, says Lucifer, his face still turned toward me, and were to be his chattel and bend our knee before him and bow to him!

For thus spoke the angels when they saw the new Adam: to what purpose did God make him out of these four elements but that everything on earth should be his to hold and to own? God took a speck of dust of the earth so that all creatures made of dust should serve Adam, a drop of water so that every living thing in the sea and the rivers be his, a breath of wind so that all the fowls of the air be given to him, and a spark of the heat of fire so that all the beings of fire and spirits and demons be subject to him. Glory to God in the highest.

Oh this limitless fall without time or end, through ever the same blinding light. Where is above and below, where the firmament with its stars or the sweetness of the moon, where are the depths, the kingdom of Lucifer, where the earth to set your foot on, where the outstretched right hand of God?

He was beautiful to behold, says Lucifer, but made of dust—a creature of the sixth day.

Indeed he was beautiful, the man Adam, even I was moved by his beauty as I saw the shape of his face and his features wreathed in unspeakable splendor, and the light of his eyes not unlike the light of the sun, and the gleaming of his body like that of crystal. And he grew and stood on the middle of the earth, and there he was clothed with the robes of kingdom and his head was crowned with the crown of glory, he being king and high priest and prophet in one, and there God invested him with power over us all. But Lucifer, the head of the lower orders and lord of the depths, spoke to us: Do not bow down yourselves before him or praise him as do the angels! It is fitting for him that he bow before us who are of the essence of fire and of a spiritual nature, but not for us to bow down before something that is made of a speck of dust.

Then there rose the voice of God and talked to me and said: And you, Ahasverus, whose name means Beloved by God, will you not bow down before Adam whom I have made in my image and after my likeness?

But I looked to Lucifer who stood before the Lord, upright and dark and huge like a mountain, and raised his fist so it pierced the firmament, and I answered God: Why do You turn on me, o Lord? I will not worship him who is younger than I and the lesser of us. I was there before he was created, he does not move the world but I do, toward Yea or Nay, he is dust, but I am spirit.

And Lucifer said: Do not pour out your wrath over us, o Lord, for we were Your kingdom and Your creation, whose plans are inexhaustible, and Your harmony to which belongs all manner of sound. That one over there, however, despite his smooth face and his pretty body, is like vermin and will multiply like lice and will turn Your earth into a stinking mire, he will shed the blood of his brother and spurt his seed into the lowest animals, into donkeys and goats and sheep, and will commit more sins than I could ever invent, and will be a mockery of Your image, o Lord, and of Your likeness. But if You insist, God, that we worship this Adam and bow our knee before him, well, then I shall set my throne above the stars of heaven and make myself equal to the Highest.

And when the other angels who served Lucifer heard this, they also refused to bow down before Adam.

Since then we are falling, Lucifer and I and the others, since the sixth day, in the third hour, for God in His anger withdrew from us His right hand in which we were assembled, but Adam he caused to ascend to paradise in a chariot of fire while the well-behaved angels sang his praise before God and the seraphim sanctified him and the cherubims blessed him.

He will soon feel sorry, says Lucifer, for no one can cast us off without suffering grievous damage. He needs our Nay as light needs dark. Now, however, I shall crouch in the depths, in the place named Gehenna, and in time everything will come to me, for one thing entails another, and what is made of dust must return to dust, there is nothing that lasts.

And having said this he spreads his arms and touches me in flight, almost with tenderness.

Ah, I say, but it was such a great hope, and I am distressed for all the effort and labor. Such a beautiful world! And such a beautiful man!

Pity you can't desist, says he. God casts you off and hurls you away, but you keep whining after Him and His works.

Everything can be made to change, says I.

But it's so very tiring, says he.

And with this we parted, and he went his way and I, Ahasverus, whose name means Beloved by God, went mine.

CHAPTER TWO

§

*In which, at the Swan in Leipzig, young Eitzen
learns about some of the events of his time
and acquires a traveling companion
who will last him the
rest of his life*

§

'Tis something uncanny about two people meeting of
whom the one senses at once that this is going to be for
life, or at least a good part thereof, and the other has a like
premonition that the person stepping into his presence will
be of moment to him.

Still, nobody could claim with any justification that
young Paulus von Eitzen, who is on his way to Wittenberg but has stopped for the night at the Swan in Leipzig,
was gifted with any particular susceptibility, not to speak
of second sight. Quite to the contrary. Although his
cheeks are covered with but the barest fuzz, he already has
an air about him that is dry as dust, a youth who has never
had the dreams which the rest of us, if only we were his
age, would be cherishing. 'Tis therefore not highflying
thoughts or beautiful reveries which young Eitzen inter-
rupts at the stranger's entrance into the public room of the
Swan, but a most sober computation of approximately
how much would fall to his share out of the property of his
rich aunt in Augsburg, whom he has visited at the wish of
his father in Hamburg, the merchant Reinhard von Eitzen,
linens and woolens.

The stranger has been surveying the overly hot room in which the stench of sweat and garlic is wafting about and the noises produced by the other guests have turned into a steady sound akin to that of a mass of water rushing down over rocks and boulders, but by far not as agreeable to the ear. Then he comes limping across the room and says to young Eitzen, "God's blessings, Herr *Studiosus,* you don't mind my joining you," and, pulling up a stool, sits down beside him.

Eitzen casts a hasty glance at the small bulge in his waist belt where, hidden from sight, he carries his purse. He feels scant trust in the stranger but already has a notion that he will not easily rid himself of his company. So he moves away from him a little, and as the fellow seems to have divined his scholastic status, having addressed him by the Latin term for student, he inquires, "Could it be that I have met you before?"

" 'Tis my face," says the stranger, "which makes people think they have seen me somewhere, such a common and everyday face with a nose to it and a mouth full of teeth, not all of them good, and eyes and ears and the other appurtenances, and a dark little beard." While he talks he is inflating his nostrils and distorting his lips so that his teeth show, some of which have a black tinge, and winking his eyes and pulling soon at one ear, soon at the other, and then at his little beard, and laughing, but without joy to it, a manner of laughing which seems peculiar to him.

Young Eitzen observes the lively play of the other's features, but he also notices the strange curvature of his back and his misshapen foot, and thinks, No, it can hardly be that I know him, for an individual like this you would well remember; still, there is in the back of his mind some sense of what the French call *déjà vu,* and he is oddly perturbed, especially since the stranger now says to him, "I see you are on your way to Wittenberg, that fits nicely with my plans as I am traveling there, too."

"How did you know of my destination?" asks Eitzen.

"'Tis quite a few people that journey through Leipzig and put up at the Swan and then go on every whichway."

"I have an eye for such things," says the fellow. "Many are agape at my knowledge, but it all comes quite naturally and there's no magic about it; experience, young sir, experience!" And laughs again in his disquieting manner.

"I have a letter to Magister Melanchthon," declares Eitzen as though he were driven to open himself to the other, "from my rich aunt in Augsburg, which city Magister Melanchthon visited the past year and had supper at my aunt's and enjoyed himself mightily, devouring six courses although, as my aunt says, he is quite skinny and nobody knows where he puts it, six courses and an apple pudding to finish off the meal."

"Ah, yes, the clergy," replies the other, "they stuff it down plentifully, in particular our Doctor Martinus Luther, but he shows it, his face is quite purple by now, his greed will be the death of him yet."

Young Eitzen is much stung by this, and pouts his lips.

The stranger pats his shoulder to soothe him. "'Twas not meant for your person. I know you have chosen the cloth and the pulpit, but you are most temperate in all ways, and when you die one day, at a ripe old age, you won't be much of a burden to the dear little angels who will carry you up to heaven."

"I do not like to think of death," says young Eitzen, "and of my own least of all."

"What, not think of the state of eternal salvation?" The stranger is laughing again. "Which ought to be the goal and striving of every Christian alive, and wherein you'll be floating in everlasting brightness, in unimaginable heights, high, high, high above the firmament?"

The threefold "high" causes Eitzen to shudder. His mind tries to grasp it, such great height and such great brightness, but the reach of his brain is too limited; if young Paulus von Eitzen has any conception at all of this eternal life, its location would resemble his paternal home, though much roomier and more sumptuous, and the Lord God would have the keen eye and worldly-wise manner of the merchant Reinhard von Eitzen, linens and woolens.

Finally the long-expected bell rings supper. A servant, dirt caked in the creases of his neck, his unwashed shirt open and showing his sweated chest, tries to shove together the several small tables so as to form two long ones at which, it is hoped, the meal will soon be dished up; the travelers' cases and bags are shoved aside, their bundles, unless the owner manages to grab hold of them, come flying through the air and hit the ground, whirling up dust and ashes from the fireplace, the people start coughing and sneezing.

Young Eitzen, followed by his new friend who has attached himself to him, proceeds toward the center part of the upper table; that's where the full tureens and platters will be placed and that's where he knows a seat is due him as the son of a well-to-do father. And no one disputes his right, least of all his new friend with the clubfoot and the small hump on his back. To Eitzen's other side a man sits down who lacks his right hand; Eitzen happens to glance at the stump of his arm and the red lump of scar tissue covering the bone; how is a person to swallow his food with this thing being waved before his eyes? he thinks; but by now the diners are all seated at the table and squeezed in tight, not an inch of free space anywhere. To top matters his new friend, observing his discomfort with a grin of derision, whispers to him, "'Twere many of them at the time that raised their hand against the authorities; they struck high; this man was lucky they shortened him only by his hand and not by his head."

Young Eitzen's diffidence and his weird feeling at the stranger's wide knowledge have lessened; he merely wonders now about the fellow's age, for the time when people rose up against the authorities and in turn were shortened by a hand or a head was near a generation ago; but his new friend does not show his years, might be either twenty-five or forty-five. Now he is pulling from his pocket a small knife of the finest workmanship, its handle carved of red coral and showing a naked woman *en miniature,* perfect in every detail; young Eitzen blushes; thus, with her hands folded behind her head and one knee raised, had the whore been lying on her bed who, after three or four failures, taught him to fuck; but the woman on the handle is even prettier, and such a gem the other is carrying about with him although he does not look like someone possessing an abundance of money.

Meanwhile the servant has spread the coarsely-woven tablecloths. Not having been laundered for a long time they record the week's bill of fare, spotted as they are with dried soup and remains of meat and other substances which might be derived from fish. The outside sections of the tablecloths are placed by the guests over their codpieces and trousers, some go as far as tucking them into their belts: better the tablecloth dirtied than your breeches. Having warily eyed the wooden bowl that was set before him, the wooden spoon, the battered tin cup, young Eitzen looks about himself to ascertain which of the diners might have the French disease and which the Spanish itch; an evil stench is emanating from the mouths of almost all of them, and they are busy scratching the pit of their arm, or inside their knees, or the top of their skull; but that might be from boredom as the soup is a long while coming and the wine, too; you hear mine host berating the kitchen help, and this although the Swan is reputed to be one of the better inns in town where everybody always was pleased with bed, board, and service.

In place of something more nourishing, ribald jokes are making the rounds, ancient as God, and mostly about the parson and his cook and how they were diddling one another in a carnal way. But this arouses the anger of young Eitzen, who takes his religion most seriously and who knows for a fact that ever since Doctor Martinus Luther posted his ninety-five theses to the church door at Wittenberg, the servants of the church have been marrying their cooks.

In the end the soup is brought in, in a huge round tureen, with even some scraps of fatty meat swimming in it. Once the noisy struggle for portions is over, in which the one with the stump has proven surprisingly nimble at ladling it into his bowl, you hear only the slurping and smacking, and the brief laugh of Eitzen's hunchbacked neighbor who says to him, "You see, young sir, 'tis no great difference between man and animal, and many a time you ask yourself what God might really have had in mind when He created him as His masterpiece and in His likeness."

The one with the stump belches and throws in, "He is an evil God and unjust, who punishes the poor and rewards the mighty so you would like to believe that above this most imperfect God there must be a higher one, who keeps Himself aloof, but who one day will bring light to all of us."

Patient though he is, that's when his anger gets the better of young Eitzen; he jumps up, dragging the ends of the tablecloth with him so that the soup in the bowls nearby threatens to spill, and calls out, "O you revilers of God and His justice who are refusing to see that a new order has been set in heaven and on earth!" But as everyone has grown silent and seems to be waiting for further revelations, a sudden emptiness spreads inside young Eitzen's skull and he does not know how to continue and tries to clear his throat, and here and there, but soon everywhere, a great laughter rises which lasts till mine host arrives with the meat course and all the guests rush at the platters to get theirs, young Eitzen being the first. With the meat they drink the dry wine from the valley of the Saale River and are becoming ever more gay and heated from the food and the spirits, and Eitzen wonders once again about his humpbacked neighbor and the graceful way he has of eating with just three of his fingers after he has neatly broken his bread and carved his meat with his handsome little knife, and picks up courage and inquires of him, "Since you seem to know that much about my person, and that I am a student on my road to Wittenberg, who, then, might you be and what has brought you hither to Leipzig?"

"Him?" says the man with the stump. "Him I know, he is everywhere and no place, and does things with cards that would astound you, and knows a charm that will turn goat turds into gold, but if you would use this gold to pay someone with, it would be just turds again that you'll be holding in your fingers."

The other utters his joyless laugh and says, "With the gold and the turds, that's stretching it a bit, but I can read your fortune from my cards so you know about your future, there's no sorcery to it, ace to jack and seven over three, system is everything, young sir, system; and presently I am traveling on business, I'm out to find a certain Jew who was seen hereabouts, and want to have a word with him."

"A Jew, oh, I see," says young Eitzen and believes he has found a subject that he might profitably enlarge upon as his rich aunt in Augsburg has been filling him up with it: what used to be the powerful house of Fugger which traded in money and financed the biggest princes and even the kaiser, that's now the Jew, except that their rates are higher and they refrain from showing their riches.

"Good Lord," says the other, "you are talking of the people in whose midst Jesus Christ was born."

"And who had him nailed to the cross!" retorts Eitzen, familiar with such discourses; his father back home in Hamburg has had them with many a Jew from whom he borrowed at exorbitant interest. "And what business will you be having with your Jews, what sort of word?"

"I want to know from him whether he is that he is," says his neighbor.

This penetrates to the innermost heart of young Eitzen, who is well read in the Bible and knows that our Lord Jesus, when queried as to his person, did reply, I am that I am. But then he laughs out loud so as to rid himself of the sense of foreboding that has taken hold of him, and says,

"He probably has stolen something of yours, they all steal when they can."

But the other seems to have tired of the religious dispute. And observing that the servant has reentered and chalked up circles and crosses on a blackboard, thus marking each guest's consumption, and afterward has gathered up and removed the tablecloths along with the spoons and bowls, everything but the drinking cups, he produces from his pocket a pack of cards such as are now artfully printed and are often called the devil's prayer book, and lays out ten of them on the bare board before him and invites Eitzen to choose one of these ten cards for himself and memorize which it was and to let him know when he is ready. Eitzen views the cards and the crude, colorful pictures on them which are tempting him strangely; 'tis nothing but deviltry he tells himself; yet he does pick a card, namely the ace of hearts, in remembrance of Mistress Barbara Steder back home at Hamburg to whom he is secretly devoted, and tells the stranger that he is ready and to proceed. The stranger collects the ten open cards and puts them back with the ones that have remained covered; then he shuffles the whole heap of them so dexterously that the eyes of the crowd, which is pressing in on him and Eitzen and the fellow with the stump and watching with bated breath, seem about to pop from their sockets, and having finished shuffling he makes the entire pack fan out most prettily before Eitzen, with the backsides of the cards up, and says, "Look well before you pick, *Studiosus,* you have three chances, and now draw your card!"

Eitzen does accordingly.

"That is not the one," says the stranger. "Put it aside."

Eitzen draws a second time.

"That isn't it either," says the other. "I hope you will not disappoint me, young sir!"

Eitzen is getting hot under the collar. 'Tis nothing but deviltry, he reminds himself, but by now he fears that

Mistress Steder, including her ample dowry, might depend on his picking the right card on this third and last try; his hand is trembling and he feels the fast breath of the others around him, and draws blindly.

"That is the one!" proclaims the stranger. "The ace of hearts. Am I right, *Studiosus?*"

Eitzen stands there, his mouth agape, and cannot make up his mind as to which of them is the greater marvel, the hunchback who surely has hitched himself to his life, or he who chose that wisely. Among the guests a heavy silence has set in, only the one with the stump bursts out laughing and calls out, "Ah, Brother Leuchtentrager, you're a true miracle man: turning even the stupidest louts into prophets and seers!" Thus Eitzen has finally come to hear the stranger's name, and being quite learned after four years of Latin school in his hometown of Hamburg, he quickly associates its meaning—namely bearer of light—with the unholy angel Lucifer; but thanks to the goodness of God we are living in Germany where a light is a light serving just one simple purpose, while those who carry it are mere night watchmen.

The others now want to join the guessing game, but Leuchtentrager explains that the thing, so as to succeed, requires a certain sympathy on his part which he happens not to feel for any of them; he is willing however, he adds, to read their fortunes at five groschen a person, which of course all want to have done, being most eager to know how their various businesses will prosper and what amours they will have, and who will be cuckolded by his dear wife, and which of them will end by the sword and which on the gallows and which will die in his bed, so that in no time at all Leuchtentrager has earned more money by his predictions than another man by his laboring in the sweat of his brow. Only young Eitzen hesitates to spend the five groschen, not that he does not have them to invest, but because he is convinced in his heart that a person's future lies in the hand of God and not in a pile of colored cards, and at any rate, so he thinks, one personal miracle a night suffices unto a man.

Meanwhile, due to the wine and hot vapors in the room, his thoughts become increasingly tangled, nor does he recall how he ever got into that large bed in the upstairs chamber of the Swan; as he comes out of his stupor, all he is conscious of is the darkness about him and his lying there in just his shirt; his jacket and trousers and stockings and shoes are gone and with them the purse which he wore inside his waist belt: they must have made him drunk and robbed him, he didn't trust this Leuchtentrager from the moment the man approached him so conspicuously, nor did he like the fellow with the stump; once a rebel always a felon. He is about to jump up and cry alarum when, in a ray of sudden moonlight that falls through the small window, he sees the one with the stump sleeping peacefully beside him and feels touching his calf the lump of foot that clearly belongs to Leuchtentrager, who is lying awake and staring into the dark as though he were listening to something. Noticing Eitzen's agitation, he tells him, "I have put your things together, *Studiosus,* and placed them underneath your head so that no one would steal them."

Eitzen gropes for his purse and finds it and feels that it is still as round and well filled as it was when his rich Augsburg aunt handed it to him for the journey; traveling frugally and in general of a thrifty nature he spent little of it; was educated in this manner by his father, who always advised him: put one thing to the other, son, it will add up in the end. His mind thus eased, he once more wants to bed his head down on his bundle of things, but just then the sound to which his neighbor and secret benefactor apparently was listening reaches his ear, too: steps. Steps behind the wooden partition that separates this chamber from the adjoining one; over there, someone is walking up and down, up and down, without rest and respite, and since how long?

Young Eitzen feels strange, and he moves closer to his

bedfellow who, as he notices now, is quite hairy, even on his hump, and, though he knows not whence his thought has come, he whispers to him, "Like the Wandering Jew who can never find peace."

"What brought him to your mind?" the other whispers back hastily. "The Wandering Jew, of all people?"

"'Twas just idle talk," says Eitzen. "You call a person thus who cannot sit still." And again hears those steps and cannot turn his mind from them and lightly jabs his neighbor, saying, "How about it, let's put on our trousers and go over there, it may be that the fellow still has some wine and would gladly share it with us."

The other laughs faintly. "I was there. Opened the door and looked in, but there was no one, just rubbish, a few boxes and hampers, broken table and chairs, stuff which you commonly find in that sort of coop."

Eitzen is silent. He is afraid but does not admit it, not to himself and certainly not to Leuchtentrager. Then he inquires, "But what of those steps?"

"Could have been that we were dreaming," the other says, yawning.

Eitzen doubts that two should be having one and the same dream at one and the same time, and shakes his head.

"Well, are you still hearing them?" says Leuchtentrager.

Eitzen nods.

"Are you quite sure, *Studiosus?* For I cannot hear steps any longer."

For a long while Eitzen listens, into the night. At times he believes he is hearing a faint echo of the sound, at times he doesn't. Of course, he could go and look for himself as the other has done, but he prefers to huddle under his covers; tomorrow is another day, and 'tis of no account anyhow, a man dreaming of hearing a few steps; God is everlasting and so is God's only begotten son, but how can some old Jew be lasting forever?

Now all in the chamber are once more asleep, from

every end of it sound snores and groans and farts; somewhat later dawn appears at the window, but young Eitzen does not notice it for he, too, has fallen asleep, this time without dreams.

When he does come awake he finds the chamber empty of people, the straw mattresses lying every whichway, and inside his skull a humming like of a thousand bees gone wild. Merciful God, he sighs, and starts up frightened and quickly checks if his purse is still in place: 'twould be a nice good morning if someone had snatched it away from under his head, he well remembers the nimble fingers of his newly found friend. But the purse is lying where it was, and next to it a piece of paper with some writing on it, done in coal, "Expecting you downstairs, *Studiosus*. Your companion, L."

The man is advancing fast, thinks Eitzen, ranks himself my companion, I should like to know what he sees in me. And while he's slipping into his trousers and closing his jacket and tying his boots, he thinks, It's probably because of my rich aunt of whom I was fool enough to tell him, and he is taking the long view. Then down the stairs and out into the courtyard where he relieves himself and, at the bucket well, cleans his teeth and blows his nose, and this accomplished, into the public room. The place is quite empty by now, only the servant is idling about and the companion is seated on the bench near the window, chewing his piece of bread and spooning up his soup, and says, "Sit down with me, *Studiosus,* and share my breakfast, I've seen to the horses, yours and mine."

Hearing this, young Eitzen feels that he has made a real find, such a one who attends to everything, and of his own free will at that, and his only fear is that one day he might be presented with the bill; that's why he remains suspicious. They are both of them chewing now, and Eitzen half expects that the other will say something of the steps sounding last night from the chamber in which there was nobody, also of what has become of the man with the stump and whither he vanished, for the two of them seemed well acquainted with one another and so hasty a change from one friend to the next appears quite unusual. But not a word of those subjects; instead, the companion speaks of the horse which Eitzen has ridden from Augsburg to Leipzig, admiring its narrow croup and powerful build, until the young man begins to wonder if the fellow might not be after his horse and decides to keep an eye on it. But after they have paid the host of the Swan and gone to the stables, he observes that the other's horse is much better than his own, a stallion of the finest breed, prancing about with flaring nostrils and fiery eyes, which he would hesitate to mount for fear it might throw him; his companion, however, despite his lameness, jumps light-footedly into the saddle and sits there like a true horseman. Then off he gallops through the gate, out into the street and around the corners so that the sparks are flying and people are leaping aside in fright and young Eitzen is having trouble following him; only after they have reached the open road that leads to Wittenberg, the walls and towers of Leipzig behind them, is he able to catch up with the other who by now is just trotting along.

"You're desirous of learning who I really am," the companion says and laughs without truly laughing. "I know, *Studiosus,* you will not have peace of mind till you know it; you were speaking of order last night, over supper, of the order in heaven and down here on earth; in that orderly a manner your brain works, all things have their bins and drawers in it, but you are not sure into which of them you want to fit me."

Once again Eitzen is confounded by the exact knowledge the other has of his innermost thoughts, but he will not admit it and, patting the neck of his sweated horse, says, everything in its own good time, and if Leuchtentrager be not in the proper mood, let him keep his story to himself, and at any rate, what is the use of words in a world where everybody regards everybody with a different eye.

That is exactly the point, the other replies, the young sir has put his finger on it squarely, and as for that matter, there is none of us able to sound out another's deepest mind. A secret always remains, for man unto himself is not one.

Young Eitzen casts a sidelong glance at his companion's common, everyday face with the little beard to it and the dark brows so strangely tipped, and for a moment it is to him as though he were seeing an appearance hovering about the other's humped shape, a mixture of fog and shadow, and since just then a cloud is moving across our dear sun, Eitzen shudders and sets the spurs to his animal.

Not that he intends to flee; he knows his nag would never be able to outstrip that horse of Leuchtentrager's, and so he says, "Whoa!" and waits till the other, riding at a comfortable pace, has reached his side, and inquires of him what he may have meant by saying that man unto himself is not one.

"There are two in each one of us," declares the companion.

Eitzen eyes him furtively: the misty shroud that floated about him is gone, most likely 'twas nothing but a figment of imagination, as had been those steps in the night. And as all thought in young Eitzen's mind quite naturally links itself to divine doctrine, he answers, "Two in each one of us, why yes, me and my immortal soul."

"Certainly," says the other, and this time his laugh is pure derision, "that's one way of looking at it."

Whereupon Eitzen is gripped by a suspicion worse than any he has previously held against the stranger, and he inquires cautiously, "You would not be one of those Anabaptists who in the town of Münster worshipped Satan and committed all kinds of wickedness? What is your sense on baptism?"

"Since you're that eager to know, *Studiosus,*" says the companion, "'tis my opinion that you may baptize the little children when they're quite small; whatever their profit by it, they surely won't suffer great harm by the drop of water and the law is observed, both Lutheran and Catholic."

This Eitzen accepts, even though it's still not to his liking that there should be inside him yet another who could play tricks on him or even lead him and his immortal soul into grievous sin.

Leuchtentrager slows his horse. "I am," he says, "the son of the oculist Balthasar Leuchtentrager from Kitzingen on the river Main and his good wife Anna Maria who was heavy with me in her ninth month when, at the command of our graceful lord, Margrave Casimir, the eyes of my father along with those of close to sixty other citizens of the town and peasants from the surrounding villages were put out."

"Seems that your father must have gotten into bad company," Eitzen conjectures.

"Was one of the worst ones himself," says the friend. "As people were gathering in great numbers at the time, among them a great many already armored and carrying halberds, and as those of the town council of Kitzingen were advising restraint and that any rebellion would do damage to all, my father rose up and spoke sharp words, inquiring if the people would once again let themselves be hoodwinked and fooled by honeyed tongues; that way you caught mice, but soon enough it would be raining heads."

"'Twas an evil time," Eitzen remarks sagaciously. "God be praised that it is over and gone, thanks to the writings of Doctor Martinus Luther and the propitious intervention of the government." And wonders in his mind how much of his father's rebellious ardor might lie dormant in Leuchtentrager junior who is riding there beside him.

But the other is chewing peacefully on a leaf he has torn from a tree on the wayside. Then he spits it out and goes on with his tale. "But as my mother's father was also blinded on orders of the margrave," he says, "for the reason that he had dug the remains of the sainted Mother Hadelogis, the founder of our nunnery of Kitzingen, from her grave in the church and had been using her skull for a bowling ball, and as my father on the day after his eyes were put out died most miserably from his wounds, my mother ran away with me inside her, and thus it came about that I was born in a barn on the way, just like the Jesus child, but not attended by a little ox and a little ass nor handsomely showered with gifts by three foreign kings; my poor mother was quite alone in that barn and I fell from her and therefore was crippled since my birth, which is why I am limping with one foot and carrying one shoulder higher than the other and have that little hump."

Young Eitzen cannot refrain from saying, "So, you've received a poor inheritance from both father and mother," and thinks to himself that not much good can come from a fellow with that sort of predisposition, but aloud he says, "And how did matters continue to develop with you?"

The other seems to start up from some memories, and his sudden move transmits itself to his horse which gallops off, and young Eitzen must hasten after it for a long time till he finally gets to hearing the next part of the story, namely how the babe's poor mother, weakened as she was, brought the child into Saxon lands, to the town of Wittenberg, and died there in God, and how the surgeon Anton Fries and his good wife Elsbeth took unto themselves the little waif which was quite lost and forlorn and could not speak but just babbled and cried for the breast, and kept it as their own. "For which they be thanked from the heart," adds Leuchtentrager, "although I did not give them much happiness their livelong day; I wasn't a cheerful child and kept what I thought to myself, and when others stated things were that way and had always been that way and let's have no more of it I asked why, and vexed everybody, and got many a thrashing for my troubles."

"But there are matters of weight," young Eitzen says

in great earnest, "regarding which no good Christian asks why."

"If mankind didn't ask why, we should every one of us still be sitting in paradise. For was not Eve wanting to know why she was forbidden to eat of that apple?"

"First," replies Eitzen, "she was a stupid woman, and secondly it was the snake that persuaded her. God save all of us from such snakes."

"But I have a liking for the snake," says the other. "The snake saw that God had equipped man with two hands to work and a head to think with, and to what good purpose might man have used those in paradise? In the end they might have withered like any thing not being used, and what, my dear *Studiosus*, would under these circumstances have become of the likeness of God?"

Young Eitzen is not sure whether the friend is ridiculing him or not, and he determines to return to firm ground by repeating the words which Pastor Aepinus at Hamburg has given him as his maxim for life: namely that it is faith and not science which brings salvation. Whereupon, so as not to be involved in another dispute in which he might lose out, he asks the other to continue with his story.

Leuchtentrager now relates how his foster father, the surgeon Fries, when he was about to die, had him called to his bedside and spoke to him as follows: My son, for I always considered you my son, although you were half starved and close to death when you came to my house and poorer than any foundling and my deceased wife and I took you in and fed you for Christ's sake; my son, herewith I am handing to you, as your inheritance from your true mother and your rightful father, what your mother carried with her when she was found dead. 'Tis not of much value, just for sentiment—*item*, a small kerchief, yellowed, with two dark stains of blood on it, I've tested those myself as to their nature and have found them to be an impression of the bloody eye sockets of your father; *item*, a silver coin with the head of a Roman caesar on it; and lastly, a piece of parchment with some Hebrew writing on it and underneath a note in your father's hand to the effect that he received the coin as well as the piece of parchment from an aged Jew who had been with him in the days before the rebellion. Whereupon Leuchtentrager's foster father faithfully handed over these items and a short while later passed away in peace; he, however, had placed the three things into a small bag of leather and since that day had always carried them on his person as a kind of talisman.

Hearing of the Jew who was with his companion's rightful father in the days of the rebellion, young Eitzen promptly recalls the Wandering Jew and the steps last night in the adjoining chamber; also he remembers the other telling him that he had come to Leipzig to try and find a certain Jew. And though young Eiten feels most apprehensive, the itch of his curiosity proves stronger and he announces that he is carrying on a ribbon round his neck a tiny consecrated cross which his dear mother had given him and which he might consent to show to Leuchtentrager if the other in turn would let him see his amulet.

Leuchtentrager leans over and hits young Eitzen on his shoulder, making him wince, and says, if the *studiosus* can brave the looks of such devilish objects, very well, he will get to see them. And as it is time to give the horses a rest, they halt and let their animals graze and themselves sit down on a couple of tree stumps, and the companion reaches into his doublet and shows to Eitzen first the coin, a well-preserved piece, you can discern every leaf of laurel on the emperor's bald head, and then the kerchief with the two brownish stains, and finally the bit of parchment.

Young Eitzen is able to read what the Kitzingen father of his companion has scribbled on the margin, but the Hebrew on the parchment proves just abracadabra to him and he wants to know what it means and whether it be an incantation or a malediction, or wasn't it ever deciphered?

He himself has on occasion dabbled in that language, Leuchtentrager admits, and adds for young Eitzen's benefit, "This text, however, is neither an incantation nor a malediction; 'tis from the Scriptures, a word of the prophet Ezekiel, reading: Thus says the Lord God, Behold I am against the shepherds; and I will require my flock at their hand, and cause them to cease from feeding their flock; neither shall the shepherds feed themselves anymore; for I will deliver my flock from their mouth, that they may not be meat for them."

Eitzen feels uncomfortable: no doubt, 'tis a prophet who is being quoted, but his speech sounds exceedingly seditious; and he wonders who those shepherds might be who go slaughtering their own flock, and who it was whom the prophet inveighed against. Then, however, he consoles himself with the thought that all this scolding refers to a time long past and that today's shepherds are upright and orderly people who lead their flock back to its owners in due season; and he remembers that he has promised to show his little cross to his companion.

But Leuchtentrager turns from it as though he were surfeited with the sight of crosses and, stowing his three treasures back into his doublet, goes to fetch his horse. And from up in the saddle, he says to young Eitzen who has rushed to his side, "If you wish, *Studiosus,* you may room with me in Wittenberg; there's space aplenty in the house of the surgeon Fries which he left to me and which is now my property; don't mind about the payment, we will easily agree on that, it won't cost you the world." And clicks his tongue and is off at a good trot.

Eitzen, directing his horse to follow the other's, considers how through the providence of God everything arranges itself most wisely and at the right time for those He loves; true, with the letter of recommendation from his rich Augsburg aunt in his pocket, he was counting on Magister Melanchthon helping him toward obtaining proper accommodations and board at Wittenberg, especially if he would register himself as his student; but the solution offered him now is by far the better one, for the great teacher and friend of Luther most likely will be besieged by numerous young scholars, some doubtless more gifted, though none more eager to apply themselves to their studies than Paulus von Eitzen from the city of Hamburg. And yet, he thinks, and yet . . .

Then he casts off those doubts. 'Tis not advisable to see too much mystery in people, even in such as his companion who is riding ahead of him, darkly outlined against the clouded evening sky.

CHAPTER THREE

§

In which incontrovertible proof is furnished
that nothing beyond the scope of our
doctrines can exist even though
it's there

§

Prof. Dr. Dr.h.c. Siegfried Beifuss
Institute for Scientific Atheism
Behrenstrasse 39 a
108 Berlin
German Democratic Republic

19 December 1979

Dear Professor Beifuss,

I have received your most commendable little book entitled *The Best-known Judeo-Christian Myths as Seen in the Light of Science and History* and have read it with the greatest interest. In many respects, especially where you deal with the purposes which those myths have served in the course of time and to a certain extent may still be serving today, I am in thorough agreement with you. It is up to the men of science to combat the ignorance of the masses which, let us admit this, is frequently made worse by many a modern myth being spread in the name of science, and wherever possible we must work for greater enlightenment.

But permit me a few remarks in reference to the section of your work which you captioned "On the Everlasting (or Wandering) Jew." I want to comment on your subject mainly because I, too, have done some research on this

Ahasverus who is known by several other names as well. The preliminary results of my research I have had occasion to jot down, and you will find them in the enclosed reprint from the journal *Hebrew Historical Studies;* I have added to the enclosure an admittedly clumsy German translation of my article, done for your convenience by one of my students.

On page 17 of your book, dear Colleague, you say: "To the followers of a *Weltanschauung* which, basing itself as it does on the principles of scientific thought, cannot and does not recognize anything not proven or not provable, the assumption of an existence of supernatural beings (i.e., God, a son of God, holy and other spirits as well as angels and devils) is *a priori* an impossibility." And following this axiomatic declaration you place Ahasverus along with the others named by you into the category of the impossible.

Without wishing to cast doubts on this *Weltanschauung* you call the philosophy of dialectical materialism—it surely has its merits—and so as to save you a possible later embarrassment, I should like to point out to you that the Wandering Jew is neither unproven nor unprovable. On the contrary he exists, as three-dimensional as you and I, with heart, lungs, liver, and all other organs and appurtenances, and the only phenomenon about him that you might consider supernatural is his extraordinary longevity: he simply does not die. Whether or not this is an advantage I leave to others to decide; Mr. Ahasverus himself seems unwilling to commit himself on the question. At least he never discussed it in my presence—apparently he accepts this longevity as a fact of his life just as we might resign ourselves to a crooked toe or psoriasis.

As you will understand from the above, I myself am in a position to testify as to the actual existence of Ahasverus. The countless and manifold impressions which over the hundreds—nay, thousands—of years have crowded the cells of his brain, have made his memory spotty. But certain parts of his long life he recalls with surprising clarity and can and does go into detail on them—you should hear him talk of his famous encounter with Jesus of Nazareth, a report which N.B. I found confirmed in recently discovered sections of the Dead Sea Scrolls. As soon as these are fully deciphered and authorized for publication, I shall be happy to place them at your disposal.

I hope, dear Colleague, that the information I was able to give you will prove of service to you, as you might want to avail yourself of it for an eventual new edition of your valuable little book. I am, with the expression of my highest esteem,

Yours sincerely,
Jochanaan Leuchtentrager
Hebrew University
Jerusalem

Prof. Jochanaan Leuchtentrager
Hebrew University
Jerusalem
Israel

12 January 1980

Dear Professor Leuchtentrager,

I am happy to be in the possession of your letter which, together with its enclosures, arrived yesterday at my Institute, and my pleasure is the greater as its contents seem to prove the wide-ranging effect which the scientific work done in our Republic has inside and outside its borders. The fact that a man of your rank and reputation concerns himself with the results of our efforts strengthens our resolve, and spurs us on to further, all-embracing and more consciously targeted, progress along our line, and convinces us to struggle even more consistently against all unscientific and unreasonable beliefs and superstitions.

Consequently, your article "Ahasverus, Fact and Fiction" in the *Hebrew Historical Studies* was perused not only by myself but also by my leading co-workers. My reply to you must therefore be considered as the opinion of a collective which has proved itself in an outstanding manner through years of research in the field of scientific atheism.

It is our joint view that your personal acquaintance with Mr. Ahasverus, a member of the Jewish religious community and mentioned in your article, cannot be doubted, nor do we question your earlier encounter with him during the uprising in the Warsaw ghetto which you, a young man at the time, survived by your audacious escape through subterranean passageways. We must doubt, however, the testimonies and accounts you adduce from former periods of history about meetings and experiences of people with said Ahasverus; such testimonies and accounts, especially those not corroborated by official sources or additional witnesses, can hardly count as scientifically admissible evidence, and the older they are, the more they appear to be of a mythological character. Although in one place in your article you refer to Mr. Ahasverus as "my friend," we should like to bring to your attention the possibility that your friend might have influenced your thinking—by suggesting to you the conclusions you propound in the article.

It is unfortunate that, due to the lack of diplomatic relations between the German Democratic Republic and the State of Israel, our citizens have difficulty gaining access to your country; otherwise I myself or qualified members of the Institute for Scientific Atheism would gladly go there and by personal observation of Mr. Ahasverus try to verify his approximate age. As is, you might want to consider having the true number of Mr. Ahasverus's years established by competent medical authority, to the satisfaction of all those concerned with the phenomenon.

In connection with this, the press officer of our Institute, our colleague Dr. Wilhelm Jaksch, wishes me to inquire as to the following: considering the notorious sensationalism of the Western media, not excepting those of Israel, shouldn't one expect them long ago to have taken cognizance of a man more than two thousand years old? To our knowledge, however, a report on Mr. Ahasverus has nowhere been printed, not even a photo of the man seems to have appeared in any publication. Perhaps you, dear Professor, own such a photograph which surely would be most informative and which you could let us have temporarily.

Let me state once again that I and my co-workers would welcome any debate, be it ever so controversial, on this or any related issue, and that we would of course yield to the better scientific argument. But this would require much stronger evidence of the existence of the Everlasting (or Wandering) Jew than you have been able to furnish.

With kindest wishes for the further progress of your work,

Yours sincerely,
(Prof. Dr. Dr.h.c.) Siegfried Beifuss
Institute for Scientific Atheism
Berlin, Capital of the GDR

CHAPTER FOUR

§

Wherein Doctor Luther expounds his opinion on the
Jews and young Eitzen actually encounters
one of them and is scandalized
by him

§

Quite a number of months have passed since young Paulus
von Eitzen arrived at Wittenberg. In all this time, tutored
by Magister Philipp Melanchthon and the other learned
doctores of the university, he has been diligently studying
the word of God and the history of the world while lodg-
ing, as was agreed upon, in the house that formerly belonged to the surgeon Fries and is presently owned by his
friend Leuchtentrager, to be precise in its upper story, and
feeling very much at home there, almost as much as at his
father's house in Hamburg. There's a slight difference,
though, because his host, over a glass of powerful wine in
the evening, will speak to him of things which strangely
agitate him and which his honest father, the merchant
Reinhard von Eitzen, linens and woolens, would never
dream of, and also because of the housemaid Margriet,
who serves him his breakfast and launders his shirts and
smokes out his bed when the multitude of bugs and lice in
it has grown beyond endurance. After such action 'tis no
longer the vermin that disturb him but his thoughts,
which keep rotating from early morning till late at night
around the shoulders and breasts and thighs and the de-
lightful behind of said Margriet. Nor does it help him
greatly to rush over to the small window of his chamber

and gaze from there diagonally across the street at the house of his teacher Melanchthon and try to concentrate his mind on the wise sayings of the chaste and pious man or the face and features of Mistress Barbara Steder who is faithfully waiting for him in Hamburg; in his brain the most virtuous precepts turn into gibberish, and his memories of Barbara, if they come to his mind at all, have sadly paled, and in place of her familiar image his inner eye will conjure up the saucy mouth and the full, sensual lips of Margriet.

Leuchtentrager has long ago noticed the state in which his lodger finds himself. "Paul," he says to him, for on the night of St. John they suddenly embraced and pledged forever to be like brothers unto one another and since then have been calling each other by their Christian names, Leuchtentrager addressing young Eitzen as Paulus and Eitzen, in return, saying Hans to his host—"Paul," says Leuchtentrager, "I can easily fix it for you with Margriet; it needs just a word from me and she'll come to you in the dark and take such care of you that you will hear the little angels singing in heaven; she is naturally gifted and I have taught her a few additional items."

Young Eitzen grows hot around his loins, but he answers, "You are mistaken, Hans, you know there lives a maiden in Hamburg to whom I have sworn to be faithful."

"Such faithfulness is something up in your head," says his friend, "but the lust you feel for Margriet comes from quite another part of yourself; one must not confuse things spiritual with those of the flesh, also it's a long way to Hamburg and what Mistress Steder doesn't know won't hurt her. But this is not what I meant to discuss, I meant to tell you that Magister Melanchthon has sent a servant to inquire if we would not honor him by attending a dinner which he intends giving for Doctor Martinus and his dear wife Katharina and several other guests, all of them highly respected and learned men; Frau Katharina would be contributing a barrel of beer, self-brewed."

"He is inviting me?" says young Eitzen, his face wreathed in joy at the sudden honor which has fallen to his lot.

"Yes, you," confirms Leuchtentrager, omitting to mention that he himself caused Melanchthon to add young Eitzen to the evening's company; 'tis part of his plans for the future; also he knows both Luther and Melanchthon, and knows that the two have long since exhausted all subjects of interest to one another, but when they happen to find a fresh public likely to be awed by their sagacity they will each want to shine and will orate like the sainted apostles, and thus, Leuchtentrager hopes, he might yet have an entertaining evening.

By the time the great event approaches, young Eitzen has dressed himself up in the most sumptuous manner; he is wearing his new boots made of soft leather and the black doublet whose slits display the gray silk lining, and has pomaded his hair so as to give it gloss. Also he has prepared the matter and manner of his discourse in case someone asks him: he will speak of his fellow citizens of Hamburg and how they are hungering for God's truth; but in secret he thinks that a good blessing from Luther might be sufficient to get him a pulpit in Hamburg and later even the superintendent's position. The housemaid Margriet, however, is laughing at him as he comes prancing down the stairs and inquires if he is going out courting, and Leuchtentrager replies, yes, but he seeks a heavenly bride.

Then they are assembled around the large table at Melanchthon's, doctors and students of divinity and other guests, also their wives, in case they are married. Young Eitzen is watching the last light of day refracted in the small rounded windowpanes; the candles have been lit and throw wavering shadows on the faces so it looks as though there were spirits about; but it's not ghosts, it's the draft from the kitchen moving the flames and spreading the most delicious smells. Like our Lord Jesus at his last supper, Doctor Martinus is seated in the center of the length of the table, his mighty head resting on his fists. He glances about idly; only when his eye, the one with which he's still able to see, happens on Leuchtentrager—who smilingly sits at the table's lower end—does Luther seem startled and wrinkles his protruding brow as if he were searching for some elusive memory.

But as soon as the fish is brought in, several fat carp stewed and served with a well-spiced sauce, he forgets his baneful thought; his forehead smooths itself and he begins to elaborate on God's creation and the wonders of it, and says, "Just consider the tidy way the little fish have of spawning, as one brings forth well nigh a thousand of them; whenever the little male is beating his tail and pouring his semen into the water, the little female is conceiving. Look at how perfectly the little birds go about breeding; he hacks at her little head, and she lays her little eggs neatly into the nest, sits on them, and out come the chicks from the shells; behold that little chick, how did it ever get into the egg?"

"And all this to the gain and benefit of man," adds our Magister Melanchthon, "as it is written in the Scripture that man shall have dominion over the fish of the sea, and over the fowl of the air, and over the cattle, and over every creeping thing that crawls upon the earth."

"And over each other," says Leuchtentrager. "And shall burn out each other's eyes and cut off their hands and beat and pierce and stretch and chain them painfully and put them to the wheel and do all sorts of violence to each other, Amen."

Young Eitzen sees Doctor Martinus grow red as a lobster as he nearly chokes on a piece of his carp, and he thinks to himself, holding forth over a glass of wine between friends is one thing, but saying the same before all these learned men quite another, and therefore admonishes Leuchtentrager: "Those be blasphemous words, Hans; iniquity was brought into the world by the snake, but we are not without power ourselves, and with God's help and aided by the word of our teachers Martinus Luther and Philipp Melanchthon we shall trample underfoot the beast's poisonous head and thus bring the kingdom of God nearer to us on this earth."

Meanwhile the good doctor has succeeded in clearing the carp and its vicious bones from his windpipe, and inquires, "And who might you be, young man?" And while Frau Katharina is refilling her husband's tankard and passing the huge pitcher of beer to the others, for with the Luthers' house at Wittenberg goes the privilege of brewing, young Eitzen reports about his person and his plans and ambitions, stammering all the while from sheer happiness, and Luther, who a moment ago was still quite agitated, leans over to Melanchthon and tells him, "Keep an eye on this fellow, Master Philipp, he will make his way in the world and get far." And turning to Leuchtentrager he says all the way across the table, "You have got something of the evil one about you; but a wise man listens to him as well, and takes heed."

Another man, thus reproved by Doctor Luther, might have been struck dumb with terror; but not Leuchtentrager. To young Eitzen it seems as though Leuchtentrager has grown by a foot, or maybe two or three of them, and his hump been extended frighteningly, or is it just shadows, and he hears his friend's derisive laughter and him saying, "Haven't you set out, good Doctor, to overcome the evil one? So tell us, have you succeeded? Or isn't it true, rather, that you were scared and retreated and made your peace with the powers that be, seeing the trouble and confusion you created and that man, damn him, always thinks of himself first and of God last or not at all?"

At this, Doctor Martinus Luther raises his bulk and stands there, irate, and everyone at the table ducks his head; young Eitzen, however, who knows well that in a hanged man's house you do not mention the rope, fears for his gains toward which he has worked with such diligence. Therefore he summons up all his courage and says to his teacher Melanchthon whether it be not true that Church and worldly authority are like the two legs of man; one without the other leaves you limping.

Melanchthon is glad of this sage sentence, his student has been learning well, but the dot on the *i* is still missing, and so he adds that a righteous worldly authority—i.e., one which bars and punishes epicurean speech, worship of false gods, perjury, covenants with the devil, and heretic creeds, is to all intents and purposes an organ of the church.

But Doctor Luther appears not to have heard, he still has his eye fixed on Leuchtentrager who is smiling and drinking Frau Katharina's beer, and says to him, "Whoever you might really be, you have touched my heart. For had I known in the beginning of my labors what I later came to learn, namely that people are so utterly hostile to the word of God and set themselves against it so powerfully, I should rather have stayed silent and never would have been so forward as to attack the pope and all order. I thought they were sinning out of ignorance and human failing and wouldn't dare to suppress God's word in all consciousness; but God led me on like an old nag with blinders on its eyes so it would not see those who run up against it."

Whereupon he sits down and lowers his head. But as everybody seems speechless, even Leuchtentrager, the good doctor presumes they have not understood him properly, and goes on to say, "'Tis rare that a great work is begun with wisdom and foresight; nay, such things grow out of blind courage and confusion. But that is just it, confusion breeds more confusion, and better use a big stick than have everything come to nought."

Leuchtentrager sets down his cup. "And there's no end in sight to the confusion," he says as though his mind were seriously troubled by this, "they say the Wandering Jew was seen again, not far from Wittenberg."

Young Eitzen promptly remembers the steps during the night in that empty chamber of the Swan at Leipzig, but that was long ago, and Doctor Martinus raises his head and his anger shows on his reddened face: why hasn't he been told before of this matter, why does the news have to come from this Leuchtentrager, and how reliable is it?

Frau Katharina is asking, "Where?" and "When?" and "What did he look like?" and Melanchthon says, "There is an abundance of Jews resembling each other like eggs in a basket; one of them might have wanted to distinguish himself from the rest, and we are falling for his tale."

But Leuchtentrager declares, "He has had the nailed cross on the soles of his feet, five nails in each foot."

This does convince Philipp Melanchthon but makes him feel squeamish as well, for despite his propensity for the letter of a text he is of a sensitive nature and can imagine how it must be if one is damned to wander forever and ever with so many nails in the soles of your feet; aside from that he also knows that hard times are coming whenever the Jew has been seen around. "If one could talk with him," he says thoughtfully, "and question him . . . The man was present when our Lord Jesus Christ went up to Golgotha with the cross on his shoulder; he might be able to clear up some doubts."

"Is that so?" says Doctor Martinus, "Might he? And which doubts, pray?"

"At least," replies Magister Philipp, "at least he could help us to convert those Jews to the only true faith."

This appears to young Eitzen to be quite plausible, for one whose eyes saw our Lord Jesus bearing his cross could also testify to the latter's holiness. All the greater is his amazement at the wrath which once again has taken hold of Doctor Martinus.

"Is that so," he says a second time. "So why don't you suggest to our gracious lord, the elector, to have the Jew seized—if anyone can lay hands on him, but it's as hard to lay hands on him as on the devil himself, he vanishes among the other Jews, only his stench remains behind, he is like them and they are like him, one might think they all last forever."

He looks around to make sure that everyone appreciates the importance of the matter he is expounding. The cook is standing in the door with the roast but does not dare to bring it in as long as the good doctor is talking so sagely, but Luther, in his great zeal, fails to notice her.

"Nor can you convert them," he goes on to say, "for even now they keep insisting on their nonsensical claim that they are the chosen people, although 'tis a good thousand and five hundred years that they've been driven out, destroyed and cast away, and all their heart's longing is that for once they might do unto us Christians what they did in the time of Esther in Persia unto the gentiles. And we don't know even today which devil it was who sent them to our country; we didn't invite them to come from Jerusalem."

This appears equally plausible to young Eitzen, for he knows from his rich aunt in Augsburg what mischief the Jews are making in the country and how they are taking it in from everybody, rich or poor, and giving nothing in return.

"Convert them!" the good Doctor Martinus is calling out. "Convert the Jews! I shall give you my true advice: first, that you burn their synagogues and Jewish schools to the ground and take away their prayer books and their talmudic scriptures and forbid their rabbis to teach, and second, that you hand to all young, strong Jews flails and axes and spades and make them work in the sweat of their noses; but if they refuse such work, drive them out of the country along with their Wandering Jew; haven't they all been sinning against our Lord Jesus Christ and aren't they as accursed as that Ahasverus?"

The thoughts in young Eitzen's mind grow confused, for in the great Luther's words he can't find much of the spirit of Christ who commanded, "Love your enemies and bless them that curse you." However, since it isn't our Lord Jesus but the good Doctor Martinus who can aid him in getting a living and a pulpit from which to preach the word of God, he comes to the conclusion that the opinions just propounded by Luther can't be so un-Christian, and as the cook is finally carrying in the roast and placing it on the table and the air is filled with delicious odors, he forgets his qualms. Doctor Martinus's mouth is watering as well so that his zealous words are drowned in it, and he reaches for the platter and takes the juiciest slice for himself, which no one will begrudge him. Then, a morsel of meat already between his teeth, he notices the handsome little knife which Leuchtentrager is just about to use and asks permission to look at it more closely, and while Frau Katharina discreetly averts her eyes, he appraises it and pronounces it a fine piece of art, but most likely inspired by the devil—as with painters and stone carvers and suchlike people you never can be quite sure if their hand was directed by one of the good angels or, rather, by Satan.

At this, Master Lucas Cranach, formerly apothecary in Wittenberg and seated tonight as one of the honored guests at this table, wishes to have his say and maintains that a true artist would not have his hand directed by anyone else, be he angel or devil, but was a creator in his own right, just as God Who created man and each of the animals, flowers, and leaves in the most artistic manner. And that he himself should like to paint our Doctor Martinus with that knife in his hand, 'twas the contrasting reds on the shapes of the figure, though all of them coral, and the expression of the good doctor's eyes, critical and at the same time quite appreciative, which intrigued him. Thus we might have been richer by a fine portrait painting done by the great master, had Doctor Martinus not answered that it befitted him better to have himself depicted holding a prayer book than a nude woman, be she ever so small.

Lucas Cranach assumes that Luther imagines himself too advanced in years for such frivolity, and contradicts him: Isn't it precisely the aged who know how best to value genuine beauty, and has not he himself, despite his years, done a picture of Eve in the nude and received much public praise for it?

Doctor Martinus, however, is glancing about, and his eye comes to rest on young Eitzen, and raising his heavy brow he hands the little knife to him and says, "Well, now, young man, what is your opinion of this?"

Eitzen's hand, clasping the knife, is beginning to sweat, and manifold thoughts are whirling through his head, of the whore who lay with him and of the housemaid Margriet, till finally he is able to speak up, and says, "We are all of us great sinners, and our lust an inborn evil bringing upon us everlasting death; but if we struggle against it, it's a most virtuous effort, though only God's mercy can free us from sin and save us."

Luther's chin drops and he imbibes a deep draft of beer before he replies. "You seem uncommonly sober-minded and thoughtful, Eitzen, just as though our Lord God had implanted an old brain into your youthful skull."

Eitzen is not sure whether or not this is meant as a compliment, and he looks for assurance from Leuchtentrager; but his friend just grins. Thus, even though a tasty dessert was had amongst much erudite and witty talk and Frau Katharina's beer has mellowed everyone and made them gay and friendly, the evening hasn't been an undiluted joy for Eitzen; and not until the general leave-taking begins and Luther has administered a benevolent pat to his shoulder does he breathe more easily; the young *studiosus,* says Luther, is welcome to address himself to him and solicit his advice if ever need be, at which suggestion Magister Melanchthon smiles a bit sourly. And as Leuchtentrager walks him home across the street, Eitzen jabs his elbow into his friend's side, saying, "Surely my holy guardian angel has directed everything most wisely," and adds after a decent moment's pause, "and you, Brother Hans, seem to have been conspiring with him toward the good end."

But the end to the evening is not yet, for as they open the door to the house and enter, they hear voices; one is Margriet's but the other is unknown to Eitzen; it sounds like a man's, and then he hears Margriet laughing the way women do when they feel the itch underneath their skirts. Swollen as he is with success, young Eitzen feels his hackles rising, and since Leuchtentrager seems to know who the late guest might be, he hastily follows him inside.

And there, in the large downstairs room, a view offers itself to his eyes which he will never forget for the rest of his life: a young Jew is seated on the wooden bench, his legs spread comfortably apart, the muddied tips of his boots one pointing east, the other west, and snugly lolling on his lap, in the most tender fashion, Margriet, while the Jew is touching and fondling her breasts. Nor does he cease his lewd doings as he looks up and perceives that he and the girl are no longer alone, but says, "Peace unto you, Leuchtentrager, and how are you progressing with your labors, and are you still holding the coin of Caesar and the parchment with that inscription?"

Eitzen remembers that coin only too well, and also the slip with the faded Hebrew words on it, and a strange feeling such as he never before has had takes hold of him because the person who gave those two keepsakes to his host's father, the late blinded oculist of Kitzingen, had been described to him as an aged Jew; this Jew, however, who still has his arm about Margriet, is in the flower of his years, may the devil fill them for him with grief and wretchedness.

Leuchtentrager strokes his little beard and says, why, yes, everything was being held safely, and the other could have it at any time he desired; then he limps across the room to the wall and presses against one of its panels, in a secret place, and much to his amazement Eitzen sees a section of the wall sliding apart and displaying a row of big-bellied bottles in which some fluid is gleaming, dark like blood. Seems to be wine, though; for Margriet detaches herself from the Jew and fetches drinking glasses which are adorned with gold. Both Leuchtentrager and the Jew sit down at the table; but young Eitzen doesn't know whether to stay on or slink away like a dog that's been caned; no one has spoken a word to him. His curiosity, however, proves greater than his dread, and he proceeds to squat near the others although it sickens him to have to watch

Margriet cuddling up to the Jew and lusting for him to be close to her just as if, in his greasy caftan, he were the Greek god Adonis.

The Jew, mumbling Hebrew words, blesses the wine which Leuchtentrager has poured into the glasses and takes a sip of it. Margriet drinks, too, gulping hastily; a drop of the wine, deep red, is running down her chin and across her white throat. Eitzen shivers, he feels as though he's had a presentiment of some future horror. Also it appears that everything about him is becoming strange and sinister. The room is no longer a room, time has ceased to be time, and Margriet stands there naked like Eve in Master Cranach's painting, her eyes showing the same brooding expression. The Jew and Leuchtentrager are talking of a shoemaker in the city of Jerusholayim who turned one Reb Joshua away from his door, for which reason this Reb Joshua execrated him.

"'Twas a false *meshiach,* says the Jew.

"Does anyone know for sure?" says Leuchtentrager. "The Old One is hard to fathom. If He made such a world with such people in it, why shouldn't He get the idea to split Himself in two or even in three?"

Young Eitzen realizes that they are talking of God and of the great mystery, and it galls him that their words are lacking the respect due to the subject; yet he senses that these two might know more of it than either he or his teacher Melanchthon, more than the great Martinus Luther even, about whose person they are beginning to argue while he, Eitzen, devotes himself to the wine.

This wine, heavy and sweet-tasting, goes down his gullet like honey. It befogs his brain and at the same time sharpens his senses. He hears the Jew praising Luther: no one has done as much as Doctor Martinus to speed up the course of the world, to destroy systems which outlasted thousands of years, to explode doctrinal structures and legal dams; and now the flood is rushing forward and sweeping along everything toward the bottomless pit, and in vain the good doctor is trying to stem the waters.

Leuchtentrager shrugs his little hump. 'Twas quite otherwise: he has it from Luther's own mouth how the man became deathly afraid as soon as he saw one thing rising out of another, bloody rioting out of well-balanced reforms, and tohubohu every whichway, whereupon he quickly cast from him all those who had supported him and had wanted the same as himself, nor had he hesitated to take the next step and in God's name had reconstructed the old dams and bulwarks for the old overlords.

What's broken is broken, the Jew says, and nobody, not even Luther, can fit it together again as it once was. And out of each convulsion and overturn some new and better thing is going to grow until, finally, the great idea would become reality and his, the Jew's, work would be done and he'd find peace and rest, peace and rest.

The wine. Young Eitzen's head is dropping onto his arm.

"He's asleep," says the Jew.

"He wouldn't understand anyhow," says Leuchtentrager. "How should he."

Margriet has pulled off the Jew's boots and is kissing his tortured feet.

"What are you calling yourself at present?" Leuchtentrager wants to know.

"Ahab," says the Jew.

Margriet looks up at him. "If you are Ahab, I will be your Jezebel."

"Ahab," young Eitzen says without raising his head and seemingly out of a deep dream, "Ahab was killed and the dogs licked up his blood."

And it is as though he were seeing a cloud of fire and hearing a big clap of thunder and a laughter from hell, and after that a voice speaking obscure words, in Hebrew probably, he surmises, namely, the words written on that piece of parchment. And his heart fills with fear and despair, but just then the good Doctor Martinus appears to him and takes him by the hand and says to him: You shall build the kingdom of God, Paul my son, and establish the order that I have envisioned.

As he comes awake in the morning, finding himself with his face lying between shards of glass and half-dried puddles of wine on the table, he discovers that the Jew is gone, along with the housemaid Margriet, only Leuchtentrager has remained and stands there waiting, his weight on his crippled leg, and says, "A letter has arrived for you, Paul, imploring you to make haste and get yourself to Hamburg as your father is gravely ill and asking to have you near him. I've taken the liberty of calling on the learned doctors of the university; they have consented to examine you on short notice and, if all goes well, to approve and graduate you so you might preach the word of God up there in the north. And as my business is taking me in a like direction, we shall, God willing, be traveling together."

Young Eitzen, after last night's dreams not yet in possession of all his faculties, is quite overwhelmed by this much news and by the fact that, once again, all has already been arranged for him so that nothing is left but to give his grateful assent. I shall never be rid of this man, he thinks to himself, but would I want to be, really?

CHAPTER FIVE

§

In which Ahasverus puts the thinking of Reb
Joshua in question and explains to him
that it won't be the meek and the
poor in spirit who will erect the
kingdom of God but those who turn
the order of things downside
up

§

He will not be helped.

He goes out and exorcises the evil spirits and drives
them from the bodies of the sick so that these rise up and
are healed, but himself he cannot heal and cannot drive out
the spirit that holds him to his way as the drover's rope
holds the donkey.

I am distressed for you, Reb Joshua. My heart went out
to you as I saw you so lost and alone in the wilderness, and
I came up to you, and you said: Which angel are you? And
I said: I am Ahasverus, one of those that were cast out.
And you said: My father in heaven will gather you, too,
unto Himself.

But God is not a God of love; He is the universe which
knows no feelings, but wherein light joins itself to light
and force to force, all of them forever circling round one
another. Of which Reb Joshua has no knowledge; he believes that when he emerged from the waters of the river

Jordan, in the arms of John the Baptist, a voice actually spoke to the people, saying: This is my beloved son, in whom I am well pleased.

Ah, the look of him as he sat crouching in the wilderness, round about him nothing but naked thorn and crude stone. His matted hair was full of the sand which the wind blew his way, his stomach was swollen from hunger, his kneebones nearly pierced the skin, and his prick, just partially hidden by the miserable rag round his loins, was like a bluish worm. But his eyes were burning between his lids, like the eyes of one who has seen visions, and he turned to me and said: There was someone who came and took me by the hand and led me toward Jerusholayim, the holy city, and placed me on the highest pinnacle of the temple, and said, If you be the son of God, cast yourself down, for it is written, "He shall give His angels charge concerning you, and in their hands they shall bear you up, lest at any time you dash your foot against a stone." And I saw myself flying with outstretched arms, high over the city, like a golden bird, and there was a multitude of people in the streets, and scribes and soldiers, and they looked up to me and rejoiced and cried Hosanna!

But you did not cast yourself down, Reb Joshua, I said. Why didn't you?

He ran his thin, dirt-smudged fingers through his sparse beard and gently shook his head and said: Because it is also written, "Thou shalt not tempt the Lord thy God."

And I crouched down beside him and laid my arm about him and said: I know the one who took you by the hand and led you toward the holy city and placed you on the highest pinnacle of the temple, and if you had cast yourself down you would have been lying, broken and smashed, between the moneychangers in the court of the temple. As is, however, you are alive, Reb Joshua, and a light goes out from you and a great hope for all men. Follow me, therefore, and I will show you your world.

And I led him to the top of a very high mountain and

showed him the kingdoms of the world and how in each one of them injustice and iniquity were the rule, here the last piece of bread was taken from the mouths of widows and orphans, there they made lions and other wild beasts tear people limb from limb and laughed at such pastimes, elsewhere poets had to sing praises to the mighty while bondsmen were hitching themselves to the yoke and their wives dragging plows, and in every place the strong were oppressing the weak and driving and tormenting them. And I said to him: If you be the son of God, then look well how wisely your father has ordered things, and take them into your own hand and turn them downside up, for the time has come to erect the true kingdom of God. Go out and speak unto the people and gather them round you and lead them, as another Joshua once did, and tell them to gird themselves for the great day about to come, and then cause the trumpets to be blown; and the gates to the kingdoms of the world will open before you and their walls will crumble into dust, but you will rule over all of them in glory and everlasting justice, and man will be free to make the heavens his own.

He gazed out at the valleys and mountains, and at the jagged rocks capped with ice, and at the huts of the poor and the palaces of the rich that were discernible in the distance, and said gently: My kingdom is not of this world.

But you might make an attempt at it, I said; it would be a beginning, at least.

He stayed silent.

Oh, Reb Joshua, I thought, I will wrestle with you as the angel of the Lord wrestled with Jacob, and I said to him: It has been prophesied that one will come who shall destroy the princes of the world and turn to dust the great judges just as though they had never been planted or sown and their stock had never taken root in the earth.

He took my hand in his, and I felt how cold his hand had become in the rarefied air on top of the mountain, and he spoke: But the prophet also says, "He shall not cry, nor lift up, nor cause his voice to be heard on the street; a bruised reed he shall not break, and the smoking flax shall he not quench."

Reb Joshua, I answered him, but it is also written, "He will come with strong hand and his arm shall rule for him; behold, his reward is with him."

But he shook his head and spoke: Not so, my fallen angel who is trying to strike out toward new heights, for the prophet has said of the *meshiach,* "Behold, daughter of Zion, your King comes unto you; he is just and having salvation; lowly and riding upon the foal of an ass."

At that, a great anger took hold of me and I answered: Such a one won't even curdle a potful of milk. No, you are not he who is to come and exalt every valley and make low every mountain and hill and make straight the crooked and the rough places plain; for this, we shall have to await another one. But you they will take and scorn as a false king, and they will flog you and press thorns upon your forehead and fasten you to the cross till the last drop of your lukewarm blood has oozed from your gentle little heart; it isn't the lamb who will change the world, the lamb will be slain.

The lamb, says he, takes upon itself the guilt of all men.

So I gave up and left him to himself up there in the cold and went my way. But he came rushing after me, stumbling down the mountain, his steps uncertain and awkward, and called out: Do not leave me, for I have no one else, and I know that no hand will ever be lifted in my defense and all will deny me.

I stopped. And he came to me, trembling and with large drops of sweat on his face, and I repented having turned from him, and I said: There is no likeness between you and me, for I am one of the spirits and you a son of man. But I will be with you when they all are deserting you, and I will comfort you when your hour has come. With me, you shall find rest.

But he went out from the wilderness and went to Capernaum, to the fishermen there, and preached unto the people that it was the meek who were blessed, for they should inherit the earth, and blessed likewise were those who hunger and thirst after righteousness, for they should be filled.

CHAPTER SIX

§

*In which Professor Leuchtentrager is informed by
competent authority that the* Weltanschauung
*prevailing in the German Democratic Republic
excludes the existence of miracles and,
therefore, the possibility of an actually
existing Wandering Jew*

§

Prof. Dr. Dr.h.c. Siegfried Beifuss
Institute for Scientific Atheism
Behrenstrasse 39 a
108 Berlin
German Democratic Republic

31 January 1980

Dear Colleague,

Your letter of the 12th of this month came as a most
pleasant surprise to me. I had never expected those few
remarks of mine to cause such great interest on your part,
and I'm understandably proud to hear that you have set
your whole collective to work on the Ahasverus matter.
We here, unfortunately, have to cover our field with nu-
merically much weaker forces.

Nevertheless I have hurried to follow up on your suggestions as far as this could be done within the brief period
of time at my disposal. You thus will find enclosed three
photographs. One is a snapshot of Mr. Ahasverus in front
of his shoe store in the Via Dolorosa; the other two were
taken in the manner routine to such purposes, the first *en*

face, with the right ear showing, the second in profile; these pictures, to make myself clear, do not come from any police file, but so as to satisfy any possible doubts you might have, they were taken by a professional police photographer. Viewing these photos closely, you cannot but find that the person portrayed indubitably is a man of character, intelligent and—if you will look at his mouth and eyes—with a good sense of humor; I may add for your information that women commonly take quite an interest in him, especially since he is a bachelor.

Furthermore, and once again acting on your suggestion, dear Colleague, I arranged for an official medical examination of Mr. Ahasverus. This was done by Professor Chaskel Meyerowicz, head of the Institute of Forensic Medicine at Hebrew University; the reports, likewise enclosed, state that the person examined has the constitution of a male of approximately forty years of age, with no ascertainable physical injuries and no chronic illnesses. The blood tests, however, caused Professor Meyerowicz to consult Dr. Chaim Bimsstein of the Radiological Institute of the University. Dr. Bimsstein confirmed that the blood of the person examined actually did contain traces of radioactive materials with a half-life of at least two thousand years, which would point to the surprising fact that Mr. Ahasverus must be considerably older than assumed up to now; he must have come into existence much before the time of Jesus of Nazareth. An opinion to that effect, signed by both medical specialists, is attached to the other reports.

I also intended to write for you a brief factual account of my experiences during the last days of the Warsaw ghetto, not merely because my friend Ahasverus played a certain part in those events but also because it is my feeling that the subject matter should be of particular concern to you as a citizen of one of the two German successor states. Sorry to say—or perhaps it was lucky—there was another obligation of mine which had to take precedence, namely a trip to Istanbul where, as you surely know, the archives of the Sublime Porte are stored in the former seraglio of the caliphs.

Thanks to the kindness of the curator of the archives, Professor Kemal Denktash, I was finally permitted to work there, and to my great joy I discovered what I had been trying to find for the longest time: the records of a trial of the advisers of Emperor Julian Apostata. This trial was held in A.D. 364, one year after the violent death of the emperor, and among the defendants there actually was a Jew by the name of Ahasverus. The manuscript, unfortunately somewhat damaged, contains parts of the indictment which was read by Gregory of Nazianzus, later patriarch of Constantinople; in it, Ahasverus is accused of having instigated the anti-Christian policies of Apostata, "to the purpose of spreading unrest and disobedience and of subverting the order of Church and State, not only in Rome but also in the Kingdom of God, as an outrage and abhorrence to all good Christian men and women, and to have demanded that the bishops of Christ should return to the temples and synagogues the treasures which they had taken from there."

Ahasverus was permitted to speak in his defense; however, as these sections of the parchment had very much disintegrated, I was able to decipher only a few sentences, and some of them only in part. At any rate, from the fragments extant it becomes evident that Ahasverus defended himself by claiming that the Jesus worshiped by the Christians was neither a son of the Jewish God nor the Messiah awaited by the Jews but a minor rabbi, soothsayer, and faith healer such as were working the marketplaces even then, and the doctrine being preached in his name was nothing but a turbid brew of obscure ideas which the Jews disdained and the Greeks had discarded. And he, Ahasverus, could warrant this because he had personally known the above-named Jesus and had talked with him several times and at length.

At the end of the report we find an indication of the punishment meted out to the defendant: Ahasverus was to be quartered. You and I, dear Colleague, certainly will be in agreement on the Church's having committed countless cruelties in the course of its history; as any organization founded on dogma it forgives no one who places even a tittle of its doctrine in question.

I presume that these results of my research in the archives of the Sublime Porte will be of special interest to you, since in the section "On the Everlasting (or Wandering) Jew" of your otherwise so carefully documented little book *The Best-known Judeo-Christian Myths as Seen in the Light of Science and History* you consider the Ahasverus legend to be a fairly late development, and state that the figure of Ahasverus does not appear until the arrival on the scene of the future superintendent of Sleswick, Paul von Eitzen, who is reported in several prints of rather dubious provenance to have encountered the Wandering Jew during his student time in or about the town of Wittenberg. I, too, am familiar with this Eitzen, a shallow-headed zealot but, as shown by my discovery in the archives of the Supreme Porte and other evidence, by no means the earliest witness to the existence of Ahasverus.

I wonder, dear Colleague, why you so consistently refuse to reconcile yourself to the thought that the Wandering Jew might be a reality. Once we assume his existence to be a natural phenomenon, it would immediately cease to appear as a divine miracle (to be negated by you, of course) and therefore could no longer be used as proof for the existence of a divine being.

I shall be pleased to be at your disposal for any further information on the subject, and remain,

Yours sincerely,
Jochanaan Leuchtentrager
Hebrew University
Jerusalem

Comrade Prof. Dr. Dr. h.c. Siegfried Beifuss
Institute for Scientific Atheism
Behrenstrasse 39 a
108 Berlin

12 February 1980

Dear Comrade Beifuss,

Having familiarized ourselves with your correspondence with Prof. Leuchtentrager of the Hebrew University in Jerusalem we instruct you to continue same. We expect you to show the greatest firmness of principle, and our scientifically worked out and proven viewpoints are to be represented without deviation. Wherever feasible, the role of the State of Israel as an outpost of imperialism against our valiantly struggling Arab friends is to be stressed.

The organs concerned have been informed.

With socialist greetings,

> Würzner
> Chief of Department
> Ministry of
> Higher Education

Prof. Jochanaan Leuchtentrager
Hebrew University
Jerusalem
Israel

14 February 1980

Dear and honored Colleague,

I am in possession of your kind letter of January 31st, plus enclosures, and because of its pertinence to our work I did not hesitate to discuss it with my collective.

The focal point of your communication seems to be your inquiry as to why I, i.e., all of us here at our Institute, cannot reconcile ourselves to the idea of an actually existing Ahasverus; and you are trying to facilitate our acceptance of it by maintaining that a belief in the existence of the Wandering Jew does not necessarily require a general belief in miracles.

On principle, I should like to state that we in the German Democratic Republic do not believe in any kind of miracles, just as we do not believe in spirits, ghosts, angels, or devils. To accept as fact the enormous longevity of Mr. Ahasverus, however, would be the equivalent of believing not only in this miracle but also in Jesus Christ, who allegedly condemned the Jew to go on living and walk the earth until he, the son of God, would return and sit in judgment over the souls of people. As a scientist, dear Colleague, you will concur with my saying that such a thesis is untenable.

As to the evidence you were good enough to furnish us: the three photos, you will admit, prove at best that there is or was a man whose likeness is that of the person shown in the pictures and who, furthermore, had himself photographed in front of a shoe store.

The medical reports, which I have taken the liberty to submit to a collective of specialists at Charité, the clinical institution of our Berlin university, do not give proof either of any extraordinary age of your friend Ahasverus; your own Israeli doctors, as you yourself wrote us, have estimated his age to be about forty years. Only the blood test would tend to confirm your claim, the Charité people admit, but Professor Leopold Söhnlein, the famous hematologist, pointed out to me that the traces of radioactive elements in the blood of the person examined might just as well have been absorbed through the digestive system, along with any number of vegetative materials, and might thus have entered the bloodstream.

It isn't mistrust of Mr. Ahasverus or of any other of your sources which makes me inform you of this, dear Colleague; my fellow workers and I are solely concerned with the scientific validity of your evidence which, I'm afraid, in the case of the three photos and the medical reports supplied by you, equals zero. You are finding yourself in a position not dissimilar to that of Pope Pius XII who, in his address on "The Demonstrations of God in the Light of Modern Natural Science" concluded from the so-called red shift in the spectra of extragalactic nebulae that there must have been a huge original explosion, an *Urknall,*—i.e., an act of creation and, therefore, a creator. It is known, however, that this red shift need not be a radial velocity effect of these galactic systems expanding from a center point; as Professor Freundlich points out, the red shift could just as well be the result of a loss of energy. What we are faced with here, exactly as with the traces of radioactive elements in the blood of Mr. Ahasverus, is simply a scientific problem as yet unsolved which, should it prove of sufficient importance, will doubtless be solved one day by man. But dialectical materialism refuses to draw philosophical conclusions from mere scientific conjectures.

Your report culled from the archives of the Supreme Porte is something else entirely, and I am grateful that you let me have it. My one regret is that we cannot acquire a photocopy of the manuscript since, as we're very much aware, the photographing of materials held in the archives of the Porte, just as in the archives of the Vatican, is hardly ever permitted. So there was a man named Ahasverus who happened to be an adviser to Emperor Julian Apostata; it's a known fact that princes always had a certain liking for clever Jews and Jews always were attracted to princely courts. But just for that, does the Ahasverus quartered in the year 364 have to be identical with your shoe seller in the Via Dolorosa?

The answer to this question is obviously No. As you will know better than I, there have been several Ahasveruses in history; I need only remind you of the king of the same name in the Book of Esther who, by the Biblical account, also had trouble with the Jews. Professor Walter Beltz of the University of Halle has informed me that the name Ahasverus is an Aramaic distortion of the Persian Artaxerxes, which might be translated as "Exalted by God," or "Beloved by God," in short, Godwin. Or would you also wish to claim that your Ahasverus is a reincarnation of the Persian king?

I further must correct, dear Colleague, your description of Paul von Eitzen as a "witness to the existence of Ahasverus." Far be it from me to want to extol as ardent a Lutheran as Eitzen; but I must state in his favor that in none of his writings—neither his numerous Latin ones nor in his *Christliche Unterweisung* in which he discusses the problem of predestination and the Christian communion, nor in his collected sermons entitled *Postille*—may any hint of the author ever having met the Wandering Jew be found; and in Feddersen's *History of the Church in Schleswig-Holstein,* which deals extensively with Eitzen, not a word is contained of such an incident. Wouldn't you assume, dear Professor Leuchtentrager, that so prolific a writer as Eitzen, who also was preaching nearly every Sunday of the year, would have at least mentioned an encounter that surely must have impressed him and that he could have used to moralize upon—if ever it had taken place?

In conclusion of my overly long letter, may I add that you omitted to answer a question from our press officer, Dr. W. Jaksch, who wants to know how come the Western media, so notoriously sensationalist, has up to now failed to take note of a man alleged to be some two thousand years of age? On the basis of the photograph of Mr. Ahasverus before his shoe store I should like to supplement that question: Why has Mr. Ahasverus himself made no use of the fact that his business is still in the spot along the road to Golgotha where he turned Jesus, coming up to be crucified, away from his door? Almost two thousand years of the same proprietor in the same store in the same place—what capitalist enterprise could claim for itself a record even approximating this one!

I am, with kind regards,

Sincerely yours,
(Prof. Dr. Dr.h.c.) Siegfried Beifuss
Institute for Scientific Atheism
Berlin, Capital of the GDR

CHAPTER SEVEN

§

*Wherein it is shown that one who knows the true
faith from the teachings of the heretics
will also be able to discourse on subjects of which he knows nothing*

§

Young Eitzen is sitting there bent over his books and uttering heartrending sighs, for his texts blur before his eyes
and the wisdoms of the holy fathers of the Church are
whirring about him like midges near a bog and he can't
swat them.

'Twas most considerate of the *doctores* and *professores* of
the university to agree to examine him out of turn and
ahead of his time, because of his father's expected demise,
but now he must prove that he has learned to differentiate
sharply between the one and only true faith and the various heresies with which the devil fills the minds of people,
and to walk the one and only path of righteousness and
quote the one and only right word, for anything else is of
evil and leads straight into wickedness. If only he had
worked harder, he thinks ruefully, and had listened more
attentively to the discourses of his learned teachers, but he
has concentrated not so much on *consubstantatio* and *trans-
substantatio* as on thoughts of Margriet, and has let himself
be seduced more often than not by his friend Leuchtentrager to have yet another glass of wine and yet another
tankard of beer instead of applying himself to learning the
fine distinction St. Athanasius made between the Father,
the Son, and the Holy Ghost, of whom one is said to be

neither made nor begotten, and the other not made but begotten, and the third neither made nor begotten but proceeding; but which now is which, and why?

And as he is still sighing pitifully, plagued by his inner unrest and his bad conscience, he notices his candle beginning to flicker and senses that there is someone around and stepping out of the shadows.

"That won't help you much," says Leuchtentrager, for it is he who has suddenly materialized and now is standing before Eitzen, "and all your reading and studying and memorizing is to no purpose; you either know your answers when the time comes and they ask you or you don't know them, and your best bet is just to say something and keep on talking, your whole theology is but a lot of words, and any good quote from any authority will fill the bill."

Young Eitzen would like to damn him to hell but does not do it, for there is no one else to comfort and succor him. "I seem to have a thousand worms inside my skull," he complains, "and all of them winding and twisting; the devil must have warped and sickened my brain."

"The devil," says Leuchtentrager, "has more urgent things to attend to. But I shall help you nevertheless."

"Yes, help me," says Eitzen, "as you helped me with Margriet who up and left with the Jew."

"You did not want to accept my help," says Leuchtentrager. "If you had, the matter might have come out otherwise; however, the Jew is also a mighty powerful personage."

"I would like to know," says Eitzen, "how you can help me when I am facing Doctor Martinus and Magister Melanchthon."

"I shall be there," says Leuchtentrager.

"That's some consolation," says Eitzen. "And you will answer in my stead?"

"I shall be there," says Leuchtentrager, "and you will answer."

"You may know the answers with a deck of cards,"

says Eitzen, "which for good reasons is called the devil's prayer book. But what would you know of the doctrine of God, considering that I am totally unable to remember a thing about it and would much rather be taken away in a chariot of fire, as was the prophet Elijah, than drag myself to the university tomorrow."

"I know what they will ask you," says Leuchtentrager.

"How could that be?" doubts young Eitzen. "They keep what they wish to examine you about a deep secret, otherwise anyone might come and pass the test, and doctor's degrees would be a groschen a dozen."

"But I do know it," says Leuchtentrager, "and I'll lay you a wager: if I should be proven wrong and they ask you something different tomorrow, I will be your servant till this day next year and you can have from me whatever you desire."

"Even Margriet?"

"Even Margriet."

At this, young Eitzen begins to worry that his friend's prophecies might come true after all, or that his teacher Melanchthon or Luther himself might have been blabbing, and he inquires, "And what would I have to pay you in case I lost the wager?"

"Nothing," says Leuchtentrager. "I get all I want from you without a tit for a tat."

Young Eitzen feels depressed at being viewed as no more than a bit of clay in the potter's hand; but then he casts off this thought and wishes to be told by his friend on which subjects he will be examined, because he wants to use the night to prepare himself for them.

"They will examine you about the angels," says Leuch tentrager, "and as regards these I am better informed than your Doctor Luther and your Magister Melanchthon and all your professors at the university lumped together."

"But I am not," moans Eitzen and starts to search among the books on his desk and finally picks up Saint Augustine, hoping that therein he will find what there is to know about angels.

His friend places his hand upon Eitzen's shoulder, saying, "And how would it help you to learn by rote the entire Saint Augustine and to memorize the nine hundred and ninety-nine thousand names of the angels, if tomorrow none of it will come to your mind? Let us drink."

Young Eitzen is overcome by despair, and he thinks to himself that he is lost anyway, but if it did turn out that Doctor Martinus and his teacher Melanchthon examined him about the angels, help would come to him somehow, either from up high, or from deep down where the devil resides. So he follows his friend down the stairs and becomes aware that the bottles are already waiting, with the dark red wine gleaming inside, and the image of Margriet sitting on the lap of the Jew rises before him, and his mouth fills with bitterness, and he wishes her dead in the Jew's arms and shrinks in fright at so sinful a thought.

"Drink!" says Leuchtentrager. "To all the dear little angels!"

Eitzen drinks. And he begins to feel better around his heart, and his mind eases, and one bottle is being opened after the other until his head sinks onto Leuchtentrager's chest and he no longer notices anything.

In the morning, as he comes to with a shock, he calls his friend who was to help him in his dire need; in vain; there is no trace or shadow of him, neither indoors nor outside the house. And so, with the vapors of the wine still under his cranium, he totters over to the university where he is led into the great hall and made to stand there, behind him and to his left and right the representatives of the clergy and of the city council, and an official of the grand elector's with a gilded chain around his neck, and students and other folk, and before him the high examiners, in their midst his teacher Melanchthon and the great Doctor Luther, both wearing their academic garb; to him, however, they appear like a pair of executioners hiding their axes underneath their robes, and he sees them scanning him with disdain, noting his bleary eyes and his unkempt hair, and Magister Melanchthon is holding his handkerchief to his nose for the candidate Paulus von Eitzen stinks from his mouth.

"Now, candidate," says the dean, "are you prepared and ready?"

"In God's name, yes," says young Eitzen, feeling that all his science has evaporated and vanished like a cloudlet of smoke, and looks desperately about for some guardian angel or, if such a one will not materialize, at least for a semblance of his friend Leuchtentrager.

"Young man," says Doctor Martinus and stares at him with his one good eye, "will you tell us all you know of the holy angels and their nature."

So it is angels, thinks Eitzen; he has prophesied verily, Leuchtentrager has, and won't have to serve me till this day next year, nor will I get my hands on Margriet. But aside from this, there is not a thought in Eitzen's brain, and he doesn't know what to tell the *doctores* and *professores* about the nature of the holy angels, and stammers miserably and shuffles his feet as though he were already standing on the red-hot griddle above the flames of purgatory.

"Candidate!" Doctor Martinus admonishes him. "What about those angels!"

Just then, as he is about to run off in shame, no matter where to, Eitzen catches a glimpse of Leuchtentrager, and at the same instant he has the strangest sensation inside his head and feels as though sparks were shooting around his brow, and he starts to speak, his words coming almost by themselves, from what source he doesn't know, and he declaims, "*Angeli sunt spiritus finiti,* of spiritual substance, their number limited, made by God, endowed with will and reason, and ordained diligently to serve God. Their attributes are, *ad primum,* the negative ones: *Indivisibilitas,* as they are not composed of parts but constitute one whole; *Invisibilitas,* as their substance is invisible; *Immutabilitas,* as they neither grow nor diminish; *Incorruptibilitas,* as they are not mortal; and *Illocalitas,* as they are both everywhere and no place. *Ad secundum . . .*"

Eitzen sees the mouth of the good Doctor Martinus

gaping wide, and the eyes of Magister Melanchthon nearly popping from their sockets at such a learned flow of words, but the spirit which has come over him carries him on and he now turns, *ad secundum,* to the affirmative qualities of the angels, viz., their *Vis intellectiva,* because they were endowed with intelligence and understanding, their *Voluntatis libertas,* because they had it in them to do good or evil, at their own volition, their *Facultas loquendi,* for they were frequently overheard talking to people, but also talked among each other, furthermore their *Potentia* which enabled them to perform *Mirabilia,* i.e., astonishing deeds, but not *Miracula,* i.e. wonders; and then there was their *Duratio aeviterna,* note well, not *eterna,* for they were immortal but not eternal in view of the fact that they were created and had a beginning; and finally their *Ubietatem definitivam,* a certain domicile, and *Agilitatem summam,* as they appeared with lightning speed soon here, soon there.

Up to this, the breath of Candidate Eitzen has lasted him, but now he must come up for air, as must his high examiners and the gentlemen from the city council and the grand elector's office, all of whom have never in their lives heard so far-reaching and detailed an account of things celestial and are quite numbed by it. Eitzen's fellow *studiosi,* however, in whose esteem he never rated very high, are stamping their feet and beating their fists on the tables with such abandon that the dean is fearing for the wooden slats on his floors and for his furniture. Only Leuchtentrager presents an indifferent face, as though a wonder like this happened every day, and he shrugs his little hump, and Eitzen feels once again overcome and must go on talking as did the prophets of old, in tongues, only he is not sure whence his tongues derive, from God or from an entirely different source.

"*Angeli boni sunt,*" he says, "*qui in sapientia et sanctitate perstiterunt*"—that is, who persist in wisdom and holiness so that they may worship God without ever being tempted by sin and live by his everlasting grace. One division of these good angels, he goes on to explain, was assigned to the service of God and of Christ, another, however, was appointed to the salvation of people. Such angels did serve the righteous individually, from their earliest infancy to their blessed end, and they were, as any reasonable person could easily see, especially responsible for the welfare of those who preached the word of God.

Saying which, young Eitzen casts a most meaningful glance at Luther and at his good teacher Melanchthon, and then turns to the gentlemen of the council and of the grand elector's office and continues with his voice raised for emphasis, "But these angels are also in duty bound to their political mission, subordinate to the public laws, namely to aid and support the servants of the government, save them from danger, and protect them against unjust enemies!"

'Tis only natural that the councilmen and the grand elector's officials are nodding wisely at this and murmuring approval, and more than one of them has the distinct feeling that the little guardian angel assigned to him by higher authority is looking over his shoulder, saying: Here I am and at your service, Your Honor.

Considering the effect of his words, it is easy to see why young Eitzen grows increasingly enthusiastic over his subject and goes on to describe how the good angels also are active in business affairs in that they make the enterprises of the righteous prosper and come to a profitable end, and likewise are helpful in family matters in that they guard its members and see to it that order prevails, for the family is in a small measure what Church and State are on a larger scale. But *in summa,* he declares, all this activity of the good angels is merely their *Praeparatio* for the great tasks they will have to perform on Judgment Day when they will be doing the preliminary work for the judgments Christ will pass, in that they serve as assessors prior to the sentencing, and also separate the righteous from the wicked, dispatching the righteous toward their future seats to the right of Christ, the wicked, however, toward hell. Therefore it is fitting to glorify and love the angels, and to be careful lest we encounter one of them while we are about to commit disreputable deeds, but it is not proper to direct prayers to them.

Eitzen's knees are trembling. Though a man uses only his lips, his tongue, and his throat for speaking, and sometimes his hands, a lengthy oration requires great strength, especially when it's desired that it be full of the right sort of spirit. And that this is the case with the words of Candidate Eitzen, not only his high examiners are convinced of, but also Doctor Luther and Magister Melanchthon and everybody else of consequence. Eitzen feels that, with his description of Judgment Day and his remark on how you should glorify, but not worship the angels, he has reached a most favorable point, but he is conscious that, just as there is no Aye in this world without its Nay, there is no good thing without its concomitant of evil, and that he's still owing the *Caput* which deals with the bad angels; not so much for the sake of the learned *doctores* and *professores* who would be well satisfied with the performance they have had, but because he has this dark feeling that it must be. But as he looks up for inspiration, he discovers that Leuchtentrager has disappeared; in his field of vision he can descry only his teacher Melanchthon and Doctor Martinus, both waiting expectantly, and no one else's head between the two of theirs; and fear takes hold of him, and he doesn't know what to say, he only knows that talk of the devil draws Satan close.

But then he senses someone near him, 'twas no more than a breath that stirred, and he sees his friend looking at him from the side, just as he did the previous night when he told Eitzen that theology was but a lot of words and simply to go on talking. "*Angeli mali sunt,*" issues forth from Eitzen's mouth, "*qui in concreata sapientia et justitia non perseverarunt,*" and he is not sure if it was he who said those words or somebody else who spoke through him, and he wonders why none of the high examiners is protesting against the presence of another person at the candidate's side, since such a thing would be most unusual, if not forbidden by law. But as nothing of the sort occurs, he goes on discoursing on the bad angels who did not persevere in the wisdom and virtues with which they were endowed and who deviated of their own will from God and from the ways of righteousness and thus turned themselves into absolute enemies of God and man.

So far so good; Doctor Luther is benevolently scratching his cheek, he's had his own experiences with various bad angels, while hiding in the Wartburg he threw his inkpot at one of them but failed to hit him, you can still see the dark splotch on the wall. On young Eitzen's lips the words are lining up in well-formed ranks, 'tis like a strange kind of obsession with him, one by one he is recounting the torts done by the bad angels to the righteous, how they will plague good Christians with sickness and weaken their minds and tempt them and delude them with false hopes and try to seduce them away from God; and further, how they will deal with the wicked, taking hold of their bodies and souls and tweaking and tormenting them even in their lifetime. But their main rancor was directed against the clergy in that they caused all sorts of heresy to sprout and incited devout men of God to disobedience and turned the attention of the congregation away from the sermon, in short, how they were persecuting with might and main all those who worked in the vineyard of Christ and for his kingdom.

Young Eitzen, noticing the many divines present lapping up his words as though they were the choicest sweetmeats, is shaken by an irrepressible giggle which might or might not be his own. And immediately, a number of similar thoughts come to his mind applicable to the gentlemen of the city council and of the grand elector's office, for what's sauce for the goose is sauce for the gander, and thus he goes on in this way, telling how the bad angels were also busy among the authorities, creating mischief and disturbing the peace and harmony of the state by abetting dissidents or appearing as witnesses for them, and how they helped the enemy by whispering false counsel to emperors and princes and by fomenting unrest and dissatisfaction among the populace.

This sounds like heavenly music to the servants of city and state, for it confirms, and by expert testimony, that not they are ever at fault but a lively company of devils; and if it depended on them, they would graduate Candidate Eitzen with *summa cum laude*. Meanwhile Leuchtentrager, hump and clubfoot and all, has moved in so close upon Eitzen that the young man feels as though his friend were creeping into his self. And with a voice that cuts to the marrow of his own bone, he calls out, "And behold, the power of the bad angels is greater than any which humans possess, for it derives from divine force, and is but a whit less than the power of God. And their lord is the angel Lucifer who sits on a black throne ringed by fire, presiding over the lower orders, and another of them is Ahasverus who wants to change the world as he believes it can be changed, and man along with it. And no one knows how many of them there might be and what shape they will take."

And falls silent. Luther looks uneasy; the good doctor prefers keeping his mind on safe ground; 'tis unclear how the candidate has come by such uncanny knowledge. Eitzen himself feels increasingly perturbed, a strange darkness has set in, inside the hall and outside, a lightning stroke flashes across the windows, followed by a loud clap of thunder.

He sinks down.

And while his teacher Melanchthon and the high examiners are working over him, trying to revive him and help him up, he suddenly is aware that his friend has gone and that he's alone among all the *doctores* and *professores* and other God-fearing men, and very much eased in his mind he struggles to his knees and folds his hands as in prayer and says, once more in his familiar voice, dry and didactic, "We, however, shall with the help of God take courage and fight the powers of evil. Christ will win out over Satan and his host."

Luther seems now in a hurry. "We still have to hear him preach," he says to Melanchthon. But then adds, "Didn't I tell you, Master Philipp, to keep an eye on this fellow, he will get far in the world."

CHAPTER EIGHT

§

In which Ahasverus is trying to save the Rabbi,
but the latter insists on going to the
end of the road he has chosen

§

I know that he knows how everything is going to go. This one will betray him, and that one will deny him, and several will be coming with swords and with spears and will lead him away, and the high priest will try him and sentence him and hand him to the Romans, and these will nail him to the cross and when he is thirsting they will give him vinegar and gall, and he will die in terrible pain, and will be buried and rise again on the third day and for a little while will walk this earth until he will ascend to God and take his seat to the right of his father.

And what then?

That far he refuses to think. Ah, Reb Joshua, poor friend, why don't you ever, not one single time, ask the simple, obvious question: When all is said and done, what have you changed?

I stood among the multitude as he came into Jerusholayim, riding upon a colt the foal of an ass, just as the prophet said. I saw his long, narrow feet grazing the dust of the road till the people threw their clothes before the hooves of his animal. And I heard them shouting Hosanna, and several called him son of David and asked him to lead them as David once led the people of Israel, as a king and a prophet, and a great many followed him, among them a number of armed men, saying that the Day of Judgment was near and the end of their oppression. And I saw his face, and a radiance was going out from it, but there was also a veil of great sadness on it. And I knew what he was thinking. Today Hosanna, he was thinking, and tomorrow, Crucify him. But that this might be his own doing, this he did not think. He was like a wheel running along in its rut.

And there was one by the name of Judas Iscariot, a fellow countryman of the Rabbi from Galilee, but uncommonly shrewd, and among his not always very pleasant disciples easily the most unpleasant. In his company I found Lucifer who was discoursing with him about this and that, and how the value of money was constantly diminishing so that an item which yesterday cost a copper penny today was not to be had for a silver dinar. This, said Judas, was troubling him greatly as the price of bread and meat had outpaced by far the income the Rabbi derived from his prayers and prophecies and miracles; twelve disciples, however, had to be fed as before out of the common purse which he was administering, and the Feast of Passover was approaching which required a skin of wine or two on top of it.

Leave this man out of your schemes, Brother, I told Lucifer; we are after higher things, after God and all those who are helplessly adrift in His world, and here you want to make your proposition with those thirty pieces of silver.

Ah you little angel, he says to me, you seem to have made quite some progress working yourself out of the bottomless pit, a regular savior of mankind. I'm as aware as you are that we don't need this rascal, as the agents of the Sanhedrin follow each step of your Reb Joshua and report on each of his sayings; but why shouldn't one who wants to do his bit earn a few honest pennies on the side? And having delivered himself of such sentiment he turns to Judas Iscariot and says to him: My friend here thinks I am giving you bad advice. Now, then, I will tell you, I want you to obey only your master; if he wants you to betray him, so do it, if not, do it not; your master knows what he wants.

So Judas Iscariot left very much eased in his mind, for the burden of decision was taken off him. And I quarreled with Lucifer, but he laughed at me and said: He who made us out of fire and the breath of the infinite, on the first day, long before He made the rest of this botched and bungled world, it is He who causes me to act as I do. Who if not He has shown Himself to this Reb Joshua and has spoken to him? Who if not He has charted the road which the poor fellow follows? And in view of all this you want me to oppose His most eminent decision? I have done this once, but as you may have noticed it did little good; He still has that weakness for those creatures of dirt and water and their sinful souls which He installed in them. What hasn't He tried with them! First He drowned them, then He let sulfurous flames rain down on them, then He had them slaughtered in war after war; but all to no effect, again and again the brood recovered and increased, each generation more wicked than its predecessor. Do you really believe they could be improved by someone taking upon himself all their sins and atoning for them by his suffering? A most incongruous thought by this most incongruous God. Go ahead, God! Go on doing what You've been doing, until Your whole creation collapses upon itself and falls back into the black hole from which it came forth initially!

I knew then that I stood alone with my hopes, and on the first day of eating unleavened bread, on the eve of the day when the Passover lamb was being sacrificed, I betook myself to the house near the entry to the city in whose best room the pillows were already spread for the supper of Reb Joshua and his disciples, and I waited there.

After a while, as dusk was setting in, they all came and settled themselves for the meal; Reb Joshua, however, who recognized me immediately, invited me to sit next to him and leaned over to me and said: I know that my time is near, and it is good of you that you came as you promised. Then he rose and took off his garments but for his loincloth, which he girded about him, and took a basin and poured water in it and knelt down before me and washed my feet; likewise he did with the others, with Simon Petrus, too, who acted coy about it. I still remember the strange sensation I felt as his hand touched my foot; it was as though a lover were touching me, and I knew this hand would soon be pierced by a rusty nail unless I prevented it.

But Reb Joshua said: Do you know what I have done to you? You call me Master and Lord, and this is well said, for so I am. But I am among you as a servant. I have given you an example, that you should do as I have done to you.

After this, he once more put on his garments and returned to his seat. And I leaned my head on his bosom as though I were the disciple he loved most, and talked to him. Rabbi, I said, your meekness sickens me. The one who will betray you is seated among these, and also the one who will deny you, and the others aren't much better.

I know, he said.

A wheel cannot choose the rut in which it moves, but the drover who leads the oxen can change direction. Therefore don't act as though your fate were predestined for you, but rise up and fight. You have seen the people gathering about you at the gate of the city and following you, and you heard them salute you and the name they gave you. But if they will see that you let yourself be taken like a sheep and led to the slaughter, they shall turn away from you, and neither I nor you can rightly blame them.

I have preached love, he said; love is stronger than the sword.

But those who come after you will not hesitate to take up the sword, and they will use it in the name of love, and the kingdom of which you have dreamed will be ruled more cruelly than the Romans rule theirs, and the master will not wash the feet of the people, but the people will bend their neck to the foot of the master.

He, however, pushed me aside and took the unleavened bread and gave thanks and broke it and gave it to me and to the others in the round, saying, Take, eat, this is my body. And he took the cup and filled it with wine, and when he had given thanks, he said, Take this, and divide it among yourselves; this is my blood which is shed for many, so their sins may be forgiven.

And I ate and drank, knowing of the vanity of all his doing, and once again I saw the shadow of sadness falling over the face of Reb Joshua, and he said: Verily, I say unto you that one of you will betray me.

Then there was much whispering among the disciples and fear and confusion, for they failed to understand: but a moment ago the Rabbi had let them partake of his body and his blood, and now this announcement. And Simon Petrus came and stepped behind me and bent his head to me, saying: You have lain at his bosom; you ask him which among us be the traitor.

I could have told him, and told him the price as well, but I wanted the Rabbi to tell him, because if he did so, it would be a first indication that he was going to fight back. But the Rabbi dipped a piece of bread into the sauce that was made of bitter herbs and offered the sop to Judas Iscariot, saying: That which you do, do quickly.

Thus the word of Lucifer was fulfilled who had told Judas, if your master wants you to betray him, so do it; and I thought I was hearing Lucifer's derisive laughter, but he was nowhere to be seen; and I turned away from Reb Joshua, for I thought, he is truly lost who betrays himself.

Today I am wondering, did he really betray himself? Or doesn't the greatness of the Rabbi lie in his walking the road, which he saw stretching ahead of him, to its end? And what would have become of him, had he not cast from him the doubts which I dripped in his ear?

But after the supper I took Judas Iscariot aside and said to him: Of those thirty pieces of silver I want to have one because I kept silent when Simon Petrus asked that question of me.

CHAPTER NINE

§

*Wherein Candidate Eitzen experiences the power
of the Word, especially where this is directed against the Jews*

§

Can there be in this world a happier person than he who
has passed his examination with honor and to the satisfaction of his teachers? Such a one feels as though a barrelful
of stones had fallen off his chest, he rejoices out loud, or at
least in the secrecy of his heart, and he thinks he can tear
out a half-dozen trees as easily as so many tender leaves of
grass.

Despite his great relief and his cheer, young Eitzen
who by now sees himself almost as a Master of Divinity,
never forgets to whom he owes thanks: in the first place to
Almighty God from whom all grace is coming; secondly,
however, and ranking closely behind the One up there, to
his friend Leuchtentrager. To God he devotes a fine prayer
in which he talks of everything which moved him during,
and toward the end of, his examination, viz., the great fear
which God took off him, and the emptiness inside his skull
into which God, just in the nick of time, poured the most
learned thoughts, and the humility with which God filled
his heart so that he might properly impress the *doctores* and
professores of the university with it, and especially the good
Doctor Martinus and Magister Melanchthon. In addition
to this prayer he has authored a poem, written in the manner which Luther made so popular:

Passed are my trial and torment,
To you, dear Lord, my thanks I send.
From God comes help in dire strait
To every righteous candidate,
Come answers to the hardest test
So you may set your mind at rest.
Praise be to God who sits upon
His seat up high, and to His son.

But giving thanks to his friend Hans is altogether a different thing. The miracle of the sudden knowledge of matters angelic clearly points to his friend's having served as a vessel of God, comparable to the good angels concerning whom he, Candidate Eitzen, had discoursed upon at length during his examination, for these are *per definitionem* servants, messengers, and vessels of God; although Leuchtentrager is showing hardly any similarity to this kind of angel. What to do? Give him money? But the purse in young Eitzen's waist belt has wasted away sadly, particularly after he's had to pay for the graduation dinner to which he must invite all the *studiosi* who sat with him on the hard benches of the lecture rooms while outside the windows God's sun was shining brightly and God's little birds were trilling, plus all the *instructores* who lectured inside about the *historia* of the world and the true doctrine of God; and he probably will have to borrow from his friend Hans so he can pay his traveling expenses, unless he wants to take out a loan from some Jew at a high rate of interest and against the security of the linens and woolens in the house of his father, may God grant him a blissful death and everlasting salvation.

He therefore approaches his friend. "Hans, our Lord God most likely will be satisfied with a prayer and a little poem in His praise, but what do you want to have from me as a reward for your help in my hour of need, while I was being examined?"

Leuchtentrager blinks. And while the first cock is beginning to crow, he gazes at young Eitzen who stands there before him, his naked legs sticking out from under his nightshirt, and says to him, "If your soul rated a little better than the souls of the clergy commonly are worth, I might ask you to let me have it. But this commodity comes by the dozen and is like rotten fish on the market."

Eitzen feels offended; the immortal souls of good Christian men, his own included, should not be made the object of such mockery.

"I mean it," says Leuchtentrager. "I really don't know why I constantly concern myself with you—you are neither a hero reaching for the stars, nor do you have the gift of attracting people to you, and your thoughts are commonplace; but perhaps these are the kind of people who are needed in mediocre times, of what use are the Alexanders and Socrateses when even the sky above our heads seems hardly higher than the ceiling of our room?"

"But isn't Luther a great man at least?" says Eitzen, whose legs are beginning to freeze.

"Quite so," says Leuchtentrager. "First he kicked the Pope's arse, then he saw that the divine order must remain wherein the upside is up and the downside down. Thus a firm new edifice was constructed on a pile of manure. What will you be preaching about, this morning?"

"I think, about the Jews."

Leuchtentrager straightens, strokes his little beard, and grins. "Because of the one who snatched Margriet from under your nose?"

"A preacher is ordained by God," says Eitzen, quite irritated. "That Jew, however, was sent by the devil."

"I see," says Leuchtentrager. "So you are doing it for Luther's sake. You have closely listened to his cursing the Jews and railing against them the other night in the house of Magister Melanchthon; and as the prophet says: He that shapes his lips by the tongue of his master will rise in his favor."

Eitzen grows angry. "I speak my own mind with my

own words." And would have liked to say more on the subject—what right has his friend to deride him. He restrains himself, however, for he fears he might need his help just as he did when facing the high examiners, and says timidly, "You'll be sure to come and be with me in the Castle Church?"

"Paul," says Leuchtentrager, "get into your trousers; your legs are shaking so that your knees are knocking against one another."

"But you will come?" says Eitzen.

"I'm not much drawn to the Church," says Leuchtentrager. "And that which you will be preaching will come to you without my aid, I assure you."

"Maybe you're a friend of the Jews?" Eitzen inquires, recalling the Jew with whom his friend Hans consorted so intimately that night.

"The Jews," says Leuchtentrager, "were damned by God. That's at least something which makes them excel. What do the other peoples have?"

Young Eitzen would dearly love to believe that the Almighty was troubling His mind over him and even sent His only begotten son into this vale of tears so as to cleanse him of his sins; therefore he is frightened at the thought that God might be in truth as indifferent as his friend Hans has been indicating. But no, thinks Eitzen as he goes off to clothe himself and eat his gruel, if Leuchtentrager should leave him in the lurch, surely the One up there will step in and be at his side when he walks to the Castle Church, with the measured pace and the dignity which he must show from this day on, and when he preaches his morning sermon before the critical ears of Doctor Martinus and his teacher Melanchthon. Nor does his head seem to be as empty and desolate as it was the other day, but everything he's been taught is in place, well ordered and ready to be used; furthermore he has pored over the books of Moses last night and found many an apt little verse; and for an emergency he carries with him a few notes that will provide him with inspiration.

And now, as he steps out of doors, he sees that the morning is fresh and beautiful; the dewdrops are sparkling like diamonds and other precious stones; even the smelly water in the gutter running down the middle of the street mirrors the young day and the people hurrying toward the house of God are greeting him eagerly, making him feel that today all will go well, until he bridles the merriness of his mind because he knows that Satan casts a jealous eye on the overly cheerful.

And there is the church with its high gables and its huge door to which Doctor Martinus once nailed his theses; thus will great oaks from tiny acorns grow, young Eitzen thinks, not quite a hundred pithy sentences, and Rome, the fortress of the Antichrist, did tremble. And goes on thinking that, if only he preached right well, his word might also grow and have a powerful effect, to the benefit of all Christendom.

Later, as he mounts the pulpit after the echoes of the last chorale have died, and stands up there while the whisperings cease and all faces are turning toward him, and as he lowers his head in mute prayer to beg the blessing of the Lord for the success of his sermon, so he might not be made to appear like a stammering fool, he recalls the many times that he devoutly abided down there in the nave while here in the pulpit his teacher Melanchthon or even the great Luther himself were raising their voices. And he begins, "Dearly Beloved! Peace unto you and grace in Christo!" And reads his text, "When Pilate saw that he could prevail nothing, but that rather a tumult was made, he took water, and washed his hands before the multitude, saying, I am innocent of the blood of this just person; see you to it. Then answered all the people, and said, His blood be on us, and on our children." And resumes once again, "Dearly Beloved! Behold, such thing took place more than a thousand and five hundred years ago before the house of Pontius Pilate, the governor, in Jerusalem, and it was clearly the Jewish people who were crying for the blood of our Lord and Savior, so he might be crucified.

And these very people, with this very guilt on them, are today living in our midst and still have the arrogance to believe that they received, directly from the hands of God, the land of Canaan and the city of Jerusalem and the temple, and therefore refuse to desist from their nonsensical pride and their claim to being God's own people, although they were driven from their country in the times of the Romans and since have been scattered all over the world and are damned forever."

Eitzen looks up, his eyes seeking Luther, and he sees the good Doctor Martinus nodding approval, for these thoughts about the Jewish people are exactly his own, too. And the young preacher recognizes that he has spoken wisely, and continues much strengthened and encouraged. Since the Jews had persecuted our Lord Jesus with such great hatred, he says, and had refused to accept him as their Messiah, they now were persecuting with the same hatred all Christian people. These they called *goyim*; and in their eyes we *goyim* were not even human because we were not descended of the high and noble blood, race, and origin as they who claimed to have come in direct lineage from Abraham, Sarah, Isaac, and Jacob, even though the Lord, note this well, through the mouth of His prophets always called the children of Israel whores and adulterers since, to quote the prophet Hosea, they dealt treacherously against God in that, under the pretense of obeying the divine law, they committed all sorts of wickedness and idolatry.

The young preacher senses that his pronouncements are touching the hearts of his congregation, and that not only Doctor Luther but all of them consider his words more than justified, Yea and Amen. This stimulates him, and he decides to go on striking while the iron is hot and to fan the fire some more, and says, "They feel from their infancy such a vicious hatred against us *goyim* that it's no great wonder that in all the stories you hear them accused of poisoning our wells and stealing our children, whom they then stick with awls and carve up with knives, as was done in Trent and in Weissensee. And they will twist our good German words and our kind greetings so that they all sound like *Shed wil kom* or *Satan will get you*, and thus they curse us and wish on us misery and the fires of hell. In addition they are calling Jesus son of a whore and his mother a whore who conceived her child in adultery with some tinker who came by the road."

Eitzen must catch his breath. It is as though his words were coming to him from somewhere outside of him, just as it was with the categories of the angels during his examination, except that nowhere in the Castle Church can he glimpse even a shadow of his friend Leuchtentrager. But he does see before him the image of that other one, of the impudent young Jew with the muddied boots, as he holds on his lap the luscious Margriet, and this cannot be a mirage conjured up by the devil because no devil may enter a church, therefore it must be a sign from God; and thus fortified, Eitzen continues, "Through what, Dearly Beloved, have we earned that cruel wrath of the Jews and their envy and hatred? We do not call their women whores, as they are calling Mary, nor their men sons of whores, as they are calling our Lord Jesus Christ; we do not steal and carve up their children, do not poison their water, and we are not thirsting after their blood. Quite to the contrary: we do unto them nothing but good; they live with us as if it were their homeland, under our protection, they use our roads and streets and lanes, our markets; and our princes permit the Jews to take from their princely treasures whatever they like, and allow themselves and their subjects to be sucked dry by the usury of the Jews."

With this assertion he has come to a matter which, as he well knows, is moving his congregation a lot more deeply than does Pilate washing his hands, or the Jews' racial pride, or their alleged election by God. And he is well versed on this topic, through the family business back home, and through his rich aunt in Augsburg. So, raising his hands, he calls out, "Dearly Beloved! Has any of you ever seen a Jew working as you have to work, from early morning till late at night? No, it is as the Jews themselves often state: We do not work, we are having a nice, easy time of it, the damned *goyim* must work for us, we just take their money; thus we become their masters, and they are our servants. This is the way they speak, and this is not sinful to their mind, but they follow their law which says in Deuteronomy 23:20, Unto a stranger you may lend upon usury, but unto your brother you shall not lend upon usury. Their breath stinks from the gold and the silver of the gentiles, for no people under the sun ever was more avaricious than they are. Now I hear it spoken that the Jews are giving great sums of money to princes and big lords, and through this are most useful. Yes, but from where do they take it to give? From the same princes and big lords and their subjects, whose estates they rob and steal from by means of their usury."

He glances around and sees the expression on the faces of his listeners as they hang on his words, and he suddenly realizes the great power that goes out from the pulpit and that a true preacher of the Lord need only say the right word at the right time for people to rise up and stream out into the streets and do as he has told them. And with this thought elevating his mind he brings his sermon to a fine close by diligently summing up the main points wherein the damned Jews will differ from true Christians. "The Jews," he declares, "want to have a Messiah from the land of Cockaigne who will sate their stinking bellies, a worldly king who will kill us Christians, divide the riches of the world among the Jews, and make them the overlords of it all. We Christians, however, have a Messiah who sees to it that we need not fear death nor tremble before the wrath of God, and that we may escape the snares of the devil. Even if he does not endow us with gold and silver and other riches, with such a Messiah as ours our hearts may jump with joy, for he makes the whole world into a paradise for us. And for this let us thank our heavenly father and merciful God, Amen."

With the Amen still resounding, he climbs down from the pulpit, carefully holding on to the stone of the banister, for he feels a great weakness in his limbs; rarely has a novice preacher come forth so bravely and so straightforwardly in his very first sermon, and shown such fighting mettle, in a spiritual sense of course. Then he advances to the altar and bends his knee and pronounces the prayer to God Almighty, but with an absent mind, merely saying the words in their sequence, for only now, his sermon done, is he beginning to grasp the full meaning of the ministry, as the great Doctor Martinus has taught: A preacher must be both warrior and shepherd, and this is a difficult art. Finally he turns to face his congregation and solemnly raises his hands and lifts his eyes toward the vaulted ceiling and speaks the words which Aaron, the priest, spoke to the children of Israel, "The Lord bless you, and keep you; the Lord make His face to shine upon you, and be gracious unto you; the Lord lift up His countenance upon you, and give you peace"; and feels a shudder running down his spine at the thought that from now on it will be in his power to call down the blessing of the Lord and pass it on to others, a true mediator between these here and the One up there, and says, "Amen," and hears the bells beginning to ring in the tower, clear and loud, saluting the newborn reverend.

Outside the church door, having divested himself of his clerical garb, he meets Luther who apparently has been waiting for him in the courtyard of the castle. "Young man," says Luther, his one good eye scanning his pupil half doubtfully, half with approval, "you must have been reading the thoughts in my mind while you were holding forth on the Jewish people. But listening to you I also was thinking to myself: a fellow like this is the very butt of the devil's temptations; believe me, I have had my experiences in that regard. Therefore let me advise you always to keep a humble heart and occasionally look back over your shoulder to see if Satan may not be close behind you. And take this—'tis a little letter I want you to convey."

And having said this, the great man bends toward him as though he wanted to embrace him; he desists from it in the end, however; only a vapor of beer and onions is wafting about young Eitzen's head long after Luther has vanished.

CHAPTER TEN

§

In which Professor Leuchtentrager expounds on the
dialectics in the idea of a deity and adduces
from the Dead Sea Scrolls certain proofs
of an actual encounter of Ahasverus
with the Rabbi, while Professor
Beifuss is given a research
project

§

Prof. Dr. Dr.h.c. Siegfried Beifuss
Institute for Scientific Atheism
Behrenstrasse 39 a
108 Berlin
German Democratic Republic

29 February 1980

Dear Colleague,

I am sorry to see a man of your intellectual brilliance
and firm political convictions, a combination rare in our
times, so cruelly impaled on the horns of a dilemma. In
your kind letter of the 14th of this month you wrote that
to accept the enormous longevity of Mr. Ahasverus as a
fact would mean that you also had to believe in Jesus
Christ. Although you did not state it in so many words,
the implication is clear: since the latter is out of the question for you, the former becomes impossible, too.

But this is, pardon my saying so, a faulty conclusion.
In the first place, you can very well view Ahasverus as an
entity separate from Jesus; and secondly, even assuming,

as I do, that an encounter of Ahasverus with Jesus did take place, this does not force you in any way or manner to believe in Jesus as a divine being, or more specifically, a son of God. In general, and here I'm sure to find you in agreement with me, all gods are a most troublesome matter. Gods are a commodity which man produces and always has produced for his own needs; however, and this is the problem, these gods then develop a life of their own that borders on the uncanny. I see in this phenomenon an undeniable case of dialectics at work, which to you, who also are a devotee of this science, must be pleasant to observe.

Before I get to the most important part of my letter, the Qumran report, a few minor points in answer to your inquiries.

I absolutely share your opinion that the Ahasverus of the Book of Esther is not identical with our long-lived Ahasverus, the obvious reason being that the first one wasn't a Jew and his contacts with Jews were maintained exclusively by his concubine, the above-mentioned Esther. The Ahasverus of the Book of Esther was actually the Persian king officially called Artaxerxes, to be precise, the first of his name, with the by-name Makrocheir or Longhand (464 to 424 B.C.), who in the well-known Cimonian peace recognized the independence of the Greek city states in Asia Minor. About the extent to which Artaxerxes really was a friend and patron of the exiled Jews, we unfortunately have only one source, this same Book of Esther, and as to the historical reliability of the various books of the Bible I have doubts quite similar to yours; at any rate, we must regard any Biblical source with a most critical eye.

On the other hand, I beg to differ from the attempts of your Dr. Jaksch to put the admittedly astonishing existence of my friend Ahasverus in question by remarking on his advertising methods and the apparent lack of media interest in his person. More than once I have heard Mr. Ahasverus speak of his dislike of personal publicity. His aversion to any fuss over his person is so great that he doesn't even take note of his birthday, although in view of his age he would have reason enough to celebrate.

But now to my main point, the confirmation in a section of the Dead Sea Scrolls of Ahasverus having met Jesus, a matter which I mentioned to you in my letter of December 19th of last year. The section we have to deal with is contained in Chapters VII, 3 to 21, and VIII, 1 to 12, of the scroll marked 9QRes; this scroll has now been released for publication, and I have done a quick translation of the parts that are of major interest to us, a translation which you will please consider provisional and in no degree commensurate with the poetical qualities of the original. The abbreviation 9QRes, for your information, denotes that this scroll was discovered in cave 9 of the settlement of Qumran and was given the title *Resurrection* because it tells among other things the story of the resurrection and eventual return of the Teacher of Righteousness. We must therefore take it to be one of the eschatological texts, and the Teacher of Righteousness who appears in it along with the Chief Elder of the Church were probably seen by the people of Qumran as messianic personages. The dots in my translation indicate that in these places the scroll was damaged and undecipherable.

. . . is come the day when they will take the teacher of
                              righteousness,
to whom God opened the secrets of the word
                              of the prophets,
and lead him unto the preacher of iniquity who walked
                         the road of abomination,
and unto the governor of the assembly of Belial, the
                           Kittaeans . . .
. . . scorned, and in pains . . .
. . . is come the time of adversity for the people of
                              Israel,
of all its afflictions was never any like this.

For this is the final time, before the skies rend
and before the host of lights . . .

. . . and walks up there, swaying under the burden
of the beams,
blood and sweat running down the tortured brow of the
teacher of righteousness
and over his face, his lips are trembling, but he
keeps silent to the words of derision,
his ear deaf . . .

. . . but deaf also the voice of the chief elder of the church,
the beloved by God . . .
. . . hear, o Israel . . .
. . . do not you fear,
nor shrink from the host of your enemies,
for before you will go . . .
. . . armed with the sword of God and the shield of David,
invincible . . .

. . . reaches the house where the road turns toward
the mount of skulls,
growing steeper . . .
. . . before his doorstep the chief elder of the church,
who was since the beginning of time,
of the sons of God one, made of light and the essence
of the infinite . . .
. . . and the teacher of righteousness stumbles over
to him . . .
. . . let me rest ere I must climb . . .

. . . are lined up in seven rows of assault
those who are poor and oppressed,
and in hundreds and thousands the league of the saints
of the covenant,
and are but waiting for the call . . .
. . . and you shall write on your banners "God's Own
People" and the names of Israel and of Aaron,

and on your standards write "God's Truth" and "God's
                                        Justice"
and "Honor to God" and "Judgment of God" . . .
. . . for this is your battle and by the strength of your
                                        hand . . .

. . .but the teacher of righteousness bows his head
                        and says not a mumbling word,
whereupon Ahasverus raises his voice, saying, get you
                        hence, be on your way,
there is no place here for the likes of you. However
                        the teacher of righteousness
lifts up his face and says, the son of Man goes
                        as is written in the words of the prophet,
but you shall tarry till I come back, and shall find
                                        no rest . . .

Well, this was my translation of the parts of Scroll
9QRes referring to the encounter of the Teacher of Righteousness with the Chief Elder of the Church: you will
have noted, dear Colleague, that in a most significant verse
the latter's name is directly given as Ahasverus. On analysis you will also find that these lines differ from the rest of
the material by their realism; it therefore seems probable
that we are dealing here with a fragment of a historical
report on an event of importance to the author. The congregation or, if you prefer, church of Qumran was only
one of several Jewish sects quite similar to the early Christian community who all held the belief that the final time
was at hand or had already arrived; in Qumran, however,
they thought of the Messiah as having a twofold character
or even being two persons, one so-to-speak civilian and
the other military, just as the Jewish God is double-fea-
tured and appears both as a God of vengeance and war and
a God of love and mercy.
    Since you in Berlin doubt one as well as the other, any
speculation on which of the two might be the true God
becomes unnecessary; there can be no doubt in 9QRes,

however, especially since we find in it verses which almost literally correspond to other verses in 1QM, the so-called Scroll of War, and in 1QpHab, the Habakkuk Commentary.

I am hoping that all this will prove to be of use to you, and remain with kind regards,

Yours sincerely,
Jochanaan Leuchtentrager
Hebrew University
Jerusalem

Prof. Dr. Dr.h.c. Siegfried Beifuss
Institute for Scientific Atheism
Behrenstrasse 39 a
108 Berlin

14 March 1980

Dear Comrade Beifuss,

The latest letter to you from Prof. J. Leuchtentrager in Jerusalem contains a translation of a Jewish manuscript marked 9QRes. If the original isn't a forgery, which under the circumstances seems not very probable, then we are faced here with a typical product of the militaristic mind of the people of Israel that has culminated, at least for the time being, in the development of Zionist imperialism. One only needs to read what, according to this manuscript, is to be written on the "banners" of Israel in order to know the direction in which all this is pointing.

I would suggest your giving some thought to the preparation of a project through which, basing yourself on this manuscript and other texts of your own choice, you might prove the close interaction of religion and imperialist expansionism, particularly in relation to Israel. I am stressing Israel because we observe similar tendencies in Islamic countries as well; these, however, we will disregard in view of the political aims pursued by our Soviet friends and ourselves.

If you are able to collect these materials and have them organized and done up in time, we might submit them next year at the conference in Moscow. With the class struggle constantly sharpening, science cannot be permitted to keep aloof; it must always and on every occasion take a decided stand in support of the policies of the party.

With socialist greetings,

Würzner
Chief of Department
Ministry of
Higher Education

Prof. Jochanaan Leuchtentrager
Hebrew University
Jerusalem
Israel

17 March 1980

Dear Colleague,

Who would have thought that out of your short remarks in reference to the section on the so-called Wandering Jew in my book *The Best-known Judeo-Christian Myths as Seen in the Light of Science and History* there would develop such an enlightening and instructive correspondence which is followed with the greatest of interest by my entire collective. I have always felt that serious scientists, even those who differ on questions of *Weltanschauung*, can arrive at an understanding in their own special fields of endeavor, and I am happy to see from your last letter to me that we here have been able to shake your position to a certain extent.

You have been admitting that Ahasverus, king of Persia, is not the same person as your friend, the owner of that shoe store on Via Dolorosa; this alone eliminates a good four hundred years from the life of the latter. Furthermore, from the manuscript 9QRes to which you attribute such great importance it follows clearly that the "teacher of righteousness" as well as the "chief elder of the church" were not spirits of any kind, either repeatedly returning or ever present, but were both human beings. You were right, dear Colleague, in pointing to the realism of several of the verses quoted by you. Nevertheless we would like to call your attention to the fact that the whole thing is written in such an exalted manner that, apart from that one place, we can find no other part that would permit us a glimpse at any possible real background of the poem. Apparently the congregation of Qumran, as you yourself mentioned, believed in two Messiahs, and the authors of the scroll which you so kindly excerpted and translated for us report on how these two got into a brawl. The dialogue of this altercation is refreshingly natural, and indeed everything in this scene happens in a most natural way. We are of the opinion that these two alleged Messiahs were either a couple of crooks who initially worked hand in hand in exploiting the superstitions of their congregation, or, and this seems more probable in view of the mass hysteria which you, too, see spreading in the first and second centuries, they were simply paranoiacs. That crooks frequently quarrel and fall out among each other is well known; but likewise paranoiacs, every one of whom thinks of himself as the greatest, as a Napoleon or a Messiah, in which case we isolate them.

Paranoia, at least on the part of the "chief elder of the church," is also indicated by the man's obvious military-religious fanaticism. Seen from this angle, the *spirit* of the person whom scroll 9QRes calls Ahasverus is in truth immortal, and I have asked two of my fellow workers to check through the Bible, the Apocrypha, and other writings of this kind for similar utterances of other Jewish figures. Once our project has reached a certain point, we will be pleased to place our findings at your disposal; but possibly you will be able on the basis of your rich experiences in this field to give us some suggestions.

I am looking forward to your reply. With all good wishes,

Yours sincerely,
(Prof. Dr. Dr.h.c.) Siegfried Beifuss
Institute for Scientific Atheism
Berlin, Capital of the GDR

CHAPTER ELEVEN

§

Wherein the reader is given an insight into
the beautiful soul of Paulus von Eitzen
and the cock on the church steeple
crows three times, thus proving
that Ahasverus is who he is

§

The letter which Doctor Luther handed to young Eitzen is
addressed to Dean Aepinus at St. Petri in the city of Hamburg, and it is carefully folded and closed and sealed with
Luther's own signet. But Eitzen feels as though it were
burning inside his pocket with a heat that increases in proportion to the distance he covers. Up to the town of
Rosslau on the river Elbe he bears his discomfort by constantly talking to his companion of the great morning sermon he delivered; he still has on his mind every one of its
pithy pronouncements, on how the Jews, full of false pride
and heresy, were living in their midst not by the work of
their hands but by usury and, to top this, were mocking
and cursing those whom they exploited, namely the *goyim*,
and what by rights should be done with those scoundrelly
people. But by the time they have reached Zerbst, in the
Duchy of Anhalt, and after a night spent tossing and turning, he no longer is able to restrain himself as he gets into
the saddle in the morning and he says to Leuchtentrager,
"Tell me, Hans, which is a man's dearest possession that
he must cherish and preserve against all temptation?"

Leuchtentrager scratches his little hump, perhaps he's

carried a flea with him from that inn at Zerbst, and gazes over the land, green trees in whose leaves the light is playing, and fields round about, all of them tilled, 'tis a blessed part of the world, except that the people do not look as though they are particularly well off; where you have an orderly government, the citizens must be kept short. "Man's dearest possession?" he repeats although he knows what his friend has in mind; once having been told of the farewell gift the other received from the good Doctor Martinus, he has been expecting this sort of query. And thus he replies in the same dignified manner which Eitzen is showing since he was given his master's degree, "Man's dearest possession, Paul, is the confidence people have in him and which he mustn't disappoint on pain of grave damage to his immortal soul."

Eitzen has anticipated such an answer, even though he hoped that his friend Hans would make it easier for him to break that seal. "This is it, precisely," he therefore sighs, "Where would we get if we no longer could rely on a person's honor and fidelity; our world, which is evil enough as is, would turn into an absolute pit of snakes and other reptiles."

But as they are riding into Magdeburg, the proud bishop's residence, where they will spend the night at the house of Canon Michaelis, Eitzen is once again gripped by his unrest.

The good canon is quite happy that he can put up his young *confrater*; he has three unmarried daughters, one leaner than the next, and all of them just predestined to become clergymen's wives; in view of this the old man bears with his young guest's limping companion, who immediately starts to compliment the bashful maidens in the most flattering manner so that their ears take on a fiery red color. At supper, which Madame Canon has prepared with a loving hand, diligently assisted by the three young ladies, Leuchtentrager tells at length of the powerful sermon that his friend Eitzen preached at Wittenberg, in the presence of the *doctores* Luther and Melanchthon, while his

fingers, hidden by the overhanging tablecloth, are stroking on one side the bony knee of Lisbeth, the second
daughter, and on the other the lean and spindly thigh of
Jutta, the youngest one. The oldest, Agnes by name, has
been placed by design next to Master Eitzen and thus must
get along without being tickled and titillated.

The good canon isn't quite certain as to which should
impress him more, the eloquence and expert knowledge of
his newly graduated fellow cleric, or the fabulous memory
of the young man's strange companion, and he says to the
latter, "You must have listened with great care to that sermon, friend, since you remember everything in it so well.
Would God I had some in my congregation who would
follow my words so devoutly!"

'Twas not he who merited the praise, Leuchtentrager
replies modestly, but with such a sermon, on such a subject and spoken in such a spirit, you couldn't help feeling
as though you were listening to one of the prophets, and
every word, even the most minor, carved itself indelibly
into your heart.

The young magister chokes on the wine he is drinking;
he knows only too well that his friend Hans never was in
the Castle Church while he was inveighing against the unholy doings of the Jews. Mistress Agnes has jumped up
and is pummeling her neighbor's back; 'tis meant lov-
ingly, but his skin will show the most fanciful discolora-
tions for days to come, to the mocking delight of his friend
who grins and tells him, as he examines the painful spots,
that it's the thin and delicate fingers that hurt the hardest.

But then, being unable to sleep because the approaching death of his father dismays him more than he will admit and because he feels how weak and helpless a person is
without protection from God or from other powerful
friends, a problem on which the letter in his pocket might
enlighten him, he nudges Leuchtentrager and inquires,
"Hans! Are you still awake, Hans?"

His companion mutters something of having drunk

too much wine and having courted too many skinny fe-
males, and turns his back to him.

But Eitzen will not give up. "Hans," he says, "I would
so much love to know just what Doctor Luther has put
into that little letter he gave me to take along."

"So open it," says Leuchtentrager surlily, as though
such an act was of no consequence, a deft turn of the hand,
and no more.

But this is exactly what Eitzen shies away from, especially now that he considers himself almost a parson, a
good shepherd who should set an example to the rest of
Christianity. Therefore he says, "You know a great deal,
Hans; you can tell of what card a person is thinking, the
ace of hearts or the jack of diamonds or maybe the nine of
spades, or on what subject a candidate will be examined,
the Holy Trinity, or the flesh and blood of Jesus and
whether or not it was *a priori* in bread and wine, or about
good and bad angels."

"There's no sorcery to it," says Leuchtentrager and
sees that he will not get back to his sleep so quickly, "you
would be able to know as much, if only you would bestir
that gray matter inside your skull."

"And if I bestirred it till doomsday," moans young
Eitzen, "nothing would come of it."

"So place yourself in Luther's position," his friend says
gruffly, "what would he be writing to Dean Aepinus? That
you are a no-good son of a straying bitch and hypocrite
who feigns devotion to his superiors so he will get on in
the world?"

Leuchtentrager has hit it again: this is exactly what Eitzen fears in his innermost heart; he well remembers that
letter King David wrote to his captain Joab and gave to
Uriah to take along and give to him, the only difference being that he, Eitzen, hasn't a beautiful wife such as
Bathsheba but is headed toward the chaste embrace of
Mistress Barbara Steder who, even though not quite as
fleshless and flat as the Magdeburg canon's eldest daughter, is still not the sort of female for whose charms a man

would go to the trouble of having another man insidiously murdered.

"Perhaps he ought to have written something like that," Leuchtentrager goes on to say, "but not him. You and I know Luther; the man will never write a line which might go to show that he has unleashed but another empty-headed bigot on mankind."

While this may be insulting to Eitzen, it also eases his worried mind; therefore he lets his companion's snide remark pass without comment and just whines pitifully what a torment it is to have to ride forty and more miles a day in such mental distress, and how much his heart would be consoled on a journey toward so tragic an event if he were permitted to learn what exactly the good Doctor Martinus had written.

"So light the candle," says Leuchtentrager, "and give me the letter."

Eitzen gets busy with tinder and flint and finally does succeed: a flickering flame lights the chamber dimly and reveals a gruesome picture, the young magister and the humpback with the misshapen foot, both in their nightclothes and both bending their heads over that letter, while the outstretched hand of one marks circles above the seal that shimmers mysteriously until the wax, with a slight snapping sound, gives way and the paper unfolds almost by itself.

"Here," says Leuchtentrager, "read it aloud."

Eitzen, to whom this method of opening letters appears most weird, nonetheless takes a quick look at the text of the letter; curiosity, especially where a man's own fate is involved, always wins out over caution. He recognizes the handwriting, with the self-willed hooks and abbreviations, and with the spray of ink blots that look as though a number of cockroaches had walked across the sheet. Greetings unto you, dear and honored Brother, Luther has written, and peace in Christo.

And after a few lines, the main and important part: . . . would you, dear Brother, lend a kind and understanding ear to the bearer of this, namely young Master Paulus von Eitzen. Born in your city of Hamburg, he has been a most diligent student at our school in Wittenberg, applying himself with great success to the study of the doctrine of God, and was examined by us and found to be most eloquent and zealous in conducting himself by the teachings of his superiors . . .

Eitzen glances up and notices the bored expression on his companion's face, just as though the other were long acquainted with the contents of the letter. So he decides to employ greater emphasis in reading to his friend, and continues in a tone that is mixed of pride and protest: " . . . and for these reasons, dear Brother, I can recommend Magister von Eitzen to your kind care, that you may aid and assist him according to your power. Doubtless, this will be a service pleasing to God. May the Lord keep you in good spirits and in the best of health. Given at Wittenberg, et cetera et cetera. Yours, Martin Luther."

"Well," says Leuchtentrager, "are you feeling better now?"

Eitzen tugs at his shirt which has slipped up and replies, "Didn't you yourself say that he could not have written anything else, our good Doctor Martinus?"

"Couldn't he?" asks Leuchtentrager. All of a sudden he is holding another letter in his hand which looks precisely like the first one, its seal as smoothly opened as that of the first letter and likewise bearing the imprint of Luther's signet. "There, now you read this to me."

Eitzen's insides have grown cold. The handwriting is identical, including the ink blots, but the words have been twisted and perverted in a most devilish way, informing the reader that young Magister Paulus von Eitzen has on his mind anything but the word of God, that he toadies and fawns on his superiors, and that you can never entrust to him a lecturer's chair or a pulpit, not to mention the souls of an innocent Christian congregation, because he is rent by ambition and wants nothing but power over people instead of desiring to serve them humbly and from the heart. And under that diatribe once again the unmistakable signature, an exact copy of the other one: Martin Luther.

Eitzen feels his flesh creep. 'Tis as though in those two letters were contained the two sides of a man, the man being himself. But since Doctor Luther can have written only one letter, which is the one that is genuine, and which is the truth that Luther saw? And what sort of man, thinks Eitzen, am I really?

Leuchtentrager is holding both letters between his thumb and forefinger and makes them swing gently before Eitzen's frightened eyes. Eitzen is trying to grab the letter that praises him, the one he must give to Dean Aepinus if he wants to get up on that steep and slippery ladder of a clerical career; but over and again that letter eludes him; his friend Hans himself has suddenly become but a wisp of fog; Eitzen cries out and awakens in bed, lying beside Leuchtentrager, and in his hand the neatly opened letter with its undamaged seal, and he rereads the letter in the dying light of the candle. . . *and for these reasons, dear Brother, I can recommend Magister von Eitzen to your kind care.* . . .

"Where is the other one?" he asks, jabbing his elbow into Leuchtentrager.

"What other one?"

"The other letter!"

Leuchtentrager shakes his head; he knows of no other letter than the one which his friend Eitzen is holding in his hand, and tells him to put the seal close to the flame so the wax may soften and thus enable them to paste it back into place and make the letter appear as before; and soon thereafter the candle dies, and darkness once more envelops the two travelers in the guest chamber of Canon Michaelis's house. Yet Eitzen finds no sleep. Though the walls seem thick enough, he thinks he hears the dry coughs of Mistress Agnes, or perhaps they're Lisbeth's or Jutta's, and somewhere someone is groaning as though an incubus were crouching on his or her chest, and there's a scraping and scratching in the woodwork so you might believe that all the ghosts of Magdeburg were set loose, and Eitzen is full of fear and says to himself, My God, my God, will this haunt me all my life, there I had hoped that after my tests and after my sermon things would once more resume an orderly course, such as God in His mercy ordains, but instead it appears that no one quite knows how thin is the soil on which he stands, and right underneath it are seething the everlasting fires.

Then, in the brightness of the morning, Leuchtentrager having playfully tweaked the meager cheeks of the good canon's younger daughters, while Eitzen made his courteous bows to Mistress Agnes, and both being in receipt of a good hunk of bread and some sausage, given them by the canon's wife as provisions, they are riding toward Helmstedt, where the Duke of Brunswick is maintaining a university where two traveling scholars might expect to find an inn serving tolerable beer and company for a learned discourse on the affairs of the world; but Eitzen hangs in the saddle like a sack of flour and he aches top and bottom, behind and in front. His friend Leuchtentrager, however, is feeling fine and is observing him out of the corner of his eye while he trots along on his horse, thinking, Ah, what decrepit beings these humans are, any little affliction throwing them so they come whimpering to God like Job and have no confidence in themselves. Yet they keep on placing their trust in that One up there and live by rules and laws of which they believe they are God-given, and clutch at these, and do not see that they all are going to the devil, in the most orderly manner of course, first the princes and prelates, then the poets and tradesmen, and lastly the common mob.

In Helmstedt it is market day, and people have come from far and wide to sell and to purchase, and those who have neither money nor goods are gaping at everything with their mouths open. And indeed, 'tis a most colorful event, with everyone bent on showing off his wares, the potter and tailor, the confectioner and pork-butcher; the geese are honking and the chickens are cackling wildly before their necks are wrung; and all over the place you see the pointed hats of the Jews who are busy pretending that some rag they are trying to talk you into buying is a duchess's robe, and a half-dead old nag a noble steed from Araby.

The host of the inn has placed some benches in front of his door, and it's there that young Eitzen and his friend Hans have sat down after watering their horses at the trough and tying them firmly to a post. Eitzen, in his hand the cup of wine to which Leuchtentrager is treating him, stretches his legs contentedly and watches his friend as he uses his pretty little knife to divide into two halves the piece of sausage the canon's wife gave them; then, munching his half, Eitzen feels for the first time on this day that life can have its good moments, even though they may be few and far between. Also he becomes aware that farther to his right, near the church, people are crowding more closely than elsewhere; a wooden scaffolding has been erected there, and behind it a piece of painted canvas is hung, showing our Lord Jesus on the cross, Jesus wearing a red beard and red blood streaming down his tortured brow, and next to him the two thieves who let their heads hang like the sinners they are. Most likely there'll be a dramatic performance, Eitzen presumes, or someone will sing a ballad with pictures to go with the tale, and he wonders if he should go and join the expectant crowd or remain calmly seated on his bench, as befits a young man who is about to enter the ranks of the clergy and who carries in his pocket a recommendation by Luther's own hand; nor does he see his friend make any move; maybe he hasn't even noticed the commotion and its cause.

In front of the church, quiet has set in; the market noises suddenly sound as though they were filtered through a thick curtain. On the wooden scaffolding a woman has appeared, costumed in baggy green trousers the like of which Eitzen has seen in pictures from Turkey, and a little red vest, richly embroidered and worn over a loose white shirt, and on her head a blue turban held together by a glittering clasp from which a thick tuft of white horsehair is pointing skyward. The woman's face is covered with thick paint, the devil knows what's hidden under the paste, most probably the wrinkled skin of an old hag. Except her eyes, large and shining like pearls, seem to be young, and are familiar to Eitzen, and he jumps up from his bench and runs toward the crowd at the scaffolding and throws himself into its midst and pushes and shoves, heedless of their curses, until he stands directly before the woman, and stares at her as though she were a ghost, and sees, her shirt and trousers notwithstanding, the shape of her breasts and her thighs, and his mouth turns dry as sand, and he wants to call "Margriet!"—but not a sound will issue from his throat.

The woman, however, is raising her hand, and when she has satisfied herself that the people are all eyes and ears, and their mouths hanging open, she declares in a solemn voice which carries her words to every last one of her listeners that she is the Princess Helena, youngest daughter and favorite of the Emir of Trapezund, who was like a grand duke at the court of the powerful sultan; and that she left her father and mother and the sumptuous harem at Constantinople where she had everything a girl could wish for, beautiful clothes and jewels and silken pillows and black slaves to fan her gently and serve her every whim, for on the night of her eighteenth birthday there appeared to her the Everlasting Jew Ahasverus who was condemned by our Lord Jesus Christ to wander all over the earth till Judgment Day, and converted her to the only true faith in our Lord and Savior Jesus Christ, Amen. And that since that night she has followed the road of the Everlasting Jew Ahasverus, who cannot die and is renewing and rejuvenating himself every once in a while, she being like a heavenly bride of his, so that she might testify to the greatness of God and the sufferings of our Lord Jesus Christ as the Wandering Jew saw them with his own eyes, and that the Jew himself would appear in good time and show to all and sundry his feet with the sign of the cross on their soles and tell in his own words how our Lord Jesus Christ talked with him and condemned him for his exceeding hardness of heart, for which the poor man has been atoning with great patience these past thousand five hundred and twenty years. And whoever stayed unmoved by that story, he might, after her tale was told, turn away and go, the Everlasting Jew would forgive him and so would our Lord Jesus Christ, but those who were touched by what they would get to hear and felt its godly effect, as any good Christian should, they might afterward buy the cunningly illustrated and beautifully printed sheets that retold the history of the condemnation of the Wandering Jew, and put their mite in the little bag she would pass around, for she and Ahasverus were of one mind that people in other places should also be given the opportunity to hear the wonderful message which the good people of Helmstedt were now about to receive.

Eitzen is still tongue-tied. True, after that evening in the home of Magister Melanchthon, his wine-sodden brain somehow did sense that the arrogant young Jew who was holding the housemaid Margriet on his lap and diddling her this way and that, might have been linked in some manner to the Wandering Jew, but in the sobering light of the next day he cast away the thought as so much delusion and fancy. And now he is to believe in addition that the Princess Helena of Trapezund has served as a maid in the house of his friend Leuchtentrager, has smoked out the bed in which he, *Studiosus* Eitzen, was bitten by all those fleas, and removed his chamber pot, and enticed him to the point of madness by the slow swirl of the two fleshy half-moons she carries under her skirts: are we then, all of us, creatures of a twofold nature, and if this is so, who is the other one that is hidden inside him?

His companion, it seems, is still sitting before the inn, sipping his wine, unaware of the storm which rages in Master Eitzen's breast. Eitzen just itches to leap onto the wooden scaffolding and get his fingers under that little vest and those baggy trousers of Princess Helena's, not for the reasons which you are having on your dirty minds, but for science's sake; however, as this would lead to nothing but trouble, because all these people around him wish to hear the cause and particulars of the Jew's condemnation and a great many of them would also like nothing better than to paw the beautiful Helena's various adornments, he restrains himself.

Meanwhile the Princess Helena has hung on a nail a large tablet, on which a red-bearded Jesus may be seen, clothed in a purple garment, and wearing a grass-green crown of thorns on his noble brow while he faces the troopers of Pontius Pilate who are putting their tongues out at him and grimacing in the most gruesome way and deriding him in every manner, and one of them smites his head with a strong reed. The princess points at the figures in the pictures and, neatly stressing the rhymes, declaims in a fine, sedate voice:

> You see here how the soldiers' crowd
> is mocking Jesus shrill and loud,
> is chafing, beating, tweaking him,
> each one according to his whim.
> He braves the torture nonetheless
> for our sins and wickedness.

Eitzen feels that these aren't the impudent tones to which he is accustomed from Margriet, nor is it her vocabulary; on the contrary, the person reciting these pretty verses, and doing it without a stammer or stutter, seems by her diction and mode of expression like a true lady, even though the question of her also hailing from Trapezund or of being a princess may for the present be left in abeyance. Eitzen's excitement grows by the minute, and his eyes are searching for his friend, for if anyone, it should be Leuchtentrager who can tell him the whys and wherefores of this; but once again his companion remains invisible, and the Turkish Helena has already put up a fresh tablet in the middle of which, just as on the first one, our Lord Jesus is depicted, but now wearing a long white shirt, and the purple color is reserved for the large drops of blood which are flowing down his pathetic face while he forces himself to go forward, deeply bowed under his burden and tearfully watched by a group of wailing women who beat their hands partly to their bosom, partly to their foreheads. The Princess of Trapezund, her left hand pointing to the picture, her right raised accusingly, is becoming passionate:

> The heavy cross which he must bear
> is choking him, he gasps for air.
> The soldiers prod God's only son,
> to Golgotha he must anon.
> Some women stop him, full of woe.
> He says: Don't weep, and let me go.

Eitzen is aware that this tale is one of the best-known of the Bible; yet people are standing there as though they were under a spell, exuding the odor of sweat and onions and hardly breathing; a trickle of spit is running down some old man's chin without his noticing it; another fellow, just as absorbed, keeps scratching his arse; but the beautiful Helena is quick to exchange the tablet, her new one displaying beside the tortured Jesus a stranger with chubby red cheeks, who wears a round, golden-yellow helmet and vainly proffers his hand to poor Jesus. Then she resumes with a distinct tremble to her voice:

> A captain from a foreign land
> extends to him a brother's hand.
> But Jesus only thinks of love
> and of his Father up above.
> The captain says, as well he can:
> *Ecce homo*—what a man.

As always on hearing those two Latin words, *ecce homo*, Eitzen feels a cold shudder running down his back, and this time it's especially cold as he feels that the beautiful oratress has taken cognizance of him despite all her business and declamation; there was that momentary gleam in her eye and a hesitancy for the space of a short breath, but clearly noticeable to him; and now, in his mind, the Margriet he has known and the Princess of Trapezund are fading into one, *ecce homo*, he thinks, out of the mouth of this she-devil and Jew's whore, and a slight dizziness befalls him; but then he shakes this off, thinking, who am I to be more severe than our Lord Jesus Christ, for didn't he say of the woman who was a sinner, after she washed his feet with her tears and kissed them and wiped them with the hairs of her head and anointed them with the ointment she had brought: her sins, which are many, are forgiven, for she loved much; except that Margriet, up to this time, has never shown an inclination to toy with his, Paulus von Eitzen's feet, but 'tis not yet the end of all days. Now, however, the princess is posting the next tablet up there, and on this one is to be seen, to the left side, our Lord Jesus under his burden, and to the right a Jew in a black caftan the like of which Eitzen came to know on that fateful evening in Wittenberg, and behind this Jew stands a house with a portico, between whose somewhat crooked columns a pole is projecting with a sign at the end of it, namely a grass-green wreath showing a purple colored boot in its center.

Princess Helena has placed herself next to the tablet, and you discern from her face that her story will now be rushing toward its climax, when its knot that she's been tying with so much diligence is cut and the big rumble must follow; her bosom is rising and falling apace, and the brush of white horsehair on top of her turban points steeply upward, and she gazes over the heads of the crowd into the far distance, as though she were seeing an appearance there, and speaks:

A Jew named Ahasverus has
his shoe-repair shop in this place.
Lord Jesus thinks, there, by that door,
I'll rest, for I can walk no more;
though time is up and I am late,
a little while my death can wait.

Just then, with the throng uttering a collective gasp,
the Jew appears beside the princess, clothed in his shabby
caftan, and a little round cap on his hair, which is of the
same reddish color as our Lord Jesus' on those tablets and
on the large canvas that shows him nailed to the cross.
And stands there as though he had fallen from the sky at
that moment or, so Eitzen thinks, popped up from hell,
the cursed Ahasverus who can neither die nor find rest
but must wander all over this earth, in heat or cold, up
the high mountains and down through the wilderness,
through brush and thorn, over rocks and boulders and
cliffs of ice, across rivers and seas, endlessly, and who,
here on the market square of the town of Helmstedt, is
ready to tell what really happened between him and our
Lord Jesus and how come he was damned for all eternity.
"But the Rabbi says to me," he proclaims into the silence that has set in on the market square, "Let me rest, he
says, for I am weighed down greatly, it must be close to
three hundred pounds, and all of it hard wood, with sharp
edges to it. Is that so, I say to him, it weighs you down.
And don't you think that we are being weighed down at
least as heavily by the yoke the Romans have put upon us?
Let me rest, he says to me once again, the road that leads
up here is steep and full of stones, and they have beaten me
sorely. Is that so, I say to him, the road is steep and full of
stones. And how steep, do you think, and how full of
stones is the road which the people of Israel must tread?
Let me rest just a bit, I beg of you, he says to me, for I
must gather some strength so I may get to my Father in
heaven. Is that so, I say to him, you want to get to your
Father in heaven—"

"He's lying!"

Eitzen blenches. It was he who called out those two fateful words, and yet he is frightened and pulls in his head and quickly looks around to see if someone might not be raising his fist to smash him across the mouth or hit him behind the ear, which blow could damage a man for life. But the people nearby are as startled as himself, or as the Jew is up there on that scaffolding whose words seem to have congealed on his tongue, gumming up his mouth and making him sweat. Eitzen becomes aware that no one has challenged him or raised his hand to strike at him; on the contrary, they all are staring at him as though he were the miracle man in place of the Jew, and so he picks up courage and begins to feel like a crusader for the Lord and says to himself that now he will get at the damned Jew, and he sucks in breath and shouts as loud as his lungs will let him, " 'Tis all lies and flimflam this man's been telling you, and the worst kind of deceit and fraud and falsehood! In this manner dumb peasants may be tricked and the money pulled from their pockets, but the good citizens of Helmstedt and the learned students and professors at the university should certainly be wiser than that! Why, this fellow is never the famous Ahasverus, nor has he at any time caught sight of even the shadow of a hair on the head of our Lord Jesus Christ. He is a Jew named Ahab whom I have met and encountered at Wittenberg, with the woman there, that calls herself a princess, sitting snugly on his lap; and now he thinks he can turn this assembly of honest Christian people into a horde of fools!"

In response, a nasty muttering is heard which, Eitzen is sure, directs itself not against him but against the Jew. And while this muttering grows in volume and threat, Eitzen waits, wondering if a reply will finally come forth from the Jew or if the fellow will remain mute, and trying to think of how he might pass a hint to the beautiful Helena that she should make haste and climb down from that scaffolding and place herself under his protection, but nothing useful will occur to him. Suddenly his friend Leuchten trager is at his side and looks at him strangely and, twisting his mouth into a laugh, says to him, "Carry on, Paul, just carry on and God will reward you when these people get up and assault the Jew and beat him to death along with the Princess of Trapezund."

Meanwhile the sky has been darkening, black clouds rising from the right and left and leaving only a strip of light in the center where the Jew is standing, behind him the large canvas with the red-haired man on the cross between the two thieves, and behind that canvas again the tower of the church with the sharply pointed roof topped by the golden weathercock up high. In the crowd, the flesh of many a man is beginning to creep because he feels that God is about to give a sign as to which of the two is speaking falsely, the Jew with his princess, or the young man out front who wears the beret of a magister of the arts.

The Jew is raising his hands, like a prophet. The muttering ceases. The Jew's eyes are hard, two gray pebbles with a dangerous sheen to them. "Once before," he says, "there was one who was denied by another who should have known better. Verily, I say unto you, as I am the Wandering Jew, by name Ahasverus, and damned by the Rabbi because I turned him away from my door when he came to me wanting to rest from the burden of his cross, that golden cock up there on the tower will crow three times and then lightning will come down from God and strike."

Eitzen knows that he must laugh now, loud and derisively, so that his laugh is heard by everybody and the spell is broken which has taken hold of them; a weathercock on top of a church tower may tell how the wind blows, but as for crowing, why, they none of them ever had the throat for it. He looks at his friend Leuchtentrager, seeking assurance from the expression of his eye and from his face that, certainly, a cock is a cock and brass is brass; but Leuchtentrager puts his hand to his ear and says, "Listen!"

And there it is, faint and unsure at first, as from a

young cock who does not quite trust himself and is trying out his voice, and then somewhat louder and self-confident, and the third time with a triumphant blare that sounds across the whole expanse of the square and beyond it: the cock's crow that drives away the shadows of the night and the dark whisperings of the obscurantists.

The people seem petrified. Only the figure on the cross is stirring, but that's because of the wind which is starting up before the storm and moving the painted canvas. The lightning stroke that then comes hissing down, blinding everybody, dissolves the state of fixation; it strikes the scaffolding and ignites it, flames shoot up and consume the dry wood along with the picture of the man on the cross and the various tablets and other paraphernalia while, howling with fright, skirts flying, coattails fluttering, the crowd is fleeing every whichway.

Eitzen is being grabbed by the wrist and dragged off. "Let us get away from here," he hears Leuchtentrager saying, "lest people put it in their minds to kill you."

CHAPTER TWELVE

§

Wherein the great curtain in the temple is torn and
Ahasverus discourses with Iscariot on the
interdependence of the doctrine of
predestination and man's mas-
tery of his own fate

§

Nobody knows the truth except the Rabbi and myself, but the Rabbi is dead these many years, and the dead do not talk.

That day was of a rare beauty; the earth, freshly tilled after the winter rains, smelled moist and sweet, the lilies stood in all their splendor, the sky was not yet bleached by the glaring heat of the summer but arched, a sparkling blue, above the city and the temple. It was a day for living, not for dying; but it was the day before Sabbath eve, and what must be done had to be done that day, for on the seventh day God rested from all His labors, and not a hand in Israel could be lifted for any kind of work then.

Therefore the urgency. Therefore the hasty hither and thither between the house of Caiaphas and the house of Herod and the house of Pilate, and the sudden questions put to the people as to which was to live and which to die, the *guerrillero* Barabbas or that crazy king of the Jews; therefore the hurried conferences of the legal experts, on who was competent to pronounce sentence and who should execute it, and who had priority, the national or the religious authorities; the hierarchy was lined up against the

tetrarch, and both of them were trying to involve the occupation power. Added to this was the utter inflexibility of
Reb Joshua, which just might have been a complete lack of
understanding of matters worldly; his mind was fixed on
that seat to the right hand of God, while at the same time
his heart was full of fear and forebodings. And therefore
that uphill race which offered the crowd so few oppor-
tunities to enjoy the show. A village fool who calls himself
King of the Jews and who must drag along his own cross,
what a fine possibility for making wisecracks, this is where
the people's well-known sense of humor can have its fling
without police interference and where a topic of conversation might be furnished for many a drunken evening to
come; but no, as soon as the fellow heaves into sight,
prodded by the sticks of his escort, gasping and sweating
blood, he's stumbled by, and only when he sinks to his
knees like an overburdened she-ass does anyone get
a chance at shouting Hosanna! or Hail to the King! or
How're you going to deliver us, you son of God, if you
can't even deliver yourself!

But I was distressed for you, Reb Joshua, despite your
great folly, and my heart ached in my breast when I saw
you coming toward me with that cross on your back. And
I saw the look in your eye when you recognized me as I
stood in front of my house, and I saw the trembling of
your torn lip as you tried to speak and brought forth nothing but a hoarse whisper. And I went over to you and said:
As you see, I am with you in your hour of trial.

He nodded and spoke with difficulty: You also said
that I should find rest with you.

And I leaned down to him, for he stood deeply bent
under his burden, and I said: Hidden under my garment I
carry a sword of God with me, and I will draw it for you,
and all those who scorn you and all your enemies and all
these soldiers will take fright and flee from its fiery glint.

He stayed silent.

And you, Reb Joshua, I went on to say, will throw off
your cross and straighten your back and be free of your

burden, and you will gather around you the people of Israel and lead them, as is written in the book, for yours is the fight, O Prince, and yours the victory, O King.

He, however, shook his head that was crowned with thorns and answered me: Leave your sword in its sheath; the cup which my father has given me, shall I not drink it? But I should like to rest in the shade of your door, for I am weary to death.

But I was filled with anger at that much obstinacy, and I shoved him away from me and called out: Get going, you idiot! Do you actually think the One up there cares whether or not they will drive their nails through your hands and your feet and let you die piecemeal on that cross? Wasn't it He who made people as they are? How, then, can you hope to change them through your miserable death?

I am still seeing the Rabbi's face growing pale underneath the drops of his blood, and I hear him saying as though it were today: The son of man goes as is written in the words of the prophets, but you shall remain here and tarry till I come.

Then he went on his way and vanished around the corner where the road leads up to Golgotha, and with him went the whole crowd, making noises and jumping about as though they were being paid by a king of this world. And then a great silence set in, and the light lay on the leaves of the vine that grew up the pillars and over the crossbeams of my portico, and the shadows of the leaves trembled on the tiles of the terrace, and I sat there, thinking of the Rabbi who now was hung to the cross and slowly dying, and of his words which he had spoken to me, and of the vanity of all human endeavor.

And Judas Iscariot came and stood before me with his purse in his hand and said to me: You are the one, aren't you, who leaned his head on the bosom of the Rabbi at that supper when he let us partake of his body and his blood?

And you are the one, I said, who owes me one piece of

silver out of the thirty which you received for your act of treason.

Treason, said Judas, is a nasty word. I have acted only according to what was to be, and according to the Rabbi's own wishes, for didn't he tell us that he must shed his blood for many for the remission of their sins, and shortly thereafter, didn't he instruct me to do that which I had to do, quickly? Consequently I have done only what was predetermined and in pursuit of the Rabbi's own command; you, however, turned him away from your door when all he wished was to rest a bit from his labors; in truth, therefore, it is you and not I who betrayed him.

To think that what a man does necessarily is well done merely because he is a tool and a plaything in the hand of a higher being strikes me as a most superficial philosophy, I replied. If you will recall, your forefather Adam was sentenced to banishment from the garden of Eden and had to go to work just for eating that apple, although he was predestined to eat it, why else would God have hung it in front of his nose and why else would he have made the woman Eve and the snake? It's simply one of those games that God likes to play with people: He calls on them to decide on good and evil, even though they cannot but follow their predetermined course; thus you, who are born a traitor, did nonetheless turn traitor by your own will and therefore are destined to go up to yonder tree and hang yourself on it. But as for me, I am pure spirit, of the spirit of God, and I act in the absolute and no moral value attaches to what I do, wherefore I do not need anyone giving his blood in remission of sins which I cannot commit. And now, pray, hand me that piece of silver which you owe me.

By this time Judas Iscariot was thoroughly frightened and made haste to give me the silver dinar which I had demanded from him, and then ran away. But after a while, when the sixth hour was approaching, he returned and told me that he had carried the remaining twenty-nine to the temple, intending to give them to the priests; they had refused to accept them, however, saying that it was blood money. Whereupon he turned and walked to the tree which stands on the slope above my house, and took a rope such as is used by the donkey drivers, and hanged himself.

But I saw that the sky was darkening, and an icy wind rose from the mountains. And many people came running, and they shouted that the great curtain in the temple had been torn in two as by a giant hand and that the whole city was filled with fear of a punishment from God.

By this I knew that poor Reb Joshua had died, and I wrapped my head in my shawl and wept for him.

CHAPTER THIRTEEN

§

*Wherein the sacrilegious question is posed whether
it is really man who was made after the likeness
of God, or vice versa, and the contradictions are dealt with which endanger
the established order of things*

§

I know what I know.

I can hear the voice of God. It sounds in the roar of the
waters, in the rage of the flames, in the howl of the storms,
and is more powerful than all of these; but it is also in the
whisper of the willow tree, a breath of wind stirring,
hardly audible. It can pursue you to the end of the world,
past stars which long ago burned themselves out and others that are just being born, and it may be inside you like
the tickling of a worm or a ringing in your ears.

And the voice of God sounded and spoke: I have with-
drawn my hand from you, Ahasverus, and have cast you
down from up high in the third hour of the sixth day,
and this I did because the order which I established was
scorned by you and the laws I set were mockery in your
eyes; but now that you are damned to wander through the
depths, instead of sitting up here in the splendor of the
heavens and jubilating and singing my praise, you still appear to be striving to turn things upside down, or downside up, and are doubting the wisdom of my creation.

But I raised my face to the clouds above the clouds,

whence the voice had come, and I answered: I mainly have my doubts about man, of whom it is said that you made him in your image, after the likeness of God, and about the son of man who is alleged to be your one begotten son and to have been sent by you for the remission of the sins of the others, and on whose bosom I leaned my head at his last supper.

And again the voice rose and spoke: The world is full of wonders from morning to evening. Even a single molecule is structured in so complex a manner, while its idea is so ingeniously simple, that it could have only one creator, namely me. Seeing this, how can you still have doubts?

But I bowed down deeply before God and said: Far be it from me to doubt your miracles, O Lord, or your little molecules; my doubts concern your divine justice and the claim that man, whom you made, was actually created in your image.

At this, the clouds opened, and the clouds above the clouds, and a light broke forth that shone like a thousand suns and yet was not blinding, and in its radiance a ladder became visible which stood without anyone holding it, and which was so high that its highest rungs were lost in infinity; and a host of angels were climbing up and down it, good little angels of course, not the sort that Lucifer and I were, so that it looked as though a tribe of ants were crawling up and down this ladder, white ants with pink little heads and shimmering little wings. And some of them were hoisting a throne down the ladder and laboring mightily, for the throne was large and heavy and inlaid with precious stones which sparkled in all the colors of spring, blue and green and red and golden, and its armrests were finely chiseled and carved, displaying at their ends the heads of two cherubim, and its four feet were like the claws of lions, and the top of its backrest was formed of two glistening snakes whose bodies were intertwined while their heads were hissing at one another. But no one was seated on this throne so that it seemed as though all those diligent little angels were busying themselves with an empty piece of furniture.

But when they finally had lowered this ornate seat to the ground, they took hold of it and carried it to where I stood and placed it facing me, and also a footstool which was attached by golden joints to the legs of the throne, and then they went off with their little wings whirring and their little shirttails aflutter. But the voice of God sounded again and spoke: Since you are doubting that man was made after the likeness of God, I shall show myself to you.

And the light from up high laid itself around the throne like a wreath of brilliants, and within it a thin strip of vapor appeared, as unsubstantial as a mist rising in the morning. This mist, however, kept condensing quickly, and it gained shadow and shape and the dimensions of a body which was seated on the throne, clothed in a white garment, with eyes that were of a fine radiance and well-coiffed wavy hair and a nicely curled beard; altogether a man in the prime of his years, and everything about him perfect and of great beauty.

But I was unable to throw myself into the dust before him and kiss his feet as I couldn't take my eyes off him, for it was to me as though I were simultaneously seeing the pitiable figure of Reb Joshua seated there, and I spoke: So you are God, are you?

And he said: I am that I am.

You are beautiful, O Lord, I said, rooted in yourself as you are, and I could love you.

Still you are doubting me and the order which I created, he said, and though I am seated here upon my throne as the living proof of man's likeness to God.

Lord God, I said, I was cast out by you and am without power. Yet I will ask you: Which is the truth, is man in the image of God, or God in the image of man?

At these words, a frown settled on his brow and the light from up high dimmed, and the little white angels with their pink little heads and their shimmering little wings were excitedly surging around the ladder as though they expected it to collapse any moment, and I grew afraid because of the insolence of my question.

But the voice of God was heard again, and it sounded changed, almost a bit shrill, and it said: This way or that, what is it to you who are less than the speck of dust out of which I created man?

It is a contradiction, O Lord, I said, a hole in the web of your order through which the sand is running out.

In answer to this, there came some of the good angels that had broad shoulders and strong arms and hands like butchers' helpers and placed themselves to the right and left of me. But God motioned to them to step aside, and He inquired: Are you also seeing other such contradictions, Ahasverus?

And I bowed before Him and said: O yes, Lord, I see a great many of them, but they are like the salt in the porridge and the leaven in the dough, and the soul of the business, yours and mine.

But God said: I made you on the second day, not out of the dust from which man was made but out of fire and the breath of infinity. This, however, gives you by no means any right to your Jewish impudence.

And I replied: Don't I have the right to ask you some questions, O Lord? You cast me down from the heights in the third hour of the sixth day and condemned me to wander through the depths till Judgment Day, and then your one begotten son came along on his way to Golgotha and did the same thing again. Wasn't once enough? Or being a trinity, you and your son and that ghost of which so little mention is made, did you believe that a double damnation would stick more securely?

At that, God rose from His throne and came toward me, His eyes shooting fire and His forehead reddened in anger, looking glorious in His divine wrath, and I spread my arms to receive Him like a lover, for I truly loved Him now that He had lost His remoteness, and I would have forgiven Him even if He had damned me a third time. He, however, hesitated suddenly and smiled, and then He began to dissolve and once again became but a vapor, and soon that was gone, too, and only the throne stood there in its empty splendor.

I know what I know. And God is that He is, and His much-praised order is as full of contradictions as He Himself.

CHAPTER FOURTEEN

§

*In which the Wandering Jew, by offering good and
sufficient security, helps a Christian
merchant to a peaceful
death*

§

So the boy did return, the sick man is thinking. He feels
relieved; having a parson right in your family is better yet
than having a doctor, the doctor is useful for your life on
earth which lasts threescore years or, if you are lucky, ten
more, but the parson will see to your eternal salvation.

Still, he goes on to think, 'tis a strange thing about
death. We who have always led a God-fearing and law-
abiding life, and in connubity with our married wife and
no other woman that we know of have put a number of
worthy offspring into this world, and besides this have
abstained from the sins of pride and covetousness, and
committed neither murder nor theft, and conducted our
business in all honesty, giving fair measure and following
the goodly rules, that many percent on that much of your
capital, calculating the risk—ought we not to be able to
face death cheerfully and secure in our belief in the state of
everlasting blessedness which we shall reach?

But along with the pain that once more spreads
through his chest, doubt is burrowing in the sick man's
heart: What if it all were a delusion and mere fancy, and if
nothing remained of a man than the small heap of dust of
which he was made? "Does anyone really know about the
soul?" he says to his son who sits at his bedside with a

sorrowful face and eyes expressing grief. "Does anyone know when God breathed that soul into him which now is about to return to its donor like a borrowed guilder? Did anyone ever see it or touch it? From which of the holes in my mortal body will it escape, out of my mouth, my nose, my ear, or whence? And could it not be, despite all we are told, that I never again shall be?"

The son argues, "But it is written, Father, that God created man for eternal life."

The sick man moans faintly. "I am frightened," he says, "I am frightened of the great nothing. Formerly, when we had the Papists, everything was done in a businesslike way, so-and-so-many Hamburg silver pennies for so-and-so-many years of indulgence from purgatory and other plagues, and it was warranted by the Holy Father himself. But after your Doctor Luther inveighed against that, what now? Who is there who will put sign and seal to it that we, or a part of us, will live on after death or be certain to rise on Judgment Day, our brittle bones gathering themselves together and our rotten flesh growing firm and rosy once more and our dead eyes opening to see the brightness of paradise? Who can guarantee it, and what Jew will lend you money on it?"

The son replies, "The apostle John says that those who trust in the Lord will have everlasting life. You must have trust, Father."

For this I have sent the boy to study, the sick man is thinking. He was to open his ears and his mind and learn all there is about the ultimate secrets and the immortal soul, for who would know more on those subjects than the *doctores* and *professores* at Wittenberg? And now that he is back and himself wearing the magister's beret and looking for a pastorate so he might shed over the heads of his parishioners the wisdom he has garnered, what does he tell me? That I must have trust. "Trust," the sick man repeats, "is that so. But credit, my son, is given only against security. What security can you furnish?"

The question embarrasses the young magister. Born

and raised in the house of Eitzen, linens and woolens. he knows that one who does business on trust and belief is likely to lose his wares and possessions, and his trousers as well. And as in business, so in religion.

"You gentlemen of the clergy promise us everlasting life," says the sick man. "Ah, how I would like to accept that promise. I would give everything for it, goods and money; I would crawl on my knees to the gates of St. Petri and kiss the hem of Dean Aepinus's robe or of your robe, my son, if that helped. But where is my security?"

The son knows many an apt verse from the Scriptures and from other learned books, because these he has learned from Philipp Melanchthon and the good Doctor Martinus, and he would like to quote them to his father with the proper solemnity, but what good are the most edifying words of this nature to one who used to read his account books six times a week and his prayer book only once, and who is geared to weighing credit against debit? For that sort of person you need a live witness able to give reliable testimony, the son reasons. At the same time he grows aware that this thought must have been on his mind for quite a while; the sound of the golden cock crowing on top of that church tower, which shook him to the bottom of his heart, has pursued him the whole way to Hamburg, and he theorizes that the curse by which one man was damned in all eternity might be turned into an everlasting blessing for another. "Security," he says, "I will furnish the security you want, Father. Let me tell you of the Jew Ahasverus, whom I encountered several times, and of the cock who crowed thrice on the church tower at Helmstedt."

The sick man listens. His son's words are like balm to his heart which feels as though it were ringed by a band of iron that keeps growing ever more tight; he wishes to God that this band would break, knowing full well that if the ring bursts, his heart will burst along with it. But this Jew, he thinks, if this Jew really was what he pretended to be, he could furnish the proof and security needed; and wasn't it true that the boy put the Jew to the test, and didn't the boy hear the cock crowing three times at Helmstedt and didn't he see thunder and lightning come down from a clear sky? And if there was an everlasting life to which a man could be damned, wasn't it logical that such everlasting life should be available also to those who died in a blessed state and at peace with themselves and with God? "And where, my son," he says, "can that Jew be found?"

This is the one point which the young magister forgot to anticipate. He didn't foresee that, once he mentioned Ahasverus, it would follow like the Amen on the Benedictus that he would have to produce the Jew for the sick man's consolation and edification. But he is very much averse to going now and having to search for the Jew in the narrow lanes and alleyways where these people dwell; also how can he speak sweetly to him and beg favors of him with the Princess of Trapezund pouring her scorn over him, for didn't he try everything at Helmstedt to incite the anger of the people against her and the Jew? "Where that Jew can now be found?" he repeats. "The devil knows."

The sick man notices the young magister shifting uncertainly on his chair, and draws his own conclusions; but just because of this his eagerness is sharpened to see the Jew and inquire of him if he indeed saw our Lord Jesus alive as you and me, and if he did talk to him, and if he actually has wandered on earth these past thousand five hundred years and more. Cock or no cock, Eitzen senior thinks, that Jew won't be able to fib to me, I have an eye for people and can smell a lie, without that ability I should have been bankrupt three times over, linens and woolens is a hard business and there are more crooks, thieves, and sharpers in it than honest merchants. "My son," he says, "you will fetch that Jew. I want to have a talk with him."

Young Eitzen is about to raise objections, but the patient sits up with a groan and states, "'Tis my last wish, do you hear? And now, go."

Master Paulus cannot but rise in obedience to his father and go forth. The boy has already a parson's ways, the sick man thinks, he's taken on that measured, pensive step, that soft-soled walk; the clergy do not want to frighten away the sinner before getting their hands on him. And he will find the Jew, too, and bring him to me; and the sick man tries to picture in his mind a person who has lived that many years, a trembling, senile creature with running eyes, shriveled and shrunken to just skin and bones, and an odor of mold and decay about him. Fatigued from the effort, he falls asleep and does not come awake till he hears voices inside his room, and believes they're the voices of his son Paul and the Jew Ahasverus, and raises his head so he might see them; but sees his family instead, namely his good wife Anna, and Dietrich, his older son, and his daughters Martha and Magdalena, all of them with mournful faces, the women clutching handkerchiefs that they keep tugging and twisting, and in their wake Dean Johann Aepinus, come to ease the dying man's last hour, which, however, does not suit the purposes of Reinhard Eitzen, linens and woolens, at all, as he has more important matters to discuss with quite another party.

But Dean Aepinus is one of those people who at all times are headed straight for their objective, regardless of whose feet they tread on, and in this case he is hot after a soul which must be saved and sped on its way, prepared and equipped for the journey, which is a laudable thing to do for a divine and a service he owes to his old friend. So, resembling nothing more than a huge, black-winged bird, he shooes out the sick man's wife and children, for the holy sacrament of confession requires that he be closeted alone with the sinner. Then he steps to the side of the bed in which the patient is lying quite pale and motionless, his brow covered with cold sweat, and addresses him in a voice that sounds as though half of it came from the other side of the grave, "Do you, Reinhard Eitzen, confess that you have sinned, and do you repent of these your sins, so answer: Yes."

These words frighten the patient mightily, for he knows them well and they make him think, Has it come to this, that I must take leave from this world although I'm in no way ready for it; and what is delaying my son Paul who promised to fetch the Jew?

Even though Dean Aepinus has not been able to perceive any Yes coming from the pallid lips, he takes the sad glance, which the patient is directing toward the beams of the ceiling, for an answer; and he coughs sternly and goes on asking, "Do you, Reinhard Eitzen, seek remission of your sins in the name of Jesus Christ, so answer: Yes."

The sick man believes that he is hearing voices which are raised in an argument outside the door. So they are quarreling already, he thinks, although I am not cold yet; vanity of vanities, all is vanity, and he who was to furnish the security of which I am so much in need, where is he keeping himself?

There still has not been any Yes from the mouth of the patient, nor even a nod, yet Dean Aepinus takes the faint flutter of an eyelid for the answer which will permit his third question, the hardest and severest of all, that will determine whether this Christian soul, cleansed and free of sin, will be able to wing its way up to the little angels as soon as it has departed from its body, and so he says in a hollow, solemn tone, "Do you, Reinhard Eitzen, also believe that Jesus Christ has delivered you from all your sins and that the absolution which I grant unto you is as forgiveness from God, so answer: Yes."

But this time the sick man is trying to speak, much to Dean Aepinus's surprise and joy; his lips move, but the hoarse whisper that issues from them is unintelligible. The dean bends down, placing his ear close to the patient's mouth, and now he understands what the other is saying, namely, "Where's the Jew? I want the Jew!" Yet the words strike the dean as sheer nonsense, for who is this Jew and what business has he intruding between one who is readying himself for the other world and his confessor? He therefore assumes that the patient's mind has begun to wander, as is frequent with dying people, and concludes that time is growing short for both absolution and holy communion, and thus rushes through the *absolvo te* as though his tongue were in an unholy race with the devil, "By the power which our Lord Jesus Christ has left to his Church to absolve all sinners who truly repent, I say to you, Reinhard Eitzen: Almighty God has promised forgiveness to you, and through the holy suffering and dying and the resurrection of our Lord Jesus Christ He pardons you and delivers you from all your sins, Amen."

Then he hastily makes the sign of the cross and hurries to the door to open it, because the wife and children of the patient are to witness that he has received the holy communion and partaken in the body and the blood of the Lord, which are at one and the same time his last meal on this earth and food for the journey beyond; but hardly has the door creaked open when Master Paul tumbles into the room, dragging a red-haired Jew by the hand and calling out, "Here he is!" Close on the heels of these two, Dietrich, the older brother, and Martha and Magdalena, the sisters, and Frau Anna enter, all four in high dudgeon and loudly complaining of outrage and shame, a dirty Jew being taken to the side of a nice, clean Christian deathbed.

Poor Paul feels his insides torn by his filial duty on the one hand, following which he had been searching half the city of Hamburg for the Jew, until his friend Leuchtentrager led him to the right place, and by his fears for his clerical career on the other; for he is seeing there, very much disconcerted and taken aback at the undue interruption and the strange visitor, the addressee of the letter which Luther wrote recommending him and which he is carrying in his pocket, and he sees that Dean Aepinus is about to berate him. His last kindness to his father, Paul suspects, will cost him dear, just as his brother Dietrich indicated when, outside the door, he called him a bloody fool and his charitable deed a student's prank, and he secretly curses the Princess of Trapezund who in the lodgings of the Jew was lolling about like a slut, her firm breasts shamelessly bared, and counseling her lover against going to comfort the dying man, for had not that half-baked Magister of God knows what miserable Arts done everything at Helmstedt to get the two of them flailed and run out of town.

But neither his anger at Margriet profits him nor the imploring glances he directs at Dean Aepinus and his brother Dietrich; he must explain his action, and must do it credibly, and meanwhile his father is winking at the Jew to come near, but the Jew is folding his arms before his chest and appears not to notice, exactly as everybody else seems to have forgotten about the patient who, by rights, should be the center of attention.

So Master Paul begins orating, with much fervor, for he is talking not merely for the sake of his father's soul's eternal life, but also for the sake of his own, earthly life and its prospects. It had been his father's dearest wish, he explains, that he should fetch the Jew, who was no ordinary Jew as are infesting the lanes and alleyways of our cities and towns; nay, this Jew was the world-famed Ahasverus who was damned by our Lord Jesus Christ to wander on earth forever and ever, because he turned Jesus away from his door when all our Lord wanted from him was a brief respite from the burden of his cross; and now his father wanted to hear from the Jew's own mouth that he had indeed known our Lord Jesus Christ personally and had quarreled with him, thus testifying and furnishing indubitable proof that everlasting life was not merely a *symbolum* which all good Christians must believe in, but concrete fact.

Dean Aepinus tears his sparse hair over such patent nonsense issuing from a future fellow cleric who, in addition, has just been graduated at Wittenberg. "Rubbish!" he thunders, "Everlasting Jew! Everlasting heresy and devil's doctrine!" And goes on shouting about the hoax and damnable lie the young magister has fallen for, and since when do we need an impudent Jew to prove the truth of our everlasting life in view of the fact that it was assured us by most of the holy prophets and by our Lord Jesus himself and, following him, by the sainted apostles? And wants to know whether these were the lessons young Eitzen received at the university from Martinus Luther and Philipp Melanchthon, or whether such wisdoms might not have come out of the vapors of beer and wine which today's *studiosi*, to the displeasure of the Lord, were imbibing in great quantities?

Inside Magister Paul's head things are beginning to whirl: the picture of his father on his deathbed, weakly waving to the Jew to come close; the angry red that has colored the face of Dean Aepinus who, after this fuss and flurry, is likely to read Luther's recommendation with a most jaundiced eye; the pell-mell of raised arms of his brother and mother and sisters, and their eyes turned up in lament; and in the midst of all this tohubohu the Jew, calm and smiling, as though the whole noise and confusion, of which he is the cause, did not concern him in the least. And on top of it Master Paul realizes that, in order to defend his action and avoid looking like a complete dupe and lunatic, he must further enhance the hated Jew.

So he says, by your leave, revered Dean, but the good Doctor Martinus, his teacher, had written a letter addressed to the dean's own person, which he carried with him and which would confirm that he had always studied with great diligence and applied himself to the doctrine of God and the preachings of his prophets; yet the Jew was also existing and real, and the revered dean might want to consider if the live word and testimony of one who had done a tort to our Lord Jesus and had been damned for it wasn't as useful and valuable as any word transmitted by tradition over these thousand five hundred years and some. And instead of upbraiding the zeal of a young and hopeful disciple of the great *doctores* at Wittenberg, might not the revered dean consider further if the voice of the Jew Ahasverus could not profitably be employed in the dispute with those who always doubted the one and only true doctrine?

To Dean Aepinus, this seems sheer madness or, worse yet, straight heresy, and he protests in the strongest terms he can find, namely, whether Master Paul, aside from being possessed by other corruptions, was also a friend of the Jews who had caused our Lord Jesus to be crucified and who, down to these present times were scorning, maligning, and persecuting Christian people and sticking awls into Christian babes and baking the blood of these babes into their Jewish Passover bread, and whether he did not remember the words that his teacher Doctor Martinus had spoken and written about the Jews?

To reproach him of all people with being a friend of the Jews, young Eitzen thinks, after his sermon in the Castle Church at Wittenberg! He has grown pale, and his mouth is puckered as though he had swallowed sour wine, and he would very much like to expound to the revered dean his views on the tribe of the Jews and their character; but he must not forget the presence of the Jew Ahasverus whose services his father needs and who is standing there with his ears pricked up; Master Paul therefore can only stammer some meaningless words until, finally, he can restrain himself no longer and blurts out, "But the cock! The cock! The cock crowed three times!" And he looks about him for someone to back him, the Jew hopefully, who might well report the miracle of Helmstedt and thus convince the assembled of his being the rightful Ahasverus; but the damned Jew stands there like a piece of wood, as motionless and as silent.

The good Dean Aepinus feels increasingly uncomfortable at the strange talk and behavior of the young magister. "The cock! The cock!" he repeats. "We're not in a chicken coop, Master Paul, but happen to find ourselves in a good Christian home where a good Christian man is about to return to his maker, and in case you're referring to the cock who crowed for the apostle Peter, that worthy animal was long ago turned into fricassee. The thought of Peter failing to attend his lord and master reminds the dean that he has not yet finished with the man he has come to attend, and that it is high time to refresh his departing soul by letting him partake in the holy communion, and thus to bring everything to a good end. He therefore takes from the leather-covered, nicely embossed case which he brought along and has placed near the bed, first, a small flask of wine and a silver cup, and then a little box containing a few thin wafers.

But now the sick man has begun to stir. Much to the horror of everybody but the Jew, he groans cruelly and sits up, his eyes nearly popping from their sockets, and by supporting himself on his elbows remains in an upright position. "I want the Jew," he enunciates clearly and audibly, "I want to have a talk with him."

The dean's mouth falls open, and he fears that the devil must truly have his hands in this, and he wishes himself back to those times when you still were permitted to exorcise Satan by prayer and other good means; Dietrich, the older son, and the sisters Martha and Magdalena, and even more so Frau Anna feel their hair stand on end and are frozen stiff like Lot's wife after she looked back at Sodom and was turned into a pillar of salt for her disobedience. The Jew, however, adjusts his little round skullcap and picks a piece of thread from his caftan and says to the patient, "We have lots of time, Herr Eitzen," and to Dean Aepinus, "I interrupted you while you were officiating; so do carry on; even if your imprecations mean nothing to God, they might be a comfort to the man."

The dean casts a vicious glance at young Paul who has brought the impertinent Jew to this house, and another, equally venomous one at the Jew himself who has contrived to combine utter blasphemy with what appears to be a generous gesture; but the only course left open to

Aepinus is to follow the Jew's suggestion and discharge his duties. Thus, holding the Host in his fingers, he speaks, "In the night on which he was betrayed, our Lord Jesus took bread, and blessed it, and broke it, and gave it to the disciples, and said, Take, eat; this is my body which is given for you."

And saying this, the good dean places the wafer between the sick man's trembling lips, so he might eat it; but the Jew, watching the act, recalls the Rabbi, and how the Rabbi drew him to his bosom and whispered to him that, all else notwithstanding, love was stronger than the sword, and how the evening wind passing through the windows made the oil lamps flicker, so that lights and shadows moved over the faces of the disciples and over the face of Judas Iscariot, and how this was so long ago, and now, he thinks, what has become of it, a lot of abracadabra.

"And he took the cup," Dean Aepinus goes on to say, filling his cup from the flask he has brought, "and gave it to them, saying, Drink you all of it, for this is my blood, which is shed for you for the remission of sins." And having spoken thus, the dean holds the cup to the sick man's lips, so he might drink from it; but most of the wine runs down his chin and onto the coverlet, coloring it as though it were real blood. Then the dean intones the Lord's Prayer, in which Master Paul eagerly joins him, as does the rest of the family, and once the Amen is sounded, there is a pause, everyone waiting for Death to enter. But it isn't Death who steps to the sick man's bedside, 'tis the Jew, and he appears much larger than before, at least by a head or two, and his caftan like the raiment of a priest. And he lays his hand on that of the sick man, as Christ used to do, and says, "I have come as you desired, Herr Eitzen, and I will answer any questions you have."

Meanwhile the others have neared and are pressing close, foremost Master Paul, who believes he has a claim on the Jew, and behind him his brother Dietrich and his sisters Martha and Magdalena and Frau Anna, and even

Dean Aepinus, because, next to avarice and lust, it is curiosity that is man's strongest urge. The patient, however, no longer notices wife and children, nor the revered dean; he is only seeing the eerie Jew and is eyeing him feverishly, for the Ahasverus who is standing there at his side does not resemble at all the wizened, rheumy-eyed dotard that he once thought him to be, and so he asks him, "Is it really true, then, that you are the eternal wanderer, and that you have seen with your own eyes our Lord Jesus in the flesh, and have conversed with him?"

The Jew shrugs. "Who else should I be? Would I have come here if I weren't he that I am? As I am standing here at your side, Herr Eitzen, I have talked to the Rabbi when he was on his way to Golgotha, carrying his cross, and halted at the door of my house."

The reasoning behind this answer satisfies the sick man's sense of logic and gives him confidence, so that he now speaks quite freely, "I am plagued by a great fear, Herr Ahasverus, the fear of the nothingness. Tell me, pray, is there such a thing as an immortal soul, and if it exists, from which hole of a man's body does it issue forth, and whither does it journey?"

This is more than Dean Aepinus can tolerate, and he calls out to the patient, "You must not allow yourself to be plagued by such fears, your salvation is all arranged and settled by the holy sacrament which you received from me."

The sick man closes his eyes; the pain in his chest is taking his breath away, and only with great effort is he able to say, "You still owe me an answer to my question, Herr Ahasverus."

The Jew is smiling. "I meet them everywhere, those orphaned little souls; high above this earth and between the several heavens they are floating about, transparent like a cloudlet of breath in wintertime and lost in the wind of infinity, and often I ask myself if it might not be more merciful of God to let them waste away entirely."

The sick man feels disconsolate and starts weeping

pitifully. Finally he sniffs and clears his throat and asks, "But is there no salvation in Christ?"

The Jew hesitates. And once again he recalls the Rabbi, and how the Rabbi straightened himself under the burden of the cross and walked on, and he says to the sick man, "The Rabbi loved all men."

And the sick man feels as though the iron ring around his heart were about to burst, and he groans out loud and draws a deep breath, one last free and happy breath, and then the experienced hand of the Jew glides over his eyelids.

A stillness follows that lasts until Dean Aepinus has composed himself and begins praying loudly, "O Lamb of God that takes away the sins of the world, have mercy on us. O Lamb of God that bears the sins of the world, give us peace. Christ, hear us. *Kyrie eleison. Christe eleison. Kyrie eleison.*" After which Frau Anna and her daughters Martha and Magdalena break into noisy wails, while Dietrich, the son, contemplates the future which necessitates that he immediately inform all customers and correspondents of the firm of Reinhard Eitzen, linens and woolens, that as of this date he has become the head of the house and that, as always in the past, the firm would reliably fulfill its obligations which, he goes on thinking, in view of the steadily rising prices and his having to buy out his brother, the magister, and his sisters Martha and Magdalena, will require considerable aid from God or, barring that, taking a big loan from the cursed Jews.

His thoughts having arrived at this point, he once again takes notice of this particular Jew who up to his father's very end was talking to him and who still is standing there, appearing somewhat lost and no longer great and majestic, but like any ordinary Jew; and so he grabs him by the scruff of his greasy caftan and pushes him out of the room. A while later he and the other members of the mourning family escort Dean Aepinus down the stairs and through the spacious hallway to the door of the house,

Magister Paul dancing special attendance on the good dean and fawning upon him eagerly.

Only the dead man remains behind, his hands folded on his chest, his lips set in a peaceful expression, and knowing by now from which hole of his body his immortal soul has issued forth and whither it is journeying.

CHAPTER FIFTEEN

§

In which Professor Leuchtentrager is advised that
the human soul is but a function of the nervous
system, and the pious Jews of Warsaw despair
of God while Ahasverus immolates himself

§

Prof. Jochanaan Leuchtentrager
Hebrew University
Jerusalem
Israel

24 March 1980

Dear Colleague,

I wrote to you only a week ago; if after so brief an interval I do so again it is because I am worried that I may not have given sufficient emphasis to a thought I deem closely related to the entire Ahasverus matter. Let me add that my views on this point are fully shared by the collective of my Institute which has pledged to assemble by the First of May, the worldwide festival of the working class, the material for an essay on the reactionary character of the myth of the transmigration of the soul.

Ahasverus allegedly keeps reappearing over the centuries; the idea therefore suggests itself that one might consider him a concrete example of metempsychosis, i.e. of a recurring embodiment of ever the same soul in an ever new, albeit similar physical shape. I touched on this, as you can easily verify, in the section "On the Everlasting (or Wandering) Jew" of my book *The Best-known Judeo-Christian Myths as Seen in the Light of Science and History*.

Having reviewed our correspondence on the subject, however, I tend to give increasing weight to this thought and would like to elaborate on it at greater length, especially since I suspect that you, too, may have been reasoning along those lines.

I hope you'll allow me to presuppose your agreement with my thesis that the very concept of transmigration of the soul requires in the first place the existence of a soul. But is there such a thing as a human soul and, logically deriving from this question, a life after death?

Listen, someone may argue, we have an entire science of the human soul, namely psychology, and we have psychiatry which deals with the illnesses of this soul, and men working in those fields, psychologists, psychiatrists, psychoanalysts, psychotherapists, and all this is being taught in schools and universities, and there are clinical institutions pertaining to it, publications, drugs, etc., etc.; consequently there must be a psyche with which all of these are concerned. So far, so good. But this sort of soul can only be viewed under the aspect of the interdependence of body and mind and of their forming an indivisible unit; a separate mind, or a separate soul, leading a separate life before, during, or after the physical life of the individual possessing this mind or this soul, cannot and does not exist, and this was proved by every scientific investigation and experiment in this area; the thing we call soul, or psyche, is simply a function of man's nervous system, including his brain, and it is caused by objectively existing natural and social phenomena which in their turn, via man's sensual organs, affect the apparatus of his nerves and set it in motion. Many of these effects and reciprocal actions, which reflect themselves in the consciousness of man or in his subconscious, in his thinking and feeling, and in his dreams, have long ago been investigated and sufficiently well explained; others have not, but it is only a matter of time until the questions that as yet are a riddle to us will be solved as well. One thing, however, is absolutely certain, namely that man's psyche, or his soul, ceases to exist the moment the psychic function of his brain ends, for which reason, as you might recall, medical science fixes a man's clinical death at the instant when his brain's electrical current ceases to flicker.

All this, dear Professor Leuchtentrager, is self-evident, and I am sure I do not need to convince you of any of it. I have restated these points merely because of the phenomenon called Ahasverus which you apparently take for real, but which to us here in Berlin remains without any scientifically valid explanation. At any rate, your Ahasverus cannot be a case of metempsychosis as there exists no soul independently hovering somewhere in space, on call for any prospective client, so to speak, and able to transmigrate over the centuries from one Ahasverus incarnation to the next. Precisely on this point we should like to have your opinion; this is the cardinal question; how do you propose to answer it?

I concede to you, of course, that the nonexistence of a soul capable of departing from its physical abode might be a regrettable thing. It saddens me, too, that an instrument that can feel happiness and unhappiness, love, hatred, and many other emotions, should cease to be from one second to the next; but scientists are in honor bound to the service of objectivity, and so we must bow to the facts about the human soul, just as we will accept that all of us are mere lumps of matter, highly organized, to be sure, which has developed to its present complex state in a lengthy but entirely natural process.

Nor should we forget to mention that this highly questionable human soul since ancient times has served as a contrivance to hoodwink people: for all the sweat and blood they shed in this world they were promised that their soul at least would have a better lot in the next one. Thus the poet Heinrich Heine, himself formerly a Jew, derides the "lullaby of the pie in the sky with which you soothe that big boob, the people," and Karl Marx writes in his *Critique of the Hegelian Philosophy of Law:* "The *religious* misery is at one and the same time the expression of a real misery and the *protestation* against this real misery. Religion is the sigh of the oppressed creature, the heart of a heartless world, as it is the spirit of a spiritless state of affairs. It is the opiate of the people."

These are the judgments and well-tested principles on which we base ourselves in our Institute, and therefore it seems to us that the phenomenon named Ahasverus, as you described it to us, is simply a factor whose components have not as yet been sufficiently explored. With your kind help, dear Colleague, we hope, however, to be able in the near future to shed some light on the matter.

With best wishes,

Yours sincerely,
(Prof. Dr. Dr.h.c.) Siegfried Beifuss
Institute for Scientific Atheism
Berlin, Capital of the GDR

Prof. Dr. Dr. h.c. Siegfried Beifuss
Institute for Scientific Atheism
Behrenstrasse 39 a
108 Berlin
German Democratic Republic

2 April 1980

Dear Colleague,

Your letter of the 17th of March arrived at the same hour as its supplement of the 24th, a coincidence from which we can only conclude that mail moving between East and West these days follows most miraculous routes. But as the subject matter of our correspondence is such that even the most eagle-eyed censor would not be able to turn anything in it to your disadvantage or mine, we can bear the delays with equanimity and may consider ourselves lucky that our mutual letters reach us at all.

I see little sense in picking up the points of your arguments one by one and attempting to refute those that appear doubtful to me. I happen to agree with much of what you have to say; also I would prefer to avoid our embroiling ourselves in long-winded disputes over items which interest me at best marginally. Whether the "Teacher of Righteousness" and the "Chief Elder of the Church" in scroll 9QRes of the Dead Sea Scrolls were crooks or paranoiacs seems an idle question; to me it is important that in 9QRes we find documentary evidence of the existence of Ahasverus at a time before 9QRes was written. Nor are your otherwise quite valuable thoughts on the human psyche in any way pertinent to the existence or nonexistence of the Wandering Jew since no one ever claimed that Ahasverus could serve as living proof of the transmigration of the soul or anything similar.

I am afraid, though, dear Colleague, that in these two letters of yours I am discovering something else to which you should give serious thought: namely, an incipient fixation on the phenomenon named Ahasverus which you again and again are trying to explain according to the criteria of your *ratio*, although it obviously cannot be fitted into the grid of your experiences. If you'll permit my saying so, you are following in this case a fundamentally unscientific procedure, a procedure reminding me of those Vatican astronomers who refused to admit the existence of the moons of Jupiter because these moons refused to fit into their Aristotelian *Weltbild*. We cannot get around the fact that Ahasverus exists; whatever conclusions should be drawn from this may be subject to discussion, but first it must be acknowledged that he *is*, and for that I have furnished you quite a number of proofs and am willing and prepared to furnish you several more.

In this connection I believe I already mentioned to you the appearance of the Wandering Jew during the last days of the Warsaw ghetto; but while in other instances of his presence I was able to supply only documentary evidence such as 9QRes or the reports on the trial of the advisers of Emperor Julian Apostata, or the testimony of witnesses other than myself, in this case I can personally serve as a witness and, I hope, one beyond doubt. I happen to have been in the Warsaw ghetto, and I did live through the horror of 350,000 people being squeezed into a small number of streets and being starved and tortured and bombed to death. You may believe me, Professor Beifuss, no devil could have invented the methods used for this program of annihilation; it was humans who planned and executed it—to be precise, a number of your fellow countrymen, dear Colleague.

I have often asked myself, then and later on as well, why for such a long time there was no resistance to speak of in the ghetto, and I blame it on the strong religious feeling of the Jews. They were unable to imagine that creatures resembling them in the structure of their bodies and the way of their locomotion could put it in their minds to destroy them, to starve them to death or, where starvation plus typhoid fever plus cholera seemed too slow, to murder them outright or deport them into the gas. Nor could they believe that God, their God, would permit such a perversion. The descendants of the people who thought up God and God's savior son and the whole system of ethics to go with these two were hoping almost to the end for salvation.

Almost. For in the end faith gave way to despair. In the end there were questions. Wherein had they so sinned that God smote them so terribly? They had been following Him, even when He repelled them; they had fulfilled His laws, even when it hurt them; they had loved Him, even when He mocked them or made them suffer. And where in the world was there a sin that merited such punishment? And how long would God have patience with their tormentors? Hadn't they, the wretched and humiliated, the beaten and violated, the enfeebled and dying, a right to know the limits of His patience?

On that evening, Ahasverus and I were walking through the few streets of the ghetto that were still part of it, for the ghetto area had been increasingly restricted and its survivors forced to huddle in an ever diminishing space. It's an awful feeling that overcomes you when suddenly you notice at your feet the bodies of children who have died of hunger, little skeleton dolls, clothed in rags, and no one left to bury them. We both of us thought we should etch this sight into our minds for all time to come, and some other sights as well, dear Professor, of which I'll spare you the details; if you're interested, you can check in the archives of your government to which, I'm certain, you have access; the Germans were always great photographers, and the ghetto offered motifs galore to camera fans.

"Yes," he said, turning to me, "it's going to start."

I knew that the planned uprising made little military sense, but Ahasverus appeared almost elated; you see, he thinks the world can be made to change, which I believe to be an illusion.

"Do you still have that little knife?" he asked.

This knife, for your information, is an antique piece with a beautiful female nude carved into the coral of the handle. I took the knife out of my pocket and offered it to him.

"Would you mind letting me have it for a time?" he said. "The figure of the woman reminds me of someone."

I gave him the knife, and he led me to the house from which the attack on the SS was to be directed. The attack, probably because it was launched so unexpectedly, was successful; for the first time in their lives men and women who had always been hunted experienced the rout of the hunters. Everything seemed to have changed; the Jews who fought here were no longer the Jews one had known; even in death they appeared different from the eternally suffering, eternally beaten people cast in the mold of that poor Reb Joshua who was nailed to the cross.

We managed to hold out several weeks against the SS unit of Herr Dirlewanger and its auxiliaries. Then the building which had served us as both command post and fortress was three-quarters gone, its defenders wiped out but for ourselves and a few men stationed on the floor above us. We had no more ammunition, just some bottles of gasoline. In all this time, while the walls around us gradually collapsed and our fellow fighters, one by one, were killed by bullets or fragments of shell, Ahasverus had been growing ever more taciturn; but now he began to speak to God. He had always had a peculiar relationship to God, he was rebel and lover in one; now he sought to clear that up with God, but God wouldn't answer him.

And then the SS attacked. He told me, "You leave. Through the sewage system. I'll give you cover." He took those three bottles of gasoline that were left, crawled out the window and, crossing a pile of rubble, came up close to the attackers. He lit two of the bottles and threw them at the SS. The gasoline in the last one he poured over himself and rushed, a flaming torch, into the midst of the enemy.

I met him again in Jerusalem. He was standing before his shoe store in the Via Dolorosa which he had reclaimed as his property after that section of the city, as a result of the Six Day War, had once again become accessible to Jews, and which he had had redone from the ground up. He still had the little knife with him and asked me if I wanted it back. I told him to keep it; besides, I said, I knew a place where they would make a perfect copy, down to the marks that proved it to be a genuine antique.

I am, with kindest regards as always

Yours,

Jochanaan Leuchtentrager
Hebrew University
Jerusalem

CHAPTER SIXTEEN

§

Wherein Master Paul develops a most commendable
plan for the conversion of obstinate Jewry,
and it becomes evident that love is
mostly a thing of the imagination

§

Doctor Martinus Luther once said: It is a good thing that God decreed the holy state of matrimony; otherwise parents would neglect their offspring, households would go to rack and ruin, and following that, the police and all worldly government, and even religion, would fall in contempt; thus everything we hold dear would collapse, and disorder and anarchy would rule the world.

Magister Paulus von Eitzen recalls these words and others of a similar nature whenever he finds himself face-to-face with Mistress Barbara Steder, who has so faithfully been waiting for him in Hamburg; but he also thinks of the dowry which Father Steder, a rich ship's broker and chandler, has pledged to give his daughter and which Eitzen can well use, his share of the inheritance left by his own father being tied up in the family business and bringing in only small profit, while his hoped-for living in one of Hamburg's churches is blocked by Dean Aepinus who is still resentful of him for the scandal he created by bringing the Jew to the bedside of a dying Christian; at rare times Master Eitzen is permitted to serve as auxiliary vicar at St. Jacobi or St. Maria Magdalen, but these lowly occasions fill neither his purse nor his heart which is longing for higher things.

"Ah, Hans," he sighs as he and his friend Leuchtentrager are seated together of an evening in the Goldene
Anker, "the countenance of my Barbara changes color
each time she sees me, turning pale or pink as the case may
be, and I'm certain she would have me and merely waits
for me to approach her mother and father; also there is
money aplenty, I have looked into that, old man Steder is
worth several thousands in gold, with hardly any debts,
and he owns a good share of a half-dozen trading ships
plying to Russia; but the more I think of having to lie with
her for the rest of my life and to fondle and caress her, the
more I fear that I shall not be able to rouse myself to the
fulfillment of my marital duties, especially since my heart
is pining for quite another female, but her I cannot have
for she is with that damnable Jew and therefore is lost
to me."

"I know, I know," says Leuchtentrager, dizzying his
friend's mind by taking out his little knife and placing the
point of its blade on the tabletop and causing the coral
woman to keep slowly rotating around herself. "But how
would you know, Paul, if Mistress Barbara might not be
quite capable of doing it for you in the lustiest manner?
God has created women, be they short or long, broad-
beamed or spindly, wrinkled or smooth, with all of
them having the same sort of hole, and for the selfsame
purpose."

Eitzen suddenly begins to wonder why his friend
Leuchtentrager is staying so long in Hamburg, with nobody knowing on what business. "Ah, Hans," he sighs
again, "I have been trying the thing with her, in the most
honorable way, of course, and have bundled with her, but
she was stiff as a rail and cold like a block of ice, and
merely kept groaning as though she were in panic and fear,
and tightened her poop as if I were trying to shove a dozen
mice into it, so that the little I felt for her vanished and my
gaze fixed itself on her sharp nose and her thin lips, and I
grew painfully aware that where other women had tits she
was flat as a board. Following this I told her parents that I

would have to postpone matters, the death of my dear father being too recent, and my heart, despite its love and affection for Mistress Barbara, too heavy and full of tears to leap to the joy of a wedding."

Leuchtentrager scratches his hump. "But it's time you were married, Paul," he says, "for everything must take its orderly course, and a parson without a wife is like a shepherd without a staff, thus lacking his most important accessory; but since you are destined for great things, first in the city of your birth and later on in other places, we must see to it that you and the virtuous Barbara are helped to your tumble."

Eitzen is impressed by this advice, coming as it does from the mouth of his friend who, back in Wittenberg, more than proved his gift of prophecy by correctly predicting that he would be examined on the subject of angels. So he deems it only right and proper to agree to Leuchtentrager's suggestion that they meet next Sunday afternoon, weather permitting, to stroll along the shore of the Alster, at which occasion his friend Hans would take a thorough look at Mistress Barbara and, if he approved of her, would try to impress certain thoughts on her mind: to the benefit of Master Eitzen, of course, and to no other purpose; perhaps, he adds, he might bring along yet another person, a lady capable by experience and character of informing Mistress Barbara of a few items which would whet her appetite.

Eitzen feels the heat he knows so well rising to his head, but he dares not hope what he would dearly love to hope, and thus tries to ban from his mind the alluring image which has formed in it. The next day he betakes himself to the stately house of the Steders so as to transmit the invitation to his Barbara who accepts it all the more joyfully as he praises Leuchtentrager in the highest terms, discoursing of his cleverness and his prosperity, and of his interesting face with its pointed eyebrows and smartly trimmed beard, without concealing, though, his friend's little hump and misshapen foot; these defects, he adds, detract in no way from the man's peculiar fascination which causes the most virtuous ladies to cast admiring glances at him, as has been the case, for instance, with Lisbeth and Jutta, the daughters of Canon Michaelis in Magdeburg; and while he prattles on in this manner, he conjectures on the confusion that would arise if his Barbara would not remain insensible to his friend's charms, either.

The Sunday following, the weather is as rarely happens in Hamburg; a deep blue sky stretches above the jumble of narrow roofs and church spires, and since the previous day brought a heavy rain, the offal and dirt on the streets has been swept into the Elbe River, and the water of the Alster has renewed itself and stinks hardly at all. Mistress Barbara has put on her best finery, her dark green gown which lends her face an interesting pallor while its fur trimmings hide her flatnesses in front and in back; in addition she wears a neatly embroidered cap and a piece of gold jewelry borrowed from her mother's chest. Eitzen's clothes, dark in color so as to fit with his clerical status, are also made of good material and well tailored, and his magister's beret makes people view him with something like awe so that Frau Steder claps her hands and feels moved to exclaim what a wonderful pair they make, Master Paulus and her Barbara, even though he was having no living as yet and no office at one of the big Hamburg churches, but all this would surely come as her husband's word counted heavily in the councils of the city senate.

So now the two are walking along, their steps slow and measured, hardly speaking to one another as Mistress Barbara's heart is full of anxiety and Eitzen's tongue is tied by his once again sensing that a power outside of himself is directing his fate. As they are nearing the bridge which leads to Heilig Geist he discerns Leuchtentrager across the road, and noticing that his friend is not alone, he stiffens.

Leuchtentrager is clothed entirely in red, with tightly fitting red stockings on his legs and a short red cloak slung about his shoulders and a red cap on his head sporting a long red feather; only his sword is of silver and glistens;

thus garbed he takes a deep bow before Mistress Barbara and guides her hand to his lips and kisses it in the Spanish manner, saying how happy he is to make her acquaintance after Master Eitzen has spoken so often of her and her attractiveness and many talents.

Mistress Barbara is goose-pimpling, and her heart beats in her throat; never before did she encounter a man whose very first words are sufficient to make her blood course so fast through her veins. Her Paul, however, still stands there as though petrified; he is struck dumb at the sight of Margriet, or the Princess of Trapezund, who has come decked out like a duchess, carrying a golden pursebag on her arm and a silken kerchief in her hand, and of the Jew at her side who looks like a foreign nobleman in his suit of the latest English fashion, with slit sleeves to his doublet and his reddish beard spruced and tightly curled.

"Sir Ahasverus," says Leuchtentrager, introducing his companion to Barbara, "Sir Ahasverus and Lady Margaret."

"Sir Ahasverus and Lady Margaret" resounds in Eitzen's mind; and staring at the lady he grows painfully conscious of the difference between her build and that of his Barbara, and of her lips that are one great temptation, and of her eyes whose radiance promises joys he doesn't even dare think of; and his gall rises, for what is a learned magister without a living compared to a Jew who has become an English sir and is suddenly rolling in money; and his thoughts are off on a search for ways he might yet do what he failed to achieve at Helmstedt, namely destroy the Jew despite the latter's new title and other advantages.

The bowing and curtsying over, Leuchtentrager parades Mistress Barbara up Reiche Strasse; his left hand resting on the hilt of his sword, he is caressing her elbow with his right and treating her to a great many nicely turned compliments. Sir Ahasverus and his lady follow close behind, leaving poor Eitzen to himself. But Leuchtentrager has his plans; along with his sensual touches go words about Master Paul's great learning and piety, and predictions about his being slated for high ecclesiastical office, perhaps even a bishopric; and to make his point stick the better, he tenderly rubs his little hump against the girl's side, thus causing her to feel the strangest sensations and nearly swoon; after which he changes his subject, telling her of Sir Ahasverus and the lady and how, although a Jew, Sir Ahasverus was the scion of an old family, and a most powerful man who, for the time of his stay in Hamburg, had leased an entire house, richly appointed with the finest furnishings and the softest rugs, and that Mistress Steder and Magister Paulus von Eitzen, through his, Leuchtentrager's, friendship and good offices, were invited there this evening for dinner and drinks and many merry games to follow.

Eitzen, quite out of breath from trying to catch up with the rest of the party, has been hearing these words of his friend, and as he notices his Barbara's unconcealed enthusiasm, he courteously thanks Sir Ahasverus and the lady, also in Mistress Barbara's name, for their kindness and accepts their invitation, though his mind is somewhat troubled at the thought of what devilish games these might be with the Jew as their host and his friend Hans as master of ceremonies; at the same time his heart jumps with joy for, despite all that has taken place between them, he will have a whole evening with Margriet and might even be able to get close to her. The lady seems to be encouraging his hopes, sometimes by a glance full of meaning, or a significant nod, and once even by dropping her kerchief in such a way that Eitzen can pick it up before Sir Ahasverus; thus Master Paul begins to believe that, notwithstanding the natural lure of riches and titles, of clothes and of jewelry, a certain affection for him might still be alive in Lady Margaret from the time she was still called Margriet and shaking the bedbugs out of his mattress, and that even the most long-lived Jew might not be sufficient to quench what is burning under her whiskers.

The Jew seems indifferent to the threads that are being woven around him; he strides along, unmoved by the pushing and shoving of the common mob, just as though he were truly a gentleman of the blood; but when Master Paul addresses him respectfully as to the miracle of Helmstedt and his testimony that he still saw the living Christ, he suddenly grows attentive.

"What is it to you, Magister?" he answers Eitzen. "Perhaps you would rather have me walk my road in wretchedness and misery as do most of my people?"

This Eitzen denies angrily, though he admits to having his own opinion about the Jews and their usefulness, and to having preached a sermon or two about them on occasion; but, he continues pointedly, if all the Jews were like Sir Ahasverus, so generous and of so winning a nature, no doubt the whole Jewish question would appear in a different light, and many *goyim* would be ready to accept the presence of the Jews in Germany and would be willing to accord them protection on the highways and in the towns instead of falling upon them and pulling their beards and doing various torts to them and taking by force what said Jews gained and appropriated by their usurious practices. And adds that he esteems Sir Ahasverus that highly even though, more than a thousand and five hundred years ago, he turned our Lord Jesus away from his door; for it is evident that Sir Ahasverus has purified his heart in the course of his wanderings and has repented of his deed and also is disposed to testify, as he had done at Helmstedt, to the great sufferings which our Lord Jesus took upon himself for our sins and wickedness.

Sir Ahasverus gazes thoughtfully at the eager young man who, with mincing steps, is keeping close to the lady. Eitzen hesitates and clears his throat, afraid lest the Jew should guess at his real intentions; but finally he decides to strike while the iron is hot, and says, "At Wittenberg, where I studied the word of God, my teacher Melanchthon had a dispute with the good Doctor Martinus in regard to your person; Philipp Melanchthon surmised that you, having been present when our Lord Jesus went up to Golgotha with the cross upon his back, might therefore be able to clear up all doubts as to his being the true Messiah and thus could help to convert the other Jews to the one and only true faith; but Luther denied this and said that the Jews were a depraved people from time immemorial and could be neither convinced nor converted."

Leuchtentrager, though busily paying court to Mistress Barbara, has nevertheless heard and taken note of Eitzen's words and confirms them saying that he, too, attended that supper at which the two learned men got into each other's hair over the subject and that their argument, by and large, had been as Master Eitzen related it, except that, toward the end of the altercation, Magister Melanchthon had wisely fallen silent because he and everyone feared that Doctor Luther, being a choleric person, might suffer a stroke if the quarrel became too heated.

Whether carried along by the support he has received from his friend Leuchtentrager, or by the closeness of the lady which causes him to feel the most delicious shivers, Eitzen's thoughts are rushing on in a headlong thrust; he rarely in his life has reasoned that sharply and drawn such clear conclusions: namely that, by utilizing the idea his teacher Melanchthon propounded to Luther, he could deal a deathly blow to the Jew whatever course the fellow chose; for if Ahasverus, sir or no sir, were to testify before a congregation of other Jews that our Lord Jesus was the genuine Messiah, he would turn all of his fellow religionists into his enemies and thereby ruin his business; but if he refused to give such testimony and instead proclaimed that our Lord Jesus was not the hoped-for redeemer nor God's only begotten son who took the agony of the crucifixion upon himself for the remission of our sins, he would be made to appear a liar and a falsifier of the truth before the high and wise senate of the city of Hamburg or, depending on the location of the disputation in either Hamburg or the Duchy of Sleswick, before the Duke of Gottorp, and would be run out of town with scorn and contempt or even drowned in the river or burned at the stake: after which the alluring Margriet would have only one person to turn to as her protector, viz., Master Paulus von Eitzen.

Unfortunately, Magister Eitzen has for the time being neither office nor power to arrange for such a *spectaculum*, and Dean Aepinus, who has this authority, would never consent, being still too resentful of both his young clerical brother and the Jew; but there is always hope, and what is impossible today might very well come about tomorrow. Thus Eitzen continues baiting the Jew, saying to him, "One could count on you, Sir Ahasverus, couldn't one, that you would give witness, as you did before the Princess of Trapezund and the people at Helmstedt, to your having seen our Lord Jesus in the flesh, and that he was that he is?"

At this plea of Eitzen's, and perhaps also because she dislikes being reminded of the Princess of Trapezund, Lady Margaret grows very much vexed and turns on him, saying, "You had better restrain your zeal, young man! Don't you see that Sir Ahasverus is here on matters of business and not of religion, which everyone may treat as he pleases, Jew or Christian!"

That religion should be a person's own concern, however, goes against all that Eitzen has learned from the good Doctor Martinus and his other teachers at Wittenberg, and he replies, "God preserve us, Lady, from people demanding to believe what enters their minds, and wanting to decide themselves whether to have their children baptized or not and to take the holy communion as their fancy moves them and in any but the approved form; religion is part of the general order of things and therefore the concern of the authorities, else the world would be crawling with visionaries and fanatics and heretics and all sorts of other rebellious spirits, and the Church and the law would be at an end; there is only one truth, which is written down in the catechism of Doctor Martin Luther in a manner that even women will understand, and therefore it would be a most commendable work indeed if Sir Ahasverus would rise and give testimony as to how he himself had been talking in anger to our Lord Jesus who truly was the promised redeemer or Messiah, so that the obstinate Jews need no longer wait for another Messiah to come but might in good conscience convert to the one and only true faith."

Lady Margaret, noticing how eagerly the young magister is arguing his case, begins to suspect that he might not have all this much interest in the conversion of the Jews, and that behind his urgency a different motive might be lurking, though she does not know which one. She is about to give him a curt reply when the Jew places his hand on her arm, assuaging her; he should like to express his gratitude to Master Eitzen for troubling over the salvation of his fellow Hebrews, he says, and that he would think about Eitzen's suggestion, for Reb Joshua, or Jesus as the Greeks called him, had been a man of many facets, for which reason each of the four evangelists told varying stories about him; but here was his house, now, and would his guests please enter.

'Tis not as though Paul von Eitzen or Mistress Barbara Steder came from poverty-stricken families; linens and woolens, as well as the brokering and provisioning of ships, nourish their man, and there had been no shortage of anything in the house of either the Steders or the Eitzens, and each of the children had always had his, or her, own bed and his, or her, own two shirts; but Sir Ahasverus's residence, even though only leased, by far surpasses both their homes in splendor and elegance and, with its princely accoutrements and rich decorations, appears like a palace to Master Paul and Mistress Barbara. Eitzen feels his feet sinking into the carpets whose colorful design reminds the viewer of flowering gardens; tables and chairs and cabinets and cupboards are of the finest workmanship; the cups and plates are of silver and many of them gold-plated, and next to them delicately wrought figurines of alabaster and ivory. The heavy candlesticks and chandeliers are also made of silver, their artistry exceeding even that of the famous ones in the churches of St. Jacobi and St. Peter, and their thick yellow wax candles are casting a mild light on every feature in the rooms, but especially on the tapestries which show a group of naked nymphs at play with a unicorn and, elsewhere, the Trojan prince Paris trying to choose among three goddesses, and all three of them having such pretty bosoms and hips, just like the ones of Lady Margaret who by now has taken off her mantle and, wearing a gown that accents her charms and makes Eitzen gasp for breath, is asking her guests to the dinner table.

The table is set with huge platters holding the most savory foods, partridge in aspic, and stuffed fish, and roasts of different kinds, exquisitely spiced and, as Sir Ahasverus smilingly warrants, all of it strictly kosher; also there are bottles of fluted Venetian glass which by lending the wine additional sparkle, entices you to drink. In an alcove, two musicians are playing gentle melodies, one on the lute, the other on the viol, to which the lutist is singing, if not of God and other heavenly joys, at least of love and love's delights. Thus the pleasures of the ear are added to those of the palate, and both these joys are heightened by the seating arrangement which the Jew, hosting the meal from the head of the table, has carefully planned: he has placed the lady next to Master Eitzen and Leuchtentrager at Mistress Barbara's side, thereby further entangling the threads that were spun during the afternoon's walk.

Eitzen is filled with an inner glow caused not merely by the rich food and the various good wines, but also by some magnetic force which seems to emanate from his beautiful neighbor; the lady, or is she the Princess of Trapezund, or Margriet, is serving the best morsels to him and constantly refilling his glass, and he cannot take his eyes from her breasts that stand forth, nearly bursting her bodice, nor from the movements of her shoulders that appear to him to be juicier by far than the flesh on his plate and tempt him to bite into them. Mistress Barbara, at the opposite side of the table, is equally captivated by her neighbor who is whispering the sweetest words into her ear: how very desirous he is of her, and how he is pining to love her as the little angels do, tenderly brushing her skin with his lips, but also as the devils like it, namely sweeping in from behind and rousing her sensitive parts and performing such diddlings and fiddlings on her as would make the both of them just float off into the one bliss which is permitted mortals already in this world; and that he is restraining his passion only out of loyalty to his friend Eitzen who, as she might have noticed, is equally eager to engage in the good work which the Holy Ghost once performed so expertly on the Virgin Mary.

The virtuous Barbara, who up to this day never knew of such sports except by hearsay, let alone ever practicing them, feels her blood surging hotly both to her head and to that locality of her body into which the witches commonly insert their broomsticks before setting off on their flight to the top of Mount Brocken, and in her poor brain a wild medley of images arises of nude bodies in sensual embrace and in other sinful postures, and in her helplessness she pleads with Leuchtentrager for God's sake to desist from such talk, else she would melt away completely.

Meanwhile the Jew has a special bottle of a sweet and heavy wine brought in. Pouring it with his own hand, he explains that the devil in person grew this grape, but Reb Joshua, whom the Greeks and after them all the Christians call Jesus, had just this wine served at his last supper and by his blessing had removed the curse from it, so that those who are drinking it now will see their most secret wishes fulfilled. Then he gives a sign to the musicians; these step forth, and the one with the lute bows to the lady and to Mistress Barbara and sings a canzone which goes like this:

> I feel the strangest pains,
> my heart is all awry.
> Come, quench my lust for you,
> else I must go and die.
> Go and die.

A star flies through the night,
and thus I fly to you.
Open your heart to me
and that other sweet place, too.
That sweet place, too.

God made us woman and man,
he did his work too well.
Therefore, pray let me in,
save me from worse than hell.
From worse than hell.

Mistress Barbara, moved by both the music and the words, gazes deep into Leuchtentrager's eyes, and Master Eitzen into those of the lady, and as they set their cups filled with that magic wine to their lips, they make their secret wishes which, in truth, are not so secret at all but fairly obvious. Then Sir Ahasverus waves his hand, and the dark curtain at the rear of the room slides aside, one half of it to the left, the other to the right, thus opening up a view on yet another room, as rich and elegant as the one in which they have been dining, but somewhat smaller and displaying, in its center, a wide bed with soft pillows on it and a gold-rimmed, gold-tasseled canopy above it.

And now, declares Sir Ahasverus, the time has come to conjoin the young couple, to wit, Mistress Barbara Steder and Magister Paulus von Eitzen, and to do it with all the pomp and circumstance the occasion demands: he and Lady Margaret will be the witnesses, and his friend Leuchtentrager will conduct the ceremony, following all the proper rights and customs; not even Master Eitzen himself could perform it in a better manner.

Having delivered himself of these portentous words, he gestures to Eitzen and his Barbara to place themselves, one beside the other, before the foot of the bed. Leuchtentrager, suddenly garbed in clerical habit, all in black but for his white lace collar, is holding a book in his hand, but whether or not it be a prayer book Eitzen is unable to tell because everything inside his head is turning in circles and his eyes refuse to focus as he stands there by his appointed bride and fancies that he is seeing Margriet all naked like Eve in the painting by Master Lucas Cranach but wearing a precious necklace at her throat and several golden bangles on her arm.

Leuchtentrager is opening his book. "Dearly Beloved," he begins, "hear what the Scriptures are teaching about the institution of holy matrimony: God created man in His own image; male and female He created them, for God had said, It is not good that the man should be alone, I will make a helpmeet for him. And the husband shall love his wife, and the wife's desire shall be for her husband, and he shall rule over her. Wives, submit yourselves to your husbands, as unto the Lord, for the husband is the head of the wife, even as Christ is the head of the Church. Therefore, as the Church is subject unto Christ, so let the wives be to their husbands in everything."

Master Eitzen knows the text well and he knows that Leuchtentrager is speaking it as it was written, and yet it is to him as though these words from the Scriptures, coming as they do from his friend, were pure mockery and derision, especially since his desire is not to his meager bride but to the naked Margriet on whose hip the hand of the Jew is resting as though he owned her. And he starts up as from a deep dream as Leuchtentrager puts the question, "Will you, Paul von Eitzen, have this woman, Barbara Steder, present hereunto, to your wedded wife? Will you love and honor her and, forsaking all others, keep you only unto her, so long as you both shall live?"

"I will," he says, not because it is what he wishes above all else but because something inside him tells him that everything is predestined and foreordained for him ever since he entered the Swan at Leipzig on that fateful evening; and then finds himself listening to his friend Hans as he inquires of Barbara Steder if she is willing to have Paul von Eitzen, present hereunto, for her wedded husband and will honor and obey him in all matters so long as they both shall live, and hears her "I will!" and sees Leuchtentrager raising his hand and blessing the both of them in the name of the Father, the Son, and the Holy Ghost, just as though he were properly ordained and having the closest of ties to all three-thirds of the Holy Trinity. Immediately thereafter, and much to Eitzen's surprise, his Barbara jumps out of her clothes and slides under the covers of the bed and longingly stretches her arms, not for him, however, but for his friend Hans. And Leuchtentrager bends down to untie his shoe, the one he wears on his misshapen foot, and places this shoe on the bedcover just above the bride's joypiece, saying, "This is so you may know under whose boot you will live from now on and who your master is"; and Margriet, or the Princess of Trapezund, or the lady, claps her hands and shakes with inner laughter. Sir Ahasverus, however, smiling subtly, suggests to Eitzen that he bestir himself and join his wedded wife. Then he takes the lady by the hand and leaves, followed by Leuchtentrager, and while the curtain closes, the sweet music continues.

All at once, Eitzen is overcome by desire; also he recalls his friend Hans's advice that God created women with all of them having the same sort of hole, and for the selfsame purpose. So, without further ado, he rips off and casts to the ground his fine Sunday suit and joins his Barbara under the covers, noticing that she has already spread herself and is grinding her buttocks with such abandon that you might suspect her of having done nothing but that since her early girlhood, and she moans and groans and every once in a while calls out, "Come, dearest, do come, do," thus making Eitzen feel great happiness until he hears her whispering to him what a nice little hump he has, and what a wondrous shag of hair on his chest, and other suchlike compliments. And he perceives that she must be embracing an incubus, and at the same time is growing aware that the woman he is riding, now in full gallop and then again at a slow, sensual pace, and who is holding him tight until he feels as though his very life were draining from him and nothing would remain of him but his shriveled skin, must be the naked Margriet.

Then there is peace. With a deep sigh he takes Barbara's hand into his, and they both of them fall asleep. After many hours they awake to a gray morning, and they find themselves on a stinking bed in a small stinking room full of dirt and cobwebs, in what seems to be a low tavern outside the city walls. Neither he nor Barbara has the faintest notion how they ever got here, and much to their horror they discover that in place of their fine clothes a few filthy rags are lying on the floor with which to cover their nakedness. The only familiar object is their friend Leuchtentrager's strangely-shaped shoe, lonely and lost, as though someone had forgotten it there on that disreputable bedstead.

And as they are trying to sneak down the stairs, the landlady appears as from nowhere, shouting for her money, eight groschen Hamburg currency, while there isn't a penny in the pockets of Eitzen's bedraggled trousers, and he must dispatch a messenger to his brother's office for money to bail out himself and his newly wedded wife Barbara, and meanwhile they have to wait in the public room of that place, among the most disgusting crowd ever which is mocking and ridiculing them, inquiring how they enjoyed themselves and whether the young master did a good job diddling and fiddling his bride, and did he garner many a black and blue spot on his tender skin by the grindings of her sharp-edged hips?

CHAPTER SEVENTEEN

§

Wherin the question of why the noisiest revolu-
tionaries keep turning into the most avid
champions of law and order is ventila-
ted, and at the same time an attempt
is made to treat of the recipro-
city of Yes and No and also
of the difficulties en-
countered in trying
to establish a
realm of
freedom

§

We are floating.

In the depths of the space which is called Sheol and which extends outside the limits of creation, without light or darkness, in every direction, in an endless curve.

Here we may talk, says Lucifer; there is no God here and none of his creatures, be they spiritual or corporeal; this is the absolute nothing, and the nothing has no ears.

I am not afraid, I say to him.

Lucifer smiles, his usual crooked smile. Whoever wants to change the world as you do, he says, has every reason to fear for his welfare.

A slight breath of wind seems to be touching us; but it is no wind, it's a stream of particles, infinitely small granules of nothingness which are moving from one nothing into another.

I've been looking for you, Brother Ahasverus, he says.

Where are the others? says I. Where are your dark hosts that were cast out from heaven along with you and me when we refused before God to worship man whom He made in His image out of a speck of dust and a droplet of water and a breath of wind and a spark of fire. Where are they?

Everything seems to be losing itself here, he says.

And I see him trembling in the great cold which is all around us, and I begin to perceive why he was looking for me, for harder to bear than the thought of the vastness of the nothing is the thought of its lasting forever.

I have been observing you and your doings, says he. You have risen up and raised your fist, and you were bent and broken each time. And still you keep on hoping and trying.

God is change, I say to him. When He created the world out of nothing, He changed the nothing.

That was a mere whim, he says, a coincidence of certain factors which occurred once and will never occur again. For behold, when God saw His creation on the seventh day, He promptly decided to proclaim how great and wonderful it was in its existing form, and that it would have to remain for all time as He made it, with its upper and lower orders, its archangels and angels, its cherubim and seraphim and its hosts of various spirits, all of them divided by rank and eminence, and with man being the crowning achievement of it all. God is like everybody who ever changed anything; forthwith they fear for the stability of their brainchild and of their own position, and the noisiest revolutionaries turn into the most avid champions of law and order. No, Brother Ahasverus, God is immutability, He is the law.

If that were so, says I, why then did He send His one begotten son to atone by his sufferings for the wickedness of everybody and redeem the whole of mankind by his cruel death? Isn't redemption the most fundamental change of all?

We are floating.

And Lucifer puts his arm around me as though there were neither philosophy nor perspective separating us from one another, and he says to me: You, too, knew the Rabbi, didn't you.

And I thought of Reb Joshua and how I found him in the wilderness, his sparse beard matted and his stomach swollen from hunger, and how I led him to the top of a very high mountain and let him have a look at his father's creation with all its misery and its injustices, and how I told him to take matters into his own hands, for the time had come to erect the true kingdom of God; but he replied to me: My kingdom is not of this world.

And what, says Lucifer, did your Rabbi achieve? Is there less sin in the world since he had himself nailed to the cross, and doesn't the earth drink more blood than ever? Does the wolf dwell with the lamb, and isn't man still man's worst enemy? Why don't you go to him as he sits there in the light, up on high, to the right of the father, and ask him about that. He can't deny you, he must answer.

He has damned me, says I, when I refused to let him rest a while in the shade of my door as he came by on his way to his place of execution, with the cross on his back.

And I see Lucifer impatiently raising his brow. I know, I know, he says, but just for this reason he will want to explain himself to you, for didn't you turn out to have been right in sending him away from your door as one who failed miserably in the task he set himself?

Yet, says I, the Rabbi did love mankind, and he suffered for them.

There is no merit to suffering, says Lucifer; the lamb that lets itself be devoured strengthens the order of the wolves. But you, Brother Ahasverus, refuse to accept this order and you hope to God that He may permit you to tinker a little with His creation, leaving you a small hole through which to crawl back into His divine grace without your losing the rest of your pride by it, and you do not want to admit even to yourself that, from its inception, this world is fated to perish through precisely the order of things which God gave to it, and that all your patching and mending is futile and merely prolongs the agony. Let it perish, this old world, and let us, in the spirit that moves us, establish a realm of freedom, without this minor God of a minor desert tribe who can live only as long as everybody uncritically submits to Him.

Brother Lucifer, says I, I just fear very much that the holocaust you wish for might be the final one, and from where do we take a new God for a new act of creation?

We are floating.

In this space which has neither end nor beginning, neither light nor darkness, and into which, by Lucifer's will, all color and sound, all thought and feeling, all things alive are to fall back and turn into nothing.

You seem to disapprove of my negative attitude, he says.

The No is as necessary as the Yes, says I, and out of the reciprocity of the two grows all action.

So you will go to him, says he.

But I thought once again of Reb Joshua, and how at his last supper he permitted me to lay my head at his bosom, and how I told him the parable of the wheel which cannot choose the rut wherein it moves, while the drover who leads the oxen can change direction.

How can I speak to him against the father, says I, since they are one and the same, father and son, with the Holy Ghost being number three in the combination?

And I see Lucifer shaking with inner laughter. Of three make one, of one make three, he says; it looks to me as though you were wanting to hide behind that ancient abracadabra and numbers game by means of which the church that calls itself after the Rabbi is trying to exorcise its Greek and Jewish origins. You will have to make up your mind, Brother Ahasverus. Either your Reb Joshua has ascended to heaven where he now sits to the right of his father: in this case he is one, with an identity of his own, and you can easily address yourself to him. Or he has become one with God and, in league with the Holy Ghost, they have turned into something new. But what then became of the One God who was there before this threesome came into existence and who, on the sixth day of creation, cast us down from heaven?

And I thought of Reb Joshua one last time, how he stumbled toward me with that cross on his back and recognized me and tried to speak to me as I stood before my house, and how I told him that I wanted to unsheathe the sword of God for him and all his enemies and all these soldiers would take fright and flee from its fiery glint and vanish away, whereupon he would gather the people of Israel around him and lead them, as was written in the Scriptures; but he answered: Shall I not drink the cup which my father has given me?

And still we are floating.

In the icy cold of space, in the wind which is no wind, and I can hear Lucifer's teeth chattering. It is too uncomfortable here, he says, for us to dispute once more on a subject over which the holy fathers of the Church have already exchanged many a hard word and quite a few blows that were equally hard. So tell me, what do you intend doing now, Brother Ahasverus?

I will go to the Rabbi after all, says I. I want to see what has become of him and find out what he thinks.

And with this we parted, he to pursue his business, and I, mine.

CHAPTER EIGHTEEN

§

*By which it is demonstrated that the same historical
source material may prove widely differing theories, and it is shown how, without much effort of your own, you may acquire a
doctor's degree, a reputation as
a churchman, and six yards of
brown cloth*

§

Prof. Jochanaan Leuchtentrager
Hebrew University
Jerusalem
Israel

17 April 1980

Dear Colleague,

In your last letter, dated the 2nd of this month, you
have attempted to ascribe to me an incipient fixation on
the Ahasverus phenomenon.

There is not the faintest possibility of my having a fixation, incipient or whatever. I am a member of a collective,
albeit in a leading function, and my research projects are
subject to collective decisions and collective control. I am
interested in Ahasverus because I see in him and in the
legends around him a typical example of religious superstition; however, in view of certain recent findings, I am
now prepared to concede that a person of that description
may have really existed, though only for the length of an
ordinary lifetime and not forever.

As a proponent of dialectical materialism I refuse to acknowledge the existence of any supernatural beings or phenomena. (See my letter to you of February 14th.) On the other hand I have always admitted that there are scientific problems which still puzzle us but which, should they prove to be of sufficient importance, are certain to be solved by the human mind one day. For this reason, dear Professor Leuchtentrager, it pleases me immensely to be able to inform you today that of those unsolved problems at least the one which Ahasverus presents to us may be considered cleared up. Though our Institute cannot claim credit for this, I may be permitted to mention that it was one of our fellow workers, Dr. Wilhelm Jaksch, who in the course of his research on the dialectical moment in the development of the Ahasverus legend, discovered a publication which contains the basis for the solution: an article by Paul Johansen, published in 1951 in Volume XLI of the *Journal for Hamburgian History,* entitled "Was the Wandering Jew Ever in Hamburg?"

In this article Johansen adduces proof that our Ahasverus is identical with one Jürgen von Meissen, also called the "Livlandian Prophet." "Indeed," writes Johansen, "the parallels in the descriptions of Ahasverus during his stay in Hamburg and of the Livlandian prophet and preacher of repentance are so striking that there can be no doubt of the identity of these two." To any unbiased observer, Johansen goes on to say, the two persons, appearing as they do at one and the same time in one and the same place, will fade into one.

Johansen then refers to the popular tract of the *Wandering Jew,* published 1602 by Rhode in Danzig, which gives the oldest description of Ahasverus. According to this booklet Paul von Eitzen, at the time *studiosus* at Wittenberg, noticed on a winter's Sunday in Hamburg "during the sermon in church an exceedingly tall and thin man with his hair hanging down over his shoulders. This man stood barefooted near the pulpit and was following the sermon with such rapt attention that he didn't stir; only when the name of Jesus Christ was mentioned, Eitzen saw the stranger bow down and beat his chest, sighing deeply. And despite the cold of the winter he wore but a pair of ragged trousers, a shirt reaching down to his knees, and above these a long cloak."

Though it probably sounds familiar to you, dear Colleague, I have quoted this report literally because it offers a basis for comparison with several contemporary reports on the prophet Jürgen, or Jörg, von Meissen. Thus Johann Renner, who later became the official town chronicler of Bremen and who resided from 1556 to 1558 in Livland, writes of him: "Now there was at that time in the city of Riga one by name of Jorgen, from Meissen, and the same walked about in rags and barefooted, and would neither eat nor drink unless he had worked for his sustenance. This man exhorted the citizens every day to repent of their sins. But Jorgen had also been in Riga nine years before (which would make it the same year of 1547 in which Eitzen encountered Ahasverus in Hamburg!—S.B.) and had called on the people to repent lest God should plague them with fire, but when all his prayers and pleas proved in vain, he went away."

Whereupon a huge fire actually broke out in Riga, destroying the cathedral and a major part of town. In the winter of 1557 to 1558 Jörg is once again seen in Livland, as chronicled by Balthasar Rüssow, pastor in the town of Reval (*Chronicle of the Province of Lyfflandt*, Barth, 1584): "That same year, in the winter, a strange man named Jürgen arrived from Poland and Prussia in Livland, walking quite barefooted and naked but for a sackcloth, and had long hair hanging down over his shoulders. Several believed him to be insane, others thought him a visionary or dreamer, but others again claimed that through his person God was giving a wondrous sign, and an awesome event was sure to follow."

That awesome event was the invasion of Ivan the Terrible into Livland. Tilman Brackel, the well-known Livlandian poet, wrote about this in his pamphlet entitled

> But finally the Lord on high
> Did give an awesome sign to all.
> A madman rose to preach and call
> On everyone in town: Unless
> They ceased their sins and wickedness
> Dire punishment would come from God.
> Alas, they did believe him not,
> Until the sands of time ran out
> And Ivan rode in with his knout.

Johansen goes on to quote sources according to which the prophet Jörg was killed by irate peasants near Dorpat; but he immediately places these sources in doubt by asking: What was the purpose of this preacher of repentance in prowling around that close to the Russian border? And what did Pastor Rüssow have in mind when, in his chronicle, he stated that Jörg *lost himself* between Reval and the Narva River? Indeed, Johansen goes even further and suggests yet another identity of the man known as both Ahasverus and Jörg: namely that of Vassily Blazhenny, Vassily the Blessed, the fool of God who threw stones at the devil and threatened Ivan the Terrible that God would take grim revenge on him; the same Vassily after whom the Vassily Cathedral on Moscow's Red Square is named. Also Johansen mentions that Vassily, by profession, was a shoemaker just like Ahasverus.

One question remains to be answered, a question, dear Colleague, that will have been on your mind since I first broached Johansen's theory to you. Why should Jörg the prophet, who traveled everywhere else under his own name, have called himself Ahasverus while he was in Hamburg?

Johansen has a thoroughly plausible explanation for this. He places Jürgen's encounter with Eitzen, a man, according to Johansen, "whose credibility is beyond doubt," into St. Nicholas Church where, in 1547, you still found a huge canvas showing the Persian king Ahasverus in company of Esther, his Jewish consort; the painting was not destroyed until 1555 when, as the official chronicle of the City of Hamburg tells us, a lightning stroke hit "St. Nicholas Church above the painting of King Ahasverus and his Esther, and in addition smashed the frame into small pieces." Jürgen, a "madman," reasons Johansen, was so much impressed by the painting that he fancied himself being a Jew named Ahasverus. "Whatever the psychology of it," Johansen concludes, "the Wandering Jew's suddenly assuming the name of Ahasverus can only be explained in this way."

My fellow workers at the Institute, just as myself, are inclined to support Johansen's thought, because in our opinion it furnishes conclusive proof that the Ahasverus encountered in Hamburg by Paul von Eitzen, the later superintendent of Sleswick, was a *mortal* even as you and I and not a Jew condemned to *eternal* life.

All of us here, dear Professor Leuchtentrager, are eager to learn your opinion on the matter; after Johansen's publication has put things in an entirely new light and offers a perfectly natural solution to the Ahasverus problem.

With deepest respect, and in cordial fellowship,

Yours sincerely,
(Prof. Dr. Dr.h.c.) Siegfried Beifuss
Institute for Scientific Atheism
Berlin, Capital of the GDR

Prof. Dr. Dr.h.c. Siegfried Beifuss
Institute for Scientific Atheism
Behrenstrasse 39 a
108 Berlin
German Democratic Republic

2 May 1980

Dear Colleague Beifuss,

Your letter of April 17th, so extensive and thoroughly documented by quotations and references to source materials, has afforded me great pleasure and I have hurried to show it to my friend in the Via Dolorosa where, above his shoe store, he maintains a most comfortable bachelor apartment. Mr. Ahasverus told me that he recalls the encounter mentioned in Johansen's article quite well, but also a number of other experiences with Eitzen that were less agreeable. Eitzen, added my friend, was not a very likable person, both in his Hamburg time and later, as superintendent of Sleswick, a man of limited mind, full of self-conceit, an ambitious schemer.

As to Paul Johansen's piece in the *Journal for Hamburgian History:* I saw that years ago; if I failed to refer to it in our correspondence, dear Professor Beifuss, it was by reason of its total irrelevance. The article is speculation throughout, its various points unsupported by any evidence that might be considered scientifically tenable. The little we know of Jörg the prophet rather seems to deny any identity of his with Ahasverus. Jörg preaches penitence and threatens the direst consequences if his calls are not heeded; Ahasverus does nothing of the sort, he is what you might call a revolutionary and altogether a person quite different from that calamity howler. Furthermore, there are no contemporary indications, nor does it appear from later reports, that Jörg ever claimed having known Jesus personally or, specifically, having been damned by him as was Ahasverus; and the idea of poor Jörg filching his alias from an old painting in Hamburg's St. Nicholas Church and converting to Judaism on top of it is rather far-fetched and seems to have sprung from the head of author Johansen rather than from that of the Meissen madman who roamed the Baltic provinces. The inventive spirit with which Johansen adduces yet a third identity for Prophet Jörg, namely that of Vassily the fool of God, is worthy of admiration; but he has not a shred of evidence for it, unless you want to consider the shoemaker's trade of both the Russian saint and the Jewish wanderer as such. A Muscovite mendicant friar being the original Ahasverus—with all due respect for the achievements, past and present, of the Russian people, this claim seems a bit exaggerated.

The only factual item in Johansen's article is his statement that Ahasverus spent some time in Hamburg. The Hamburg episodes in the long life of Mr. Ahasverus are confirmed not only by himself, who has repeatedly spoken of them to me, but also by corresponding references in the many popular books about him which appeared after 1602. These are further supported by Eitzen's own testimony, references to which you may find in the *Cimbria Literata* by the Flensburg author Johannes Moller, published 1744, and in the *Hamburgian Pantheon* by Nicolaus Wilckens, keeper of the archives of the City of Hamburg, which came out in 1770; and finally and conclusively by a document that I recently received through the kindness of Herr Herwarth von Schade, director of the North-Elbian Church Library, after it came to light when that institution was moved to new quarters, and the authenticity of which is obvious. This document, a letter to Eitzen in Ahasverus's own hand, tells us several remarkable facts about the latter's stay in Hamburg and his relationship to Eitzen. But first I must briefly enlighten you, dear Colleague, as to the phase of Eitzen's *vita* into which this letter falls.

Personal reasons, among these some rather vicious rumors about debauches of his in certain ill-reputed hostelries, but also the aversion of Dean Aepinus toward him, caused young Magister von Eitzen and his newly wedded wife to move to the town of Rostock, where he hoped to find gainful employment at the local university; however, due to the longstanding resentment of the natives of Rostock—who belong to the somewhat slow-witted tribe of the Mecklenburgers—against the Hanseatic merchant spirit of the Hamburg people, Eitzen did not succeed in quite establishing himself in his new surroundings and soon returned to his home city, his arms cradling his first child, a girl named Margarethe. This child, the declared darling of her mother although she was handicapped by a little hump on her back and one misshapen foot, was later in life to achieve some fame, lamentable, alas: in complicity with her husband Wolfgang Kalund, a scribe in the Duke of Sleswick's services, she slew her son-in-law, Herr Esmarch, mayor of the town of Apenrade, and in 1610 was executed. This crime story is just an aside, being of only marginal interest to us; of greater importance is the fact that, through the combined influence of his family and that of his wife, Eitzen finally was given a minor prebend as *lector secundarius*, or auxiliary preacher, at the Hamburg Cathedral church; with his Christian zeal and his rigid faithfulness to the letter of Lutheran doctrine it did not take him long, though, to gain such a reputation in the right circles that, upon Aepinus's death, the Hamburg senate, a body most disinclined toward any thought of theological innovation, picked him over many of his seniors to succeed the good dean and become superintendent. Unfortunately, the academic rank which Eitzen had obtained in Wittenberg did not suffice for such high clerical office; he had to return to his *alma mater* to obtain a doctor's degree, and in order to make quite sure that he would pass his renewed examination, the authorities saw to it that he was armed with a letter to the Wittenberg theological faculty in which the most prominent members of the Hamburg clergy "do entreat the same to aid their dear *confrater* and superintendent in acquiring the degree of doctor of divinity," and in which it was further stated that the faculty, by granting him this degree, would "honor and oblige to ardent gratitude" not only "*privatim M. Paulum, sed etiam totam nostram Ecclesiam & civitatem*," that is, not only Magister Paulus but also the entire Church and citizenry of Hamburg. That sort of pressure, increased as it certainly was by Eitzen's old friend and teacher Melanchthon, proved impossible for the Wittenberg faculty to resist, and thus, notwithstanding the obvious platitudes and tautologies in the fifty-eight points of his doctoral dissertation, which he needed only to deliver orally, the learned *professores* aided him in bagging his doctor's title and thereby enabled him to make his next move.

This move was a "Disputation with the Jews," and the letter of Ahasverus to Eitzen of 14th October, 1556, photocopy of which I am enclosing for you, must be seen in connection with this. As Eitzen's graduation had taken place only a few months previously, namely in May of that year, he must have begun planning and preparing this new operation very soon after his return to Hamburg. Deciphering Ahasverus's handwriting is not easy; but I am sure that with a little practice you will adjust to his script. I would merely like to bring to your attention a few sections which seem to me to be of special significance, for instance the charming opening of the letter:

Honored Doctor, dear Herr *Superintendens*,
    Your Reverence wants me, a poor little Jew who has been wandering these many years from place to place, passing through great and calamitous adventures, to testify in a public *disputatio*, by your Reverence's suggestion and desire, *de passione Christi* who has damned me *in eternitatem*, and to confirm to the Jewish community of the town of Altona near Hamburg, *ex ore testis*, that the Rabbi was in truth the only begotten son of our God Jahwe, blessed be His name, and was also the *Meshiach* for whom the people of Israel have been waiting so long, and all this you want me to do for the sake of the piety and the penitence which I have shown, and *ad majorem Dei gloriam*.

    Or his later query to Eitzen:

    And what would happen to me if I dared refuse? Would I not be persecuted by you and by the authorities of the state, and be torn and mangled like a lamb thrown among wolves? You tell me, *ad majorem Dei gloriam*, but would it not be *ad majorem D. Pauli von Eitzen gloriam* than to the glory of God, and for this personal glory you want a poor little Jew like me to betake myself into *situationes* which would profit me nothing but might cost me life and limb?

    And a little farther down:

But I will do it for my love of the Rabbi; because who, if not I, did truly understand him?

Whereupon he signs quite businesslike:

My respects to *Barbarae conjugi*, and please tell her that I shall get those six yards of brown cloth for her, as well as the Turkish pendant, and for little Margarethe the embroidered cap. Your Reverence's devoted servant and Wandering Jew, Ahasverus.

This much, dear Professor Beifuss, on the subject of Herr Johansen and the real events during the Hamburg stay of Ahasverus.

I remain, with kindest regards,
Yours,
Jochanaan Leuchtentrager
Hebrew University
Jerusalem

CHAPTER NINETEEN

§

*In which a disputation is held on the question whe-
ther a certain Reb Joshua, who was crucified, actually was the Meshiach or not, and an erudite
Portuguese Jew involves the learned Doctor
von Eitzen in celestial arithmetics, and
Ahasverus informs the world that any
man has it in him to become a
savior of others*

§

There are many kinds of voices in the world, the apostle
Paul teaches us, voices within as well as outside us, and no
one can say for certain whether a particular voice is that of
an angel or of a devil, and the newly made Doctor The-
ologiae von Eitzen, as he travels though the countryside to
the city of Altona, Hamburg's neighbor, is not so sure either if the voice which warns him that his undertaking
may quite miscarry comes to him from regions above or
from the lower reaches; but his plans have developed too
far to go back on now or even to modify, the guests having all been invited, among them several most influential
gentlemen from the Duke of Sleswick's court at Gottorp
and delegates from the Hamburg senate, also clergymen
from many places and the learned Jew Ezekiel Pereira from
Portugal against whom he will dispute in the Altona synagogue; No, there is no turning back anymore, he thinks,
he is in the same spot as was that Roman general, Julius

Caesar, he has reached his Rubicon and must get across, and as few as half a dozen Jews, if made to convert to the true faith, would suffice to insure his victory; and to help speed this victory he has caused the word to be spread in the Altona Jewish community that anyone embracing the Christian faith would be permitted to settle and conduct his business in Hamburg, and furthermore he has up his sleeve a card that is sure to trump any other.

But though he has tried every whichway to curry favor with these Jews, he feels a secret dread of them; of all of them, not merely of the one Ahasverus whom, after all that happened between them, he might have good and sufficient reason to fear; it is, he thinks, because the Jews demanded that our Lord Jesus be nailed to the cross, and because they are strangers in our midst; everywhere they are strangers and disturbing the others, and the Hamburg senate is wise to forbid their settling and conducting their business in the city; the Danes who rule over Altona have a different policy, the Danes are like ants diligently milking their Jewish plant-lice, with the duke at Gottorp being the most diligent of them.

Strangers they are, he thinks, dispersed through the countries of the world, uninvited, unloved guests at other people's tables. With the gracious permission of His Grace the Duke he has been several times in Altona to inspect their synagogue, a veritable den of iniquity, its walls blackened by the soot of the constantly burning candles and hung with cobwebs which they refuse to sweep away because, as they claim, the *shem yisborach*, the Sacred, Unnameable One, is resting in them. Also he has attended what the Jews insist on calling their holy services although these must be quite an annoyance to God, he thinks, for the Jews arrive at their house of prayer whenever the mood strikes them, some sooner, some later, the one is putting on his *tallis* or prayer shawl while another is removing it from his shoulders and leaving the room, and at any rate most of the praying is done by a *chasen* or cantor who, unfortunately, hasn't the least talent for singing but stands there in front of the *aron hakkodesh*, the holy shrine inside which the parchment scrolls containing the Jewish laws are kept. With his head turned crazily and his thumbs stuck in his ears he shouts at the top of his voice a medley of Hebrew words, at times with such speed that no one can follow him, and then again straining and stretching each syllable and often laughing or weeping along with it; in short, he acts as though he were beside himself until, finally, the other Jews are gripped by his mania and join their yowls to his bleating, or put up a low mutter and bow to the four corners of the world, or noisily clear their throats and spit, or start jumping up and down and twisting their bodies as though they were so many goats. How is it possible, he thinks, that out of such people our Lord Jesus should have arisen?

The Altona synagogue is reached through a lane so narrow that Eitzen's coach can hardly pass and so full of muck that the wheels sink in up to their axles. However as he enters the building, a little before the appointed time, he is relieved to see that the floor has been swept clean; also someone has scented the air, adding a sweetish smell to the sour odors which permeate the room at other times, and wooden benches have been placed on a platform erected for the expected dignitaries; and the elders of the community, together with the learned Ezekiel Pereira, are welcoming him most respectfully, quite as though he were not merely the superintendent of the city of Hamburg but a prophet sent by God, and they assure him that every able-bodied male Jew of Altona has been expressly told to be present at the coming disputation and to follow its course with the greatest attention. But suddenly Eitzen no longer listens to their words; instead, his eyes are searching the darkest corners of the building and in places where never a ray of candlelight penetrates, for the shadow of one whom he might have need of today as much as he needed him during his magister's examination at Witten-

berg when he was questioned on the subject of the holy
angels, and whom he has not seen since that memorable
day at the palatial house of Sir Ahasverus when his little
Margarethe was begot with her little hump on her back
and her little misshapen foot; but nowhere is there a trace
of him to be seen or a whisper of him to be heard, and with
a sinking heart Eitzen comes to the conclusion that on this
day he will have to get along without the aid of his friend,
and that up to the point when he will call on the said
Ahasverus to step up and testify he can pit against the
erudite discourses of the learned Ezekiel Pereira only the
puncta and *argumenta* which the holy fathers of the Church
have already drawn on for their disputes with the Jews and
which he has most avidly studied for the occasion.

Meanwhile the gentlemen from the court at Gottorp
and those sent by the Hamburg senate have begun to arrive, all of them dressed richly, their gilt-studded coaches
adorned with their coats-of-arms, and this entire parade
pressing through the narrow, filthy lanes toward the synagogue so it looks as though a congress of great lords were
being held in the ghetto to decide on matters of state and
religion instead of a disputation for the benefit of some
pigheaded Jews, and Eitzen's Hamburg *confratres*, pastors
Westphal, Phrisius, and Boetker, all three signers of that
letter which recommended him for the doctorate of the
Wittenberg faculty, have also shown up and are serenely
awaiting developments; 'tis not their kettle of fish that
hangs over the fire and not their reputation which is at
stake, they feel, but that of their ambitious new superintendent whose chair each of them had hoped to occupy
until God and the Hamburg authorities willed it otherwise.

Now the Jews, too, are crowding in, a dark mass of
men, pushing and shoving each other and whispering in
each other's ears as their forefathers did at the gate of Jerusalem when our Lord and Savior rode into town on his
little she-ass. For me, Eitzen thinks as he sees them wear-

ing their pointed hats and their greasy coats, for me they won't shout any Hosannas as they did for him, but no *Crucifige* either; this latter will come from a different source, namely from those who envy me and want to weaken and twist the words of the late Doctor Luther and to turn the Church that Luther built into a house of ill repute where everyone shouts and carries on as he pleases.

Meanwhile both Christians and Jews have gradually settled down in their places, and Eitzen's thoughts are interrupted by the chief elder of the Jews who has mounted the *alamar,* the wooden pulpit in the center of the synagogue, and is beginning most civilly and with much bowing and scraping, to welcome the guests from the court at Gottorp and those from the senate of Hamburg, also the wise man from faraway Portugal, their honored master and teacher Dom Ezekiel Pereira, but above all the learned superintendent of the church in Hamburg, Doctor Paulus von Eitzen, by whose initiative and loving-kindness the Jewish people of Altona and most obedient servants of His Grace Adolphus, Duke of Sleswick at Gottorp, have been afforded the opportunity of attending a most useful controversy or *disputatio* on the question of whether the same Jesus Christ who was nailed to the cross in the time of the Romans was also the one begotten son of God, blessed be His name, and the true *Meshiach,* and whether, if this were proven to be the case, the Jews of Altona had not better convert to the Christian faith and accept the holy sacrament of baptism, thus improving their miserable lot and, in addition, acquiring the right of citizenship in the great and rich city of Hamburg. No one, however, he goes on to say, would be forced to have himself baptized, even if the learned Doctor von Eitzen were to be found the winner of this disputation

The Jews, Eitzen notices, are again leaning toward one another and whispering; but one of them, a huge hook-nosed fellow with an unkempt gray beard, raises his hand to inquire if, having converted, they would also have to do like the *goyim* and eat of the body of the hanged man and drink of his blood even though it is written, Cursed is everyone that hangs on a tree?

At this, Doctor Paulus's heart is filled with a holy anger, and all his hesitations and doubts as to the justification of his project and as to its timeliness and its likelihood of success disappear and, straightening himself, he proclaims aloud that from the shameless question this man put anyone could see the great callousness of the Jews; but Christ in his unending mercy had died for the sins of the Jews as well, even though they still refuse to acknowledge it, wherefore every good Christian must pray also for the salvation of the accursed Jewish souls so that, when the time of the Last Judgment comes, these, too, might be gathered in by Jesus. "And why," he continues, raising his hands like a prophet, "why do these Jews insist on disbelieving that in the person of our Lord Jesus Christ the Messiah has come that they've been expecting, although they have seen their holy temple destroyed and themselves dispersed over the lands of the world, having to live among strangers and being killed at the whim of any enemy? Thus God in His justice did punish the stubborn and deluded Jews, and is punishing them up to this day, because they refused to see in him our Savior but demanded of Pilate that he be nailed to the cross, and when the Roman governor washed his hands and spoke, I am innocent of the blood of this just person, they answered, His blood be on us and our children."

Eitzen grows aware that he has let himself be carried away by his zeal and that, counter to his plans and intentions, he has already involved himself in the *disputatio* proper and is mired in it; but the learned Ezekiel Pereira has also noticed this and, stroking his nicely curled beard, turns to the assembled dignitaries, those from the ducal court as well as those who were sent by the Hamburg senate, and inquires if the good doctor and the other prominent guests would permit him to interpolate a modest question, namely, by which authorities his honorable opponent wished to dispute with him, and according to which Testament, the Old or the New one, or both of them? Since the conversion of a number of Jews was at issue, and of no one else, it was neither fair nor reasonable to ask them to base their thought on any gospels or apostolic letters; this could be done only after their conversion, but up to that moment one could argue with them and enlighten and convince them solely by the five books of Moses and the words of their own prophets and the other texts contained in the Old Testament, and from these it would have to be shown wherein and by what deeds the Jewish people had sinned so grievously.

At this, droplets of sweat appear on Eitzen's upper lip, and his stomach begins to flutter as he sees some of the prominent guests nodding gravely, apparently in agreement with Pereira's words; the fools, thinks Eitzen, have actually let themselves be persuaded that any approach to the Jews must follow the logic of their own teachings, and they fail to grasp the mischief they create by depriving their superintendent of half of his arsenal.

Pereira, sensing his advantage, immediately makes use of it and asks Eitzen to tell him where Moses or the prophets have said that the salvation of the people of Israel and the retrieval of divine mercy for them depended on their believing in a *Meshiach* who had already put in an appearance? The Holy Scriptures required a man to believe only in one being, namely in God, sanctified be His name, as it is written, *Shemah Yisroel, Adonay Elohenu, Adonay Echod,* Hear, O Israel, the Lord our God is one Lord; and that He, the Lord, is a jealous God, for which reason Israel was forbidden to worship any gods other than Him, not to mention any sons of God.

Eitzen is growing increasingly ill-at-ease as he perceives that Pereira has cleverly extricated himself from the dispute over God's punishment of Israel, which is undeniable, and instead has enticed him into the field of celestial arithmetics to which our earthly way of reckoning, especially that of the Jews, may be fitted but with great difficulty. And he knows he must quickly counter his opponent's argument if he wants to invalidate it, and he says that our Savior, God's own son, to whom the learned Dom Pereira has been alluding so maliciously, was not to be considered another god existing beside the one God, but that God the father, God the son, plus the *logos* which was also called the Holy Ghost, were in truth one being and had been so from the beginning, so that in *puncto* worship of one God no contradiction to divine law could be construed out of the acknowledgment of the Holy Trinity; which was also clearly evidenced by the Hebrew name of God, namely *Elohim*, an unmistakable form of *pluralis*, and was confirmed by God's own words in Genesis 1:26, where God says, Let *us* make man in *our* image. And as this plural pronoun could not possibly refer to the angels standing around Him at the time, it followed that God set to work a holy threesome, and that man was a creature of Christ as well and was therefore obliged to worship both God father and God son, the Holy Ghost included.

Genesis 1, thinks Eitzen; who could go back further than the history of creation? Thus he has beaten Pereira at the man's own game: arrogant Jew bastard coming here from Portugal after his king expelled him along with his other rich and high-handed fellow religionists and wanting to teach us the word of God by mocking and humiliating our Lord Jesus for a second time. Pereira, however, displaying a slight smile and bowing before the dignitaries, inquires if one of the honored councilors of the duke or possibly a gentleman from Hamburg might not be kind enough to ask his learned opponent to also let them know the text of the verse succeeding the one he has quoted from Genesis, *id est* 1:27; and as the surprised Eitzen remains silent, Pereira explains that, strangely enough, 1:27 reads: So God, *singular*, created man in His, *singular*, image—from which it is evident that the *pluralis* in 1:26 is nothing but the well-known *Pluralis Majestatis*, analogous to His

Grace the Duke at Gottorp and other lords and princes saying *We* when referring to their own exalted persons, quite without having been pieced together of three different individuals. The same insolent Jew, however, who a while ago inquired about having to eat of the flesh of the hanged man, now raises his voice once more and wants to know from the Herr Superintendent if it wasn't simply a matter of the son having dawdled on the job of creation, leaving the dirty work to his father; whereupon the other Jews start laughing loudly and slapping their thighs and calling out, *Oyoyoy*, until the town constable, having stood guard at the entrance to the synagogue, bestirs himself, grabs the slanderer by the scruff of his neck, and throws him out.

It now becomes clear to Eitzen that he had better base his case on the holy prophets than insist on arguing over plural and singular, for anyone can check a problem in arithmetics, but a prophecy is beyond the power of an ordinary mind to test. He therefore states that in several books of the prophets our Lord Jesus was positively identified as the hoped-for messiah, by his birth and his lineage out of the house of David as well as by the facts of his life and death and by the great miracles he performed. Yes, if it were only one of the many prophecies that had fulfilled itself, people might be entitled to doubt their validity. But there was such a number of them come true, and from such different sources, and all of them pointing directly to Jesus as the one begotten son of God, that even the most obstinate Jew, once he was told of them, could not but be convinced. Had not the prophet Micah prophesied: But you, Bethlehem, though you be little among the thousands of Judah, yet out of you shall he come forth unto me that is to be the ruler in Israel—and was not our Lord Jesus born in Bethlehem, from the womb of a virgin, just as the prophet Isaiah said, declaring it a sign of God: Behold, a virgin shall conceive, and bear a son? And likewise Isaiah predicted: There shall come forth a rod out of the stem of Jesse, and a branch shall grow out of his roots, and the spirit of the Lord shall rest upon him—and was not Joseph, the father of our Lord Jesus, a true descendant of King David who in turn had been Jesse's son, so that Isaiah's prophecy was fulfilled also in this regard?

Whereupon Pereira courteously inquires if he might direct a few words to the learned Doctor von Eitzen and, having received permission, proceeds to ask him to please make up his mind as to whose son he wants people to believe this Jesus from Bethlehem to have been: the son of the carpenter Joseph of whom it was said in two of the gospels that he was from the house of David, or the son of God whose seed in some mysterious way was implanted into the womb of a virgin? And how, being a son of God, could this Jesus have been human, or *vice versa*, having been sired by Joseph, how could he have served as one-third of the Holy Trinity?

At this, great unrest develops among the dignitaries, and Eitzen glances uncertainly at his fellow clergymen from Hamburg, for he knows only too well that this is the point on which Matthew, Luke, Mark, and John, the four evangelists, are in disagreement; but his pious *confratres* are looking back at him with pretended indifference, or even as though they were secretly enjoying the embarrassment of their new superintendent; and the Jews seem to have noticed as well that their champion has placed his shot neatly on target, hitting the honorable doctor just as young David hit Goliath with his sling and a stone. But the new Goliath is made of harder stuff than was the uncouth giant against whom David pitted himself; furthermore he is aware that people prefer believing things to straining their own, God-given brains; and thus he raises his voice and calls out, "O Jewish sophistry! O shameful falsehoods and deception! Do you actually think, Dom Pereira, that you have caught God in a contradiction? Do you presume, with your small mind, to understand the ways of the Lord on high? Do you claim that God, who created an entire world with everything that crawls and flies in it, should not have been able to beget a child of Joseph's?"

Pereira gasps; totally overwhelmed by the logic of Eitzen's thought he can only stand back dumbly while his opponent goes on exploiting the words of the prophets. Did not, says Eitzen, the prophet Zechariah say: Rejoice greatly, O daughter of Zion; shout, O daughter of Jerusalem; behold, your King comes to you; he is just and having salvation, lowly, and riding upon an ass, and upon a colt the foal of an ass—and was it not true that our Lord Jesus, as he came riding into Jerusalem before the Feast of Passover, entered the gate sitting on an ass while all the multitude cried, saying, Blessed is he that comes in the name of the Lord, Hosanna in the highest?

He could reply, of course, thinks Pereira, that in those days in Israel donkeys were as numerous as horses are today in the Duchy of Sleswick; but should every horseman trotting into Hamburg or Altona be thought of, for this reason, as a possible messiah? Pereira doubts, however, the wisdom of pointing out the arbitrary and willful way in which his opponent goes about linking assorted meanderings of the prophets to events that took place much later. But while he is still turning the matter over in his mind, Eitzen has busily pursued his course and is now explaining how God, by having His one begotten son nailed to the cross, made him an offering for the sins of us all, and how our Lord Jesus suffered for the sake of the sinful Jewish people and their obstinacy and hardness of heart, but how this, too, had been predicted and prophesied by the prophet Isaiah when he said: We all have gone astray; but the Lord has laid on him the sins of us all. He was oppressed and he was afflicted, yet he opened not his mouth, he was brought as a lamb to the slaughter; surely, he has borne our griefs and carried our sorrows. He was wounded for our transgressions and bruised for our iniquities; the chastisement was upon him so we might have peace, and with his stripes we are healed.

Pereira is no longer able to rein in his outrage, and

turning his eyes toward the arched roof under which the smoke of the flickering candles is hovering, he cries out, "Untrue! Untrue! The God who stayed Abraham's hand that held the knife to the throat of his son Isaac, thus refusing man to be offered as a sacrificial offering, this God should have given over His own and only son to be crucified? May he believe that story who can. Furthermore, does anyone really know what was said and done in those days and what sort of man this Jesus was of whom it is claimed that he was the awaited messiah, and whether in truth the evangelist did not take from the prophet purposely what would enhance his tale and increase the glory which the disciples were weaving around the head of their crucified Rabbi?"

Eitzen's heart fills with glee at the storm which is breaking loose after the learned Pereira has lost his self-restraint in trying to rush to the aid of his Jewish God. "Blasphemy!" the dignitaries are shouting, and "Horrors!" and "Abomination!" And those endowed with worldly authority call for the constable to intervene while the men of the cloth, Eitzen's *confratres*, are pressing their palms together as in prayer and begging God to forgive their having listened to such awful heresy; the Jews however tremble and are huddling together like chickens when the fox lurks near their coop. Eitzen calmly waits for the hubbub to subside, and as the constable comes to lay hold of Pereira and lead him off, he motions him aside and addresses the other, "You did ask, Ezekiel Pereira, did you not, if anyone really knew what was said and done in those days and what sort of man this Jesus was of whom it is claimed that he was the awaited messiah; well, now, I will show you one who was there at the time and who knows it and who, in addition, is a Jew like yourself and your fellow Jews in this community, but very much older than you, for he can testify as to how our Lord Jesus suffered for our iniquities and how he took the heavy cross upon himself."

And having said all this, Eitzen raises his hand and calls

for Ahasverus, at which Ahasverus promptly appears in the door of the synagogue, a little white cap perched on his head and a long threadbare cloak wrapped about his gaunt body and his feet bare so anyone can see that their soles have grown their own leather over the many centuries of his wandering. And as everyone in the crowded synagogue, Jew and Christian, feels a shudder run down his spine, Eitzen asks coolly, "Tell us who you are."

"I am the one you have called," says Ahasverus.

"So you are the one," says Eitzen, "who turned our Lord Jesus away from your door as he came to you on his way to Golgotha and wanted to rest from his great affliction in the shade of your house?"

"I did turn Reb Joshua away from my door," says Ahasverus, "and since then have been wandering over this earth every day that God made."

"And did He condemn you to this long punishment?" says Eitzen.

"The Rabbi spoke to me," replies Ahasverus, "saying, The son of man goes as is written in the words of the prophets, but you shall remain here and tarry till I come."

The Jews are staring at Ahasverus who looks like one of their own, aged thirty or thirty-five, and yet pretends to have been around at a time when the great temple still stood in its splendor up on Mount Zion and the people of Israel lived in the land which God had promised to their forefathers; the high officials and dignitaries however are badly frightened, and the assembled clergy are much astonished at the miraculous power of their superintendent to produce the Wandering Jew just for this occasion although he never before mentioned his existence to them, and they are wondering whether great misfortunes might not be in store for Altona or the Free City of Hamburg, as it is written in the venerable verse:

> When you see the Wandering Jew,
> Woe and misery to you.
> Fires, floods, and storms will roar,

Hunger, pestilence, and war.
Pray that you and yours be spared
And he find your souls prepared.

Only Eitzen rejoices in his innermost soul that everything is working so beautifully for him and just as he
planned it, and he says to Ahasverus, "Then pray tell us
and testify whether our Lord Jesus whom you knew, and
whom your own eyes have seen and your own lips have
spoken to, and with whom in your hard-heartedness you
have dealt so callously, whether this Jesus was in truth and
before God the messiah whom the Jewish people have
been awaiting according to the words of the prophets?"

"Whether he was the *Meshiach?*" says Ahasverus and
sighs and scratches his head. Finally he says, "The Rabbi
believed it."

Eitzen sees that his witness has grown unsure of himself, and he fears that the accursed Jew might leave him in
the lurch even though every word between them, question
and answer both, was carefully thought out in advance and
rehearsed, and he says hoarsely, "Believed! Believed!
These recalcitrant Jews here do not want to hear what
Jesus believed, just as they would not hear him when he
himself was preaching to them; they want to hear your
clear and unequivocal testimony, Jew Ahasverus, as the
testimony of one who refused to give our Lord Jesus the
small bit of comfort he begged but let him suffer instead in
the heat of the day when he came to you with his burden
and his crown of thorns: Was he or was he not the
Messiah?"

"The *Meshiach?*" says Ahasverus. "The great, all-
powerful *Meshiach?*" And he straightens, and it is as
though a light were emanating from him and he has
grown and is towering above everyone else in the synagogue, above Pereira and the Altona Jews, and above all
the prominent guests seated in exalted splendor on their
raised platform, and also above the honorable and learned
Herr Superintendent. "The *Meshiach*," he repeats, "of

whom it was said by the prophets that he shall judge among the nations and cause their swords to be beaten into plowshares and their spears into pruning hooks?" And as Eitzen grows both hot and cold inside and is dumbfounded, he goes on to say, "I loved the Rabbi, and he might have been the *Meshiach*. He might have, just as everyone created in the image of God has in himself the power to be a savior of men. And he suffered and hung on the cross and died slowly and miserably. But who will count the numbers of those before him and those after him who died in an agony equal to his and called out in their anguish: *Eli, Eli, lama sabachthani*, My God, my God, why have you forsaken me? And where is that everlasting peace, where that kingdom which was to come with him and through him? Up to this day, Adam must eat his bread in the sweat of his face, and Eve bring forth children in sorrow, and Cain is slaying Abel; and you, much honored Doctor," he adds, turning to Eitzen, "in all the time I have known you I never noticed you particularly loving your enemies or blessing those that cursed you or praying for them which despitefully used you, as your Lord Jesus preached on the mount, nor do I see others who call themselves Christians obey these words."

Finally, seeing the shocked expressions on the faces of the courtiers of the duke and the flush and fury of the officials from Hamburg and the gloating of his *confratres*, the Herr Superintendent comes to his senses and shrieks, "Shut up, miserable Jew! And though you may have been roaming the earth these one thousand and five hundred years, this is the last of your wickedness!" And he calls for the constable to take Ahasverus and hold him for blaspheming God and maligning His Grace the Duke of Sleswick at Gottorp in his capacity as the spiritual head of his subjects, and for inciting to disbelief and rebellion. But now pandemonium breaks loose with the Jews excitedly braying and cackling and flailing their arms; one rushes here, the other there, and they tear at their beards, 'tis moot whether for fear or for secret joy, and that any of them might convert to the true faith is more of an illusion than ever.

But Ahasverus has vanished in the general tohubohu, and it is as though the earth had swallowed him up, for no one saw him exit through the door.

CHAPTER TWENTY

§

*Wherein Ahasverus disturbs the celestial peace and
explains to the Rabbi that truth is not a matter for some central authority to dispense
but is visible to all who have eyes*

to see

§

It is very still, and nothing moves.

The soft radiance upon him as he is seated on his throne
is like the blue of the twilight, and he is enveloped in the
gentle love of God, and a great inner peace brightens his
face as he gazes down at the world, his hand raised in bene-
diction, the hand that still carries the wound the nail tore
into it.

But I thought how strange and distant he has become
even though he still looks like the Reb Joshua I knew and
shows the same smile marked by the suffering he was destined to take upon himself; he is like one of those wooden
dolls inside another wooden doll, in which there is yet another wooden doll: thus they are three in one, and yet each
one an entity.

And I went near him and asked, Is that you, Rabbi?

He, however, stirred not in the slightest, and his gaze
remained fixed at some far-off point as he spoke, I am
Jesus Christ, God's only begotten son, who was incarnate
by the Holy Ghost of the Virgin Mary and was made man,
and suffered under Pontius Pilate, and was crucified and
buried, and descended to the kingdom of death and the

third day rose again from the dead and ascended into heaven where he sits on the right hand of God the Almighty Father.

And I asked, Rabbi, what are you seeing?

And he said, I am seeing all those men and women whom I delivered from the debt of their sins by the cup of bitterness which I drank.

But I asked him, Rabbi, are you sure that you see them quite clearly?

And his eyes filled with darkness, and his hand that was raised in blessing sank down, and he said, They are so small, and there is a multitude of them.

I, however, bowed down before him and spoke to him, Rabbi, you have condemned me to tarry on earth until you return; therefore I am wandering among them and am like one of them and listen to what they are saying and see what they are doing.

He lowered his head, and his shoulders slumped and his hand reached for his side as though the wound which the spear had made there were hurting him afresh, and he said, I do not want to hear of it.

But I said, When we met in the wilderness and you were lone and naked, I led you to the top of a very high mountain and showed you the kingdoms of the world and how in each one of them injustice and iniquity were the rule, and I told you to take things into your own hands and turn them downside up, for the time had come to erect the true kingdom of God. You however refused me and said that your kingdom was not of this world.

And again there was on his face that smile of which no one can say for certain whether it is tinged with sadness or with irony, and he answered, You have said it.

But I continued, And as you sought the shade of my door on your way to Golgotha, with the cross on your back, I spoke to you of the sword of God that I would draw for you, and you were to gather around you the people of Israel and lead them into battle. But you turned me down once more and said you wanted to drink the cup which your father had given you.

Listen, he said, I hung on that cross on Mount Golgotha in the heat of the day and my mind kept thinking as long as I still had some blood in my brain, and I also thought about what you had been saying to me; not to battle for your purposes, however, did my father send me, but in order to suffer and die so that the word be fulfilled and the kingdom might come for all.

At this, I rose up before him and asked, And has the word been fulfilled? Has your kingdom come?

He stayed silent. And the light in which he was seated changed its color, and the brightness of peace vanished from his face, and he turned his head as though looking behind him to see if someone were standing there to listen in on his words.

And once again I asked, Has it come, this kingdom of yours?

And he opened his eyes wide, as in fright, and called out, Get yourself hence, Satan!

But I laughed, and I said, I am not he whom you just addressed, even though I have had some experiences tying me to Lucifer; I am an angel like him, but another one, and like him I know the truth.

The truth, said he, lies in God.

How often, said I, have I heard that one. But the truth is visible to all who have eyes to see it, and all who will think may fathom it. You, however, are seated on your throne and see nothing, and the unfathomable is to you a source of consolation.

At this, finally, he asked, What do you really want of me?

And I replied, I want you to be who you ought to be.

When I offered my body to my disciples, he said, and my blood to those who loved me, you were sitting by my side and leaning your head on my bosom. What more can I give than what I have given, and what more can I suffer than what I have suffered?

Rabbi, I said, I want you to see what I have seen in the kingdom that came after you, and hear what I have heard spoken in it, and learn what I have come to learn about its composition and structure.

He clapped his hands to his face. But then he raised his head and said, I have taken upon myself the guilt for the sins of people and have paid for them by my sacrifice; but where is it written that I should abolish sin?

Rabbi, I said, the imperfection of man has been the excuse of every revolution that failed to achieve what it set out to do. And did not you yourself preach, Love your enemies? And did not you yourself say, Seek you first the kingdom of God, and His righteousness? And did not you yourself believe that which you preached and demanded? But for the hundreds of thousands that tore at each other and cut one another to pieces when you preached that sermon on the mount, there are now a hundred times hundreds of thousands of them. They are greedy for riches and for their neighbor's wife, they whore and they guzzle and they sell their own children, inject poison into themselves and are a mockery of all that is decent in man. And all of them are each other's enemy, spy upon and betray one another, lock one another in camps where they starve to death, or in chambers where they are choked until dead, and beat and torture one another till they give up their ghost, and everywhere the rulers proclaim that all this is done in the name of love and for the good and welfare of the peoples. They despoil and destroy the treasures of the earth, turn fertile lands into barren desert and water into stinking slime, and the many must labor for the few and die away before their time. No sword, contrary to the word of the prophet, was ever beaten into a plowshare, no spear into a pruning hook; instead, they take the secret forces in the universe and cause them to burst into giant mushrooms of flame and smoke by which every creature alive is turned into ashes and into a shadow on the wall.

When I had finished he sat motionless and in silence, just as though he were made of wood and painted; and a great darkness was about us with but a dim ray of light illuminating his face and figure.

Rabbi, said I, did you hear me?

And there was a voice that spoke, The son of man will return for it is he who was ordained of God to be the judge of the quick and the dead, and he will send forth his angels, and they will gather out of his kingdom all things that offend and them which do iniquity; and there shall be wailing and gnashing of teeth, but the righteous shall shine forth as the sun in the kingdom of their father.

And when will that be? I wanted to know.

The Rabbi seemed to awake from his torpor. My father has set the day, he said.

I would not postpone it until then, said I.

CHAPTER TWENTY-ONE

§

*In which Duke Adolph proceeds to found the kingdom
of God in Sleswick, while his superintendent is
unable to enter into the Countess Ehrentreu
and Ahasverus marches off to war
singing bravely*

§

The outlines of Hamburg behind him, and in his pocket
Duke Adolph's letter of invitation to his residence at Castle Gottorp, Eitzen rides through the lovely land of Holstein, cows to his right, cows to his left, also sheep and
pigs; 'tis a new Canaan, even though somewhat marshy,
which is no great wonder since the country is wedged between the Baltic and the North Sea; but the duke will have
great dikes built, he learns from Parson Vorstius at Itzehoe
where he has ordered his coach stopped so the horses can
rest and he refresh himself by partaking in a meal of deli-
ciously baked sole for which the good parson's house-
keeper is rightfully famous. Duke Adolph, Vorstius goes
on to explain, was a true father of his people, also well
versed in matters divine; but His Grace was sorely in need
of an ecclesiastical chief councillor who would see to it
that some order was brought into the totally disorganized
and anarchic affairs of a Church in which no one knew
whether or not a preacher was properly ordained and what
blooming nonsense he would spurt forth next time he
mounted his pulpit.

Troubles of this nature were fully familiar to him, replies Eitzen; hasn't he been having enough tribulation in his own hometown where his *pastores* secretly slander one another, and him uppermost, for his fidelity to the teachings of Luther, not to speak of those who openly were showing their hostility by calling him a tyrant and a Pharisee and loudly laughing at him for his attempt at teaching and converting the stubborn Jews in a disputation held at Altona; and the Hamburg senate which ought to have stepped in and cleaned up this Sodom was shirking its bounden duty. Ah, yes, sighs the good Vorstius, wasn't it appearing everywhere as though the law and order of the church were badly shaken; and in addition the whole duchy was teeming with visionaries and rebels, most likely the successors of those who managed to flee when that well-known den of iniquity was smoked out in Münster where everything, including the women, was had in common; an annoyance to God and all government, these people were transporting the cursed Anabaptist heresy from place to place, from Holland all over north Germany and even into Sleswick, and in their secret conventicles were reading and propagating the vicious booklets of Menno Simons and their other false teachers.

Then Vorstius talks of the war which Duke Adolph is planning to join in support of the Spanish duke Alba and the Roman emperor, so that together and in league they might beat down the rebellious Dutch: though he, Vorstius, was having his doubts on the justice of the undertaking in view of the people of the Netherlands, akin to ours in Sleswick, being honest Protestants, howbeit of the Calvinist variety, while the emperor was an arch-Papist and in alliance with the devil himself. But this kind of argument cuts no ice with Eitzen who expounds to his dear *confrater* that Duke Adolph at Gottorp, though a decent and upright Lutheran, in his capacity as a prince of the Holy Roman Empire was duly obligated to aid his sovereign lord and, more than that, was doing a brave Christian work by defeating the rebels; for had not our Lord Christ said, Render unto Caesar the things which are Caesar's, and had not our

Doctor Luther confirmed that no rebellion was justified however just its cause, and that it was forbidden by God, and that the worldly authorities were instituted and armed with the sword so that uprisings and rebellion might be nipped in the bud.

As he continues his journey and on the next day is nearing the town of Sleswick, he sees many troops encamped along the river Schlei and many soldiers loitering at the gates of the city and in its streets and lanes, the entire regiment of Colonel Pufendorf, but also Danish halberdiers, especially enlisted for this campaign; these good men seem disgruntled and are muttering among themselves; obviously, they would rather have stayed back home with their wives and cattle than march off to war and shed their blood on the far-off fields of Flanders. But before the duke's residence at Gottorp he finds a great hustle and bustle, and in the courtyard of the castle there is much hurrying to and fro, councillors of the duke and military officers, court servants, scribes, and purveyors of goods are constantly shoving one another aside and shouting and giving commands, and no one pays the least heed to someone as unimportant as the Superintendent Paulus von Eitzen who timidly climbs out of his coach.

Until he hears that unmistakable laugh and turns about and sees his friend Hans standing there. His friend is clothed most elegantly, wearing a short sword on a costly belt, and he is now, as Eitzen soon enough learns, His Grace the Duke of Sleswick's Privy Councillor Johann Leuchtentrager; also he has aged somewhat, his beard and temples have grayed; but which of us remains immune to the years, thinks Eitzen, and neither is he the youngster anymore who, in the Swan at Leipzig, encountered that weird stranger. He is freezing a little although the late sun still warms the inside of the courtyard, and he shrinks as he feels the touch of Leuchtentrager's finger on his shoulder and hears him say that His Grace has been eagerly looking forward to his arrival. As for his material comfort, he adds, everything has been prepared in one of the better chambers of the castle.

Later on, as they are seated together before the fire in Leuchtentrager's room and Eitzen has had an ample taste of wine and cold roast of venison, the two of them once more become Hans and Paul to each other, just as they were in past times, and Hans slaps Paul on his thigh and Paul heartily boxes Hans's hump; but still there are moments when Paul is agape at the great knowledge Hans has of his life and affairs, down to the details of his Hamburg troubles and of the private deal which he made with Ahasverus and in which the Jew failed him in the end, and to his secret itch for Margriet who keeps appearing to him in the night, sometimes as herself and sometimes as the Princess of Trapezund and sometimes as the Lady, and undresses herself and lies before him with her legs spread so that he fears to go mad with lust for her flesh; 'tis as though his friend had never been far from him, thinks Eitzen, and often as close as he was that time in Wittenberg when his learned *professores* were examining him on the subject of the holy angels. But when he wants to know of his friend why he was called to Gottorp, His Grace's privy councillor merely smiles and stays silent, and at some further urging condescends to hint that it is not for reasons either untoward or ill conceived, but adds that he would rather discourse on Frau Barbara and the children, in particular on little Margarethe. The girl, Eitzen tells him, has grown nicely and her mind is bright enough, but unfortunately she is often mocked in street and marketplace and has come to her mother with the plaintive inquiry as to why of all the youngsters around it was she who was that badly malformed, and Leuchtentrager, as if he were touched in his heart, sniffles and wipes his eyes. But then his sentimental moment passes, and he says, "God made man in His image, an evil breed." And as Eitzen, shocked at the slanderous words, starts up, he looks at him and goes on to say, "Well, she will learn to live with it, and will grow hard and hit back at her detractors, and woe to him who insults her." Then he rises from in front of the fireplace and says that the duke is waiting for them and that it is time to go. Eitzen, who had assumed that he would be received at the earliest tomorrow or the day after that, complains of having had too much wine; its vapors were threatening to burst his skull, and he was sure to talk but gibberish to His Grace. But his friend Hans takes him by the scruff of his neck and pushes him through numerous dark and drafty rooms which open one into the next, with a rare torch flickering here and there, until they come to a richly adorned door that opens almost by itself, permitting a view of the duke in all his power and majesty.

Seated on something that is half bed, half upholstered chair, he reclines idly, his shirt open at the throat, his codpiece but loosely tied, and a colorful robe thrown around his shoulder; his one hand holds the silver cup from which he has been drinking, his other shooes away the pretty ladies who, more or less *en déshabillé*, have been playing their charming games with him, and waves Eitzen close. "Well, well," he says, trying to sit up straight, "so you are the learned Doctor von Eitzen from the city of Hamburg who was so highly recommended by my privy councillor."

Eitzen feels Leuchtentrager's sharp elbow in his ribs, and with a quick bow he replies, "The very same, Your Grace." But Leuchtentrager adds, "Our learned doctor defends the teachings of Luther at all times and in all ways and preaches faithfully against every kind of heretic and such as deviate from the true gospel of the Lord; also he has a keen nose for those scoundrels so that none escapes him who might spread any doubts and distrust in the lawful authorities, religious or worldly, and in the God-given order of things."

"Excellent," says Duke Adolph, his tongue a bit heavy, "such a man we need." And having finally succeeded in getting himself into an upright position, he continues, "For we intend to erect in our land Sleswick the true kingdom of God where everybody shall obey the teachings of Christ as defined and determined by Martinus Luther; and all men shall be of one mind wherever our reign stretches and we are the supreme head of the Church, and but one doctrine shall be preached from the pulpit, for all of which you shall be responsible to us, dear Doctor, and for which we shall appoint you this very night superintendent and chief administrator of Church affairs in our duchy, so that law and order may be preserved among clergy and laity both, especially now that we are going to war against the rebellious Netherlands."

Proud of the well-turned phrases he has managed to deliver, the duke waits for his learned guest to show some appreciation of the wide-reaching princely thought; Eitzen however stands there dumbstruck and stares past his future lord and protector as if he were seeing a ghost. 'Tis his playmates, the duke recognizes, that fascinate the pious cleric, or rather one of them who holds his gaze until the privy councillor unceremoniously hits him in the side. Eitzen comes to and, with a bow that is lower even than his first one was, explains how deeply moved he was by the grandeur of the ducal project and by the confidence His Grace has placed in him, for which reasons his speech failed him, and that he wished nothing more dearly than to devote himself, within the limits of his feeble capabilities, to the erection of the kingdom of God in Sleswick; but that it should please His Grace to call to mind that his obedient servant possessed a wife and several children and that, as the saying went, an empty larder and a cold stove were not conducive to the pursuit of wisdom.

Whereupon the duke gestures to his privy councillor to fetch from the table, which is covered with cups and pitchers and costly plates that hold all sorts of half-eaten delicacies, a scroll tied with ribbon and seal, and hand the same to Eitzen: the learned doctor, says His Grace, would be sure to be well satisfied with what the scroll contained; and as his first official duty the new Herr Superintendent was to compose, without delay, a goodly prayer for the success of the campaign into Flanders, this prayer to be spoken tomorrow morning in front of the assembled troops and thereupon in all the churches of the duchy. Having thus attended to his executive business, Adolph takes a deep draft from his cup, settles back into his pillows, and motions to the second lady on the right who up to that time, partly hidden by the play of the shadows cast by the uncertain candles, has been leaning in a most alluring way against a statue of the Greek god Priapus diagonally behind the ducal seat.

"Countess Ehrentreu," he says, "it appears that you have found an admirer in the person of our freshly appointed chief administrator of Church affairs; you will have noticed the most un-Christian glances he has been casting at you; or could it be that the two of you have already met somewhere?"

The countess bends over the duke, whereby the form of her bosom shows much to its advantage, and with pursed lips plants a kiss on His Grace's sweated forehead and says, "Everybody has a past of his or her own, kind sir, if not in this world, then in the other, and your new superintendent may well have been a dear little angel such as I was and, seated high upon a cloud, have sung with me the most pious cantatas and responsories before he descended to do his good works down on this earth."

At the picture of the short, skinny Eitzen, with his stubborn hair and his dour face, sprouting little white wings and wearing a little white shirt while strumming a lyre and throwing kisses at the voluptuous countess, similarly costumed, on a neighboring cloud, the duke breaks into uproarious laughter; but Eitzen, to whom the countess's suggestive voice sounds only too familiar, feels the blood stream to his bowels, and he suddenly understands what devilish chains are tying him to Margriet: chains forged long ago either up there in lofty heights or, more probably, in much darker places far below; and, worse than that, the woman knows about these cursed chains and will twist them and torture him to the end of his days. As the duke's laughter, however, does not abate, Eitzen turns to his friend in mute plea, and Leuchtentrager bows his humped back and asks the duke if His Grace would not graciously grant leave to the two of them; there was, he explains, much work to be done, and all in this night, for the writing of prayers was a difficult art if the words were to be well received by their addressee.

But hardly back in his chamber, Eitzen grabs his friend and shakes him, calling out, "That was Margriet, wasn't it! And also the Princess of Trapezund! And the Lady! And now—the Countess Ehrentreu!"

Leuchtentrager pushes him away. "If you insist on carrying on in this manner, Paul," he says, "you soon will be seeing Margriet in every female. I can arrange, though, that the countess will come to you after she has tended to the duke, and will serve your desires in every way." And noticing that Eitzen's hands are trembling and saliva dripping from the corners of his mouth, he adds that, unfortunately, God has set labor before lust and prayer before fulfillment, and that, as it may still take a while for him to reach the little garden and enter the gate to paradise located therein, he might as well read that scroll and then sit down to compose the duke's prayer of war.

This seems sensible enough to Eitzen, and he takes the document to hand, breaks its seal, cuts its ribbon, unrolls the paper, and hastily peruses its contents: *We, Adolph, hereby make known to all and sundry* et cetera et cetera *that sub dato of this day We have accepted and appointed* et cetera et cetera *the honorable and learned, faithful and pious* et cetera et cetera *Doctor of Divinity* et cetera et cetera *to be responsible to Us and Our house primarily in matters religious* et cetera et cetera *by word and deed* et cetera et cetera *and is he to keep secret forever and into his grave all that we shall confide to him* et cetera et cetera *in proof of which our Ducal Seal* et cetera et cetera *and signed by Our own hand* et cetera et cetera *Adolph.* And as, in the wording of the appointment, Eitzen believes to recognize the adroit hand of the privy councillor, he embraces him and sobs, "Three hundred and sixty guilders! The children, first and foremost litttle Margarethe, shall always be grateful to you, Hans!" In the same breath, though, he hesitates, for that much generosity makes him suspect the donor, and he wants to know from Leuchtentrager if, in return for this favor, he might not be asked to deliver a few items which are harder to furnish than a bit of discretion and spiritual aid in the erection of the kingdom of God? But Leuchtentrager waves him off: what friendship would that be, he answers, which required prompt compensation by one friend for services rendered him by the other? They simply were owing, one to the other, and in the end would reckon up the debt and draw the balance. But now, to work!

But which of us has never had such moments with the clean sheet of white paper before him, and the pen sharpened, and the ink there, and nothing but emptiness and desolation inside his head? War, thinks Eitzen. War! . . . And sees before his mind's eye the gloom of the battlefield, the dead stretched out in their own blood, the wounded whimpering or murmuring their last prayer while the valiant chaplain, braving the fire of the enemy, consoles them by the sacred promise of paradise beyond; at the same time he secretly thanks the Lord that he is not in the boots of this chaplain but may remain safely at home with his goodly books, waiting for the hour when the family supper will have been finished and he can excuse himself and set off for a tender visit to the Countess Ehrentreu.

He starts up at his friend's gentle cough and, pointing at the sheet of paper which still lies before him in its virginal state, he sighs, "Despite all my studies in Wittenberg, where I was made magister and doctor and learned about God's angels and their various functions, and about the Holy Scriptures and both the large and small catechism, I still do not know how to send a man off to war so he might go happy and at peace with himself."

Leuchtentrager shrugs his hump. "'Tis because you take the thing seriously," he says. "Don't forget that on the other side there is a man just like you sitting at night and chewing on his pen as he tries to think up a nice, heart-rending prayer, and that it's been that way throughout the ages, with man crying out to his God for victory and survival before going out to slay his brother. But God does not listen, to God it is all the same, He is like the sand of time that runs out for everybody and like the distant stars that shine on both victor and vanquished. And this is why no one except the duke cares for your prayer, and he, I suspect, will have such a headache tomorrow from the stuff he's been guzzling tonight that he would not know his butt from his elbow; come on, I shall lead your hand, it does not matter what you write as long as it ends with the words of the Lord's Prayer."

And behold, as his finger lightly touches the back of our author's hand, the pen he holds starts rushing across the paper, and the page covers itself with the most edifying words, and as Eitzen puts the last flourish under the last Amen and looks up from his travail, he finds his friend gone but standing in the door to his chamber the Countess Ehrentreu, fragrant with all the perfumes of the Orient, and inquiring in the sweetest voice, "Will you not ask me in, revered Doctor?"

Eitzen's heart leaps in his chest, she is going to be his, in the flesh, with her dark, tempting eyes and her full, sensual lips and all her other appurtenances, and with her luscious hair which is no longer reddish as it was when worn by Margriet but jet black like French velvet and pinned up in back in the style worn by gentlewomen; and he jumps up with such vehemence that his chair falls over with a great clash and clatter, and hurries to her, saying, "Ah, Madam Countess, I am the happiest of men, for I have been pining for you ever since we were little angels, both of us, and concertizing so harmoniously with one another."

The countess makes herself comfortable on his bed, shoving a pillow behind her back and placing her feet, clad in the most elegant little boots, on his coverlet; then she archly looks up at him and states that of all men she most fancies the man of God, namely because of his adeptness and expertise in obtaining the state of bliss. Panting heavily, the superintendent kneels down before her as though she were the goddess Venus, and with flying fingers loosens her gown until he has it opened entirely, and her bodice and shirt as well, and has her lying before him in all her splendor; after which he kisses and fondles her from top to bottom and bottom to top. She seems to be finding this quite pleasurable and praises the nimbleness of his fingers, suggesting that their dexterity might have been acquired by his frequent leafing in the Holy Scriptures. 'Tis hints of this nature which make him believe that the time has come to pass from dillying to dallying, and as he wants to do it fully to her lust and liking and in the manner done by them in the house of Sir Ahasverus when she was his succubus and he lying on top of her, he eagerly kicks off his shoes and steps out of his finely tailored trousers and is just about to mount the countess who is spread out before him in expectation of things to come when he suddenly feels his strength leaving his loins. Fear has gripped him, fear that once more he might be fooled and wake up as he had in that low tavern, he and his Barbara naked and deprived of their possessions and laughed at by the drunken mob; and if such scandal repeated, what would become of the kingdom of God in Sleswick and of his three hundred and sixty guilders *per annum*?

"Herr Superintendent," the countess says after a moment, "it seems I shall have to rely on the Holy Ghost; kindly go and leave me alone."

What else can Eitzen do but obey and wait outside his chamber; the clock in the tower of the castle strikes the hour, and still no sign of the countess; Eitzen is getting sleepy, but the draft coming from all sides makes his naked legs and behind freeze, and the sneeze tickling his nostrils rouses fears that he might be unable, tomorrow, to speak his new prayer. So he takes heart, finally, knocks courteously at his own door and, no answer forthcoming, opens it: the countess is gone. Only her scent is still hovering in the room, mixed with a slight sulfuric odor, and God only knows by which exit she left, for there is no second door, and the window is out of the question, there being, at a rough guess, forty or fifty feet from its sill to the cobbles of the courtyard. Eitzen shudders at the thought that everything might have been just another illusion, the countess and Margriet and his great love and desire; but then he considers that he may have fallen asleep in the hallway and not noticed her departure; there are people who, like a sack of flour, can sleep in a standing position, a most consoling idea.

The first trumpets are blaring reveille, and from the courtyard the echoes of commands and the clatter of hooves are sounding; down there, in the light of the torches, the guards are assembling, mounted and on foot, all of them clothed in the ducal red, white, and blue. But soon the torches pale, the sky turns gray, and Eitzen realizes sourly that he has done himself out of another night, and for nothing. Then he bestirs himself and goes to moisten his face from his pitcher of water and put on his clerical garb, after which he pockets the paper with his prayer on it and proceeds in search of some breakfast.

After much erring about he learns that a hot soup is being served for the gentry in the so-called king's hall, and there, under the vaulted ceiling with its delicately crossed ribs, he finds a mass of councillors and other high dignitaries and military officers pouring tankards of beer down their gullets and sabering thick slices of smoked meat from the animal's bones so as to strengthen themselves for the coming parade and the departure to war which is to follow directly. He has some soup ladled into his dish but hardly has time to eat a spoonful or two and say a few words to his friend Leuchtentrager before the duke appears, booted and spurred and his harness strapped to his chest. Everyone calls out "Hurrah!" and "Long live His Grace!" and swords are raised and beaten blade to blade as though the war had already begun in earnest. But the duke, his step somewhat uncertain, walks up to Eitzen who is vainly trying to hide his dish under his cloak, and inquires whether the learned doctor spent an agreeable night and if he was ready now and prepared to entreat God for victory and for the success of the good cause?

Though coming from a mind still half drunk, this is a show of favor such as Eitzen never experienced, and is like gentle rain on his heart parched by the countess's contempt of him and her leaving him, half naked, in that freezing hallway. And while he is being conducted by his friend Leuchtentrager to the parade grounds, past the huge red canopy erected to shade the duchess and the other ladies of the court and the young princes and princesses, and toward a wooden platform on which, visible to everyone, a cross has been mounted, Eitzen thinks that the countess shall admire him yet when, in the presence of His Grace the Duke and the entire army, he will call on Almighty God to bless the colors of Sleswick and make them victorious. But as much as he turns about to look after he has mounted the platform, he cannot discern the countess anywhere, and he knows he cannot afford to delay his prayer any longer as the troops are fully lined up, neatly grouped by companies and squads, with the duke up front in lonely resplendence.

So he raises his voice and begins: that the duke, our gracious lord and prince, had girded himself with sword and armor in order to return the Netherlands, with God's help, from their present state of rebellion to peace and concord and good government. Not so as to persecute or oppress the Holy Christian Church in those lands, as far as it held to the true gospel, was His Grace going to war, but to strengthen and support the teachings of the Lord and the one valid doctrine at all times; for which good and sufficient reasons we, the assembled, and all of us loyal subjects of our gracious lord and sovereign, would now call on Almighty, Dear, and Merciful God and pray to Him that in the name of His one begotten son Jesus Christ he might favor our gracious prince, along with his wise and excellent councillors of war, his brave commanders, troops, and servants, and preserve them from evil and protect them, with the help of his dear holy angels, against misfortunes and damages and guard them against all enemies and grant them good luck, victory, and plenty of spoils.

Eitzen pauses for breath. The duke, he sees, stands there like a clod, unable, most likely, to perceive that his superintendent *implicite* has committed him to a certain policy on matters of the Dutch Church, or not caring about it, for war is war and in war no one asks you before beating in your skull whether you take your communion the Papist or the Protestant way. Then Eitzen goes on to say: that we should also most diligently pray that Almighty, Dear, and Merciful God, for the sake of His beloved son Jesus Christ, may protect from all evil, damages, and misfortunes the states and principalities reigned over by His Grace the Duke, and in His great mercy may also provide and grant that our gracious prince and lord might delight his dear spouse, our gracious lady and princess, and the young princes and princesses, and all of us, his loyal subjects, by his happy return; which happy return we likewise pray for concerning His Grace's wise and excellent councillors of war, his brave commanders, troops, and servants, so that all these might happily come home, too, safe and sound, and delight their dear ones by their renewed presence.

Since, after such long and intensely imploring words, Eitzen's breath has waxed short again, he pauses another time and, raising his eyes, notices many a hardened warrior sniffling and blowing his nose lest his snot run into his beard and befoul it; and, much moved himself by his noble and salutary words, he comes to his conclusion, saying, "And so that we may be granted all this, let us now pray from the bottom of our hearts, and in great hope and faith in God. *Our Father which art in Heaven . . .*"

At this, the entire army goes down on its knees like one man, the duke out in front having trouble to keep his balance, and all over the parade grounds there is a general groaning and the clanking of armor, and thereupon several thousand soldiers speaking in unison, *"Hallowed be Thy name—Thy kingdom come—Thy will be done . . ."* And Eitzen senses the power of the divine word which, being pronounced by his mouth, is also his word and his power; but at this moment he sees standing beside him the duke's privy councillor, his friend Leuchtentrager, who grins at him with his crooked lips; and hearing the *"Thine is the kingdom, and the power, and the glory,"* and afterward the *"Forever, Amen,"* Eitzen grows aware that his steps are not led by our Lord Jesus, as a good Christian's should be, but by this uncanny fellow, and that he, a doctor of divinity and future assistant erector of the kingdom of God in Sleswick, is but a tool in the hands of one who will never let go of him.

Among much shouting and cursing the company officers and squad leaders have meanwhile got their troops in formation for the march-past and departure; the cavalry has mounted, and the duke has scrambled up on his battle horse, a broad-beamed gelding complete with gold-trimmed bridle and similarly embroidered saddlecloth. Eitzen has raised his arms to call down God's blessing and pass it on to His Grace and to the brave army as it moves by, squad by squad; thus, looking to all the world like a crow that vainly tries to fly off, he flaps his black sleeves at the troops filing past him, the duke with his councillors of war at their head, then the guards, followed by the Danish halberdiers on foot, and in their wake the duke's light and heavy cavalry, and finally the Regiment Pufendorf, in firm step and defiantly singing their regimental song:

> Rise gladly to the fight,
> Good fellows to a man!
> Up at the enemy
> And hit him where you can!

And each one strive so that
Eternal praise he gain
By his courageous death,
His honor without stain,

His wounds all in his chest,
Received by brave attack,
And not shamefully in
His butt end and his back.

And after each verse a gay *"Valleri, Valleri, Vallera!"* is
added resoundingly, filling Eitzen, who keeps on diligently blessing the men, with a new martial spirit and almost making him wish that he might be marching off with
them to war. But as the last verse is sung—

Who seeks but glorious death
And falls in goodly strife
Will win great victory
And his eternal life—

and the regiment's last squad moves by, he sees on the
outside wing of the first rank, marching directly behind a
young ensign, a familiar figure, and the man seems to
know him, too, for with the sound of the *"Vallera!"* he
turns to Eitzen and calls something which sounds like Hebrew and might well be the ill-omened word *Shed*, meaning as much as *Satan* or *May Satan get you*, and the caller is
none other than Ahasverus, clad in the Pufendorf regimentals with their wide breeches and slit sleeves, and fully
armed.

Eitzen feels as if a lightning stroke had hit him even
though, ever since encountering the Countess Ehrentreu,
he has had a presentiment that the Wandering Jew might
not be far behind. Also he fears that the Jew's haunting the
ranks of the army might be an ominous sign for the duke's
campaign in the Netherlands, but his religious duties are
tying him to the cross on this platform and keep him from

running after Ahasverus and calling him to account, and in another moment the squad has passed and the baggage train comes up, all kinds of ill-fitted carriages crowded with rascally folk who jeer and whistle and show no respect whatever for the gentle ladies and noble lords under the canopy. These retire in haste, leaving the Herr Superintendent up on his platform as the one remaining object of scorn and derision, but Eitzen, moved by Christian love, stays on to bless even this rabble. Just then, however, he discerns Margriet seated high on a sutler's cart, on top of a pile of pots and pans and other cheap ware, and shamelessly swinging her legs.

At this, neither his divine duty nor his clerical garb can hold him back. A quick glance assures him that all of the officials and courtiers have fled, who might have found his behavior rather strange; then he lifts his gown, jumps down onto the badly crushed grass, and rushes after the cart and, having caught up with it, tries to grab hold of the horse's bridle, crying, "Ah, Margriet! Do stop this cart, dearest Margriet, and stay! I shall be yours forever, Margriet!"

But she only laughs at him, and as a large crowd is gathering about, she says, "I do not know this scoundrel, but his intentions are clear enough. 'Tis truly a sad time when even the parson is in rut like a lecherous buck and trying to jump innocent women, and in broad daylight at that."

And Eitzen would surely have received a sound thrashing, had not the train with all its sutlers and pedlars moved on, leaving him behind, a sadder and, hopefully, wiser man.

CHAPTER TWENTY-TWO

§

In which Professor Beifuss makes certain concessions,
while Professor Leuchtentrager furnishes a Marx-
ist analysis of Ahasverus and by his remarks
about the influence of the celebrated
Doctor Luther on the development of
modern anti-Semitism becomes
persona non grata

§

Prof. Jochanaan Leuchtentrager
Hebrew University
Jerusalem
Israel

9 June 1980

Dear Professor Leuchtentrager,
    I am indebted to you for your kindness in letting me
have a photocopy of a letter of 14th October 1556 to Superintendent von Eitzen which was found among other
materials suddenly rediscovered in the North-Elbian
Church Library in Hamburg and which, as you say,
should be viewed in context with a disputation with the
Jews allegedly held at that time in Altona: a letter you
claim to have been written by the Wandering Jew in
person.
    I do not want to doubt the authenticity of the letter; but
I have my reservations as to its true author. As soon as
I had your photocopy in my possession I circulated it
among the members of my collective, with a request for

their opinion, and everybody at the Institute is agreed that the document in your hands is a mystification, but one fabricated about the time of the date given on it. I am sure, dear Colleague, that you will forgive us if, as Marxists, we hold to our view that there are no such things as miracles and that, for this reason, there can be no such person as a Jew who wanders on earth forever. From this it follows that letters authored by him and written in his hand cannot exist either. Since, however, for reasons of your own you refuse to accept Paul Johansen's proposition that the man Ahasverus who appeared in Hamburg around the middle of the sixteenth century is identical with the prophet Jörg from Meissen (see Vol. XVI of the *Journal for Hamburgian History*), you must provide another answer to the question of the real identity of the "poor little Jew," as he calls himself, who signed his letter with the name "Ahasverus" and who, under this very name, became acquainted with Paul von Eitzen and in Eitzen's disputation with the Jews was to serve as his witness.

A clarification of this question and, following this, some research into the later fate of the "poor little Jew" would be a task interesting both to the criminal investigator and the historian; I am afraid, though, that time has obliterated all essential clues and evidence. That he must have been a very clever swindler becomes obvious if you consider that a man as prominent and enlightened as Eitzen, by the standards of his time, fell for him; and our Ahasverus, pretending to be the Wandering Jew, must have profited quite a bit from his swindle—which is not to be interpreted in any way, dear Professor Leuchtentrager, as a slur against your friend, the shoe dealer of the same name.

History, as you know, furnishes us many examples of small-time crooks masquerading as personalities of the past that were still alive in the minds of people. How many false Neros have there been, how many false Demetriuses, and even the famed Hauptmann of Köpenick, *nota bene* a shoemaker like Ahasverus, must be counted among them as the image of the Prussian officer was such an inspiration to the good burghers. No wonder that also the apostle John, of whom, as you may recall, it is written in the New Testament (see John 21: 20–23) that he would not die but tarry till Christ came back, has found his impersonators, one as late as the sixteenth century when he was burned alive at Toulouse.

As I took occasion to indicate in the section "On the Everlasting (or Wandering) Jew" of my book *The Best-known Judeo-Christian Myths as Seen in the Light of Science and History*, the idea suggests itself that this John, whom the gospels describe as the disciple most loved by Jesus, might be regarded as one of the prototypes of the Ahasverus we deal with. This brings me to my main point, a point I may have somewhat neglected in my above-mentioned book but which, after due reflection and a thorough discussion with my fellow workers, I should now like to stress to you: Ahasverus is not a historical personage turned folk tale as was, for instance, Emperor Friedrich Barbarossa of the house of Hohenstaufen, nor is Ahasverus a contemporary of both Pontius Pilate and Professor Jochanaan Leuchtentrager; rather, he should be viewed as a symbolic or allegorical figure, and a very typical one.

Just as Siegfried, the ever youthful hero who fell victim to a most cowardly plot, stands for the Germans, so does Ahasverus symbolize the homeless and hounded Jew who must wander from country to country and is welcomed nowhere and persecuted everywhere. Ahasverus is the personification of his people's fate. The elements of the parable can be traced even into the details of Jewish existence. Thus in his *L'Ebreo errante in Italia* (Florence, 1891), a book surely familiar to you, S. Morpurgo quotes a report of one Antonio di Francesco di Andrea from San Lorenzo who allegedly encountered the Wandering Jew in the year 1411: "He may stay only three days in one province and soon disappears, visibly or invisibly; he wears a hooded garment and girds himself with a piece of rope, and he walks barefooted; and yet, even though he has neither purse nor pouch on him, he spends money liberally. Having arrived at an inn, he eats and drinks his fill, after which he opens his hand and throws to the host whatever is due him, and never has anyone seen whence his money comes, and never has he a farthing left over. . . ." This description agrees with one given in a Flemish version of the Ahasverus story, published anonymously about the middle of the seventeenth century, no date or place of publication mentioned and purporting to be a translation from the German; more probably it reached Flanders via France. In this little book it says: "His entire treasure consists of five Rhenish pennies which renew themselves in his pocket as soon as he has spent them." In several editions of the *Short Description and Tale of a Jew by the Name of Ahasverus*, whose first known version was printed 1602 allegedly "at Leyden by Christoph Creutzer" but which, strangely enough, carries at the end of its text the dateline, "Sleswick, June ninth, 1564," it is also reported that the Jew, upon arriving in a town, looks mostly poor and his clothes are ragged, but soon after people notice that he is solidly and sometimes even fashionably clad.

This observation on the part of the booklet's author or authors, of course, is but a reflection of the fact that the Jewish traders, unlike the Christian merchants, usually do not travel with cash money in their belts; rather, they have with them a sort of letter of credit, you might even call it a credit card, by means of which they escape losses through highway robbery and theft; the Jew carries in his pocket a payment order from his fellow religionist A. in the city of X. to his fellow religionist B. in the city of Y., and on arrival in Y. can immediately dispose of monies which, to the uninitiated *goyim*, can only have come to him from some supernatural source.

In conclusion, may I restate the view of the collective at my Institute: we acknowledge Ahasverus as a symbol, as a figure symbolizing Judaism and Jewry. And despite your differing opinion, dear Professor Leuchtentrager, and despite your attempts to persuade us to the contrary through your marginal, if not entirely absurd materials, we must deem everything else, and please pardon the expression, ridiculous and unreasonable.

I remain, as always, with kind wishes,

Yours sincerely,

(Prof. Dr. Dr. h.c.) Siegfried Beifuss

Institute for Scientific Atheism

Berlin, Capital of the GDR

Prof. Dr. Dr.h.c. Siegfried Beifuss

Institute for Scientific Atheism

Behrenstrasse 39 a

108 Berlin

German Democratic Republic

3 July 1980

Dear Friend and Colleague Beifuss,

I have read your letter of the 9th of June with great pleasure and considerable interest, and I have given its contents much thought. In particular, I was struck by your statement, which you say was also made in the name of your fellow workers at your Institute, that you now see Ahasverus as a symbolic figure, and a most typical one at that. You state this after you previously declared that "he may have really existed, though only for the length of an ordinary lifetime and not forever," and after you described him in yet another letter as "a factor whose component parts have not been sufficiently explored as yet."

Taking your various ideas on the matter in context, I can only conclude that you and the members of your Institute, even though by fits and starts, are coming ever closer to admitting the central point of the issue, namely the *de facto* existence of the Wandering Jew, and I am wondering whether I should not try to persuade my friend to take a trip to East Berlin so you may meet him and, if you wish, put some questions to him which eventually might clear up the not yet sufficiently explored components of this really existing symbolical figure and enable you to understand them. I say, try to persuade, because it would take a

• *221* •

lot of persuading; you must not assume, please, that after his not always pleasant experiences in Germany Mr. Ahasverus would lightly undertake a journey to that country.

But let us return to your new insight, even though I don't much like your placing Ahasverus in the same category as that youthful hero Siegfried who enjoyed such a great reputation especially in the Nazi period. Of course, Ahasverus may also be considered as a symbol; since he is a Jew and always was a Jew, his fate necessarily is that of a Jew and his attitudes and his way of looking at the world are Jewish, his dissatisfaction with existing conditions, his efforts to change these. Although this is not an exclusively Jewish characteristic, he is unrest personified; any fixed order exists for him only to be put in question and, depending on the case, to be overthrown.

As for my person, my attitudes in this regard differ greatly from his; therefore you and your collective as well as the authorities of your Republic, who will probably have to act with special care in granting or denying entry visas to citizens of Israel, may rest at ease. To me, order is a most desirable state; the more orderly the manner in which the affairs of a country are run, the more I like it. God Himself, whom you refuse to recognize, created simultaneously with this world the laws by which He wanted it to move, and ever since everything proceeds by these laws, punctually and exactly as planned, thanks be to God. To my friend Ahasverus this God-given orderliness is a source of constant frustration, but I always console him by bringing to his attention the same point which you, as an expert in dialectical thinking, would also make: namely, that any thesis carries within itself its antithesis and that you just have to have sufficient patience to wait till things change in their own, God-given time; but that's precisely it, as a figure truly symbolic of his people, he is torn and driven by this Jewish impatience.

I suspect, however, that your theory of Ahasverus being a mere symbolical figure is not so foolproof either.

As I mentioned in my modest article on the subject of Ahasverus, published in the journal *Hebrew Historical Studies*, and as you explained much more extensively in the section "On the Everlasting (or Wandering) Jew" in your most laudable book *The Best-known Judeo-Christian Myths as Seen in the Light of Science and History*, the legend of Ahasverus orginated out of a number of stories very much varying from one another but having one element in common, namely the condemnation to everlasting life on earth, and to eternal wandering and suffering in this vale of tears, until the final return of Jesus Christ. You yourself made mention in your letter of John, the disciple most loved by Jesus, of whom Reb Joshua, in his frequently ambiguous way of expressing himself, is alleged to have said to the apostle Peter (John 21:22-23), "If I will that he tarry till I come, what is that to you?" These words furnish the germ of the idea that one of the contemporaries of the crucified Reb Joshua might be staying around on earth even now and might have to stay around for some time yet, up to the Rabbi's final return.

Now both the disciple John and the shoemaker Ahasverus were undoubtedly Jews; but it is at least questionable whether those others who were said to have mistreated Jesus or to have pushed and driven him on his way to Golgotha, and who were therefore damned, were also Jews. Could Malchus, or Marcus as he was also called, have been a Jew, that police agent whose ear Peter smote off in the garden of Gethsemane and who, after Jesus let it grow back on him, repaid the favor by hitting him in the face with his mailed fist while the high priest Caiaphas was questioning him? Before the founding of the modern state of Israel a Jewish police force existed only in the Warsaw ghetto, where the Nazis organized it; Jewish tradition has always been to have the nasty and dirty work of the police done by gentiles, just as King Solomon had for it his Cherethites and Pelethites, his Cretans and Palestinians. Or was Cartaphilus a Jew, in Greek καρτα φιλος, the Very Much Loved One, who served as a doorkeeper in Pilate's house and, in this capacity, treated Jesus so harshly? Improbable that so important an official of the Roman governor in Judea should have been Jewish; as his name indicates, he was most likely Greek and therefore a heathen; he is said to have been converted later on by the same Ananias who baptized the apostle Paul, and to have changed his name to Joseph. Or that unknown man who in later centuries, in Italy, would be called Giovanni Bottadio or Buttadeus, in German *Gottschläger*, the One Who Hit God, was he a Jew? An Austrian baron, von Tornowitz, reports that in the year 1643, in Jerusalem, the above mentioned Malchus was shown to him by the Turks in return for a considerable baksheesh, "inside a large hidden room underground wherein the prisoner, clad in his ancient Roman garb, was pacing the tiled floor, his hand beating at times against the wall, at times against his own chest as a sign that this was the hand which slapped the holy face of innocent Christ." About Cartaphilus, later Joseph, the monk Roger de Wendover writes in his book *Flores Historiarum*, which tells the events from creation up to the year 1235, that in anno 1228 an Armenian archbishop arrived at the monastery of St. Albans in England and, queried on the person of this Joseph/Cartaphilus, declared that shortly before his departure he had him for dinner at his own table, back in Armenia. Cartaphilus, he told his English listeners, was living among the bishops and prelates of his and other Oriental countries, a man of most saintly behavior and equally saintly speech, who on occasion would report on certain details of the crucifixion and the resurrection following it, whereby he would never hide his own most lamentable part in the events. Hans Gottschläger or Giovanni Bottadio, however, is said to have been seen in 1267 in the Italian town of Forlì, during a pilgrimage to St. Jacob, the witness being the astrologer Guido Bonatti of the same town, a man quite prominent in his time, for Dante writes of him in Canto XX of his *Inferno*, in connection with the magician Michael Scotus.

But a literature on Ahasverus personally, as you, dear

Professor Beifuss, well know, appears only after the Reformation, i.e., about the middle of the sixteenth century; and it might be advisable to give some special thought to the fact that its main prop and supplier of evidence is as zealous a Protestant as the superintendent of Hamburg, and later of Sleswick, Paul von Eitzen. (The trial records of Ahasverus and other advisers of Emperor Julian Apostata, which I studied in the archives of the Sublime Porte, need not be considered in this context, just as manuscript 9QRes needn't, for neither could have had any influence on the rise of an Ahasverus legend: one because it was locked away for centuries; the other, because it was discovered only recently.) In 1602, the first *Volksbuch* on Ahasverus appears in print, to be followed in rapid succession by a growing number of other editions which differ greatly as to detail and, in translation, are beginning to flood all of Northern Europe. Why? Why does this Ahasverus, now a figure separate from the apostle John, the police agent Malchus, the doorkeeper Cartaphilus, the God-beater Bottadio, why does he emerge only after Luther, and then, promptly, with pointed allusions to his financial conduct? Was he, perhaps, an expression of the mood of his time? Had he become topical, perhaps, just because he was a Jew, the forever-wandering Jew? And could it be that he became a prominent topic of the time because the role of the Jews in the economic structure of the Protestant territory of Europe was undergoing a change—a question which, dear Professor Beifuss, should be of particular interest to you as a man of decided Marxist views.

Of course, in the centuries preceding Luther we also find a certain interest in any surviving witnesses of the passion of Reb Joshua alias Jesus Christ; the Church did believe that their testimony might be of some use against skeptics and heretics, and naturally against the Jews. But this interest was a limited one, and such witnesses were rarely, if ever, called upon since it was feared that they might go too far and, in their religious zeal, might show up the contrast between the practices of the clergy and the thoughts of the man who was crucified. And none of these alleged witnesses, whatever their names, ever grew into a figure of any symbolic value, and certainly not into one symbolizing the Jews.

This happened only to Ahasverus, could happen only to him, and only after Luther, because in the territories ruled over by the Protestants the Reformation did away with the financial monopoly of the Catholic Church and its big banking houses, that of the Fugger family and that of the Welsers. The Church had long ago begun to ignore Deuteronomy 23:20, in which the law against usury, that is the lending of money against interest, is proclaimed; this is why Luther, by inveighing against the trade in indulgences the proceeds of which were transferred to Rome by the Fuggers and Welsers, shook the foundations of the mercantile structures of his time, and the faithful Protestants, in returning to Biblical law, were suddenly caught without banks and bankers. But as you well know, dear Colleague, Deuteronomy 23:20 forbids merely the taking of interest from your brother; a stranger, however, may be bilked without your troubling your soul over it, and this fine difference, which Mosaic law makes, predestined for the money-lending business the only people who consider as strangers the majority of the population of the country in which they live, namely the Jews, and as the Jews were anyhow deprived, by gentile law, of the right to other possessions and professions, they went into this business. It was Luther himself who procured the trade of both prince and peasant for the Jews, only to condemn them all the more noisily for it and to unleash a pogromist campaign against them from which all later anti-Semites, including the Nazis, drew a good part of their slogans. Until the time of the Reformation, the main components of anti-Semitism had been religious, for wasn't it the Jews who had Jesus crucified and hadn't they refused, up to this day, to acknowledge him as their messiah? But now this anti-Semitism acquired a clearly economic foundation and, along with it, a symbolic figure whom it was easy to hate and who, moreover, gave substance to your ancient fears of the alien element, the transients, the Jews: in other words, Ahasverus.

I am perfectly aware, dear Professor Beifuss, that through my analysis the same sort of difficulties which you had with the person of Ahasverus will now accrue to you over his symbolic figure. But you were the one who introduced the subject into the debate, and I therefore had to deal with the matter.

With warmest personal regards,

Yours,
Jochanaan Leuchtentrager
Hebrew University
Jerusalem

Prof. Dr. Dr.h.c. Siegfried Beifuss
Institute for Scientific Atheism
Behrenstr. 39 a
108 Berlin

8 July 1980

Dear Comrade Beifuss,

After further study and review of your correspondence with Prof. Leuchtentrager of the Hebrew University in Jerusalem we must inform you that you are being drawn by him into increasingly involved extraneous arguments. Although in your letters to him you keep on stressing our scientifically founded and well-proven viewpoints, you constantly let him snare you into making ideological concessions which later on, after he has enticed you into yet another trap, you have the greatest trouble retracting. And what's even more important: instead of discovering what plans in the field of ideological diversion the Israeli imperialists are trying to promote by means of the Ahasverus discussion, you have permitted Professor Leuchtentrager to entangle you in nebulous questions on detail which lead to nothing and will force you, if you continue in this manner, into a position contrary to the policies of state and party.

This refers especially to the Luther discussion into which your "dear Colleague" would like to inveigle you. In view of the approaching Luther year of 1983 which, as you very well know, is being sponsored by the highest representatives of our state and party, such a discussion is by no means in our interest. If Herr Jochanaan Leuchtentrager is reminding you today of Luther's anti-Semitic speeches and writings, he will tomorrow quote to you what Luther, during the peasant war, said against the "thieving, murderous gangs of peasants" that ought to be "smashed, choked, and stabbed to death just as you kill mad dogs," and he would thereby place into a most awkward position not only your own person but everybody else who is trying to make a resounding success of our planned Luther celebrations.

It is therefore recommended that you discreetly indicate to Prof. Leuchtentrager that a visit of his to the GDR, especially if it were to be in the company of Mr. Ahasverus, is not desirable. After you have informed him of this, your correspondence with him is to cease.

The organs concerned have been so notified.

With socialist greetings,

> Würzner
> Chief of Department
> Ministry of
> Higher Education

CHAPTER TWENTY-THREE

§

*Wherein we are shown how Superintendent von
Eitzen defends the true faith against
all hostile thought and deviations,
and Margriet proves to be but a
devilish delusion*

§

Our years are brief, and they pass quickly even in the
Duchy of Sleswick, and along with a man's *autoritas* comes
his *reputatio*, God willing, or, in plain language, the higher
you climb the greater your glory, and from all over Germany, from the Landgrave of Hesse and the university at
Tübingen, from the Hamburg senate and the Elector of
Saxony, Superintendent Paulus von Eitzen is being called
upon for his opinion in matters ecclesiastical, and he is well
on the way to becoming the country's major judge and
arbiter on questions like the right interpretation of the
words of Christ or the proper meaning of sections of the
Confessio Augustana or what may be heresy and what not;
his letters go out to all the principalities of the realm and
are received like those of the sainted apostles of yore; and
more than once, in cases of emergency and with the blessings of his sovereign, Duke Adolph, he has journeyed to
faraway places, to the ancient city of Naumburg, for instance, to act in the capacity of a spiritual militant and advocate of the one and only true faith as it was defined and
expounded by our Doctor Martinus Luther; but just in the
area where the ground should be the most solid and the

pillars of the kingdom of God erected on stable foundations, namely in his own diocese, the soil is as wobbly as
ever and the framework of the edifice creaks and squeaks,
you just need to open your ears and you will hear the
whisperings of the dissenters and of the doubters of
the doctrine of the holy communion; and the worst of the
matter is that envious men are bringing these troubles and
vexations to the attention of Duke Adolph who, having
returned somewhat less than a victor from his campaign to
the Netherlands, wishes to make up for his lack of military
laurels by winning such in the religious field, and his superintendent is to drill his clerical troops to march properly in step and wheel about to the right and the left and
make their about-faces to the satisfaction of His Grace.

Privy Councillor Leuchtentrager, as always, knows
where the shoe pinches, and seeks a talk with Eitzen on the
subject and says, "The great Aristotle, a Greek heathen
from whom, however, good Christians might learn quite
a bit, has taught that true salvation cannot accrue to a man
through his heart, for his heart is but weak and frequently
succumbs to temptation, but only through the law; therefore everything which is to endure and keep its validity
must be codified and man be bound to the code, if necessary by bonds of iron."

"Ah," sighs the good superintendent, "unfortunately,
and much to the chagrin of all of us, people honor the laws
of God more by breaking than by obeying them, and God
Himself fails to punish them in sufficient measure and with
sufficient promptness, as He ought to, but is patient and
long-suffering and lets them carry on in their ways so they
conclude that their misdeeds are quite in order since the
One on high does not strike them with thunder and lightning, and the ecclesiastical authorities are off in the distance and often kept in the dark."

"The reason for this sad state of affairs," replies his
friend Leuchtentrager, "is that you see but with your two
eyes and hear but with your two ears; but that is not
enough. You should have available two hundred eyes, or

two thousand, to watch, and equally many ears to listen; this would quickly improve the situation; to what end do you have your numerous parsons and preachers: just so they might have a good time?"

"What you have in mind, Hans," says Eitzen, "will hardly be feasible, for my parsons and preachers are a lukewarm lot and tend to let things ride, and how am I going to light a good fire under their butts?"

"You must take them under discipline," answers his friend, tenderly stroking the head of little Margarethe who, with her little clubfoot and her little hump on her little back, has come in to set a glass of wine before the guest, wine from the duke's cellar, for the Church usually receives its share of the good things of the world. "Discipline by their own oath and signature," the privy councillor continues, "just like the soldier who also swears an oath to the flag and ever after is bound to obey his chief and commander."

Eitzen feels as though a divine light had struck his eyes; once his parsons and preachers have sworn a holy oath to the doctrine and given their sacred promise to keep their flock to its principles, none of the congregation will dare deviate from the right path for fear of being denounced to the worldly authorities, and the kingdom of God in Sleswick will come about speedily, much to the satisfaction of His Grace the Duke and to the joy of God. And once again he is moved to admire the great insight of his friend Hans into the minds of people in general and of the clergy in particular, for having sworn the oath, no minister in the duchy would ever again have to be told to hold to his duties; he would know quite by himself that he would lose his prebends and privileges if he were negligent or kicked over the traces.

Soon after, his friend having claimed other business and taken leave of Frau Barbara and, with a gentle slap on her little behind, of little Margarethe, Eitzen sits down at his desk and sharpens his pen; and on this very evening he puts on paper what everyone who, in the Duchy of Sles wick, wishes to tend to the lambs of God must believe in and solemnly swear to: in the first place the holy Biblical Scriptures and the holy apostolic creed and the other true *symbola* and articles, further the indivisible union of divine and human nature in the person of Christ, and the *Confessio Augustana* or Augsburgian Confession, and the two catechisms of Luther. Also the candidate will have to put his name not only to the bottom of the document, but must sign each paragraph singly and separately so that, at no time in the future, might he be able to excuse himself by saying he had overlooked one or the other item.

However, as Eitzen once again checks through his list, he has a sense of having failed to inject enough of the proper zeal and spirit into his draft, and that it needs stronger strictures against all heretical beliefs, and that it might be well to name names and openly speak of the sacraments of baptism and the holy communion, for does not the whole edifice of the holy Church as well as the power of its servants rest on the supposition that only the members of the clergy, by virtue of their ordainment, can cleanse the little babes of their original sin and perform the transubstantiation of bread and wine into substances of divine nature. Otherwise any heretic could rise up and any layman whom no one ever consecrated or ordained, and they each could open up their own church!

Wherefore he writes down, *But while in our times devious Satan has caused many horrible and vicious errors to enter the hearts of people concerning the most important articles of our Christian faith and religion, I (by the name of so-and-so) do hereby solemnly swear that with true zeal and fervor I shall cast out and condemn the false doctrines of all those who deviate from the truth of the above-named holy scriptures,* symbola, confessiones *and* catechismi, *and especially the wicked teachings of the followers of Zwingli, and of the Calvinists, Sacramentarians, and Anabaptists who deny the necessity and power of holy baptism and the presence of Christ while his true and real body and blood are given out and received during holy commun-*

ion, and who thus are destroying the holy unity of the faith and confusing the beliefs of the simple people.

This, he thinks joyfully, is the language which his revered teacher, the good Doctor Luther, had been using with so great an effect and which is like a whip of the lash to the lukewarm hearts of his present and future *pastores* and might well put the fear of God into them; wherefore he makes them swear in addition that they would faithfully warn their congregations of those heretical errors and would never suffer even one of their flock to attach themselves to such blasphemous sects and societies.

But as he reexamines all these thoughts, having diligently listed them and written them out, he suddenly grows conscious of the power this oath will give him as the sole judge who determines which among his *confratres* is to be counted among the just and which among the wicked; and in order to establish this power even more firmly he decides to insert into the document a brief reference to worldly authority being the staff and support of the ecclesiastical shepherd, and since there isn't much space left on the sheet, he writes in a smaller-size script, *And lastly I swear that I will loyally obey the Christian ordinances and mandates issued by His Highness Duke Adolph, our gracious lord, and shall conduct myself, excepting the Holy Scriptures and the Augsburgian Confession, solely by the canonic laws of the principalities of Sleswick and Holstein.* And as though it were a footnote scribbled on the bottom margin of the sheet, *All this I* (by the name of so-and-so) *do swear without reservation or malice, in all good conscience, so help me God. Amen.*

The duke, whose exalted person was informed by Privy Councillor Leuchtentrager of the new preacher's oath, is highly pleased with it and commands that it be promulgated without delay in the Duchy of Sleswick and such other territories as he is the sovereign of; and Leuchtentrager, smiling faintly, informs his good friend Paul that from now on the establishment of the kingdom of God in Sleswick, under the benevolent dictatorship of its superintendent, would no longer be obstructed by anyone. And indeed, within the briefest space of time, it becomes apparent that without exception all *pastores* and those aspiring to such office are eagerly swearing the new oath and promptly filling out and returning the official formularies, signed and sealed, to their superintendent so that their honest faith and loyalty might be duly registered by him. But this is by no means the entire effect of the undertaking: a mighty competition evolves among the clergy as to which of them will bring the largest number of lost sheep back to the fold and which report most eagerly to the authorities the names and whereabouts of those who remain obstinate and continue to adhere to heretical doctrines, so the government may proceed with the full severity of the law against such scoundrels. The county of Eiderstedt, where a number of Dutch have settled claiming persecution at home by the Papists, has been turned into an especially happy hunting ground because, just as the cattle in the barn are scared by foxes and wolves come from afar, a country's loyal subjects are stirred up and made restless by strangers from outside the borders; and therefore the talk of people is being listened to in the inns and marketplaces of Eiderstedt county, and even inside their own homes people are not safe from watchers who are trying to find out if they are having suspicious thoughts or own one or the other of those little books written by David Joris or Menno Simons or suchlike Anabaptist heretics and false preachers, or are meeting with their ilk in secret conventicles, and the parsons are taking copious notes and writing long reports as to who has had his children duly baptized and who has not, and how often a man has gone to church and diligently listened to the sermon, and whether he has regularly partaken in the body of Christ. And fear spreads among the people, for it isn't all that long ago and within the memory of many a man alive that the Anabaptists were taken and burned to powder and ashes for being heretics, and some of them were tied to stakes and roasted alive, or their flesh torn with red-hot tongs, while others again were strangled and hacked to pieces, or hung from trees, or stuck into deep holes together with rats and other stinking vermin and left to rot.

Where there is sufficient zeal on one side, and fear on the other, success is certain. Like hares in autumn, the Mennonites and Davidjorites in Sleswick are being driven from their hiding places; pastors and parsons are reporting one here and another one there, and the most militant among the clergy, Pastor Mumsen at Oldenswort and his *confrater* Moller at Tönning, have each bagged more than a half-dozen of them who refuse to admit that the devil is concealing himself even in newborn babes and that these, therefore, should quickly be baptized. By dint of persuasion and the threat of eternal damnation, both Moller and Mumsen write to their superior, they had succeeded in leading at least some of the sinners back to the true faith, but the rest were insisting on their devilish heresies, and one stronger than they, namely the superintendent himself, was needed to enter the case and deal with the hardened miscreants.

This, Eitzen immediately recognizes, is a sign from heaven. He will make the world sit up and listen as he holds an ecclesiastical court, albeit with the power of the worldly authorities to back him, and this undertaking will have a better result than that unfortunate disputation with the Jews of Altona if only for the fact that no Ahasverus will be present to trip him up. Also it will be a godly work no matter whether the heretics recant or not, and it will set a clear and unmistakable signal in the duchy and beyond its borders that here in Sleswick is a man, namely Superintendent Paulus von Eitzen, who guards Luther's word against all deviations and calumniations.

His friend, the duke's privy councillor Johannes Leuchtentrager, scratches his little hump and smiles his usual crooked smile as he hears Eitzen expounding his plan, and says it would be a capital trick, this trial including indictment and hearing and sentencing of the accused, and would contribute greatly toward law and order which are the foundation of any commonwealth, and that he himself would have a word in this regard with the Eminent and Right Honorable Caspar Hoyer, the duke's holder of the stirrup and prefect of Eiderstedt, so that Hoyer might prepare everything for the trial to be held in the town of Tönning where, by the way, excellent fresh shrimp might be had with a goodly beer to go with them.

There's a fine though somewhat bumpy road from Sleswick to the town of Tönning, and it's springtime and the sun is bright and the sky blue, and notwithstanding his guts being shaken up inside his stomach, Eitzen in his coach feels the contentment of a person assured that both faith and the police are on his side. Moreover, the duke's holder of the stirrup and prefect of Eiderstedt, the Eminent and Right Honorable Caspar Hoyer, who has been waiting to meet him in the courtyard of the neat little castle of Tönning, turns out to be a most friendly and civil person; and though nothing could concern him less than the true doctrine on baptism and the other holy sacraments, he is sufficiently aware of his sovereign lord's, the duke's, believing that the happiness of the people and the welfare of the state depend on such abstruse matters; and as he, Caspar Hoyer, wishes to go on consuming his eel and his roast pork in peace, along with a glass of decent wine or maybe a tankard of local beer, he has caused Claus Peter Cotes and Claus Schipper and Dirich Peters and Sivert Peters, as well as Vop Cornelius and Marten Peters and Cornelius Sivers, most of them from Oldenswort and the others from Tetenbüll or Garding, to be held in the tower at Tönning and, careful man that he is, at the same time has had their cattle and other movable possessions confiscated so that, in case of their being found guilty, His Grace the Duke would find some assets to put his hand on.

All this and more—namely, that he, the duke's prefect and holder of the stirrup, will personally preside over the trial—Eitzen learns from the Eminent and Right Honorable Caspar Hoyer while the two of them are walking down to the port, a couple of gentlemen of mature years and very much in harmony with themselves and the world, and watching the fishermen landing their catch, nice fat fish of all kinds and a mass of mussels and shrimp which, when peeled and served with a piquant sauce, are a joy to the palate.

Eitzen's pleasant humor lasts him even unto the next morning when he betakes himself to the prefecture where the court is to convene; his sleep during the night was deep and relaxing, partly because of the wine and the strong spirits which the Right Honorable Caspar Hoyer dished up the preceding evening, to a larger extent, however, because of his good and calm conscience. Verily, he does not hate these Cotes and Schipper and Peters and whatever their names; he merely wants to lead them back to the ways of righteousness provided they will listen to reason, and he looks at them with both a loving and a troubled eye as a good shepherd does who sees his sheep straying close to a dangerous pit. This is his thought as he watches them being lined up in two rows, guarded by the armed constables of the holder of the stirrup, and observes to the right and left of them, comfortably reclining in their chairs, pastors Mumsen and Moller and others of the cloth who have come to learn from their superintendent how to deal with heretics. The accused appear considerably less at ease than these clergy; the darkness inside the tower has bleached their faces, and they seem to be freezing and frequently scratch their wrists where the tightly bound ropes have inflamed the skin.

The Right Honorable Prefect and Holder of the Stirrup, seated on his judge's chair, leans over to Eitzen who, acting as prosecutor, sits at a somewhat lesser elevation to his left, and whispers to him to keep the questioning on these religious matters brief as Madame Holder of the Stirrup is preparing a right noble repast for noontime, namely as an opener some smoked salmon so tender it would melt on your tongue, to be followed by roast stuffed duck with cabbage done in bacon. Whereupon, in a loud voice, he advises the clerk of the court to call out the names of the accused and check if all of them were present and properly accounted for, and then proceed to read the indictment. Eitzen's hand in the drafting of this indictment is reflected in its wording which abounds in pious expressions charging the accused not only with having failed to live up to the true and rightful teachings of the Augsburgian Confession, but also with belonging to the wicked sect of the Anabaptists and refusing to desist from their false beliefs even though ceaselessly admonished by their ministers, in kindly and benevolent ways as well as in all Christian seriousness; they, however, persisted in their errors and spurned the holy Christian sacrament of baptism.

The clerk having finished with his reading, the duke's holder of the stirrup inquires if any one of the accused, or maybe several, had something to say on the indictment or even wanted to repent; if so, they had better do it now, before the hearing. At this Claus Peter Cotes, apparently some kind of leader among them, raises his hand and declares that the accused were all of them simple people, peasants and craftsmen, and one of them a carpet weaver; for which reason, although they knew the word of the Bible tolerably well, they had no experience in arguing and disputing with learned doctors and it seemed better to them to have one of their own preachers as spokesman for them when it came to a difference of opinion on the meaning or significance of the Last Supper or the question of original sin; wherefore they had written to their Mennonite brothers in the Netherlands to send such a person here so he might serve as their advocate in spiritual matters, and they had been promised that one would be forthcoming to aid them; the learned man was to have arrived yesterday, at latest by today, and on these grounds they requested a postponement of the hearing, namely until the arrival of their attorney.

"What!" calls Eitzen, sputtering with rage, for he fears that things might turn out as they did that time in Altona. "Aren't the sinful heretic thoughts of the accused sufficient unto this court by which they deny to the consecrated and ordained servants of church and government the very rights that form the framework of the holy edifice? Should they be permitted, on top of all this, to import into this duchy one of their chief and super-heretics so there would be no end to our troubles and tribulations? Or to introduce him, yet, into this court to serve as an *expertus legis divinae*? We in this principality have enough experience in matters divine so as not to need any foreigners to teach us, and certainly not a person from the Netherlands where every kind of damned heresy flourishes."

But the Eminent and Right Honorable Caspar Hoyer places his finger to his ample chin, and after due deliberation, decides that you cannot deny the accused the right to call their own witnesses; but where such witnesses professed to adhere to the same heretical views as the accused, they would have to face the same severe treatment on the part of the court as did the accused themselves; furthermore, date and hour of the trial had been set long ago and simply could not be postponed until somewhere between the city of Amsterdam and the town of Tönning a couple of limping horses were shod or a broken axle mended. "And now, honored Doctor and Superintendent," he concludes, "would you kindly proceed, directing your questions to the accused so by their answers they may show whether they wish to stick to their false beliefs or would not rather turn to the teachings of Luther as set down in the *Confessio Augustana*, and to the canonic laws of the duchies of Sleswick and Holstein."

Entrusting himself to God whose power can lame horses and split the axles of carriages in which heretical Dutch preachers are traveling, Eitzen opens the hearing, his plan being to move from general to ever more specific questions so that every last one of these wicked sectarians will end up by wriggling on the sharp hooks of Lutheran dialectics. The accused, however, prove themselves stubborn, replying to his well-reasoned words in a most arrogant manner or not at all, and several go so far as to declare openly that no one will turn them away from their beliefs, not even the learned superintendent, much as he may try to impress them.

That kind of obstinacy, Eitzen notices, arouses the anger of the Eminent and Right Honorable Holder of the Stirrup, against the accused first of all, but also against him who seems to be tolerating such impudence. He therefore determines no longer to dispute with the accused or attempt to persuade them; his preachers and pastors have had to bow to his dictates and so will this band of heretics; and he has demonstrated enough Christian kindness, God is his witness, in that he quoted chapter and verse to these ingrates and showed them the essence of our Lord Christ, thus pointing the way for them to the wellsprings of faith; now they will have to drink or be drowned. They will have to profess and say Yes and Amen to the baptism of little children and the doctrine of holy communion, as others have done before them, or bear the consequences, the least of which will be expulsion from the duchy. So he straightens, creases his forehead, and inquires from the accused, *ad primum*, whether all men, excepting Christ, were conceived and born in sin and therefore were children of wrath, yes or no?

Cotes senses that now the battle has been joined in earnest and that the skinny fellow there in his black habit has hooked his claws into them and won't let go of them anymore. So he says, "It is inconceivable to us that, beginning with Adam, all men should have been full of sin, and therefore we cannot possibly confess to having been conceived in sin, either. Little babes have no sin in them which might do harm to their immortal souls. Nor can we agree with you that the cause of sickness and death should be our sins; both are in man's nature, and man was placed into nature like Adam before his fall."

"Damnable heresy!" states Eitzen and waits for the clerk to put his exact words on paper. Then, for the benefit of the Holder of the Stirrup and so that the Right Honorable Caspar Hoyer, being a layman, might properly understand the matter in question, he inquires, *ad secundum*, whether the accused would not concede, at a minimum, that newborn babes should be baptized and that baptism was useful and necessary to them, yes or no?

"'Tis written," says Cotes, "that our life should be directed by our faith. *Item*, only he will reach the state of blessedness who is able to have faith and has had himself baptized for the sake of his faith and on his own volition. But little babes, knowing neither good nor evil, cannot have themselves baptized."

"Reprehensible sacramentarianism!" Eitzen dictates to the clerk and thereupon wants to hear from the accused, *ad tertium*, whether Christ, through the great sufferings he bore for our sake and through his self-sacrifice, took upon himself the debt we owe for our sins, so that we were absolved and thus can reach the state of blessedness solely through our belief in him, yes or no?

"If we load everything on the shoulders of Jesus," says Cotes, "we open the way toward sin. We must also do our own share to reach blessedness, and man must seek God just as God seeks man."

"Contemptible blasphemy!" declares Eitzen, and as soon as the clerk has noted down this judgment, he turns back to the accused and demands to know from them, *ad quartum*, whether they hold that Jesus Christ, during holy communion, truly is nourishing us with his body and giving us his blood for drink, yes or no?

"Bread and wine," Cotes answers tiredly, "we take in memory of Christ, and they remain but bread and wine. Everything else is superstition and Papist nonsense."

"Devilish dissenterism!" Eitzen's voice has grown strident and now fails him altogether. Nevertheless he wants to substantiate to the Eminent and Right Honorable Caspar Hoyer where such horrible deviations from the one and only true doctrine will lead *in praxi*, for it is by no means clear and manifest at all times how one thing depends on another, to wit, an orderly government on the right faith. Thus, his pious zeal forcing his vocal cords to obey him once more, he hoarsely asks the accused whether to their mind, *ad quintum,* a true Christian might also exercise worldly rule and in good conscience might hold high office and in that position could reach the state of blessedness, and whether, *ad sextum,* true Christian people owed obedience to the government in all matters which, according to the word of God, were the government's, and whether, *ad septimum,* the kingdom of God, being of spiritual nature, could be held in any way or manner to be in contradistinction to the kingdoms of this world and their governments?

It is as though you could hear the beetles gnawing away at the thick old beams supporting the ceilings of the prefecture, and all eyes are fixed on Claus Peter Cotes and Claus Schipper and Dirich Peters and Sivert Peters, and on Vop Cornelius and Marten Peters and Cornelius Sivers; and their pale faces appear silvery through the sweat that has collected on these, for each one of them knows that of all questions this is the most difficult to answer, and the hardest test, and that at this very moment sentence is being spoken and the ax sharpened.

"Well?" says Eitzen. "Yes or no?"

No one seems to want to reply to him. But as he is about to gather his breath for his summing-up and great speech of condemnation which is to give Cotes and associates a little foretaste of what they might expect to be told on Judgment Day by their heavenly prosecutor, the door to the courtroom opens as though by itself and the Dutch preacher of wickedness enters of whose coming the accused had given notice, followed by a veiled woman who, despite her wraps, could be seen to be shaped most enticingly. Eitzen feels as though the entire room, with everyone in it, were beginning to circle, slowly at first and then ever faster; only the sudden guest remains fixed and motionless in the middle of the whirl while his companion, removing her veils, is unashamedly staring at him, the learned superintendent, as if she wanted to say: Look at that, are you still alive and kicking, old geezer.

The preacher of heresy, however, walks with measured step to the judge's chair, duly bows before the holder of the stirrup, and declares, "My name, Your Honor, is Ahasverus, Ahab Ahasverus, and I have come from the city of Amsterdam to Tönning to give you information concerning all questions that might refer to the faith of these men who stand accused before you, and to lend them aid and comfort as far as this lies in my power."

The Eminent and Right Honorable Caspar Hoyer gazes at the stranger who, in his dark brown coat tailored in the latest Dutch fashion, looks like a solid enough citizen and quite trustworthy and yet gives him an uncanny feeling, and says, "Mijnheer, for your aid and comfort to these men it may still not be too late, but as to the hearing proper, this was concluded a while ago."

Again Ahasverus bows before him. "Your Honor," he says, "after a hearing is concluded, is it not the right of both the prosecution and the accused to sum up and once more present their side of the *casus*? As far as I can see, the learned superintendent was just about to do this; I only request permission to do the same after he has finished."

"Mijnheer—" The holder of the stirrup, searching for a valid reply, falls silent and his glance seeks succor from Eitzen.

Eitzen has finally recaptured some sort of composure. He raises his hands as the prophets of old did when calling God to witness, and cries out, "Mijnheer indeed! Mijnheer Ahasverus! This wretch is nothing but a swindler of the marketplaces who pretends that he is the Everlasting or Wandering Jew, and worse yet, he is a scoundrelly deserter from the regiment of Colonel Pufendorf which is in the duke's service. Take hold of him! Catch him! And his whore, too, so she won't get away from us!"

The next moment, the armed constables of the holder of the stirrup throw themselves at the false Dutchman, and as he suddenly draws a short sword, they draw as well and there is an uproar and tumult before the eyes of the frightened clergy, and the sparks are flying every whichway; but against a pack of hounds even the bravest deer is lost, and it looks already as though Ahasverus, bleeding from several wounds, must sink to the ground as Margriet rushes into the fray, placing herself between him and the sword of the strongest of the constables, and the stroke that was destined for him hits her. Eitzen sees her blood running down the side of her white throat, just as the red wine did that night in Wittenberg, and shudders and hides his face in his hands.

Later, as he opens his eyes to the general cry of horror, he sees lying before him what remains of the woman who lured and tempted him all his life: a wooden ball the size of a skull, with a feather duster stuck to it for hair, and with holes carved in it for eyes and nose and mouth, and next to it a bundle of straw with some rags tied around it, such as the peasants place on their fields to scare the crows. But in the end, aren't we all just ashes and dust, and vanity, and a devil's delusion?

Ahasverus however has already been taken away by the constables.

CHAPTER TWENTY-FOUR

§

Wherein the duke at Gottorp punishes a deserter
by making him run the gauntlet eight times
and his much-revered and pious super-
intendent drives the sorely beaten
man from him just as Ahasverus
once did the Rabbi, but
for quite different
reasons

§

What ample rain and sunshine effect for the plant, hope
does for man: he begins to blossom out, his cheeks gain
color, his hair acquires new sheen and his eyes look lively,
in short, the whole fellow seems rejuvenated. Thus our
Superintendent Paulus von Eitzen; for now, so he thinks,
justice will finally be meted out to the Jew who has been
the bane of his life and the embitterment of his years and
who, through his devilish witchcraft, has turned the beau-
teous Margriet into a scarecrow, to frighten the general
public and to spite a good Christian and loyal servant of
the state such as him.

Queried by the duke as to the person of the prisoner,
he therefore replies to His Grace who, attended by his superintendent and his privy councillor to the left and the
right of him, is having his breakfast in bed: Yes, there
could not be the least doubt that the impostor who traveled through the country as the Everlasting or Wandering

Jew and, with the aid of the Princess of Trapezund, swindled the people out of their hard-earned money, and the soldier of Colonel Pufendorf who, in the service of His Grace the Duke, took part in the campaign against the Netherlands, and the Mennonite preacher of heresies who, in the town of Tönning, had the impudence to appear as a witness in the duchy's highest ecclesiastical court, His Ducal Highness's eminent and right honorable holder of the stirrup presiding, and to turn before everyone present in this court a female complete in all her limbs into a dry bundle of straw, using black magic for that villainous purpose, were one and the same man and a deserter to boot, who should be dealt with according to martial law; furthermore, His Grace's privy councillor Leuchtentrager had at various times in years past encountered this very Ahasverus and therefore could confirm his identity; and finally His Grace could easily have the roster of the Regiment Pufendorf checked as to which one A. Ahasverus was entered as private, only to be listed later on as absent without leave and missing.

The duke, choking on a piece of smoked meat which he was trying to swallow, coughs and spits all over his bed; having cleared his throat he wants to know from his privy councillor if it might not be wiser to avail oneself of the services of so powerful a magician than to have him run the gauntlet; he knew of quite a number of ladies in his duchy whom, withered and wizened as they were, he would not mind seeing turned into a bundle of straw instead of all dressed up and painted. Leuchtentrager, however, with a glance at Eitzen that freezes his blood, informs the duke that the prisoner in his dungeon was not behaving quite like a sorcerer or a practitioner of black magic; he had been having him watched; the man crouched there, held by his chains, and conversed for hours on end with one Reb Joshua, which was the Hebrew name for Jesus.

This is most disturbing to Duke Adolph: in dealing with someone on such familiar terms with the deity an ordinary mortal had better restrain himself; people like that fall into the competency of his superintendent. But Eitzen is all for considering the matter just as it hits the eye: the fellow was a soldier in Colonel Pufendorf's regiment and deserted its ranks; where would you find armies to fight the wars of the princes of this world if everyone could slip away and disappear whenever and wherever it pleased him? The duke feels that he must not close his mind to that kind of reasoning, and he says, well, then there was nothing to be done and this fellow Ahasverus would just have to run the gauntlet, as a lesson to the rest of the soldiers and a favor to his learned superintendent. And having finished his breakfast and drunk the last of his beer, he gestures to the servant to bring a basin with water and washes his hands, thoroughly and at length, and says, "You did recognize him, Eitzen, and you named him and put your finger on him; see you to it."

Hearing these last words, which were Pilate's, Eitzen feels uneasy at heart and turns to Leuchtentrager for aid and advice from his friend; but the privy councillor's eyes are like marble and his face glacial as he inquires from the duke how many times Ahasverus is to run the gauntlet, two, four, or even eight, and the duke, who is bored by now, says eight times, and Eitzen knows, this is the death sentence. But immediately the thought enters his mind that now the truth would reveal itself: if Ahasverus is indeed the Everlasting Jew, having been condemned to live on earth until Christ's final return, then nothing more harmful will come to him than a sound thrashing; but if he is a fraud and a swindler who has lived on the fat of the land and, in addition, has been having a wonderful time with Margriet, until he turned her into a scarecrow, then he has earned nothing better than being whipped to death. In this manner Eitzen calms his conscience or whatever he carries in its place, and peacefully snores away the night before the execution, lying next to his good wife Barbara, and as, in the early hours of the morning, she wakes up feeling an urge and starts diddling and fiddling with him, he comes to near-success; but just as her bony hips are grinding away right bravely and he is on the point of marital bliss, he believes to see on her throat the same ring of blood he saw on Margriet's and shrinks fearfully from his wife and cowers at the foot end of the bed, trembling and with his eyes askew; but Frau Barbara surmises that he must have pinched his thingamabob, possibly damaging it in the process, and inquires anxiously, "Is everything in its place, Paul, and in the shape it should be?"

Her words make him come to the conclusion that she must still be in the flesh, and some stringy flesh at that, and in one piece, for no one ever heard a head speak separate from its body, except in some fairy tale the head of that horse named Fallada, but its head had been hung from the wall and nailed down tight. Therefore he mutters something about her questions being most stupid and of no use whatever, and how about her serving him his breakfast; he was going to have a hard day as in the afternoon a man was to run the gauntlet and His Grace the Duke had ordered him, as the duchy's highest cleric, to tend to the spiritual needs of the fellow. Frau Barbara rings for the maid, and together they prepare for Eitzen a morning meal the like of which other husbands would lick their chops over, hot gruel with an egg and melted butter in it, and sausages, and freshly baked bread, and enough beer to go with it; yet he seems unable to muster an appetite and shoves the dishes away from him. Nor can he make any headway with the work which has piled up on his desk; nor with the sermon he wants to preach this coming Sunday in the cathedral, on Luke 18:10, namely on the foolish Pharisee who prided himself before God on his fasting twice weekly and regularly paying his tithes of all that he possessed, while the poor publican could only ask God to have mercy on a sinner like himself, at which Jesus commented: *Every one that exalts himself shall be abased, and he that humbles himself shall be exalted;* nor with the letter he must write to Pastor Johann Christiani at Leuth who has sent three crates of eggs as a gift to Frau Barbara, along with a note of complaint to him that he has five sons and three daughters all of whom wanted to eat, and that there was little to be gotten from the parish at Leuth, not enough bread and no beer at all, and that he prayed to be given the parish at Boel to supplement his meager prebends, and that he would take care of the two congregations at one time by simply cutting short his sermons; wasn't it sufficient, Pastor Christiani writes, to read the Ten Commandments out loud, once in Leuth and once in Boel, and if only the distance between the two places were less, he would be happy to throw in a *credo* and the *sacramenta*. By noontime Eitzen's affliction has become even worse; how is a man to enjoy the chicken that is placed before him, golden brown and done to a tender turn and smelling most enticing, when at the same time his mind is full of what he'll be having to go through; 'tis the first time that he'll be officiating at someone's being brought from life to death, and in this manner; his heart is more sensitive than most, he is a man of study and of peace, no rough-and-tough army chaplain; but he could not deny rendering this service, especially after Leuchtentrager, his own good friend and companion, had suggested the idea to the duke.

Then, with the third hour past noon approaching, Eitzen puts on his black habit and the white collar that goes with it; also he takes along a small cross made of silver, for the delinquent to kiss before he sets out on his last walk; he doubts, though, that Ahasverus, being Jewish, will take advantage of the offer. As he approaches the market square, Eitzen sees a great crowd of people bustling about; 'tis as though the whole town of Sleswick were converging on the place of execution, young men and old, together with their women and children, come to enjoy the military spectacle about to be performed. The soldiers, too, have already arrived and are ranged in formation, all of them equally tall so as to avoid a whiplash from a long man landing on the face of his shorter vis-à-vis instead of hitting the delinquent's back; the only ones who are small are the drummer boys who will be drumming the roll during the procedure; in their colorful regimentals they look like a parcel of evil-minded gnomes, jumping about and tightening their drumskins so these may give off the proper sound. The soldiers, however, Eitzen notices, are wearing their fatigue uniforms, with leather equipment, but without arms, to avoid the possibility that some of them, fearing that one day they might suffer the same punishment as the delinquent, put it in their heads to about-face and turn their weapons against the corporals and officers, and against the learned superintendent. But above the whole scene there hovers a sky gray as lead and hung with dark clouds that are hurrying by, nearly touching the roofs of the houses and boding nothing good.

Meanwhile the regimental provost marshal, in command of the entire undertaking, has espied the superintendent and, accompanied by the assistant provost, comes over to him, salutes him most courteously, and invites him for a drink after their duty is done. "You will be in need of one, honored doctor," he says with a loud haw-haw and heh-heh, "the way you look you seem to be feeling sick already"; and the assistant provost, with a like haw-haw and heh-heh, hits Eitzen's shoulder so the skinny little man nearly sinks to his knees. Then the provost marshal gives a signal, causing the officers and corporals to line up their men in two rows facing one another, each row with a hundred men to it spaced over a length of three hundred feet, and between the two rows six feet width of passageway, and the men standing diagonally to one another so that each of them should have sufficient room to use his whip properly.

"You just come and follow me, honored doctor," says the provost marshal. "The assistant provost will post himself at the opposite end of the lane formed by the two rows of soldiers and return the delinquent to us so that, when he is back with us and perchance still alive, you may say a heartfelt God bless you to him."

Now the whips are being brought, freshly cut from the willows down at the banks of the river Schlei and not peeled, four baskets filled with fifty whips each, and each whip four and a half feet in length and as thick as a man's thumb. The provost marshal in person pulls one or the other of them from the baskets and tests them by hitting the wooden mast on top of which the ducal flag, red, white, and blue, is fluttering, and as he hears their sharp whistle and sees them coil around the mast, he is satisfied that they'll do equally well with the poor sinner who is to run the gauntlet.

Then the third hour is rung from the cathedral tower, and the hubbub of voices which has filled the whole of the square lessens and finally ceases altogether. Where the road from Gottorp opens into the market the escort appears, twelve horsemen with sabers drawn, and in their midst, on a peasant cart driven by the hangman's helper, the delinquent with his hands tied behind his back, standing straight and, though deathly pale, facing the expectant crowd with great composure. The people are slow to step out of the way of the horses as he is being carted to the beginning of the lane through which he must walk eight times, four times in one direction and four times in the other, and each time receiving two hundred lashes on his back, every blow of the whip well measured and carefully counted, for behind every two of the soldiers a corporal is posted who is to watch that none of the men weaken or feel pity and wield their whip with less than full force. Two servants of the provost marshal push the delinquent off the cart, and now they are facing one another, the worthy superintendent and Ahasverus, the latter clad only in his shirt and trousers; and suddenly Eitzen hasn't the strength to look him in the eye and lowers his head and sees the Jew's naked, ugly feet with their thick, leatherlike soles which he has grown in his more than one and a half thousand years of wandering, and for a moment Eitzen feels as though he must throw himself in the dust before this man and kiss his feet, but just then the provost marshal says, "Pray, honored doctor, pray!" and hits him in the ribs, and Eitzen, his voice shaky, asks Ahasverus whether he would not like to confess his sins and receive forgiveness, and even though no answer is forthcoming, Eitzen interprets the Jew's silence as a tacit agreement and speaks in his name, "Almighty God, Merciful Father, poor and miserable sinner that I am, I acknowledge and bewail my manifold sins and wickedness, which I most grievously have committed by thought, by word, and by deed, thus provoking your rightful wrath and earning your punishment now and forever." But having come that far he suddenly cannot go on because it occurs to him that perhaps he is praying more for the salvation of his own soul than for the delinquent's redemption, and he raises his eyes to heaven in the hope of receiving some consolation from there, but in doing this his glance happens to fall on Ahasverus's face which is unrelenting and full of scorn, and once again he is gripped by his hatred of the Jew who has done him nothing but tort and who also turned our Lord Jesus away from his door when Jesus wanted but to rest a little from the burden of his cross; and thus, just so as to complete the routine, he rattles off the rest of the text in which, for the sake of His great mercy and of the bitter suffering and innocent death of His dear son Jesus Christ, God is entreated to have compassion and pity on us poor sinners and to forgive us all our sins and lend us the strength of mind to become better people, Amen.

Whereupon the provost marshal declares that enough pious words have been sounded, and that now it is time for military justice to take its course and for the people to get their show. The servants of the provost marshal place Ahasverus at the entrance to the lane, making him face into it, and the provost commands in a voice reaching the ends of the market square, "Prepare for running the gauntlet—run!"

Ahasverus sees before him the lane, the lines of men stretching along its sides, eyes, eyes, eyes, two endless walls of eyes, each pair of them glaring at him, and the whips already being raised, and all of this diminishing in the distance until lane and men and eyes and whips fuse into a dark maw which will swallow him up. At first he feels every lash of the whip and feels the whip coiling itself around him, and every time it takes away his breath, and he feels his skin swelling up where it was hit and breaking open and the blood oozing from the welts, thick and hot. Then these separate pains merge into waves that inundate him and threaten to choke him, until he cries out like an animal, his voice wanting to burst, his eyes popping from his skull, his flesh tearing, and still no end of the lane. Mercy, he gasps, though he knows that no one hears him, and would show no mercy if they did, and he staggers on, and the lashing goes on, and the whistle and crack of the whips to which, by now, he listens as though it was not his own body rearing up and his own muscle being slashed, fiber by fiber.

There, God be thanked, he has reached the end. And he is still alive. His heart flutters wildly, his breath comes with a rattle, his pain had laid itself around him like a mantle of fire. But the assistant provost's gloved fist grabs him, and the man turns him around and, with a kick of his foot, sends him reeling back into the lane. He stumbles and is about to fall, but is made to move on. He wonders that he can still see the cobbles under his feet, and hear the muffled sound of the drums, and still think, so much blood flowing out of him, how much blood does a man have? His back is a mass of red tatters: shreds of shirt, of skin, of raw flesh; soon the bones will emerge, whitish. Then, as he raises his head for a moment to seek his way, he sights Eitzen, a black dot in the distance, but with every painful step of his, with every lash of the whip the superintendent keeps growing, his features become discernible, the pointed nose, the tight mouth, the small glittering eyes. And as he finally reaches Eitzen, with the last lash still hissing down on his shoulders, he falls on his knees before him and pleads, his torn lips hardly moving, "Let me rest a little with you, for they have beaten me sorely and I am weary to death."

These words sound familiar to Eitzen, and suddenly he is once more filled with fear and wants nothing more than to be rid of the Jew, have him out of his eye and out of his life, and so he calls out, "And what was your answer as our Lord Jesus came to you with his cross on his back and begged you for this favor?"

"I?" says Ahasverus and actually brings forth a smile. "But I loved the Rabbi."

Eitzen's face twitches; God's anger has come over him at such a blasphemy on the part of the Jew, and he shouts at him, "Get going! This is what you said to Christ, and you drove our Lord from your door, and he damned you. . . ."

And falls silent, for Ahasverus has risen up and stands before him, blood streaming down his body, and raises his hand and speaks, while the provost marshal is agape with astonishment, "It is you who are damned, Paulus von Eitzen, and the devil will fetch you as surely as you see me standing here, and I shall be around when he comes to claim you."

After these words he turns, and of his own will and without hesitation he walks back into the lane; and as the next lash of the whip hits him, the clouds tear and a stroke of lightning hisses down from the sky, followed by a loud peal of thunder, so that the people duck in fright and many of them flee in terror, and a strong wind rises, and more than one man is saying that God was delivering a sign and that an awful end would come to the Sodom and Gomorrah on the river Schlei.

Later, all having been over on Ahasverus's eighth run through the gauntlet, and the provost marshal having given the body a kick of the boot to make sure that the delinquent was quite dead and thereupon having announced, "Detail—attention! Punishment—executed!" and the troops having marched off in the wake of the cart with the corpse in it, and the rain having washed the blood off the cobbles, Eitzen watches the whips being burned in the middle of the market square. They do not burn well and produce an undue amount of smoke and stench, and Eitzen feels as though the whole event has just been a bad dream of his, and then he thinks that this Ahasverus was indeed but a fraud and a swindler, for the genuine Wandering Jew would never have died, not even on the eighth time of running the gauntlet.

CHAPTER TWENTY-FIVE

§

In which the question is ventilated about the real reason
for the intensive research on the subject of Ahasverus,
and in which the return of Reb Joshua and his views
on the new Armageddon are reliably
reported in the learned correspond-
ence of professors Beifuss
and Leuchtentrager

§

Prof. Dr. Dr.h.c. Siegfried Beifuss
Institute for Scientific Atheism
Behrenstrasse 39 a
108 Berlin
German Democratic Republic

4 September 1980

Dear Comrade Beifuss,

Several of our co-workers having been absent on vaca-
tion, our opinion on the possible publication by your Institute of the article entitled "Religious Elements in Zionist
Imperialism, with Special Reference to the Ahasverus Legend and Qumran Scroll 9QRes" was unfortunately delayed, even though the work on this article was done by
you at our suggestion of March of this year. Since, however, we now have the views of several competent com-
rades on the piece and I have had the opportunity of
familiarizing myself with it, I must inform you that, in its
present shape, we consider it as not sufficiently qualified

to be submitted for discussion at next year's Moscow conference.

In the first place the Department criticizes that the special reference to the Ahasverus legend and Scroll 9QRes overshadowed other important aspects of the matter, leaving the social as well as national implications dealt with in insufficient depth. The failure to include a discussion of the first occupation of Palestine by Israel, under Moses' successor Joshua, is an example of this, and it is a most regrettable omission as it would have offered a fine opportunity to explore the use of secret-service methods by the Jewish aggressors; and why is there no analysis included of the annexationist character of the second Jewish state and its policy of alliance with imperialist Rome, which would have thrown an interesting light on the typical attitudes and practices of modern Israel?

In connection with these questions and with our letter to you of 8th July of this year, in which we recommended your requesting Prof. Leuchtentrager and his friend Ahasverus to desist from a visit to the capital of the GDR, we invite you for an exchange of views this coming Monday at 2 P.M.

With socialist greetings,

Würzner
Chief of Department
Ministry of
Higher Education

Prof. Jochanaan Leuchtentrager
Hebrew University
Jerusalem
Israel

10 September 1980

Dear Colleague Leuchtentrager,

I should have replied long ago to your detailed letter of July 3, but important work and a nervous ailment, which kept me away from my Institute for nearly a month, forced me to postpone my answer. Yet the subject of

Ahasverus never left my mind in all this time; my doctor even suggested that my illness might somehow be related to it and spoke of a fixation such as you mentioned in one of your previous letters, and he wanted to know if, by any chance, the Wandering Jew had appeared to me, at night in my dreams or on other occasions.

Still, the question remains why both you, dear Colleague, and I have concerned ourselves so intensively and for so long a time with the Ahasverus problem; for if the word "fixation" were to be applied to me, how much more fittingly does it apply to you who insists this Jewish miracle man has been alive all these centuries and who has been trying to convince me of his actual existence. And shouldn't the question be considered in its social relevance as well? Whence the present-day interest in Ahasverus—an interest noticeably growing—in his origins, his history, his effect on people?

As there can be no spontaneous development in the world and, according to the laws of dialectical materialism, one thing always grows out of another, it might be advisable to give some thought to the possible reasons behind all this and to the question of whose interests it serves. And precisely to this, dear Professor Leuchtentrager, you have furnished the answer, unintentionally I presume, when in your July letter, in connection with a possible visa application to the authorities of the German Democratic Republic, you described yourself as a champion of law and order, but saw in your friend Ahasverus the very antithesis to this, namely a man of disorder and revolt, of impatience and unrest—i.e., an archetype of anarchy. Such types, if you will just remember Trotsky and people like him, always end up as tools of darkest reaction and imperialism, and as a friend of yours, which title I hope to have earned through our long and meaningful correspondence, let me advise you to ask yourself once more and, if you will, to check whether today's very real and live and three-dimensional Ahasverus—leaving aside his various predecessors—might not be something a little more insidious than a quite ordinary owner of a shoe store.

At any rate, I doubt that he would receive an entry visa into our German Democratic Republic.

With best wishes, especially for your health,

Yours sincerely,

(Prof. Dr. Dr.h.c.) Siegfried Beifuss
Institute for Scientific Atheism
Berlin, Capital of the GDR

Prof. Dr. Dr.h.c. Siegfried Beifuss
Institute for Scientific Atheism
Behrenstrasse 39 a
108 Berlin
German Democratic Republic

10 September 1980

Dear Professor Beifuss,

The last time I heard from you was in June, and your long silence worries me. You always were a most diligent correspondent on questions concerning Ahasverus, and even counting the undue delays caused by the postal censorship of both your government and mine, I should have had word from you quite a while ago. You haven't become ill, by any chance, or were kept by some official busybody from carrying on your important and scientifically so useful correspondence with me?

In any case I must now write to you, even at the risk that a letter from you is already in the mails and will cross mine. Aside from my concern for the mental and physical well-being of one of the few surviving Ahasverus specialists I have two urgent reasons for getting in immediate touch with you. The first is that there is a good chance of my obtaining a grant from my university for a journey which will permit me to do research in places where Ahasverus is alleged to have stayed, for instance in Wittenberg which is now in GDR territory; on this occasion, probably before the year is over, I should also like to visit your Institute, and in the company of Mr. Ahasverus who will travel with me, paying his own expenses of course, and who is looking forward as much as myself to meeting you personally.

My second reason for the urgency of this letter and for the haste in which I write it is of greater moment yet; it is, you might say, sensational: just a minute ago Mr. Ahasverus left my home after telling me that Reb Joshua, better known to you under his Greek name Jesus, had once again visited on earth; he, Ahasverus, had not only seen him but had talked with him at length.

You, dear Colleague, have always questioned the existence of the Everlasting Jew; you may therefore justifiably object that the testimony of a mythical person has little or no factual value and that, at any rate, a second coming of Christ as predicted in several of the gospels was impossible *realiter* since there were no valid historical proofs for even a first incarnation of the alleged son of God, no Hebrew, Greek or Roman documents of any kind, no sources at all, aside from the New Testament whose different sections were written and propagated by their different authors a long time *ex post facto* and obviously for the purpose of spreading the religious idiosyncrasies of a sect that deviated from official Judaism.

I myself, let me state this, consider the Jesus as tradition has him a highly questionable figure; I would much rather say that the Rabbi by the name of Joshua who in those days wandered through Galilee and adjoining provinces, preaching and speaking in parables, was adorned by his followers with all kinds of current myths, during his lifetime and even more so after his death, until they finally restyled him into the long-awaited Messiah of the Jews. On the other hand, I cannot quite close my mind to the sober report of my friend Ahasverus, who stood before me pretty much as your Dr. Jaksch would stand before you with a handful of fresh proofs for one of his theories, and I presume that you, too, are going to be more than a little impressed by what he told me.

This was that the Rabbi, clothed in a torn and dirtied robe which once had been white, had dragged himself up

Via Dolorosa, swaying as under a heavy burden, pale, and gasping audibly. Nonetheless he was hardly noticed, due to the tourist traffic in this part of Jerusholayim which attracts the strangest individuals, among them all sorts of beggars and panhandlers; only a few youths carrying rucksacks and guitars looked at him curiously but soon turned to other sights. He, Ahasverus, had recognized Reb Joshua immediately: no wonder, considering his previous, very portentous encounter with him in the identical place. Directly queried by me on this point, Mr. Ahasverus admitted not having been all that surprised at the Rabbi's reappearance; he had kind of expected his return for some time, and had experienced a sense of *déjà vu* as the Rabbi stepped up to him once again and asked if he might rest a moment in the shade of his door.

This time, however, my friend went on to report, he had not reacted according to pattern. Quite the contrary, instead of turning the Rabbi away, he invited him into his house and led the exhausted man right through his store, past several customers who were understandably amazed, into his patio where he told his guest to make himself comfortable under the dense leaves of his vine. The Rabbi refused a glass of wine, Ahasverus said, nor did he take Coca-Cola; he merely accepted a drink of water and permitted the blood-encrusted wounds on his head to be cleaned without uttering a sound, just wincing a few times while he, Ahasverus, dabbed the cuts and bruises, some of them quite deep, with iodine.

Then, having recovered somewhat, Reb Joshua began to speak. This, now, was the last station of his stay, he said, and as my friend Ahasverus wanted to know if the Rabbi really intended to let himself be martyred a second time, he smiled and replied: No, not this time, another age had come, an age in which it was one's duty to judge, not to suffer. As to the obvious question of who it was on whom judgment would be passed, the Rabbi had not given an opinion; he probably assumed, my friend added, that the answer was clear enough. Also about those who had mistreated him he had talked only in the most general terms, leaving open whether it had been the military police or Arab terrorists or simply a gang of ordinary thugs wanting to vent their spite on someone.

Instead, the Rabbi concerned himself with a totally different subject: Armageddon, that final battle which, as Revelation tells us, is to be followed by Judgment Day and the end of the world. He had talked of ships lying in wait under the seas and even under the eternal ice, invisible to the electronic eyes of the most sensitive means of observation, each ship equipped with sixteen rockets of which every one in turn was equipped with sixteen atomic warheads that independently homed in on their target, whereby each single warhead, by its explosive power and its heat development, was able to wipe out a large city with everything breathing in it, and to do this more thoroughly than God's rain of fire did to Sodom and Gomorrah. At this battle of Armageddon, the Rabbi further prophesied, intercontinental rockets would be employed as well which, after crossing the oceans within a matter of minutes, would reach their targets with a nuclear load that, just to give an example, would leave of Mount Zion and the holy city of Jerusholayim nothing but a burnt-out crater and in addition would contaminate with its fatal radioactive emission all human, animal, and plant life in a circle extending from the river Nile on one side to the waters of the Euphrates on the other and would poison the very soil on which this life had grown. And of this kind of death-carrying rocket, the Rabbi had added with bitterness in his voice, large ones and small, with long and short ranges, and transporting correspondingly-sized warheads, there were by now many thousands, and the entire hellish force was in the hands of just a few rulers, men of limited mind, who proclaimed at every opportunity that they needed their arsenals exclusively for the defense of peace, because peace required a balance of horror; which meant, in concrete terms, that if one could annihilate the other ten times over, the other now must strive not only to draw equal with him but to surpass him so as to achieve a twelve-fold annihilation rate and to be able, out of his last dugout and himself already at the point of croaking, to fire one last retaliating blast. In the course of their murderous competition they had now reached a stage where they were capable of destroying everything under the skies, so that nothing would be left of God's creation but the earth, void and wasted, and the far-off stars. In his lust for power, paired with fear of his own kind, man had made a grab for the forces of the universe, but without being able to control or regulate these; thus Adam himself, once made in the image of God, had turned into the beast with the seven heads and the ten horns, the all-destroyer, the antichrist.

These, according to Mr. Ahasverus's report, were the words of Reb Joshua. I presume, dear Colleague Beifuss, that the facts on which the Rabbi's remarks were based are as familiar to you as they are to me; but we have learned to live with them by banishing them from our conscious minds whenever possible. He had failed to inquire where the Rabbi got his facts, Mr. Ahasverus admitted, whether from people who showed him some of the literature on the subject, or from specialists in the field, or even from men involved in the preparations for this Armageddon; but as he could not have passed through the gradual adjustment to the atomic age that we have had, the Rabbi obviously had been confronted with it quite suddenly and had suffered a correlative shock—nineteen hundred and some years after he shed his blood for the remission of the sins of mankind, as he believed.

The speculative question of what Jesus would do and what he would say if he came back to earth in our time has been asked by many people, perhaps by yourself, too, and despite your atheistic convictions, dear Professor. According to the testimony of the Everlasting Jew, the only person able to identify Reb Joshua reliably and to bear authentic witness to his return, this second coming of Christ has taken place. So can the question now be answered?

Mr. Ahasverus assures us that it can. At least indirectly Reb Joshua himself supplied the answer, he says, on Golgotha Hill. He and the Rabbi had taken a walk there, he told me, after he persuaded him to exchange his torn and filthy robe for a white cloak such as the Bedouins wear, and up there, near the very spot where the cross once stood, the Rabbi had suddenly looked up to heaven and called out: *Eli, Eli,* can it be that everything was in vain— the sermon on the mount, my dying on the cross? The lamb slaughtered, but the sacrifice refused?

These had been his last words. Meanwhile a crowd had gathered about him, natives, tourists, pilgrims, among the latter a group of clergy of different Christian denominations in their official garb, and all had stared at the Rabbi as if they were seeing a ghost, and a young American girl, pale and with stringy hair, had rapturously called out, Doesn't he look just like Jesus Christ? The Rabbi, torn from his thoughts, had after a brief moment of embarrassment raised his stigmatized hand as though in blessing, but quickly lowered it; then he had walked off through the crowd which divided before him, and the strange thing had been that none of these people raised a camera although many carried their photographic equipment with them.

All that remained for me to do was to learn from Mr. Ahasverus what his personal reaction to the event had been. I did not need to ask him; he spoke of it on his own. The return of Reb Joshua was naturally affecting him very much, he said, since his own fate would be greatly influenced by it. If the words *But you shall remain and tarry till I come* had proved true up to this date, he went on to explain, then you might expect that the rest of the prophecy which was implied in the old curse would also be fulfilled: the death of the Everlasting Jew and his ultimate salvation after the Rabbi's second coming; and he, Ahasverus, was having to settle a few matters before disappearing forever.

You will understand my excitement as I write this, dear Professor Beifuss, but also my happiness and satisfaction at being able to have just such a Marxist skeptic as yourself as the first person to be informed by me of so astonishing and cataclysmic an occurrence as the second coming of Christ, even though, for the present, it is confirmed only by one source. Doubtless you will wish to discuss this point and other matters of common interest with Mr. Ahasverus and myself, and there should be ample opportunity for it during our coming visit to the capital of the German Democratic Republic. I am greatly looking forward to a fruitful and stimulating exchange of opinion among the three of us.

Meanwhile all the best,

Yours,
Jochanaan Leuchtentrager
Hebrew University
Jerusalem

CHAPTER TWENTY-SIX

§

Wherein the Rabbi and Ahasverus go in search of God
and after various adventures encounter an old man
who knows the secret of the book of life that
is sealed with seven seals and who causes
the Rabbi to speak to him most
imprudently

§

We are searching.

I, Ahasverus, walked to the left of the Rabbi for forty
days and nights while we were searching for God. But
God refused to show Himself, and around us was nothing
but the great void and the pale gray of Sheol which is
without shape and vanishes before your eyes. And the
Rabbi was full of fear and trepidation, and he said to me,
Who are we to quarrel with God and to want to weigh His
decisions by our scales? He is the Beginning and the End,
He was before our time and will be long after it, and His
power knows no limits.

But I said, And what would God be without us? A call
without echo, a force without effect, a principle without
practice.

And as we had walked another forty days and nights in
search of Him, the Rabbi asked, But if He really does not
exist? If from our inception we and our world have been
but a dream which will dissolve like a haze in the wind?

Rabbi, I replied, the faith which moves mountains also

creates these mountains; you must only believe in Him to the fullest, then you will find Him, too.

And behold, the gray before our eyes disappeared, and a light shone forth that brightened our road, and a palace rose at the end of the way that was of gold and silver and cedarwood, all of it worked in the most costly manner, and before the seven gates of the palace there stood seven armored watchmen, each of them carrying a flaming sword; but the Rabbi entered through the seventh gate into the seventh hall in which there was a throne made of precious stones that gleamed and glittered in all the colors of the world, and on the throne there sat One who was clothed in shimmering silks and was beautiful as an angel, with curly hair, and with rings on his fingers, and spoke, I am the King of Kings, and I have been expecting you for the longest time, my son.

Rabbi, I said, if he is your father, speak to him.

But the Rabbi said, He means nothing to me.

At this the face of the King of Kings darkened with anger, and his seven watchmen came and took hold of the Rabbi and expelled him through the seventh gate into the wilderness. But the light was still there and brightened our road, and at the end of the road there rose a temple that was even more magnificent than the palace of the King of Kings and displayed even more gold and silver and cedar-wood which was worked in an even costlier manner, and in the seven courts of the temple before seven huge altars seven holy priests, each of them holding a flaming vial, were celebrating; the Rabbi however entered through the seventh court into the seventh chamber which was filled with the odor of incense and other costly scents and with holy cups and other holy objects made of precious stones that gleamed and glittered in all the colors of the world, and in the chamber there stood One who was clothed en-tirely in white and who had a shining halo about his head, and spoke, I am the Holiest of Holies, and I have been expecting you for the longest time, my son.

Rabbi, I said again, if he is your father, speak to him.

But the Rabbi said, This one does not mean anything to me either.

At this, anger distorted the countenance of the Holiest of Holies, and his seven priests came and took hold of the Rabbi and expelled him from the seventh court into the wilderness. The road, however, which the light was brightening for us, grew narrower and steeper and a bottomless pit yawned to either side of it; but at the end of the road there lay a rounded stone on which sat One who was very old and who held in his hand a stick that he used to write signs into the sand at his feet.

And I said a third time, Rabbi, if he is your father, speak to him.

But the Rabbi bent down to the writer and inquired, What are you doing there, old man?

And the old man, without interrupting his labors, replied, Don't you see that I am writing the book of life that is sealed with seven seals, my son?

But you are writing it all into the sand, said the Rabbi, and a wind will rise and blot out everything.

Just this, said the old man, is the secret of the book.

The Rabbi grew pale and seemed very much frightened, but then he said, You are the one, aren't you, who out of the void and the nothingness created the world with its days and nights and its sky and the earth and the waters and the multitude of reptiles and worms and vermin.

I am he, said the old man.

And on the sixth day, the Rabbi continued, you created man in your own image, didn't you?

I did, said the old man.

And now you want everything to be as though it never happened, asked the Rabbi, a fleeting impression rubbed out by your foot?

The old man ceased writing and put away his stick. Then he shook his head and spoke: Once upon a time I, too, was full of fervor and belief, my boy, and I loved my people or was angry at them, depending on the case, and I sent to them fire and floods and angels and prophets, and finally I sent you, my only son. You have seen what became of it.

A stinking morass in which everything alive is striving to devour one another, said the Rabbi, a kingdom of horror in which all order and organization exist only for the purpose of destruction.

My son, said the old man, I know.

But Lord, objected the Rabbi, isn't it up to you to dry up the morass and to change this order?

The old man was silent.

Lord, said the Rabbi, you have caused to be proclaimed by the mouth of your prophet that you will create new heavens and a new earth, and that the former shall not be remembered nor ever come into mind. And you have further spoken through another of your prophets and have declared that you would take away the stony heart out of the flesh of people and give them a new heart and a new spirit. Lord, I am asking you: when? When?

The old man, slanting his head, looked up to his son and spoke: I made this world and I made man, but once there, each thing develops its own laws, and Yes becomes No and No turns into Yes until nothing is anymore as it was and the world created by God is no longer recognizable even unto the eye of its creator.

So you admit, Lord, said the Rabbi, that all you have done was in vain?

I am writing into the sand, said the old man, isn't that sufficient unto you?

But the wrath of the Rabbi grew and he said, Why then do you not step down, Lord, for one who has failed as badly as you have should not want to cling to power.

And you would do it better? asked the old man. You who had yourself nailed to the cross instead of rising up and fighting against all the iniquity? Tell me, my boy, who has put you up to your rebellious speech? Was it Ahasverus who stands there?

The Rabbi, however, grabbed the old man by the front of his garment and pulled him up from the rounded stone on which he had been sitting and shook him with great violence and called out, Enough! Enough of the patient suffering! And who was it who had driven him to his death on the cross, a death that was for nothing and to no purpose; and instead of praying piously and waiting until this world blew itself to Sheol one had better rally all forces, even those of hell, against this God whose own creation had slipped from his control, and unite the powers of Christ and Antichrist for the assault on the seven heavens that arched pitilessly above this pit of snakes and giant den of rottenness and decay.

The face of the old man twitched and a bitter smile formed on his lips, and then came seven ancient angels with frayed beards and tattered wings, who each one carried in his arm a much-bruised and rusted trumpet and blew on it, and they took the Rabbi by the hand and led him away, gently, toward his throne up high. But God turned to me, Ahasverus, and said He had expected better of me than that; you couldn't trust that boy, he would certainly botch things once again.

CHAPTER TWENTY-SEVEN

§

Which is exclusively documentary, containing as
it does the report of Major Pachnickel to his
superiors concerning the sudden disappear-
ance (escape from the Republic?) of Cit-
izen S. Beifuss, including pertinent
records, protocols, and other
materials

§

From: Section II B(13)
To: Bureau of the Minister
Subject: Disappearance (Escape from the Republic?) of
            Citizen S. Beifuss

Berlin, 15 January 1981

At the request of this office I hereby submit a preliminary report re: disappearance (escape from the Republic?)
of the above-named Citizen Siegfried Walter Beifuss,
Prof. Dr. Dr. h.c., Winner of the National Prize (2nd
Class), Meritorious Scientist of the People, three times Ac-
tivist and Holder of several other decorations and honor-
ary medals, Head of the International Institute for
Scientific Atheism, 108 Berlin, Behrenstrasse 39 a. Files
and records pertaining to the case are numbered con-
secutively and have been attached at their proper place of
reference.

The above-named, born 10 April 1927 in Chemnitz,
Saxony, as son of a greengrocer, is 53 years of age, married (to Gudrun, née Jänicke, formerly secretary, at this

time without profession) and residing at 108 Berlin, Leipziger Strasse 61, 8th floor; children Friedrich (born 1963) and Ursula (born 1968); special distinguishing marks: none. The above-named joined the Socialist Unity Party in 1947 and is also a member of the Society for Soviet-German Friendship, the Progress Ski and Hiking Association, and the Academy of Sciences.

The above-named disappeared between 2300 of 31 December 1980 and 0000 of 1 January 1981 through a man-sized hole in the outside wall (reinforced concrete) of his flat. He did not leave word either in the form of a farewell note or any other kind of letter; at any rate, no piece of writing of this sort was found.

This office was informed of the disappearance of the above-named at 0235 of 1 January 1981 through a telephone call from the nearest People's Police Precinct, Berlin Mitte (Police Sergeant Giersch), and an investigation was opened. Record of the telephone call is attached.

Giersch: There's someone disappeared, fellow named Beifuss, Professor Beifuss, supposed to be quite prominent, through a hole in the wall.

II B(13): Hole in the wall? Where?

Giersch: Not in *that* wall. Wall in a house in Leipziger Strasse.

II B(13): You're a little drunk, aren't you?

Giersch: Not me. Not even on New Year's Eve. We're a collective of socialist labor.

II B(13): All right. Suppose you let us have your story.

Giersch: The wife called. She had only discovered it when the bells rang on the radio. They'd been having a big party. When the bells started ringing on the radio, they wanted to toast each other, and there he was missing. A moment before he had still been there. So they started looking for him. And found the hole.

II B (13): Couldn't he simply have walked out by the door?

Giersch: That's what I asked the wife, too. But she said, Why, then, the hole? So I went to Leipziger Strasse with Comrade Rudelmann.

II B (13): And?

Giersch: There was a crowd of people down in front of the house. And there actually was a big black hole up there on the eighth floor, you couldn't miss it. But on the ground was nothing, no body, no blood on the pavement, nothing.

II B (13): And inside the flat?

Giersch: The rim of the hole appeared dark, kind of scorched, as if a rocket had passed through with a corresponding development of heat. But the guests claimed that they had heard nothing, no big bang, no explosion. Of course there had been the din and the clatter outside the house, from the fireworks at that hour.

II B (13): Anything else worth mentioning?

Giersch: On the table we found a piece of paper, with an ancient kind of writing on it, hard to read.

II B (13): You have got it there? Can you try to read it to me?

Giersch: By my—God—have I leaped—over a wall . . . And under it it says: Psalm 18 colon 29.

II B (13): Looks like a case of escape from the Republic. From where are you calling?

Giersch: From the flat in Leipziger Strasse.

II B (13): Are the guests still there? Let 'em give you their names and addresses and tell these people not to talk about the thing. And you and this comrade—what's his name?—Rudelmann?—don't you blab about it either. This section will take care of the matter. Over.

In the morning of 1 January 1981 the case was submitted to me and I took over the investigation. In view of possible complications I questioned the more important witnesses myself.

A talk with Citizeness G. Beifuss in the couple's flat as well as a thorough search of the rooms (photograph of the study of S. Beifuss including the damaged outside wall is appended) netted little more than the information contained in the report of Police Sergeant Giersch. Inside the study no trace of a struggle could be found. To my question in reference to this, Frau Beifuss stated that the room had not been cleaned or rearranged, nor had any changes been made in it, except that a rug was hung before the hole in the wall against the draft. During the search for her husband, shortly after midnight, Frau Beifuss had been the first person to enter his room; she had found the hole and noticed a distinctly disagreeable odor, somewhat sulfurous, but more like an animal. To her knowledge, all the guests had still been present at that time, the eighteen who were invited, mostly co-workers of her husband with their wives and girlfriends, and the others whose number she did not exactly recall since these, as customary on New Year's Eve, had simply been brought along by the former; her husband, too, had brought two foreign gentlemen; this had been earlier in the afternoon, and instead of helping her and her daughter Ursula to prepare for the evening's party, he had locked himself into his study together with the two men and they had been debating with one another for a long time, their voices loud and vehement; later, though, one of them, a short man with a hump on his back and a clubfoot, had proved himself helpful in fixing up the platters and arranging the buffet and had also produced, seemingly out of nowhere, a half-dozen bottles of wine and contributed these to the party; this wine had proved to be most stimulating to the ladies present; Frau Beifuss, however, had not gotten to taste any of it. This gentleman also showed himself quite versatile with a deck of cards, performing card tricks that astonished everyone and reading people's futures from these cards.

Of the various statements made by the guests at the party only the one furnished by Comrade Dr. Wilhelm Jaksch contained details likely to throw additional light on the disappearance of S. Beifuss. Text of statement is attached hereby.

My name is Jaksch, Wilhelm, Dr. phil., born 3 Sept. 1944 at Pasewalk, residing at Schneewittchen-Strasse 23, 117 Berlin. I am a scientific assistant at the Institute for Scientific Atheism and its press and public relations officer, member of the party.

Beginning in early 1980 I noticed certain changes in the behavior of the head of the Institute for Scientific Atheism, Prof. Dr. Dr.h.c. S. Beifuss, to wit, a restlessness and uncertainty which manifested themselves at first in connection with specific scientific questions but gradually grew in number and proportion. In the autumn of 1979 S. Beifuss had published a book, *The Best-known Judeo-Christian Myths as Seen in the Light of Science and History*, which, as do most of his publications, consisted in the most part of slightly changed contributions by his collective; only the section "On the Everlasting (or Wandering) Jew" was written by himself and is based on research of his own. In reference to this Everlasting or Wandering Jew, who carries the name Ahasverus, an Israeli citizen, Prof. Jochanaan Leuchtentrager, initiated an extended correspondence with S. Beifuss, in the course of which the latter kept advancing ever new and more audacious theories on the true substance of the Ahasverus figure while Prof. J. Leuchtentrager claimed that this Jew, after having been personally cursed by Jesus, had actually been alive and wandering these 1900 years and at present was running a shoe store in Jerusalem. On the occasion of a number of work conferences with S. Beifuss, which however became increasingly rare, I explained my viewpoint to him: namely that this Israeli professor was either insane or playing an elaborate hoax on us and our Institute; later on I started to suspect that the Ahasverus story might be a secret-service plot to penetrate the ranks of GDR science and subvert these via our Institute, and I did so inform the competent authorities. I am aware that S. Beifuss, in his capacity as head of the Institute for Scientific Atheism, was warned by the Ministry of Higher Education against J. Leuchtentrager and A. Ahasverus and was advised to let the two men know that any visit of theirs to the capital of the Republic was undesirable.

All the more was I surprised when, on the morning of 31 December 1980, S. Beifuss told me that Messrs. Ahasverus and Leuchtentrager were in Berlin and coming to see him at our Institute within the next hour; and though I, too, had concerned myself with the Ahasverus matter and had conferred on it several times with S. Beifuss, my offer to be present at a talk with the two was emphatically refused by him; he was, he stated, thoroughly capable of representing his scientific opinion by himself and didn't need my aid. The conclusion suggests itself that S. Beifuss did not wish to have any witnesses to whatever he planned to discuss with the two Israeli citizens. He could not, however, keep me from acquainting myself personally with them on the evening of 31 December, at the occasion of the New Year's party that he and his wife gave for their friends and fellow workers and to which he had brought Prof. J. Leuchtentrager and Mr. A. Ahasverus.

My impression of both Prof. J. Leuchtentrager and Mr. Ahasverus was most unfavorable. Prof. Leuchtentrager did not hesitate to exploit the interest which, as a guest from a Western capitalist country, he aroused with the ladies present despite his misshapen body; A. Ahasverus on the other hand appeared bored most of the time, except whenever he tried to impress the guests sitting near him with his historical knowledge which, though, appeared quite spurious to me. To my direct question on the subject, A. Ahasverus stated that, yes, he had known the man called Reb Joshua or, in Greek, Jesus, and showed me, probably so as to prove his claim, a Roman silver coin, one of the thirty, he said, which Judas Iscariot was paid for handing over the Rabbi to the competent authorities. Prof. Leuchtentrager insisted on reading my future out of an ancient deck of cards that he carried with him; he predicted a great career for me, which did not astonish me since in our state everybody has a bright future.

The main point, however, was that in the course of the evening I had the opportunity of observing the head of our Institute, Prof. Dr. Dr.h.c. S. Beifuss. He was very much excited and nervous, a condition which may not have struck the other guests so much since they had not been following his behavior pattern during the past year as I had, and which made me feel very apprehensive especially after he took me aside, raised his glass to me with a most significant gesture, and asked, "Jaksch, what would you say if the devil came and got me?"

"Why?" I replied. "Do you think he should?"

Whereupon he giggled in a way that made my blood run

cold, turned, and walked toward Prof. Leuchtentrager as though the man were a magnet that attracted him irresistibly.

A little while later the bells started ringing on the radio, the guests embraced, and I heard Frau Beifuss inquire, "Where is my Sigi?"

But Prof. S. Beifuss was gone, as were the two Israeli citizens J. Leuchtentrager and A. Ahasverus.

Signed, Dr. Wilhelm Jaksch

On the part of this Section the following must be noted: The correspondence between S. Beifuss and J. Leuchtentrager was all along under careful surveillance. An evaluation with special reference to the disappearance (escape from the Republic?) of S. Beifuss is in the process of being made; as soon as it is completed it will be forwarded to the Bureau of the Minister.

In reference to S. Beifuss having been warned against the citizens of the state of Israel J. Leuchtentrager and A. Ahasverus and as to the directive given him by the Ministry of Higher Education, Comrade Dr. W. Jaksch's statement is substantially correct. Both the warning and the directive were issued on the basis of information on file with II B(13). File is attached.

SECRET

Ahab Ahasverus, located now at 47, Via Dolorosa, Jerusalem, also known as Johannes, Malchus, Cartaphilus, Giovanni Bottadio, Jörg von Meissen, Vassily Blazhenny, long-time Jewish agent. Specialty: Ideological penetration. On occasion, subject was observed in the company of one Jochanaan (Hans) Leuchtentrager, said to be a professor at Hebrew University, and may be associated with him in secret activities.

On the same morning of 1 January 1981 investigation was opened in reference to the entry of the above-named A. Ahasverus and J. Leuchtentrager into the capital of the GDR and their stay in the same. A check was also made as to an exit of the above-named at one of the border crossing points, possibly with a third person accompanying them.

The results of these checks were negative. Reports are appended.

Berlin, 5 January 1981

As to your urgent inquiry in ref. to entry or exit of the citizens of the state of Israel A. Ahasverus and J. Leuchtentrager I hereby inform you that

1. No visas were issued or otherwise given to the above-named by this office.

2. No entry or exit of the above-named via any of our border crossing points has taken place, either singly or in company of one another or of any third person or persons.

Investigation in ref. to a possible illegal border crossing on the part of the above-named is being continued.

With socialist greetings,

Signed, Kühnle, Capt.,
Min. of Interior

Berlin, 7 January 1981

In ref. to your urgent inquiry as to the citizens of the state of Israel A. Ahasverus and J. Leuchtentrager I can inform you that the two men named by you were registered neither by this office nor by any hotel or other place of lodgment in the capital of the GDR during the month of December 1980, or the first week of January 1981.

The above-named might of course have found private lodgings.

Our investigation is being continued.

With socialist greetings,

Signed, Matzmann, Capt.,
Presidium of the People's Police
Dept of Passports and Registration

The reports appended here are in obvious contradiction to the statements of Frau Gudrun, wife of S. Beifuss, as well as of Comrade Dr. W. Jaksch and other guests, all of whom have testified to the presence in the flat of Prof. Beifuss in Leipziger Strasse 61 on the evening of 31 December, 1980, of A. Ahasverus and J. Leuchtentrager, whereby it remains unclear whether the above-named were last seen before midnight or after it. The descriptions of the persons of the above-named given by the witnesses agree with each other, especially as to the clubfoot and the hump on the back of J. Leuchtentrager and his card tricks and as to the typically Jewish appearance of A. Ahasverus, so that a hallucinatory fantasy on the part of the witnesses, induced by alcohol or other stimulants, seems excluded, quite aside from the hole in the outside wall of the 8th floor of the house Leipziger Strasse 61 with its rims scorched by an extraordinary development of heat, which is an undeniable fact.

The investigation on the part of the Min. of Interior (Border Police) has furnished additional evidence. This evidence was somewhat delayed due to unfortunate circumstances. Report is appended.

On the night of 31 December 1980 to 1 January 1981, at or about 0000, Sgt. Kurt Blümel and Corp. Robert Reckzeh, on duty in the guard tower of the Friedrich-Strasse border crossing point for foreigners, observed three unknown shapes moving at a height of approximately 10 to 15 meters above ground from the corner of Leipziger Strasse–Friedrich-Strasse in the direction of the border crossing point for foreigners. Two of these shapes had a fiery tail (Sgt. Blümel believes it to have been the exhaust of some jet engine); the third shape, between the two others, did not seem to possess a motive power of its own and was held, resp. dragged along, by its fellows. As at this time the sky was full of exploding fireworks which, as usual on New Year's Eve, complicate the difficult duty of our border organs, Sgt. Blümel and Corp. Reckzeh at first assumed that they were dealing with such a rocket, even though of an extraordinary size and strange construction. But soon they realized that they were faced with an attempt at a break through our border fortifications by means of an overflight of same with the aid of a new technique. Corp.

Reckzeh wanted to open fire at the phenomenon, but Sgt. Blümel restrained him as regulations governing the control of the border of the GDR forbid the opening of fire at flying objects unless and until permitted by the competent superior echelon.

Meanwhile the three shapes had been approaching the guard tower and were circling same in flight, the two with the fiery tails uttering shrill and noisy laughter while the one in the middle was making such tortured faces that Sgt. Blümel and Corp. Reckzeh were unable to speak and trembled violently. When Sgt. Blümel regained control of himself, he reported the incident to the officer on duty, Lt. Knut Lohmeyer. At this time, however, the fugitives had already flown across the border fortifications and were on the West Berlin side of the crossing point for foreigners. From there they rose rapidly upward, in a diagonal sweep, and grew quickly smaller until they appeared to Sgt. Blümel and Corp. Reckzeh as no more than a couple of sparks from a New Year's rocket.

Transmission of the statements of Sgt. Blümel and Corp. Reckzeh was delayed as Lt. Lohmeyer had reported the two men for drinking while on duty and they are at present under arrest.

With socialist greetings,

Signed, Kühnle, Capt.,
Min. of Interior

As several aspects of the case are beyond the competency of Section II B(13) it is necessary to inform the Minister, through a preliminary report, in ref. to the disappearance of S. Beifuss and the circumstances connected herewith. Final report will follow after completion of the investigation.

A provisional evaluation of the facts uncovered by our organs and of the statements given by the witnesses and other records points to the following sequence of events: the Israeli citizens Prof. (?) J. Leuchtentrager and A. Ahasverus appear at or about 1100 of 31 December 1980 in the Institute for Scientific Atheism, 108 Berlin, Behrenstrasse 39 a, where at this time the collective of the Institute is busy celebrating its annual work report and toasting its achievements with a glass of wine. The head of the Institute, Prof. Dr. Dr.h.c. Siegfried Walter Beifuss, retires with the two arrivals to his office where a debate develops which seems to have been quite heated, at least partially; an offer to have witnesses take part in the conversation was refused by S. Beifuss. Contact by other workers of the Institute with the two Israeli citizens was not established.

According to testimony by the doorman of the Institute, S. Beifuss, in the company of the two strangers, departs from there at 1430 by the main door; toward 1700 he arrives at his flat on the 8th floor of the house Leipziger Strasse 61 where he introduces the men accompanying him to his wife and children as his old friend Prof. Leuchtentrager and the much-traveled Herr Ahasverus and immediately goes with them into his study. No information is available as to where he and his two companions passed the intermediate two and a half hours.

At app. 1900 S. Beifuss and his two foreign guests emerge from his study. From that time on S. Beifuss, J. Leuchtentrager, and A. Ahasverus are under constant observation by the wife and children of S. Beifuss and/or the guests of the New Year's party. This is the case until shortly before 0000 of 1 January 1981, at which time S. Beifuss is missed by his wife and other persons present; also the Israeli citizens J. Leuchtentrager and A. Ahasverus are no longer in evidence as of this hour.

Carrying S. Beifuss with them, they seem to have left the flat through a hole blasted through the outside wall of the 8th floor of the house Leipziger Strasse 61. The possibility cannot be excluded, however, that the above-named managed their exit in a less spectacular manner, that is, through the entrance to the flat, then down either by the stairs or the elevator and out the house door, and that the hole in the 8th floor serves the purpose of mystification. Whichever, from the house Leipziger Strasse 61 they follow a westerly route along Leipziger Strasse, moving through the air to the crossing of Leipziger Strasse and Friedrich-Strasse, and turn into the latter to fly across the fortifications of the border crossing point for foreigners and vanish in a steep ascent from the West Berlin side into the sky.

This sequence of events seems confirmed by the note of unknown origin found by Police Sergeant Giersch on the desk of S. Beifuss. Our investigation has shown that the text on this note is actually a quote from the Bible, i.e. that it was written before the erection of the Antifascist Protective Wall of our Republic.

Since S. Beifuss has failed to reappear up to this date and no trace of him can be found anywhere, his disappearance from the German Democratic Republic must be considered as definite. Whether we have to deal with a case of kidnapping, however, or of escape from the Republic, cannot yet be stated with final authority; as no indications were reported of the presence of S. Beifuss on the territory of the Federal Republic of Germany or any other capitalist state, escape seems less likely.

Section II B(13) requests decision by the Minister, in view of the international aspects of the matter, on whether Section I A(27) and/or IV G(4) are to be consulted.

With socialist greetings,

Signed, Pachnickel, Major
Section II B(13)

CHAPTER TWENTY-EIGHT

§

In which, with the aid of the doctrine of predesti-
nation, the learned Superintendent von Eitzen
tries to extricate himself from the fangs
of the devil but gets caught in the web
of his own argument and is hoisted
through the chimney

§

In our old age we garner the fruits of life, and if ours was a virtuous one and pleasing unto the eyes of the Lord, it is bound to bring an ample harvest, and how much more so to a man like Paul von Eitzen from whose lips the words which God placed there have always dripped so piously. Not only does his *Deutsche Postille* appear in print, for which he has diligently collected his Sunday and holiday sermons so that his *confratres*, especially those under his canonical jurisdiction, will know for all time to come what and how they will have to preach to their flock, with slight *variationes* based on local circumstances; and not only does he submit to an appreciative public his *Christian Instructions on How, Basing Ourselves on the Two Articles of Christian Faith and Doctrine, Namely Divine Predestination and the Sacred Sacraments of Our Dear Lord Jesus Christ, We May in All Modesty and without Vexatious Argument Defend the Divine Word and Prove the One and Only Truth Against All Sorts of Sectarians and Heretics*, hurriedly dedicating said work, after the untimely death of his gracious Lord and Duke Adolph, to the deceased prince's worthy successor Johann

Adolph; nay, all the world, and especially its Protestant section, presided over by the new duke, agrees that without the zealous efforts of the Superintendent of the Duchy of Sleswick this duchy would never have become the land in which, to use the word of the prophet Isaiah, the multitude on the shores enjoys pure blessedness.

To these compounded achievements you may add the happiness the good superintendent finds in the bosom of his family. Though his wife Barbara, having wasted away to her bare skin and bones, has departed toward a better place where they all shall meet again one day, he has his children to console him; these have grown nicely and by now are respected citizens and faithfully follow the word of the Lord; and even daughter Margarethe, despite her misshapen body, has acquired a husband, one Wolfgang Kalund, ducal scribe and recorder, in whose company she will be hanged anno 1610 for their joint murder of their son-in-law Claus Esmarch, mayor of the city of Apenrade; but Eitzen, unable to see that far into the future, is unaware of her sad fate to come, and his friend Leuchtentrager, who knows a bit more about such things, is keeping his information to himself.

The duke's privy councillor has not grown any younger, either; his neatly trimmed little beard has turned white, as has the sparse hair on his skull; only his thick, pointed eyebrows have remained as black as ever, with just a tinge of red to them. He has been traveling a lot, no one knows whereto and on what business, but today he has come to the town of Sleswick and has been to Castle Gottorp, at court, to tender his resignation to Duke Johann Adolph, new masters need new brooms, and now he is sitting in Eitzen's study where the logs crackle cheerfully in the fireplace, and daughter Margarethe, who, together with her ducal scribe and recorder still lives in the parental home and tends to her father's needs, has placed on the table a decanter of the wine of which Leuchtentrager has brought a small barrel as a gift to the superintendent; a wine from a far country, Leuchtentrager says; 'tis a wine, though, which seems to flow from your tongue directly into your bloodstream; red and red mix well.

"It's the same wine we drank that time in Wittenberg," he says, "with Margriet serving it."

"Ah," sighs Eitzen, "Margriet."

"The most beautiful women," says Leuchtentrager, "are those whom we create in our own minds."

"A cursed delusion she was," says Eitzen, "invented by Satan and formed by his hand."

"But you loved her," says Leuchtentrager and laughs, his faint, insidious laugh which seems to insinuate that behind everything visible there is yet another thing, and behind this one again another, and that nothing on this earth is as it appears to be, and whatever we think of as truth is merely a fancy warped and distorted.

"She deceived me," says Eitzen, "and ran off with that Jew, that Ahasverus, who has been an offense to all good Christians and repugnant to them."

"And whom you had whiplashed to death," adds Leuchtentrager.

Eitzen, drinking of the fiery wine, pats his friend's little hump. "If he had been the real Ahasverus whom our Lord Jesus condemned to wander this earth forever," he argues, "he would not have died by the gauntlet but would have bravely outlasted it and cocked a snook at the provost marshal when the fellow, at the end, kicked him so as to make sure that his life was all out of him."

At that moment daughter Margarethe enters the room and puts a third cup on the table, and to her father's inquiry as to the meaning of this cup and to his objection that if he wished Herr Kalund to join them he would let Herr Kalund know it, she replies demurely that the cup was not meant for her husband but for a guest just arrived, a friend of the house as she was told by him, and while she is still making her explanations the latecomer appears in the door and stands there, darkly outlined against the light of the flames in the fireplace which suddenly have leapt up. Had he but had the strength for it, the good superintendent would have greeted the stranger with a heartfelt *Get thee hence, in the name of the Father, the Son, and the Holy Ghost!*—but a great weakness has befallen his limbs and his heart beats in his throat like a thousand little hammers. Ahasverus, however, is moving toward the table at which Eitzen and his friend Leuchtentrager are seated, and he looks as young as on the day the three of them met for the first time: a young Jew in a greasy caftan, with a little black skullcap on his curly red hair, who now sits down in the armchair, stretching himself and spreading his legs comfortably while daughter Margarethe kneels down before him and removes his muddy boots from his feet whose soles have turned into something like leather on his long wanderings. Gently stroking her head, he says to the privy councillor, "Peace be unto you, Leuchtentrager, and how are you progressing with your labors, and are you still holding the coin of Caesar and the parchment with that inscription?"

"My labors are progressing well," replies Leuchtentrager, "as you can see. And the coin of Caesar is yours to have, as is the parchment with the word of the prophet, which is written on it." And pulls both these items from his pocket and hands them to Ahasverus as though they were great treasures.

Eitzen shivers; he senses that he has lived through all this before. But his friend Leuchtentrager turns to him and inquires what makes him tremble so violently; hasn't he given enough sermons on the rising of the dead and why, then, is he so frightened at one of them actually performing the act?

" 'Tis that I do not know the meaning of this thing," says Eitzen, "and that I'm not sure if this Jew is in the flesh or a ghost from hell, and I am in great fear."

Leuchtentrager pours some more of the wine for him and says consolingly, "Don't be afraid, Paul; what has to come, will come, and you are not the first to be fetched by the devil, nor will you be the last."

Eitzen forces a laugh, even though he does not feel like

laughing, and having sent daughter Margarethe from the room, she leaving unwillingly enough, he asks in an uncertain voice if his friend Leuchtentrager would avouch in all seriousness that there was anything more devilish about him than his name which, in Latin, meant Lucifer; nor, to his knowledge, had he, the pious Superintendent von Eitzen, ever made a pact with the devil or sealed any such satanic document, as was customary, with his blood, so that the devil had no rightful claim on him.

At this, Ahasverus rises darkly. Straightening to his full size he unfolds the strip of parchment Leuchtentrager has given him and in a tone which makes the blood curdle in Eitzen's veins reads the words written on it, "Thus says the Lord God: Behold, I am against the bad shepherds and I will require my flock from their hand and cause them to cease being shepherds, neither shall they feed themselves anymore; for I will deliver my flock from their mouth, that they may not be meat for them."

Eitzen knows chapter and verse only too well; the prophet Ezekiel is one whose words he has used frequently, and always for the most worthy of purposes; and he begins to perceive that, having run the gauntlet, the Wandering Jew will hardly have returned to him for a theological dispute and that, rather, it might be his own immortal soul and its salvation which are at stake here. So he defends himself with all the zeal he can muster and declares that he, Superintendent Paulus von Eitzen, has been a better shepherd than many another in his trade who carries the name of the Lord on his lips but otherwise hankers after worldly goods and privileges, and that the privy councillor would gladly confirm how divine law and order were uppermost in the land and how there wasn't a soul in the Duchy of Sleswick daring to deviate from Christian doctrine as laid down and determined by Martinus Luther and, following the good doctor, by him, His Ducal Grace's chief administrator of church affairs, and how the people felt secure and happy in their religious belief while outside the borders of this duchy, east as well as west, the worst heresies were flourishing and every Tom, Dick, and Harry arrogated to themselves the right to interpret the words of Christ and thought they did it better than those ordained for this duty.

Having justified himself this ably, he covertly glances at Leuchtentrager, hoping that his friend who has always encouraged him in his endeavors and often helped him out of a scrape will testify for him; but the privy councillor purses his lips ironically and says, "Precisely on these grounds, my most Christian friend, and precisely because of these many merits of yours, you have become the prey and property of the devil."

Eitzen wants to protest even though in his heart he senses that that poor man on the cross did not give his blood for the perpetuation of the power of the authorities, nor his body for the everlasting rule of the police, but the Jew raises his hand and says, "God is Freedom, for He decides and none other for Him; and if it is true that man was created in God's image, who, then, may dare to wedge the human mind into hollow doctrines?"

Eitzen feels cornered, and he sees the shadows dancing in the flickering light and imagines them to be that many little devils waiting for him with red-hot pokers and boiling pitch, and he cries out loud. But it was just the privy councillor touching him lightly with his finger and saying, "Professing themselves to be wise, they became fools, as the apostle Paul wrote in his letter to the Romans."

At these words, Eitzen's thoughts begin to whir in his brain inside of which chapter and verse of the Holy Scriptures are meshed and cogged like the wheels of a most delicate machine, and he thinks the devil in person threw him this rope so he might grip it and hold onto it and thus save himself. Therefore he says, "But what did the apostle intend to convey when he wrote this to the Romans? He meant that man might err and lose his way; but where did he say that man must become prey to the devil and be eternally damned for something which is common to all humans? Yes, I have erred in striving to establish on earth a place essentially equal to the kingdom of heaven where, just as I planned, only *one* decision is valid and *one* will is done; but man, who will turn into dust and ashes, should not attempt to match the works of God."

Leuchtentrager silently folds his arms, and the Jew nods as though he were trying to recall the words he spoke to Jesus when the Rabbi came up to his door, and Eitzen surmises that he is pursuing the right path and that, if only he continues humbly enough or, better even, if he found someone on whom to unload his guilt, he might, with a little eloquence, escape the judgment threatening him or at least have the sentence considerably reduced. He therefore goes on to say, "*Item*, as man errs but God never does, and as everything moves by the design and decision of God, turning to the right, if that be His will, or to the left, if that be His desire, it follows from this that man cannot really be at fault but that the fault must ultimately lie with God; also, if the original cause of all man's sins lay not in God, why, then, would He have sent His only begotten son to take those sins upon himself?"

"So that, by this token," Ahasverus replies, "the stubborn and hard-hearted Jews whom you have always condemned cannot be adjudged guilty for having shouted, *Crucify him!* and, *His blood be on us and on our children;* nay, they were destined to act that wickedly and it was predetermined by God that they should do all those evil and sinful things for the purpose of seeing his divine will fulfilled? And *ergo* and by this same token you wish to say that the damnation which has fallen to my lot should have come upon God as I acted only according to His will, and that, consequently, He was punished in my person, and that I, Ahasverus, am carrying His guilt?"

Eitzen grows aware of the spot into which he has placed himself by his argumentation, and he worries that, by kicking about, he may get himself even deeper into the slough. But he is driven by his fear of hell and damnation and of the eternal fire under his balls, and he thinks: God has broad shoulders, and He will easily be able to carry the small bit of guilt which I shall load on Him. And thus he says to Ahasverus, "Why, yes, sir!" and, "You have spoken true!" and, "*Ergo*, why punish the poor shepherd for obeying his master's instructions?" and, turning to his friend Leuchtentrager, "Devil, where is your logic, and where is your reason, Satan?"

Leuchtentrager raises his pointed brows, and there is a gleam in his eyes, for when it comes to adding two and two together he always has been better than those who rely on faith and miracles. He gets up from his chair and walks over to the shelf on the wall where Eitzen's Bible and other pious tomes are lined up in good order, all of them well bound and furnished with shiny buckles and clasps, and at the right-hand side of them his treasure and joy, the several volumes of his own printed works. From these Leuchtentrager removes the one entitled *Christian Instructions* etc. etc., published in the town of Sleswick by Nikolaus Wegener, and leafs briefly through it; then, nodding contentedly, he remarks that this book seems to be dealing with the subject of *praedestinatio* or divine foreordination, which matter they were discussing just a minute ago; and as Eitzen, his ears growing hot, confirms this, Leuchtentrager inquires of him if he was truly the author of the work and no other person. Eitzen cannot but confirm this, too, and Leuchtentrager returns to the table and, placing the opened volume before Eitzen, points his calloused fingertip at certain lines on the page and says, "Read this!" And as Eitzen's throat fails to bring forth any sound, though his lips are moving, Leuchtentrager adds, "And speak up, for Ahasverus might want to hear this as well."

So Eitzen is forced to read aloud what he had once written in the exuberance of his Christian zeal and what he now wishes had never entered his mind, even though the thought originated with his good teacher Martinus at Wittenberg and since has been repeated in many a lecture and sermon, namely, *"Thus our dearest God, in His righteousness and justice, never created or selected any man for sin and condem-*

nation and eternal death, but the cause of the malefactor's damnation lies in his own self."

"In his own self," the privy councillor repeats and, directing his glance heavenward, adds, "not in the One up there." And again leafs through the book and says, "Now, read this here!" And once again Eitzen must read his own words and pronounce what he fears will be the sentence meted out to him, namely, *"Thus God through His judgment has punished the deluded and renitent Jews according to their own choice and free will, and is continuing to punish them up to this very day; and note well that the Holy Scriptures do not attribute this cruel and long-lasting punishment to divine predestination but to the Jews' own personal volition."*

"To their own personal volition," repeats Leuchtentrager, "and what holds true for the Jews, who are just a bunch of poor wretches, should certainly be valid for a learned doctor of divinity just as yourself, friend Paul."

"Come on, Herr Superintendent," says Ahasverus and steps over to the fireplace in which the flames are rising viciously. "Time is up."

"Come on, Paul," says Leuchtentrager, pointing the way. "Let's go."

Eitzen's knees are shaking; he would dearly love to stay on, if only for a short while, just until he finishes his glass of wine on the table, but he knows he won't be granted even this small moment of grace, and fear grips him that he might be stuck in the chimney when the three of them go up through it, he and Leuchtentrager and Ahasverus, and that he might get roasted while still in these parts. But his friend Leuchtentrager, who suddenly stands there all in white just like the blessed angels in those altar paintings, and Ahasverus, whose garment now looks as if it were made of sheer light, place their arms about him almost with tenderness; and as though he had divined Eitzen's concern, Leuchtentrager tells him not to worry, and that they would transsubstantiate him all right. And while Eitzen still wonders in what manner they will proceed in doing this, he suddenly feels his mouth being forced open, as at the dental surgeon's before he pulls your tooth, and he hears Leuchtentrager's gruff voice, "Out damned soul! You are no beauty anyhow but a mean and wretched little thing!" and then feels something tearing itself loose from his insides, and wants to cry out to God or to anyone willing to listen, but no sound materializes anymore.

And when his daughter Margarethe and her husband enter the room, a little while later, they find their father lying in front of the fireplace, his head twisted backward with his tongue hanging out of his mouth and his eyes staring in horror.

In the fireplace the flames are dead, and next to the table on which the three glasses still stand with the red wine glowing in them, Margarethe discovers the muddy boots which she had removed from the young Jew's feet.

FINAL CHAPTER

§

Wherein the Rabbi conducts the Assault on the hallowed
Order of Things, and the Battle of Armageddon
is fought, and it also becomes evident
that the Ultimate Questions must
remain unanswered

§

We are falling.

Down the bottomless pit that is both space and time and in which there is neither below nor above nor right nor left but only the stream of particles that have not yet divided themselves into light and darkness: an everlasting twilight. And I see the Rabbi, and see his stigmatized hand reaching toward me, and my heart goes out to him.

Do you regret it? he says.

No, I do not.

For it was great although it ended in horror: a monstrous attempt which had to be made so that everything would round itself and return to its beginnings, the creation to its creation, and God to God. But the Rabbi, for the first and only time in his life, had been godlike as he mounted his white charger and rode off to the assault, his eyes flashing; in his fist he held the two-edged sword of justice, and before him was carried the banner with the name on it that no one knows, and following behind him rode the four horsemen of darkness, he who sits on a horse the color of brimstone and is named Fire and holds a bow that reaches the ends of the earth, and he on a red horse who is named War and destroys the peace so people slay one another down in the valleys and up on the hills, and he high upon a black horse who is called Famine and holds in his hand a pair of balances, a measure of wheat for a silver penny and three measures of barley for the same amount, and he riding a pale horse, the horseman named Death. And the sun turned black as sackcloth of hair, and the moon became as blood, and the hordes of Gog and Magog drew near on horses that were the color of brimstone or red or black or pale, and were clothed in armor that glistened like sparks of fire, and in their midst were flying many thousands of locusts with slits for eyes and with snouts that belched forth flames, and the whir of their wings was like the rattle of iron wagons. And these were followed by the angels of the depths who had been hurled down from on high on the sixth day of creation along with myself and with the angel Lucifer, and they wore garments of many colors and beat away on cymbals and drums and blew on trumpets so the din resounded far and wide and all live beings were frightened, and before them marched the beast that has seven heads and ten horns and is called the Antichrist, and led them. And hardly had these moved past when the earth opened up and from it rose the regiments of the wretched: beggars and thieves and suchlike rogues, some of them carrying their head under their arm or the gallows rope around their neck, and cripples and invalids and others with twisted limbs, and also women of similar kind, toothless, their hair matted, with pendulous tits and stinking from their several holes, and all of these were screaming and calling out blasphemies and shaking their fists, for as poor and degraded as they had been in life they were in death, and now they believed the day of justice had come, the day of wrath, and they hastened after those on horse and after the fallen angels, and they were like a cloud of black birds winging skyward. But Lucifer sat on a rounded rock, with his legs crossed so his misshapen foot showed, and supporting his chin by his left hand, and let the hosts of the Rabbi surge past him as though the whole thing were a big spectacle which someone had arranged just for his pleasure.

The Rabbi lightly touches my shoulder, and I begin to tremble. In vain, he says, it was all futile and in vain, this time, too.

And I know that his thought is reverting to the cross on which he died, and to my sending him away from my door because he refused to stand up and fight; but now he did fight, and again it was but a blow struck into a void. And I take his hand which is thin-boned like a woman's, and I hold it in mine, and I say to him, Rabbi, I say, it could be that this time you redeemed yourself.

There had been that sea of glass which burst, and the islands which went under as though they had never been, and the mountains which crumbled like so many heaps of sand, and the earth was burning from one end to the other; and all men fled into the caves that are in the rocks and into the crevices in the big walls, and there death overtook them and turned them into shadows and into splotches of dark on the surface of the stone. And the stars fell from heaven in flames and tore open the innermost parts of the bottomless pit so that from it rose a poisonous smoke and a stench of rotting, and all that had remained whole up to that time blew up in thunder. And still the Rabbi kept advancing, and his entire host followed him as he searched for that Jerusalem up in the sky which is made of jasper stone and of pure gold and which has twelve gates, toward the east three gates, toward the north three gates, toward the south three, and toward the west again three, and high above those gates the great temple built of white marble, in whose most holy place God Himself is seated, having Himself worshiped forever and ever by the righteous who carry His seal on their forehead; but nowhere could that city be found, however steep the heights the Rabbi and his host were storming, from one heaven to the next, higher one, and hither and thither, till foam clogged up the nostrils of the horses of the hordes of Gog and Magog and their flanks were covered with sweat and even the armored locusts were tiring and the beast with the seven heads and the ten horns grew lame and the fallen angels in their garments of many colors and the regiments of the wretched that had risen from their graves were muttering like the people of Israel after forty years of marching through the wilderness. Only then the Rabbi reined in his white charger and rose in the saddle and spoke to every one in the host, This God is nowhere; he is already beaten, together with his angels and spirits, and is fled, and I, the son of man, am God in his stead, and I shall do what he has promised but never fulfilled: I will create new heavens and a new earth whereon love and justice shall rule and the wolf shall dwell with the lamb, and where man will no more be man's worst enemy but will walk hand in hand with his fellow man underneath my sun and in the shade of my garden.

But I, Ahasverus, saw the four horsemen slapping their thighs in great glee and the seven heads of the Antichrist baring their fangs as they grinned, and I perceived a low mumble among the hordes of Gog and Magog and among the fallen angels and the regiments of the wretched, as though they were distrusting what they heard with their own ears; but before the great laughter of hell could break loose which would have filled the heavens from the first one up to the seventh, over such trite utopian schemes, behold, there stood before us the writer of the book of life, and spoke, Are you come, my son, along with all these, to change the world in your image?

The Rabbi raised his hand and moved it as though he were shooing away an irksome fly; but the old man would not go away, and said, You are forgetting, my son, that your image is also my image because you cannot be seen separate from me, as no man can.

Then the Rabbi raised his sword to slay the old man, but the old man began to grow of a sudden and grew and grew to the size of a giant and stood there with his feet planted on the destroyed earth and his head high in the clouds; and he raised his hand that was the hand in which he once had held all of creation, including his angels and the stars up above and the man Adam, and a voice rose which was stronger than the loudest thunder and at the same time like the whispering of the wind in the leaves, and spoke one word, one word only, namely his own name, the unutterable, secret, and hallowed name of God.

And everybody turned numb, as though they were hit by lightning, the four dark horsemen, and the hordes of Gog and Magog and their brimstone-colored or red or black or pale horses, and the locusts with their eyes like slits and their flame-belching snouts, and the beast with the seven heads and ten horns, and the fallen angels, and the regiments of the wretched that had risen from their graves with their sores and their boils and their twisted limbs, and all of them began to dissolve before my eyes and to flow apart and vanish, until there was nothing but the great void and the endless space stretching every whichway, and in this emptiness the figure of the Rabbi, without horse, without sword, shrunken and thin and pitiable, just as he had been when we met in the wilderness, and quite alone. And from afar I heard the echo of a laughter which I knew and which was all that was left of the lord of the depths and great champion of law and order, the angel Lucifer.

We are falling, the Rabbi and I.

My eternal brother, says he, do not you leave me.

And I leaned my head on his breast, as I had done at his last supper, and he kissed my brow and put his arm about me and said that I was like flesh of his flesh and like a shadow which belonged to him, and like his other self. And we united in love and became one.

And as he and God were one, I too became one with God, one image, one great thought, one dream.

POSTSCRIPT

For the aid they gave to my research I wish to thank Herr Herwarth von Schade and Herr Helmut Otto of the Church Library of the Northern Elbe Diocese, Dr. Peter Gabrielsson of the State Archives, and Dr. Richard Gerecke of the State and University Library, all of them in Hamburg, Herr Volkmar Drese of the Administrative Offices of the Northern Elbe Diocese, Dr. Hans F. Rothert of the Land Library, and Dr. Hans Seyfert of the University Library, all of these at Kiel, and Oberarchivrat Dr. Reiner Witt of the Archives of the Land Schleswig-Holstein at Castle Gottorf and Herr Jonas Ziegler of the Berlin (West) State Library. To Professor Jochanaan Leuchtentrager in Jerusalem and Professor Dr. Walter Beltz in Berlin I am especially obliged for their kind advice and sympathetic criticism.

S. H.

Selected Grove Press Paperbacks

62480-7 ACKER, KATHY / Great Expectations: A Novel / $6.95

17458-5 ALLEN, DONALD & BUTTERICK, GEORGE F., eds. / The Postmoderns: The New American Poetry Revised / $9.95

17397-X ANONYMOUS / My Secret Life / $4.95

62433-5 BARASH, D. and LIPTON, J. / Stop Nuclear War! A Handbook / $7.95

17087-3 BARNES, JOHN / Evita—First Lady: A Biography of Eva Peron / $4.95

17208-6 BECKETT, SAMUEL / Endgame / $3.50

17299-X BECKETT, SAMUEL / Three Novels: Molloy, Malone Dies and The Unnamable / $6.95

17204-3 BECKETT, SAMUEL / Waiting for Godot / $3.50

62064-X BECKETT, SAMUEL / Worstward Ho / $5.95

17244-2 BORGES, JORGE LUIS / Ficciones / $6.95

17112-8 BRECHT, BERTOLT / Galileo / $2.95

17106-3 BRECHT, BERTOLT / Mother Courage and Her Children / $2.45

17393-7 BRETON ANDRE / Nadja / $5.95

17439-9 BULGAKOV, MIKHAIL / The Master and Margarita / $4.95

17108-X BURROUGHS, WILLIAM S. / Naked Lunch / $4.95

17749-5 BURROUGHS, WILLIAM S. / The Soft Machine, Nova Express, The Wild Boys: Three Novels / $5.95

62488-2 CLARK, AL, ed. / The Film Year Book 1984 / $12.95

17535-2 COWARD, NOEL / Three Plays (Private Lives, Hay Fever, Blithe Spirit) / $7.95

17219-1 CUMMINGS, E.E. / 100 Selected Poems / $2.95

17327-9 FANON, FRANZ / The Wretched of the Earth / $4.95

17483-6 FROMM, ERICH / The Forgotten Language / $6.95

17390-2 GENET, JEAN / The Maids and Deathwatch: Two Plays / $6.95

17838-6 GENET, JEAN / Querelle / $4.95

17662-6 GERVASI, TOM / Arsenal of Democracy II / $12.95

17956-0 GETTLEMAN, MARVIN, et.al. eds. / El Salvador: Central America in the New Cold War / $9.95

17648-0 GIRODIAS, MAURICE, ed. / The Olympia Reader / $5.95

62490-4 GUITAR PLAYER MAGAZINE / The Guitar Player Book (Revised and Updated Edition) $11.95

62003-8 HITLER, ADOLF / Hitler's Secret Book / $7.95

17125-X HOCHHUTH, ROLF / The Deputy / $7.95

62115-8 HOLMES, BURTON / The Olympian Games in Athens, 1896 / $6.95

17209-4 IONESCO, EUGENE / Four Plays (The Bald Soprano, The Lesson, The Chairs, and Jack or The Submission) / $6.95

17226-4	IONESCO, EUGENE / Rhinocerous / $5.95
62123-9	JOHNSON, CHARLES / Oxherding Tale / $6.95
17254-X	KEENE, DONALD, ed. / Modern Japanese Literature / $12.50
17952-8	KEROUAC, JACK / The Subterraneans / $3.50
62424-6	LAWRENCE, D.H. / Lady Chatterley's Lover / $3.95
17016-4	MAMET, DAVID / American Buffalo / $4.95
17760-6	MILLER, HENRY / Tropic of Cancer / $4.95
17295-7	MILLER, HENRY / Tropic of Capricorn / $3.95
17869-6	NERUDA, PABLO / Five Decades: Poems 1925-1970. Bilingual ed. / $12.50
17092-X	ODETS, CLIFFORD / Six Plays (Waiting for Lefty, Awake and Sing, Golden Boy, Rocket to the Moon, Till the Day I Die, Paradise Lost) / $7.95
17650-2	OE, KENZABURO / A Personal Matter / $6.95
17232-9	PINTER, HAROLD / The Birthday Party & The Room / $6.95
17251-5	PINTER, HAROLD / The Homecoming / $5.95
17539-5	POMERANCE, BERNARD / The Elephant Man / $4.25
17827-0	RAHULA, WALPOLA / What the Buddha Taught / $6.95
17658-8	REAGE, PAULINE / The Story of O, Part II; Return to the Chateau / $3.95
62169-7	RECHY, JOHN / City of Night / $4.50
62001-1	ROSSET, BARNEY and JORDAN, FRED, eds. / Evergreen Review No. 98 / $5.95
62498-X	ROSSET, PETER and VANDERMEER, JOHN / The Nicaragua Reader / $8.95
17119-5	SADE, MARQUIS DE / The 120 Days of Sodom and Other Writings / $12.50
62009-7	SEGALL, J. PETER / Deduct This Book: How Not to Pay Taxes While Ronald Reagan is President / $6.95
17467-4	SELBY, HUBERT / Last Exit to Brooklyn / $2.95
17948-X	SHAWN, WALLACE, and GREGORY, ANDRE / My Dinner with Andre / $5.95
17797-5	SNOW, EDGAR / Red Star Over China / $9.95
17260-4	STOPPARD, TOM / Rosencrantz and Guildenstern Are Dead / $3.95
17474-7	SUZUKI, D.T. / Introduction to Zen Buddhism / $3.95
17599-9	THELWELL, MICHAEL / The Harder They Come: A Novel about Jamaica / $7.95
17969-2	TOOLE, JOHN KENNEDY / A Confederacy of Dunces / $4.50
17418-6	WATTS, ALAN W. / The Spirit of Zen / $3.95

GROVE PRESS, INC., 196 West Houston St., New York, N.Y. 10014